Books by Scott William

Available on Amazon.com
and at other fine bookseller

- PRE-PUBLICATION EDITION-

Final Editing in progress; reader may encounter
content, typographical, or punctuation errors.

Neptune's Trident

www.scottwilliambooks.com

TOOTH

By Scott William

Alpha Psi 1246 Publishing Co. Ltd.
P.O. Box 9422
Greenville, SC 29604

Cover by: Steven J. Catazone
Interior Design: Scott William

This book is dedicated to the memory of my father,

Robert,

who succumbed to cancer's third go before the
last chapters of the first draft
could be read to him at his bedside.

Foreword

There are so many things to say about the adventure presented herein, but the trick is to do so in as brief a manner as possible so as to not detain the reader any more than necessary for those inclined to read Forewords. Fortunately, there is a website, scottwilliambooks.com, that can relieve some of this burden by sharing some of the juicer nuggets of the back story for readers after the tale is concluded as kind of a desserts of compatriots, if you like.

Tooth started out as an exercise for me to learn the craft of being a novelist. Initially, that's all it was. But then the fever set in. The Creative Fever. The absolute joy of creating a tale to entertain others is an addiction difficult to ignore. So the re-writes started, erasing my initial prosaic flounderings leading to a crisp narrative and finally a tale I felt worthy of asking for your time. In this case, this was a journey of years. And there were many who contributed to this book's final disposition. While I take sole responsibility for the contents of this book and any of its errors, there were many hands that stirred the pot helping to shape, mold and, finally, defining the story by paring the detritus that accumulates from an author's hubris. Others provided inspiration, and always at the right time. It is now time for this unseen cast to take a bow.

There are always two voices in every book, that of the author, and the more subtle voice of the editor who is adept pointing out when not to say something or when to stop writing because the mission is accomplished. In this case, editors were often recruited by threat of violence because of the need for their perceived skills coupled with the author's desperation to give a yarn without interruption or distraction due to grammatical or punctuation transgressions. In this endeavor, I hope we were successful. If not, please accept my apologies. The editors for *Tooth* include but are not limited to Gayle Barnhouse, Sally Lauterio, Heather Burden, Danielle Fisher, Rob Nielsen, and Kim Jones. Their insights, guidance and inspiration were greatly appreciated.

The biggest inspiration to bring this literary effort into fruition belongs to my loving wife, Linda. The many, many hundreds of hours devoted to this story were hours sacrificed by her. Without her indulgence and those of other authors' spouses, we writers would never have had an opportunity to launch. I would also like to thank the many readers, perfect strangers, who have been so kind to write me with praise for my efforts. Believe it or not, I never counted on this. My joy was in the creation. And those kind words have had a profound impact upon me, inspiring me to continue to feed my creative addiction. For this, I thank you.

Scott William

PROLOGUE

11,000 years ago off the Pacific coast of the Baja Peninsula...

    The vibrant, azure tropical skies above gave no indication of violence. Heavy afternoon clouds of white with shadings of gray, formed by the sun's relentless evaporation of the ocean, were gently being pushed towards the coast of the Baja Peninsula's land mass by convection currents. Where the sky met the sea, the ocean's surface undulated in gentle swells of a foot and a half spaced well apart, the remnants of a tropical storm on the other side of the Pacific that had traveled the width of the ocean to die in a gentle caress upon the white undisturbed sands of what would be called the Central American coast. The serene portrait of earth, sky, and water allowed the seagulls, pelicans, and terns to wheel in the sky and look into the sea's clear, brilliant blue waters. This avian watch of comings and goings, a vigilance stretching back for millennia of the aquatic realm below the ocean's ceiling was occasionally punctuated by their intrusion into the aqueous realm's life and death struggles, plunging through the margin to consume an unsuspecting inhabitant before returning to the world of air. The birds were inured to the cycles of birth and death that eternally played out below them; their only point of interest was finding a meal when hunger was upon them. So the titanic struggle that was taking place below the surface seemed only right, only natural; ordinary to their limited consciousness.

The largest predator in the sea, a megalodon shark more accurately known as *Carcharodon megalodon*, was swimming at a fraction of its top speed and only in short spurts now. Its right pectoral fin was shredded and tattered, trailing a stream of blood along its superbly streamlined body into the clear blue waters off the Pacific coast, its energy ebbing in its desperate effort to escape the pursuers. Occasionally, it would find strength to sprint up to half speed for a few seconds before the buildup of lactic acids, keratins and carbon dioxide in its muscles and blood became greater than it could remove by its already saturated vascular system, forcing the giant fish to drop out of exertion and glide. Although a few predator fish were poikilothermic - maintaining an internal body temperature higher than the ambient surrounding water - the megalodon was a true homeotherm, or hot-blooded organism, allowing it to react and move faster than cold-blooded fish it mostly preyed upon. This evolutionary advantage had helped it become the top predator of the oceans for eons but was now no match for its attackers, whose cardiovascular systems were far more advanced. It could feel its attackers all around it through its network of lateral lines, little openings along the length of its body that allowed it to sense movement and vibrations around it.   Its attackers were not interested in subtlety, though. The megalodon's ear could hear the clicks and whistles of the antagonist bombarding it from every direction.   A constant stream of directed sound waves pelted it from the eight pursuers always just slightly behind in trail.

The other thing that made the situation worse for the megalodon shark was its full belly.   In the last five days, it had found only a few dozen or so of king salmon and the odd sea otter, hardly enough to fuel its forty-eight foot, nine and a half ton body.   Just a few hours ago, it had followed a rich scent-stream of blood-like bodily fluids in the offshore currents until it arrived in a cozy bay occupied by a whale and its just born infant whose jerky, uncontrolled movements ignited its hunger pangs. The megalodon had circled lazily below for several minutes before finding the right attack approach.   The morsel rested on the surface next to a much larger animal that constantly shifted itself between the newborn whale and the megalodon.   Finally, the larger accompanying animal was distracted by the infant momentarily and was late in shifting, giving the megalodon the opening it needed. With surprising quickness for an animal its size, the megalodon had arced into a vertical climb, charging its near fifty foot mass from nearly straight below the newborn and accelerated to full speed in two body lengths.   When it hit the tiny whale, its five-foot maw of razor-sharp, serrated triangular teeth sliced right through it; only a few hours old, the infant whale's muscles, tendons, and ligaments had not yet hardened from use and offered no resistance to the shark's crushing bite.   The megalodon took the front third of the baby whale on the first bite. The two hundred pounds of warm meat was carried aloft in its jaws as the megalodon breached skyward until its momentum dissipated and lazily arched over to re-enter the ocean, curling to its left along side the larger animal in a towering eruption of sea, spray, froth and blood. The shark took the meat to a depth of sixty or so feet and after several gyrations of semi-spitting the huge chunk of meat out and repositioning in its mouth, the megalodon finally had the head of the morsel in the right spot to pass it down its gullet to its stomach. Still hungry, the megalodon rose slowly to the surface for another bite of the baby whale's carcass. The larger animal circled slowly around the blood-red pool of water, squealing and clicking incessantly. The megalodon slowly nuzzled the corpse a few times before lunging and extending its huge jaws around the still warm meat. The megalodon bit down with incredible force, easily severing the spinal cord and another one hundred fifty pounds of meat was passed down its maw. Once the meat arrived at its destination, the megalodon was filled to the point of ignoring the remaining tail that now bobbed on the surface. The shark lazily flicked its tails in its most economical speed and descended to the depths to start digesting its latest meal.

As the shark descended, it heard a mighty blast of squeals from the larger creature above, that continued ever more faintly as the shark found the depths.

The pod of killer whales had been summoned to the scene of the attack by urgent distress calls for help from the young female of the pod. She'd splintered off from the pod earlier in the day to seek a sheltered deep-water bay to give birth to her first baby. When the pod arrived it was clear something was very wrong. The young female, weak from having just given birth hours before kept nudging the lifeless black tail of what should have been her baby. The water was heavily scented with amniotic fluid from birth and blood from death. Through a series of clicks and whistles the Alpha Male of the pod interrogated the hysterical female as to what happened. The distraught and exhausted female only kept repeating the squeal for the killer whales' mortal and hated enemy, the Giant Shark. This shark was the only creature stupid and bold enough to prey upon the young of killer whales. Because of this threat to the young and juveniles of their kind, all killer whales of all clans killed the Giant Sharks whenever they were found. The old timers in the pods who had killed many Giant Sharks in their day kept the hatred alive by indoctrinating the young whales of their clans. Many of the young whales had never seen a Giant Shark, having witnessed a marked decline in numbers in the last two generations.

After some gentle nudges and nuzzles from the alpha female of the pod to the young would-be-mother to calm her, she was able to get the young mother to the surface for some deep breaths of air to steady and soothe her distress. The young female's own mother started to caress her stricken daughter allowing her to calm enough to give the Alpha Male the direction taken by the shark and an idea of time since the attack measured in increments of tide changes.

The trail was fresh.

The Alpha Male swiveled to look at each member of the small pod arrayed around the young mother and clicked at those old enough to participate in what was about to transpire. He chose seven of the strongest males and females from the pod. Having chosen his warriors, the Alpha Male positioned his himself vertically in the water, head down, and let loose a mighty blast of sound.

TTTTHHHROOOOM   click-click-click-click,
TTTTHHHROOOOM   click-click-click-click,
TTTTHHHROOOOM click-click-click-click.

Then the other seven warriors of the clan eased their heads down to add their voices to their leader's in the War Cry of the killer whale.

TTTTHHHROOOOM   click-click-click-click,
TTTTHHHROOOOM click-click-click-click.

Pursuit started in the direction the young mother had indicated. The killer whales fanned out, racing at their top maintainable speed while using their echolocation sense to search the seas before them for the Giant Shark. The killer whales wove back and forth, up and down, keeping track of each other's position through echolocation clicks that could carry for tens of miles in the ocean, searching for the killer.

The killer whales were able to search vast stretches of the ocean in this manner.

Less than a quarter of a day later, the older female on the left flank found the Giant Shark one hundred twenty feet down, two miles off the coast in an offshore current that was moving south. She summoned the closest pod member who in turn called in the next member in the search pattern until all were assembled three hundred yards behind the Giant Shark.

The Giant Shark had heard and felt the whales gathering behind it but was unconcerned. It was full, so it wasn't interested in them as a meal, and they were far enough behind it so as not to constitute a threat or harassment; as a mature apex predator, it had never known fear or been hunted.

That was about to change.

For many of the killer whales, this was their first hunt of a Giant Shark. However, for years the elder members of the pack had taught them the war techniques learned from millennia of trial and error. First, they would pursue the Giant Shark to tire it out, to dull its reflexes, and delay its reaction to provocation. They wouldn't survive an attack against the shark until it had been slowed. It was faster, larger and more powerful; its massive, five-foot wide jaws were filled with huge serrated teeth that could cause massive tissue damage to the whales with just a glancing bite. But the advantages the killer whales had in close quarters combat were maneuverability and quickness. The big paddle fins of killer whale positioned by evolution close to the front of the whale's frame allowed it to turn in tighter circles. The shark's pectoral fins were smaller in surface and placed further back on its body due to the gills and respiratory system; it had evolved for speed but was less maneuverable to the killer whales.

While the Giant Shark could easily out-sprint the fastest

killer whale due to its sheer size, killer whales had learned that the Giant Shark tired more quickly and used that to their advantage.   Despite an ultra hydro-dynamically efficient body shape and a heart configuration that made the megalodon the marathon runner among sharks, it couldn't keep up with the sustained activity level of the killer whales.   The killer whales were oblivious to the technicalities of their advanced cardiopulmonary system bestowed upon mammals by millions of years of continued evolution; they only knew that they could run anything in the ocean to ground.

The killer whales had another advantage: their echolocation.   They had the ability to focus the sonic energy produced by a cartilage structure in their head into a tightly focused beam.   When focused on the shark, this beam overwhelmed the megalodon's sensory suite, blinding him to what was going on in the sea around him. It also caused pain.   To put their superior physiological advantage into play, along with the sonic disruption, one of the members of the pod would move forward to press and harass the Giant Shark while the others of the hunting pod would lag slightly behind.   The shark would easily sprint ahead and then return to its normal cruising speed when it felt it had put enough space between them for comfort.   But the killer whales' relentless pace would soon catch up to the shark.

By lagging behind, pushing and harassing their prey, the killer whale pack accomplished two things. First, they conserved their strength and energy. Secondly, should the shark turn to attack, those lagging would be able to scatter in different directions and draw attention away from the lone pusher placed closer, giving it an opportunity to get away and the pod an opportunity to regroup. Try as it might, every time the Giant Shark turned to confront its harasser, the pod's tactics of scattering, diving, weaving, and bobbing so distracted the Giant Shark that it was never able to get its mouth on any one of them. They were just too quick and agile for the Giant Shark.

It was a nervy game for the killer whales. Yet, it wasn't without its own dangers. The shark could sense the attacks coming from its rear quarter and would initially turn back to challenge the attackers.   While the killer whales remained fresher, it was a relative state compared to the Giant Shark. The effort had tired them also. The youngest female on her first Giant Shark hunt let her mind slip as she grew fatigued. She didn't initially see when the shark turned abruptly to challenge its attackers again. It was only by waiting to the last instant to turn away that she avoided being raked by the shark's jaw. She'd learned from her elders through centuries of trial and error that the Giant Shark possessed no eyelids; when the shark went to bite, it rolled its eyes back into its head to protect them, temporarily blinding it. At that moment, a burst of speed or an agile turn could save a killer whale from a vicious bite or mortal wound.

The Giant Shark was larger than even the Alpha Male by a full quarter. Yet, the conical spike teeth of the killer whale could easily puncture the shark's thick, sandpaper tough hide; the deep tooth roots penetrated into and anchored to the killer whales' skull and jaw; this anchored them to the whales' bodies allowing them to apply the mass of their body, delivering tremendous leverage and torque that could shred, rake, and break a prey's body. With these few, meager physical attributes the killer whales needed every advantage that their intelligence, communication, team work, and endurance their warm-blooded metabolic rates could provide.

Given all the physical advantages to the shark, the killer whales had to be very circumspect and delicate when going about the business of killing.

The pack of killer whales ran the shark in a giant three-mile circle, constantly herding it in a giant loop. Knowing the game plan, half of the killer whales would chase the shark while the other half rested and cut the center of the circle to the other side to wait on the other side of the loop. As the tired whales passed by pushing the shark, the rested whales relieved tired ones in a relay to pick up the chase. With each push, the Giant Shark sprinted a shorter and shorter distance ahead until the whales could no longer goad the shark into a sprint and it was struggling to move forward at anything above a slow swim.

By the end of the fourth circuit, the Alpha Male killer whale determined the speed of the Giant Shark had diminished sufficiently; the exhaustion level of the giant fish had reached the point at which the attack could begin. The Alpha Male killer whale signaled to all the attack members to form up for the next phase of the hunt. The Giant Shark was too big for them to kill outright. A fish his size had to be cut down to size, piece by piece. That process started with taking away its ability to maneuver and by attacking from the rear, away from its jaws.

The terns, seagulls, and pelicans circling above watched as the killer whales commenced their attack. Sensing that the time was nearing when the scraps of a mighty battle might lead to a feast for their vigilance, a flock of birds started to gather over the Giant Shark.

The killer whales arrayed themselves into a trailing circle to the sides, top, bottom and rear of the Giant Shark at a distance of about twenty yards behind. On the right and left were two pairs of the largest males in the pod below the Alpha Male. On top of the circle was the Alpha Female and on the bottom was the female in rank below her. Another female, the youngest whose mind had wandered earlier, trailed the Giant Shark from directly behind. Her job was to continue to pelt the Giant Shark with sonic energy, blinding it from the others' actions. The Alpha Male trailed below the formation. From this vantage point he could coordinate the attack and deliver the coup de grace when the moment came. This attack formation wasn't happenstance. These positions had been assigned by the Alpha Male based upon size, strength, speed, nerve and risk to the pack members. The Giant Shark posed the greatest risk to whales on the sides. The Giant Shark could most easily turn to the side and bite; it had more difficulty in diving or climbing to bite due to the location of its snout and jaws. The safest position was directly behind the shark.

On signal from the Alpha Male, the two flanker males from each side and the females top and bottom accelerated and made a shallow, gliding approach to the Giant Shark.

The two side whales watched each other to gauge and adjust their attack vector so they both had the same angle, distance and speed. If done right, the Giant Shark would sense the closing killer whales from all sides and with the threat being equal on all sides, the shark would be confused enough to swim straight away from the closing noose. This would put the flankers in a position to do their business.

The Alpha Male's job was to call out signals to the attacking killer whales because in their final attack the pursuers would be blind to the position of the others, shielded from sight and sense by the body of the Giant Shark. It took a lot of courage and nerve to swim in such close proximity to the Giant Shark for the length of time for the attack to fully develop, guided only by the calls of the Alpha Male.

On the first attack run, the female on the bottom was slow to position and the Giant Shark chose to sprint and dive from the closing noose of the attackers. After a quick run to the surface for a lung full of air, the killer whales reformed for a second attack.

On signal from the Alpha Male the six perimeter killer whales started their attack glides again. This time, the timing was perfect. When the flankers were in position, swimming along side just behind the Giant Shark's pectoral fins, the Alpha Male made another click. The two flankers lunged at the pectoral fins of the Giant Shark. The left flanker missed as the Giant Shark turned to the right and into the right flanker's bite which sank its conical fangs deep into the Giant Shark's right pectoral fin at the base where the fin joined the shark's smooth streamlined sides. When the right flanker felt his teeth sink deep into the Giant Shark's flesh up to his gums, he rolled violently to his left into the shark. Unlike the slashing, cutting teeth of the Giant Shark, the stout pointy conical teeth of a killer whale interlocked. Curving to the rear of the mouth, the teeth were designed to bite and hold while the interlocking action crushed tissue between the teeth, incising a circular hole on flat surfaces or raking flesh off larger objects. As the right flanker rolled into the Giant Shark, it used its body's leverage at the contact point as a fulcrum, dislocating and breaking the shark's cartilage fin with an audible snap. As the shark jerked away from the pain, the fin was ripped through the right flanker's teeth, shredding and tattering most of the remaining fin. The right flanker rolled right, low and away as the sandpaper skin and underlying flesh was strained through his teeth.

A blood-trail now flowed from the shredded tatters of the Giant Shark's right pectoral fin, trailing along its superbly streamlined body into the clear blue waters of the Pacific coast.

As the right flanker finished his attack, the left flanker peeled off left; the top and bottom killer whales shifted back to the points from which they started and the two remaining flankers rotated into to the original start position of the whales who had just delivered the first attack. The first two flankers rejoined the formation and took positions as the outside flankers for the next attack.

The successful attack run just completed destroyed the Giant Shark's ability to turn to the right. This time the shark's only options were to turn to the left, climb or dive.

The Alpha Male, from his position, signaled the third attack run with another click.

The whales started their convergence, again keeping an eye on the others, more confident this time. The veteran killer whales after two attack attempts were now assured that the first timers wouldn't now break or lose their nerve.

Closing until the flankers were right alongside, the Alpha Male's click released the flanker's lunge again. An instinctual, brutish eating machine, the Giant Shark's primitive brain reacted to impulses and programming that couldn't change its desire to turn away from its hurt pectoral fin. It turned left and smack into the mouth of the flanker on that side with identical results.

Giant Shark with its pectoral fins dismantled could now only turn by arching its body left or right and using its momentum against its dorsal fin to change direction.

Another quick run topside for a breath of air was needed before the killer whales formed up for the final phase of the hunt. On this attack run, the shark could only marginally pitch up or dive without its pectoral fins. With the Giant Shark semi-disarmed, the Alpha Female now took center stage. Again, on signal all the black and white whales started to converge on Giant Shark. This time, the Alpha Female's attack to the dorsal fin was more assured and every bit as precise, vicious and brutal as the males. The dorsal fin was left broken and laying on the shark's right side in tattered ruins.

All the Giant Shark could do now was limp straight

ahead making it and easy target for what was to come next.

With a long billowing blood trail streaming from the shark's mangled appendages, the killer whales headed once again to the surface and air. The shark wasn't going to go anywhere they couldn't find with more than a few echolocation clicks. Due to the extended exertion of the chase and tension of close water attacks on a very dangerous enemy, the killer whales took a long pause on the surface to take several deep lung fulls of air through their blow holes before returning to the hunt.

The fourth attack run in many ways was the most difficult and dangerous. Now that the Giant Shark could only swim straight ahead, it made a much more predictable target. The last phase of the attack for the killer whales was to destroy the shark's propulsion by dismantling the caudal or tail fin. Because this was one of the most heavily muscled and powerful parts of the shark, one wrong calculation on the attackers' part could get a killer whale crippled or killed by a crushing stroke. This was a job for the largest, most powerful and boldest killer whale; this was the Alpha Male's job.

The killer whales found the shark where they expected it and assumed their now standard attack formation. At the Alpha Male's click, the attack noose started to contract on the Giant Shark. The whales could tell that the Giant Shark was agitated. It might be a big dumb fish, but it was still an animal that could respond to the stimuli of pain. Having endured three previous attacks, the Giant Shark desperately wanted to escape the attack it sensed coming.

The Giant Shark summoned its last bit of energy and did the only thing it had left and put its waning strength into a dozen strokes of its caudal fin before it was totally spent.

The killer whales had expected this surge and through a series of clicks and whistles, they coordinated to keep the big fish tight in their noose.

The Alpha Male trailed from below, watching and waiting until the Giant Shark started to glide, exhausted from its last surge. With a burst of acceleration from powerful strokes from its fluke, the Alpha Male maneuvered into first a dive and then a near vertical climb with speed one wouldn't have expected an animal of its size to possess. He covered the forty feet between him and the Giant Shark in an instant, homing in on the narrowest part of the Giant Shark's anatomy, the juncture just before the tail fin joined the streamlined body. Just feet from making contact, the Alpha Male rolled to his right into a spiral with a flick of his pectoral fins to align his mouth to bite into the juncture. At the last moment the Alpha Male opened his mouth, the shark's body slid between his jaws, and the Alpha Male snapped down with its four inch conical teeth in a crushing bite. In a fraction of a second, the killer whale's teeth punctured the shark's sand paper skin, piercing the tendons that joined the shark's powerful muscles to its tail and imbedded into the cartilage that comprised the Giant Shark's skeleton. With the Alpha Male's body still in a corkscrewing power climb, the pierced and weakened ligaments and cartilage couldn't take the sudden, immense torque delivered by the whale's spinning eight-plus tons of momentum. The

Alpha Male's jaw filled with a jolt of pain as the physics of torque tried to wrench his lower jaw from his head. But he held on with grim determination fueled by anger at the death of the infant whale of his pod born and died this very morning.

Snap!

With a tremendous thud, the Giant Shark's tail fin was broken in an instant, well past perpendicular to its body. The impact of the collision between the titan bodies carried the Alpha Male in an arc while forcing the Giant Whale's head down before spitting out the fish's destroyed propulsion plant. Flipping to his left, the Alpha Male descended slightly in a big sweeping dive to reposition himself behind and below the Giant Shark for another attack. From below, he was able to inspect the damage delivered to the hated monstrosity of a fish.

The Giant Shark, somersaulted over by the attack to its tail, hung head down in the water, the tail fin set at a grotesque angle to the right. The pain of the attack and injury burned into its primitive small brain triggering a reflexive shuddering that it couldn't control. In between quivers, the shark attempted to stroke its tail fin to escape. When it pulled to the left, the tail merely folded out of the way on the hinge of sinew and skin that was still holding it to the body; when it stroked to the right, the tail provided a little propulsion, but only enough to lurch it forward a few feet, which wasn't enough to force sufficient water over its gills to give it life sustaining oxygen.

The other killer whales, who had peeled off as the

Alpha Male delivered his bite, now gathered at close distance to watch as the Giant Shark quivered and convulsed from the lack of oxygen. The Alpha Male, satisfied that the Giant Shark no longer posed a serious threat, gave the order and honor of finishing what he'd started to the youngest female of the attack pack that had been in the safest position of the noose below the shark. She'd not yet had an opportunity to taste the blood of her enemy, serving so far only as a blocker and distraction in the attacks. She circled tentatively gauging her attack and when she was sure her approach was right, she accelerated. Using the same technique as the Alpha Male, she approached the disfigured tail fin from the shark's bottom side. This time, she corkscrewed to the left, biting into the Giant Shark's tail. A smaller pop was heard as the remaining damaged tendons on the right side of the shark's tail snapped in her jaws. As was the culture of the this killer whale tribe, in this way the young of the killer whales of the clan were able to watch, learn and taste the blood of their enemy.

Now fully disabled, the Giant Shark hung at a forty five degree angle head down in the water on its back, in immense agony, slowly suffocating.

With the eternal enemy prostrated before them, the assembled killer whales now gave up the control of the precision-guided attack needed to bring down their larger enemy and let loose the fear, anger, and emotions they had carried in them throughout the day. They all let loose a tremendous chorus of the killer whale War Cry…

TTTTHHHROOOOM   *click-click-click-click,*

TTTTHHHROOOOM click-click-click-click.

In an uncoordinated melee, the killer whales charged at full speed and rammed the Giant Shark in a display of pure animal savagery and blood lust, beating to death the once mighty killing machine with their foreheads. The blows to the shark's gills, heart and internal organs delivered by the killer whale's head butts crushed organs and shattered arteries deep within the Giant Shark.

As their adrenaline subsided giving way to exhaustion, the killer whales, one by one gathered on the surface until all had vented their pent up emotions and the fears to which the brutal beatings gave release. Below them, the last remaining megalodon shark on earth slowly slipped to the ocean floor that lay a hundred fifty feet below to feed the sand fleas, crabs and other bottom dwellers that lived on the detritus of the lighted waters above. Within a week the massive carcass would be rendered into a fleshy skeleton; in three weeks time, even the cartilaginous skeleton would be gone, leaving nothing but a few scattered teeth to mark this once great killing machine's passage on earth.

Though the killer whales didn't know it, with their final savagery, they had ended a feud of hatred that had lasted for hundreds of thousands of years. A feud that started as the population of killer whales grew and spread into the range of the megalodon. A feud that had been concentrated as the ice age's pack ice had slowly squeezed the combatants into the small, contested waters around the equator. With the death of this shark, the last living Megalodon, the climax of Megalodon's extinction reached its zenith and brought final resolution and peace to the clans of the killer whales...

1

Eric McCallister finished packing the last of the day's gear into his eleven-foot rigid inflatable tied to the rear of the right hull of his catamaran, the *Pacific Chanteuse*. He found that for his work it was easier to anchor up in a centrally-located bay and use the smaller, semi-rigid hull boat that was much faster and less intrusive to locate and track his study subjects. The last thing he needed was to go to the galley to retrieve the cooler, which harbored his packed food and beverages for the day.

Once that was accomplished, he stowed and lashed all his gear to the inside compartments of the front and rear wells of the rigid internal hull. Survival food and boat gear in the rear well, his computer and acoustical gear in the front. He found it much easier to work out of the front of the boat once he was at a study site because it was quicker to drop his acoustical sound heads and submersible speakers from the front of the boat without fouling on the outboard engine, the down drive or fuel line hose at the transom of the boat.

Eric was typical in most respects. He was neither handsome nor ugly. His twenty nine year old body was six foot tall, one hundred seventy five pounds. A hint of paunch around his middle hinted at the sedentary nature of his work as a cetacean linguist. His yearly summer research stints here in Southeastern Alaska's Alexander Archipelago didn't give him much of an opportunity to stretch his legs except for a few days every other week when he headed into Ketchikan to get supplies and spend a few precious hours with his girlfriend, Melanie. What wasn't ordinary about Eric was his very agile mind and exquisitely sensitive hearing. When he was younger while aspiring to be a musician, as a joke someone gave him a recording of whale songs. This couldn't have had a more profound impact on his life. He could hear a pattern and purpose to their 'songs' which intrigued him and he'd spent his life trying to unlock their meaning. His passion had found a home at PKMI, Pacific Ketterman Marine Institute, in Portland, Oregon, as a researcher studying whale languages.

It looked to be a gorgeous day for Southeastern Alaska. The skies were clear, and the light breeze tousled his light brown hair in the early morning light. *Today might be the day*, he thought. He vowed each year to take off his shirt on at least one day of summer. He did this as a tribute to his friends in the lower forty-eight and all the pool parties his work made him miss. So he waited for the least cold day of the summer to execute his tribute and this mid-July day had the potential to be that day. Southeastern Alaska was the southern most part of the state, and presumably, it was the hottest. "Hottest," he chortled to himself aloud, "now that's a relative term if ever there was one." By anyone's standards, the hottest day in Southeastern

Alaska would be considered downright tepid with a daytime summer high of seventy-two on land and even less on the water.

And Southeastern Alaska was all about water.

It was an archipelago of thousands of islands, innumerable bays, and scores upon scores of channels. All but a miniscule portion of the sky, land and water was pristine wilderness with a singular lack of any of man's flotsam or jetsam to destroy the impression that you could be the very first human to ever see this particular bar or that island. However, one would be wrong to believe that illusion. Seward's Folly, as Alaska was known in its infancy, was purchased from the Czar of Russia for seven million dollars and change in 1867. At that time, the czar's Russian-American Company had been charged with exploring the Alaskan Territory for the purpose of exploiting its abundant fur resources. The Company had charted some of the interior of the state and only the coastal areas along the south. And over the years, at one point or another, most areas had been charted by various governmental agencies and private citizens. However, in much of Southeastern Alaska, the charting only captured the gross outlines of the coast and very little was known of the interior aspects that couldn't be discerned beyond the satellite topography. The seabed was even less well known, which made life exciting for Eric. Despite the best oceanographic maps, he often found new rock formations as he explored the unnamed bays looking for whales.

As a cetacean linguist, the closer he could get to his subjects, the clearer the nuances of their communications

would be to his sound gear. Eric was in this part of Alaska
to study dialects of killer whales in the interior waters
inhabited by the pods of resident killer whale clans. In the
early days of studying whales, researchers had tried to use
active sonar to locate and identify whales, but this had had
the same effect as trying to herd cats using firecrackers.
The whales were sensitive to the emitted pings and were
constantly moving to get away from them. Trial and error
taught that the best way to find whales was the old
fashioned way. For Eric, that meant cruising up and down
a sector he thought likely to contain whales, cutting the
engine, and drifting while scanning with binoculars until
he spotted whales breaching or the misty clouds of
exhalation blows. If he was lucky, he might be able to spot
the towering black and white fin of an adult male. But
more often conditions required him to fire up the
outboard motor and go investigate what species had
caught his eye. Spot and stalk.

On a day like today, it would be a pleasure.

He untied the bow of his boat, kicked away from the
catamaran, and scrambled over the front section of the
skiff to his seat at the rear. After attaching the forty-foot
safety cord and the engine kill switch cord to his chest
harness he twisted to the rear to switch ON the battery.
The thirty-five horse outboard coughed and caught with
the first turn of the electric starter. After letting it idle to
warm for a half a minute, Eric engaged the drive, throttled
up the gas and put the boat into an arching turn heading
for the bay's mouth of his anchorage and the bigger
channel beyond.

******

"Bingo!" Eric exclaimed from behind the heavy set of binoculars. After a few hours of spotting and stalking, Eric had moved twenty or so miles south down the channel before he thought he'd spotted a pod of killer whales heading into a large bay of an island. He gunned the motor and roared after them.

Eric knew this island but had never been in this particular bay before. As he entered the three-quarters-mile-wide bay mouth, his sight was greeted by a four mile- deep by two mile wide bay with the typical topography of towering hills and ridges of two to three thousand feet plunging to meet the water at a narrow rocky beach.

Eric spotted his quarry at mid-bay and determined that it was a group of minke whales. *Not exactly what he was looking for, but they would do for today*, he thought. Steering his boat off to the western side of the bay, he killed the engine and drifted. Due to hundreds of hours spent in the tiny boat, Eric no longer even noticed its wobble as his weight shifted to the boat's front section and his sound gear. Powering up his laptop computer, he prepared to lower his speaker and both the broad spectrum and directional microphones. Once he was sure that his momentum had abated and that his sensitive sound gear wouldn't be hampered by the sound of water flow generated from being dragged through the water by the boat's dying impetus, he spooled out line from cable reels he'd rigged for the speaker and broad spectrum microphone, lowering them over the side. The directional microphone sat at the end of a ten-foot-long telescoping pole that mounted to a bracket that flipped up over the side of the boat. It had a handle on top so that Eric could steer the pickup head and a twist grip to change the angle up or down. Mounted above the directional control mic was the latest equipment that had really moved the study of cetacean linguistics light years forward. Three small rectangular panels, each about six by four inches were attached; the center panel to the down boom and two panels attached to two-and-a-half foot outriggers that could be folded up for storage. This was the Turbulent Tracking and Categorization System, or TTACS as it was called, and was the heart of Eric's research.

It stemmed from Navy research aimed toward creating a new form of passive sonar to aid in the detection of foreign submarines. Research went into detecting and tracking the vibrations or acoustic signatures created by the turbulence of a body moving through the water. The theory was that design or imperfections of protrusions from a body moving through the water would make turbulences at the trailing edges, junctures and margins. The three panels Eric used provided stereoscopic data collection that allowed target aspect changes to the tracking computer as well as ranging information by measuring the milliseconds between sounds arriving at different panels.

The Navy ultimately abandoned the research because it proved to have a too limited range for their purposes, but it proved perfect for scientific research when it was de-classified. Previously researchers could only record whale communications and try to correlate them with surface observed behavior, never knowing which individual had made the vocalization or what they might be doing below the surface. The PKMI technicians had figured out a way to compact the size and calibrate the system for whale research. Because each whale species has a unique body, each species had a unique acoustic signature. In addition, scientists had long known that each whale had unique scars and fin deformities, which had been used for decades for visual identification. Now those unique scars and fin formations could be used to identify individual whales acoustically by their turbulent signatures. With enough computer power, the signatures of individual whales could be tracked and displayed in three dimensions on a computer screen. This allowed researchers to link vocal emissions from specific individuals to underwater behavior, something they had never been able to do before.

Additionally, PKMI technicians had slaved high resolution video cameras to the directional mike boom so that visual markings could be recorded and matched to acoustic signatures and vocalizations. Now one could watch the proceedings in real time, with icons that depicted the size, sex, identity, voice print, and name of each whale in the pod as they swam and frolicked in the ocean. And Eric loved every minute of it. As a result of their advances, PKMI now had a dozen researchers in seas and oceans all over the world doing the same thing that Eric was doing.

Once his equipment was all set, Eric situated himself on

a seat at the nose of the boat, nestled amongst his gear all at arm's reach and donned his headphones to monitor the feeds to his laptop computer. His laptop didn't have enough computational power to visually show what was going on below the surface, but recorded all the different feeds at the same time for playback and analysis later. It did have various filters and visual display modes so that he could better understand what was going on in the seas around him, but its primary function was to show Eric where to steer the directional boom apparatus to keep it on target and record all the acoustical data gathered from the various systems. Later that night, he would upload the data to the computers on his catamaran and use their greater computing power to watch what really transpired that day. Over time though, Eric's keen ears and observations of the previous days' data let him surmise with a high degree of accuracy what was transpiring below.

Even though his work relied on good ol'-fashioned methods like binoculars, note pads, camera, and Mark-I eyeballs to observe and document what he saw, his laptop was really the center of his work. But, in addition to recording, it could also simultaneously broadcast selected whale vocalizations from the hard drive's library of translated calls. His library even allowed him to select and broadcast the vocalizations of selected individuals, which he used in a rudimentary way to try and communicate.

Although Eric specialized in killer whale dialects, he spent a good amount of time studying all whale speech.

Just like linguistical anthropologist studied human language to help determine the genealogy of man, he was helping to put together a genealogy of whales through their language. PKMI was a private foundation devoted to the repopulation of cetaceans, and Eric was obliged to his employer to gather data on *all* whale species, but the Institute understood that if given two different whales groups to pursue, killer whales or something else, he was going to track the killer whales. During the summer, his main focus was to gather as much data on as many species as he could. When the weather finally shut down field collections, he would return to the PKMI acoustics labs in Portland, Oregon to analyze and catalogue all that was gathered.

As Eric placed the headsets on his ears, he was immediately met with the whistles, clicks, and low moans that told him that several whales were feeding -- and the feeding was good.

"Well hellooo Mister and Misses Minke Whales. How's everyone doing today?" Eric said as he tried to determine if he'd heard these particular whales before. His job kept him isolated from other humans most of the time and it is only human to try to talk to the whales, even if they couldn't hear him. After all, his exquisite hearing allowed him to identify a good number of individuals from each species by their unique vocal signatures, and he could follow the conversation pretty well. In a sense, he felt like he was actually part of the conversation. And with that, he selected a greeting call from the library of minke whale calls on his laptop and broadcasted his introduction to the whales below.

******

From below, a pair of eyes driven by hunger examined the strange looking whale that rested upon the surface through the jellyfish filled waters. Its senses picked up small electrical currents being given off from the salt water in contact with the different metals of the outboard motor, potentials of electricity which made it feel like a live animal to the hungry eyes. Its ears could hear squeals and clicks emanating from the still, floating form. The strange looking whale started to quiver and rock from side to side. All this served to confirm to the hungry eyes that this was food. Its tiny brain targeted the tapering end of the whale and accelerated into a vertical attack at full speed; when it was less than ten feet away it opened its gaping maw filled with rows of razor sharp teeth to rip a huge chunk of flesh from the sunning whale.

******

Eric's boat had drifted to within four hundred yards of the shore; two hundred of those yards were covered by a kelp bed that started just off the rocky beach. It was almost eleven and Eric felt thirsty, so he set down the headphones and got up, stepped over the middle hump to rummage in the cooler for a soda when he suddenly found himself launched in a long, high-arcing flight through the air over the rear of the boat. Blue sky tumbled with green water, and time seemed to slow to a crawl.

Eric flailed his arms and pumped his legs wildly as the apogee of arc was reached and he started his descent.

2

Twenty five years ago…

The raindrops fell from the night sky straight into Dr. Christina Katzburg's eyes, each one seemed intent upon landing on her face. They formed somewhere high in the darkened sky in gray, low scudding clouds unseen above. As the raindrops squeezed from the clouds, gravity's gentle tug started them downward. Gradually they traveled earthward, at first gaining mass by colliding as fine mist droplets within the cloud to form larger drops before reaching terminal velocity crashing straight at her head. Or so it seemed, as the drops entered the night's halo of the street light above her on the pole just a few feet from where her broken body lay. Right for her face they came. She was powerless to stop them. She could feel the cold rivulet of rain running in the gutter her body lay across and partially dammed. She could feel warm blood leaking from her shattered leg, imagining it mingling with the night's rains to make a red streamlet meandering down the gutter to the sewer. She could hear the rhythmic pop and fizzle as rain drops hit the hot cylinder head and exhaust of her motorcycle that lay on its side, piled up somewhere outside the circle of the street lamp's light.

And voices.

Excited voices -- but vague, mixed with the sound of gentle patter of rain joining with the world around her. *'I'm going to die here,'* the sudden thought popped into her head with finality and surprising gentleness.

'How did it come to this?' she asked herself. And the shame washed over her, threatening to squeeze the remaining dregs of life from her before it could ooze slowly from her fatal wounds. *'My secret, my shame,'* she mused quietly, *'will die with me. How the hell could I have been so foolish?'* At least she prayed for that outcome. Because right now, all that was left to carry on in the world of Dr. Christina Katzburg, Ph.D., was her reputation and the immortality of her publications, but only if they didn't discover her folly.

In the distance, a siren's wail was just beginning to emerge from the soft murmur of the rain's caress of Seattle's Queen Anne Hill's neighborhood around her. She could sense people gathering around her, indistinctly murmuring.

'What was I thinking? How could I have been so reckless? My life's work will be ruined,' she mentally moaned, and in a blink of her mind's eye she saw how easily it started the day she started drifting from the path of scholarly rigor to which she'd devoted her life. That day started with that interview...

******

"Hi, you must be Dr. Christina Katzburg," said the casually dressed man with the foppish hair and bookish glasses as he offered his hand to shake while entering her office. "I'm Dennis Mortonson with Scientific Inquiry

Magazine. Thank you for seeing me. I'm sure our readers at Scientific Inquiry Magazine will be interested in learning more about one of the world's premier ocean biologists and shark experts."

"Please, have a seat." Christina motioned to the unoccupied, plain wooden chair in front of her desk, which was the only chair not covered in computer printouts or paper-clamped journal articles. She came around her desk to shake his hand, formalizing the introduction. "I'm not so sure about how entertained they will be. Most of what I do day to day would bore drying paint."

"Oh, I don't know about that," he interjected, smiling, "you're one of the preeminent authorities on sharks in the world, and the public has always been fascinated by sharks...mindless killing machines, not afraid of man, and all that."

"I don't know if I would call them 'mindless killing machines'. I think of them as finely tuned eating machines with just the right amount of brain power to get the job done; a balance that has lasted the test of time through hundreds of millions of years. In fact, studies have shown that many different species of sharks have long term memory and basic reasoning skills by returning year after year to the same spots when and where food is plentiful. Hammerheads show up at certain sea mounts at the same time every year, great whites show up at seal birthing beaches and tiger sharks return to albatross rookeries when hatchlings trying to take flight, to name just a few."

"See, that's what I mean. Our readers like to hear about

these sorts of developments. But before we get back to that, I'd like to ask you a few back ground questions to help the reader to get a sense of you as a person rather than some 'lab rat' of sorts."

"Sure, fire away."

"Alright, then," he paused to pull out a spiral topped note book out of his satchel, flipped it open then snatched a pen from his shirt pocket, clicking it open in the same swift move. "So where did you grow up?" he asked settling in his chair and giving her an inquisitive look.

"I grew up in a quiet, middle-class neighborhood outside St. Petersburg, in Florida; nothing special, just your everyday American neighborhood."

"How about growing up? How would you describe your childhood?"

"Well, everything revolved around going to the beach when I was growing up. I was probably a little awkward socially, so going to the beach for me was more about the sea creatures than the social life. I would rather spend my time wading in a tidal pool than building sandcastles. Even from an early age, I remember being fascinated by all the creatures that I found along the shore and gazing out at the sea trying to imagine what else was out there that I couldn't see. Later on, that pattern seemed to become more prominent as I entered high school. My curious nature tended to express itself in direct questions for my classmates, which I'm sure they deemed inappropriate. Fortunately, I had a science teacher, Mrs. Kendrich, who saw my curiosity and inquisitiveness as a boon and helped me focus on school and particularly science. She really opened my eyes to the world of science. In my senior year she used her contacts to help me land a full scholarship to the University of Florida, because she knew how good their marine biology department was and she wanted me to have the best opportunity."

"So off to Florida you go...anything happen to you there that stands out in your mind?"

Smiling wickedly, she said, "You mean aside from the hunt for a football national championship every year? Well, yes and no."

"What do you mean?"

"Well there was no one singular event that was life-changing, but a series of smaller events. I already knew that I wanted to study marine biology and sharks. But my horizons expanded once I got there. For example, I remember taking my first genetics class and I saw instantly that you really couldn't look at only half of an animal to study it."

"I'm not sure I understand; can you explain?"

"Sure. For example, how can you observe a shark's physiology, or for that matter, its behavior, without understanding its genetic heritage? I had an epiphany about this early on when applying evolutionary principles to lower phylum creatures. Under Darwin's theory, nature favored certain characteristics in the ever-changing environs of the world. Yet, it isn't really the characteristics that nature favors, it's the genetics. Characteristics, both physically and behaviorally, are the expressions, the manifestation of genes, especially in the lower orders. So in order to truly understand a creature, like sharks, you steel industrial door at the end of the hall into a large warehouse-type cavern.

Tom immediately noted the stone topped lab benches cluttered with the beakers, Bunson burners, centrifuges and micro pipettes that one would find in any microbiology or genetics lab. There were several groups of men and women in their mid or late twenties wearing white lab coats working with what he recognized as genetic separation tools.

"This," she indicated with her arms, "is our lab area."

"What is your lab currently working on?"

"I received a grant to start the first genomic sequencing library of shark DNA. We receive samples of different shark DNA from all over the world. My grad students you see here store the samples cryogenically and we are starting the DNA sequencing. The thought is that sharks are one of the most, if not the most, successful super-orders in any kingdom. They first appeared four hundred eight million years ago in the Devonian Period and have been around every since. They have survived numerous extinctions and the reason is believed to be its DNA seems to have a unique ability to adapt quickly to the changing faces of the earth. If we can understand why and how their DNA seems to adapt more readily than, say, mammals, perhaps we will find medical cures to cancer and DNA based diseases."

"How would knowing that help, exactly?"

"Because since there is a wide variety in shapes, habitats, behaviors and food sources in a group of very closely related fish, it is reasoned that the diversity spread colors. Simultaneously, two more moved to either side of the seam of the clam-shell doors to grasp large metal handles welded there. He noticed for the first time that water was dripping from the seam. "Earlier today, we slipped the shark scheduled for exam a Mickey-fin."

Tom looked at her to see she was smiling back devilishly. "That's what the students call it. It's a fish laced with sedatives so that after a few hours the shark is docile enough to allow us to handle it." Tom watched as the divers were near the top of the ramp, their heads and shoulders clear of the water up to their chest. He watched as they slowed and seemed to position themselves for something.

"Sharks exchange oxygen and gases produced by metabolic activity by moving forward, passing water over their gills. In a moment, the divers will be backing the shark into position and the forward flow over their gills will cease. The shark may panic if it can't breathe. The timing on this will be critical. To counteract this as soon as the shark is spun, one of the students will hit a switch," she indicated to the student standing by the palm-push buttons, "and start a gentle water current up the ramp which evacuates down through grates in the bottom of area behind the metal doors. This small current flow will also help to 'cork' the shark. When it's corked, we will switch the flow of water to grates at the top of the ramp creating an artificial flow of water to pass over its gills and keep it comfortable while we examine it."

Tom had to fight back his journalist impulse to ask questions and forced him just to watch the carefully choreographed ballet that was unfolding on the monitors.

The two swimmers were now at the top of the ramp and without pause, at a prearranged spot, one diver stood still, pivoting, while the other walked the shark around to head in the opposite direction. Tom heard a set of pumps kick on and caught a slight movement out of the corner of his eye where the man was standing by the buttons. The water started trickling faster from the door seam as water started flowing through it. With shark centered in a square opening and one hand each cradling the shark, the divers reached behind them to swing heavy, clear plastic doors behind them closed. As the doors converged on the shark, he could see that round notches were cut in middle, clear, soft heavy padding was attached around the round notch and along the seam to create seals.

"This is probably the most dangerous time for the shark," Christina intoned as Tom watched the process unfold. "With the shark's tail still in water, it can still produce propulsion; it could panic and bolt, injuring its tail trying to get out of the hole in the door. We use clear plexiglass doors so that it can't see the doors closing on them and because the plastic does not emit electrical impulses like a metal door would that could overwhelm its electrical sensory organ, the ampullae of Lorenzini. For the same reason, the divers handling the shark are covered in neoprene and their diving tanks and gear are made of plastic or non-electro conductive material.   We learned that lesson the hard way. Several sharks and divers were injured before we learned not to put so much trace electrical current in the water so close to the sharks."

The divers expertly shut the doors around the shark's body, at which point the hole acted like a vacuum cleaner with the current being pulled through it and sucked the shark firmly back into the padding.   The shark was corked.   The man who was standing by the palm-push buttons had been watching the monitor intensely, quickly punch several buttons in rapid succession. Tom heard the sound of the pump stop, then a fainter set kicked on, presumably the ones at the end of the ramp to create water flow over the sharks gills. A split second later, the sound of a giant toilet being flushed behind the metal doors drowned out all other sounds.   It took two to three seconds, but when it diminished to a gurgle the two lab coats on either side of the door quickly threw the latches holding the clam-shell door together and yanked them apart.

What met Tom's eyes was a sight he could never have imagined. A little more than the back third of the shark was sticking out of the plexiglass doors, its tail waving lazily back and fourth. Another student, a woman, moved in and quickly attached a sling to the shark's tail which was hung from an eye-bolt in the ceiling and cinched it up taking the weight off the tail.

"In the water," Christina started from Tom's elbow, "the tail is buoyant, hanging in the air puts a different strain on the animal that it wasn't designed or used to. This way it can continue its instinctual impulse to stroke its tail without hurting it or interfering with our examination." The ultrasound cart was wheeled over to the shark, where the student prepared to give the shark an exam by smearing gel on the ultrasound head and shark's flanks where its uterus was located. "We start with an ultrasound before we move to insert the endoscope that way we know if there are any problems, obstructions, and where the pup sharks are."

Christina moved closer to the procedure; Tom followed. Both watched fascinated, for different reason as first ultrasound pictures in grainy black-and-white pixels on one of the screens produced images that Tom couldn't really understand but clearly meant something to the others on the dais. After a few moments of the ultrasound technician fiddling with knobs and capturing screen shots while sliding the ultrasound head all over the shark's rear third, she abruptly stepped back to let another grad student step forward that was holding an endoscope probe. Briefly they conferred over the images on the ultra sound machine pointing at this feature or that grainy blob before he stepped away applied some lubricant to the probes end and inserted it into the shark.

Endoscopic images moved across a different screen on the wall. Two shark pups were clearly visible in the camera's eye broadcast to the monitor. Their forms were starting to morph into the sleek form like their mother's.

What seemed all too soon, the probe was retrieved, the carts moved, and the students prepared to release the shark. The reverse process went much quicker as the tail was un-slung, the doors were closed, locked, and water was pumped into the area behind the tail. Christina and Tom watched as the Caribbean Reef shark was literally shot out the doors as the water pressure behind the metal doors blew open the Plexiglas doors closed on the tail. The divers had departed and the shark swam lazily back into the reef pool, the sedatives starting to clear from the predatory fish's system.

Christina took a look at her watch and noted that the morning was almost gone. Turning to Tom, she stated what was on her mind. "I have a busy day scheduled and were a little over the time I allotted for this interview. Is there any other questions that I can answer for you?"

"No," Tom hesitated as he did some mental calculations, "I think I got everything I need for an article."

"Good, then," she said briskly pacing towards the door, while tossing over her shoulder, "let me walk you to the door."

In silence, mostly because Tom could never catch up and pull even with Christina, they made their way to the lab's front door where Christina shook his hand and bid Tom a brief adieu before waving at him as she ducked back into the building. Her thoughts, having been disturbed by the reporter's presences needed to be refocused. She decided that the best way to accomplish that would be grabbing a quick lunch. She snatched up her coat and headed for the door.

3

When Christina arrived back from lunch she found Dr. Ken Hendles, Dean of the School of Biology waiting just inside the laboratory's front door with a Cheshire-cat-grin on his face.

"What are you so happy about today, Ken?" Christina chirped, his infectious smile mirrored on her face, "You look like a grinning fool."

"Well, my little marine biology superstar, you've done it again," replied Dr. Hendles, relishing his little intrigue with her. Dr. Hendles was of man of medium height, mostly bald with a fringe of sandy brown hair, a gaze that held you steady in its lock and a meticulous dresser in an average sort of way; nothing flashy, just traditional patterns and combinations. To Christina's inner scientist, everything about him screamed politician, having gotten out of the field research years ago for budget battles in conference rooms with other school heads. But he was loyal and fair, and Christina had always been glad she'd had him to watch her backside in the politics of the university.

"What exactly did I do that merits such happiness on your part, and what have I repeated?" She replied somewhat cautiously, realizing that she was clearly missing something here.

"You're just not going to believe what just happened. I

got a call early this week from James Svodas, the Vice President of the University, to discuss an opportunity that had come across his desk, so I went to see him an hour or so ago. You know that the university has an agreement in place with the State of Alaska to provide educational and research opportunities for Alaska and its citizens, because it has such a small population and cannot support an extensive higher education system, right?"

"Yaaaahhh", Christina replied, still not knowing where this was going.

"The indigenous tribes of Alaska have formed corporations to control lands and resources that they were granted as part of the Alaskan Natives Claim Settlement Act of 1971. Well, it turns out that one of the larger native corporations, owned mostly by the Tlingit tribe, in Southeastern Alaska, which owns all sorts of Islands and a large percentage of the mainland between Canada and the coast, has come into some considerable money." Dr. Hendles said warming up to his subject and switching to his lecturing mode. "The tribe was already doing very well, having discovered large gold deposits on two of the islands they own; now they have discovered a diamond pipette on a portion of land inland close to the Canadian border.

"The Tlingit are a sea going people, having fished and harvested from the sea all that they needed prior to the arrival of Sino-European culture to Alaska. And like most indigenous people, sea creatures as deities heavily influence their religious belief system. One of their deities is named Chagatash which, as it turns out," Dr Hendles paused, his grin beginning to emerge again and finished with a flourish, "is a little known shark. The salmon shark to be precise."

An inkling started to creep into Christina's mind. But she was still unsure what she'd done or what the connection was, so she threw out "I know of this shark, Lamna Ditropis, a member of the Order of Lamniformes, Family Lamnidae; the family generally known as Mackerel Sharks: the same family as the great whites, makos and portbeagle. But I haven't done any research on salmon sharks, Ken."

"A perfect segue, my dear." Dr. Hendles said, gently taking Christina by her elbow and steering her towards her office. "That's what I am here to talk to you about." Once they were settled into their respective seats in Christina's office, Dr. Hendles continue, "The tribe is very flush with cash at the moment and is concerned about their fish god, Chagatash, and possible declining stocks. The shark is very mysterious and seldom encountered in the wild. Salmon fishermen seem to be taking a toll on them. The gill-netters end up drowning the younger sharks not big enough to break through their nets. And the salmon pursue-seiner fishermen kill the larger ones that get caught in their nets just for spite, because the big sharks tear up their gear so badly. The purse-seiners cut off the tail fins and tie them to their masts as trophies then throw the sharks over board to watch them thrash in vain trying to get water over their gills. The only thing the sharks can do is dive slowly. But that only lasts so long until they hit the sea floor, where they slowly suffocate."

"Sonsofabitches" Christina muttered

"Anyway," Dr. Hendles continued in a much cheerier voice, "the tribe contacted the State of Alaska. Alaska sent them to Svodas's office to make the connection. I just met with Tom Greenlee, an official from the tribe and James Svodas. Actually, I guess this Tom Greenlee is a shaman of some sort within the tribe. He had an incredibly interesting offer for the biology department. They had done some homework on who's who in shark reproductivity research and they want you. They want to fund the department's General Research Fund to the tune of five million dollars as part of a larger grant if the department will conduct some focused research on the salmon shark."

There it was: the connection. Christina knew that although grant money was flowing to her lab, the rest of the department didn't fare as well, and five million dollars would really have a positive impact on the rest of the department. But, Christina didn't like being told what to do. In fact, up to this point, she'd always done pretty much whatever she pleased. This whole proposition was beginning to smell of departmental politics. If she didn't take the project the other scientists in the department would know about it. Try as they might to be polite, it was only natural that there was a touch of jealousy because her projects were always so well funded, while most others were struggling to find adequate funding. And at a research university like the U of W, 'publish or perish' wasn't just a quaint afterthought to education; it was the only thought, with education a distant second. If she didn't accept this project, it would give others in the department reason to bring out the long knives and label her 'not a team player.' Not that she needed the other scientists, well, at least not right now anyhow. If she accepted this direction in her research, she might be laying a terrible precedent and no longer be her own woman in control of her destiny. She had always been a bit of a maverick and a non-conformist, choosing to ride a motorcycle rather than the preferred conveyance like a Saab or Volvo that was so in vogue with the other professors at the U of W. *Well, I better find out just how bad this is going to be,* thought Christina. "Just what exactly do the Tlingit want when they say 'focused research,' Ken?"

Having teased out enough line, it was now time to reel in his prize. And Ken Hendles was a master of the art. He knew that, when it came to Ph.D.-sized egos, frontal assaults were wasted efforts. The people who he admitted to his department got there because they were genuinely curious by nature. So he played to their strengths. "The Tlingit would like a full genome survey done on the salmon shark for posterity, and a survey of genetic diversity among the current population."

'The first wasn't so bad', thought Christina. *'We are already doing similar work, and this could easily be handled by one of her grad students.'* This project was partially underwritten by the University of Washington because of the support of Dr. Hendles. He truly believed that the core principle of the science of biology was the preservation of all life forms, and that all research and knowledge should serve that purpose. From Christina's

standpoint, this would be an easy project. All that was required of her was to structure and supervise the process, and edit the findings, while turning the routine, repetitive, monotonous work over to graduate students eager to get their doctorial or masters thesis published.

But the second condition may be a bit of a bear though. "Ken, it's going to take a ton of time, man hours, and money to collect samples from the current population off the Western Coast of North America and, quite frankly, I just can't break away right now to do this."

Good, thought Dr. Hendles, *no objection to the first part, only issues on the collection program. Time to set the hook.* "The Tlingit seemed to have worked that out for you already, Christina. They are willing to pay for and distribute hypodermic sample kits and instructions on how to gather fish biometrics, plus take and preserve the sample through the Alaska Fish and Game Department to every commercial fishing license holder. It seems that the Tlingit have some clout with the Department of Fish and Game in Alaska; and the Fish and Game Department have total say over the commercial fisherman. The Fish and Game Department has let it be known that there will be a two thousand dollar fine for every shark tail found on a boat and that the Tlingit will pay a six hundred dollar reward for each viable sample taken, accompanied with video evidence of the sample being taken and the safe release of the sample salmon shark."

"That will work," mused Christina, pretty much talking to herself, "a little carrot and a lot of stick. A fine to give the fisherman pause to think before they kill a shark just because their paths crossed, tied to a financial reward to send them on their way alive. I like it!" After a pause, Christina continued talking to herself, "So really this would just be data collation on the biometric and standard genetics diversity spread on key genetic markers which a couple of my grad students can do." Christina had been staring at her desktop and snapped her eyes up to meet Dr. Hendle's quizzical expression.

And now for the final nugget of the pitch: "And last but not least, the Tlingit would like a full study on the gestation of the salmon shark." crooned Dr. Hendles.

"What?" gasped Christina. "That's just not possible. I would have to have live subjects for that and my tank is currently configured and stocked with tropical water sharks. I would have to stop all my current research programs, release my test subjects, and repopulate the reef microenvironment with coldwater flora and fauna. That would take months and just be too disruptive! There is just no way I'm going to do that!"

"Tlingit will grant you five million dollars with a contingency of another five million for the cost of another holding tank," Dr. Hendles deadpanned in almost a whisper. "You did hear me say 'as part of a larger grant' didn't you?"

Christina's indignant sputters froze on her face for a moment and then turned to confusion. "That's ten million dollars; that can't be right!" Christina wavered. In marine biology, a three hundred thousand dollar grant was the upper limit and rare. A new holding tank with all the buzzers and whistles of her wildest dreams would cost half what they proposed; five million would keep her research funded for ten years, easy, and she wouldn't have to stop any of her current research projects. Plus, she would be preventing the senseless slaughter of benign shark species.

"Well, just think about it, Christina," said Dr. Hendles, slapping his knees as he pushed himself up and out of his chair.

Christina was still wrestling with the incongruity of it all as Dr. Hendles disappeared through her office door. After the shock wore off, there really wasn't much to think about. In the morning she called Dr. Hendles and accepted.

And so Christina's slide into her own private hell started.

4

Two years later, the genome project for the salmon shark was nearing completion; the samples collection program was a huge success, with over a hundred samples collected the previous summer and a hundred fifty this year. These two hundred fifty samples gave a fair baseline of the genetic diversity, and over time, the program would be able to tell if there was any narrowing of the genetic pool to indicate the health of the salmon shark's stocks.

The gestation program was just getting underway. A new holding tank, designated the cold water tank, had been introduced four months ago and the flora and fauna population had been completed two months before. This part of the project had turned out to be less difficult than setting up the tropical holding tank because most of what she needed was available out in Puget Sound, not more than ten miles from her lab. The only thing different that she had to do with this holding tank was to add refrigeration units to keep the waters at forty-two degrees to simulate littoral water temperatures just off Vancouver Island on the Canadian/U.S. border.

Christina had two adult male salmon sharks, identified not only by their size, about seven and a half feet long and weighing in at four hundred twenty-five pounds, but also for the claspers organs near the pelvic fin, and three females who were slightly larger at eight and a half feet and four hundred eighty-five pounds. While there were reports of some salmon sharks reaching fourteen feet long and weighing nine hundred pounds, the sharks Christina had were typical of most mature salmon sharks for their gender, which made them larger than most tropical reef shark species, but smaller than tiger sharks. Their usual color was blue-gray with brown splotches; the belly was white. The body form was typical of *Lamnidaes*, with a cruciform tail fin of near equal proportions above and below the spinal cord-tail juncture. The *Lamnidaes* body architecture was a very streamlined form designed for speed and efficient cruising. The U.S. Navy had clocked salmon sharks at just over fifty-seven miles an hour, making the salmon shark one of the fastest fish in the ocean and by far the fastest shark species. *Lamnidaes*, collectively known as mackerel sharks, were distinguished by having no nictitating eyelid to cover the eye as the shark bites. Instead they have developed a different strategy to protect their eyes by rolling them to the back of their head for protection when biting. Their last distinguishing characteristic was that they were homeothermic, a form of warm bloodedness. But even among homeothermic fish, the salmon shark was unique, having the highest recorded body temperature of any fish in the ocean, which was probably responsible for the incredible speeds salmon sharks were capable of reaching. Salmon sharks were stockier in the body than their cousins, the makos, probably an environmental adaptation to the colder waters of its range since thicker bodies have less surface area to mass and therefore lose heat to their surroundings at a slower rate. They looked more like juvenile great whites except for the confirmation of their teeth, which were triangular with serrated edges like all *Lamnidaes,* with smaller barbs called cusplets at the ends of the tooth where they met the gum line. The great white's teeth by comparison were stouter, equilateral in shape with serrated edges that were capable of more crushing force without breaking. The salmon shark's teeth were more slender, adapted to catching and consuming its primary food source of light-skinned and boned salmon, squid, sablefish, herring, and the occasional sea mammal that swam mainly in the upper layer of the ocean warmed by the sun.

Although salmon sharks have been spotted as far south as the Baja Peninsula and in open ocean waters, they generally preferred the continental shelf and coastal waters above the fiftieth parallel and range as far north as the Arctic Circle. The sharks were not highly aggressive towards humans, with no known attacks. This was probably due to the fact that the Northern Pacific coast is one of the least densely populated areas of North America and shark/human interactions were statistically minimal. The salmon shark was usually solitary in nature, but was known to collect into groups of up to five around river mouths when salmon started to collect prior to their run up river to mate, breed, and die. So Christina felt that five salmon sharks could be kept comfortably in the holding tank, and their introduction to each other and the holding tank had been uneventful.

As the last of the specimens was transferred to the holding tank by a sling, Christina was captivated. She was enamored with all things shark, but this particular one was really beginning to fascinate her. As her fascination with the salmon shark grew, Christina was glad that her arm had been twisted, however so lightly with a velvet wallet, to study this shark among sharks.

Now that she had her test subjects in place, all that was left of her initial commitment was the gestation study. Female salmon sharks mated every two or three years in the fall, giving birth to live pups in the spring after a nine-month gestation. When test subject females were being rounded up in Alaska, Christina had no way of knowing which sharks would come into season this fall and be viable for gestational studies. Christina's plan was to harvest sperm from the two males and perform in-vitro fertilization on the females who might present for mating in the fall. This approach would eliminate as many variables as possible, the fear being that the new surroundings of the holding tank and living in proximity to other sharks for a prolonged period of time might change the natural cycles and alter the males' instincts for mating. If the changes and new surroundings didn't impact the males, Christina would have the added benefit of studying mating rituals and habits, provided at least one of the females came into season. Christina felt her best chance statistically to have at least one female come into heat was to have three females, with a good probability that two of the females would present positively. In addition, it wasn't known if salmon shark pups committed in-uterine cannibalism, eating their womb-mates to ensure survival of the fittest. This had been discovered recently in other species of sharks and Christina had a hunch that this would be the case with salmon sharks. So the more successful embryos that were produced, the more likely her gestational study would be completed successfully.

So Christina had waited through the summer for the mating season to begin. She'd plenty to do during this time. She had study projects going on in her original tank that had now been dubbed the tropical tank, five Ph.D. candidates doing their doctoral theses under her supervision, about a dozen graduate students doing their masters theses and a small army of undergraduates who volunteered in the lab to do the grunt work of keeping the place clean and running smoothly. She left the supervision of the undergraduates to her Ph.D. candidates, because she felt that in order for a Ph.D. to have a successful career, managerial skills were important. This arrangement freed her from interacting with most of the undergraduates and let her have some personal time to enjoy the outdoor lifestyle of the Pacific Northwest, one of the main reasons she had settled there in the first place.

While Christina tried not to be aloof from the undergraduates, she was usually so preoccupied with her own thoughts while in the lab that she didn't always see or acknowledge those who volunteered to help.

One Tuesday night late in July, Christina had stayed late to do some documentation from her latest research project. She was a little restless and bored, not really wanting to go home just yet, so she got up to walk around the lab to stretch her legs. As she moved around the lab, she heard a commotion in one of the utility rooms to the side of the lab. Thinking she was alone in the lab, she approached the door with some curiosity. As she pushed open the door she saw a young girl in her early twenties standing over a utility sink full of suds with a scouring pad in hand briskly going at a steel fish pan the lab used to prepare food for guests in the holding tanks. A brunette with shoulder-length hair and of medium height, she was heavy boned in the true sense that she wasn't fat but thickly proportioned. Christina, not wanting to startle the young girl, softly said, "Good evening" to her back.

Startled nonetheless, the girl whipped her head around, taking a moment to register Dr. Katzburg standing in the doorway before responding to Christina, "Oh, good evening, Dr. Katzburg. I didn't hear you open the door."

Christina recognized her now, having seen her around the lab. Carol, her name was, or at least Christina was confident enough to throw it out and see if she got it correct. "You're staying late tonight, Carol," she said as both a statement and a question.

She could see the girl blushed at being called by name by the head of the laboratory as she put down the scouring pad while turning to face her. "Yeah, well I really didn't have much of a social schedule tonight. At least here I always feel like there is something useful I can do, if you know what I mean," Carol said, trailing off, realizing that she might have said more about herself than she wanted.

Christina knew exactly what she meant. Carol wasn't unattractive, but she wasn't really attractive either. She'd the raw-boned wholesomeness of a Mid-westerner and carried herself with a chosen plainness that didn't require a lot of makeup to make her feel comfortable in her own skin. Her upper lip was very slightly disfigured by a faded vertical scar from some long ago accident; not enough to be obvious, but just enough to subtly alter the symmetry of her face. But she had a smile that could light up any room, and she was smiling now, lifting Christina's funk. "Summer can be either really exciting and busy if your friends are around, or a real bore if everyone has gone home for the summer. How about you? Any of your friends still in town?"

The young girl cast her eyes to the floor, and shuffled her feet. Christina could well guess that she was still a little uncomfortable talking to a noted scientist on a personal level, heck on any level, for that matter. She'd not said more than a few dozen words to Christina the entire time she'd been volunteering in the lab, and most of that was just returning "hellos." And now, here she was, asking about her friends. "Nah," she said leveling her gaze to Christina's, "most of my close friends here at the U have gone home for the summer. It was cheaper for me to stay here and work rather than go back home, so at nights I come down here just to keep busy and look at the sharks."

Christina was really feeling the need for some human companionship after plotting and analyzing data from statistical runs all day. She wanted to keep this conversation going. "I remember some summers like that when I was doing my undergraduate work. Summer is a kind of netherworld caught in between the cycles of learning. I'm glad that you came here tonight because, frankly, I can use the company."

"Really?" Carol asked, obviously surprised. "I mean, you're always are on the go around here, and the lab is always full of people."

"True, true," Christina continued, "but even my job gets boring sometimes, and I've been stuck, cooped up in my office all day doing one of those boring analyses. I mean, I *am* glad for the results it yielded and excited by the knowledge it brings, but it can be a little monotonous getting there." Changing subjects, "Aren't you a junior?" Christina tossed out, guessing.

"Next year I'll be a senior."

"So tell me, what core classes did you take last year in your major?"   Christina knew full well what the junior-level core requirements were for her department, having taught many of those classes over the years. But she truly loved to help and counsel undergraduates, especially those who were serious enough pursuing their majors to help as volunteers in her lab. Marine biology was so exciting and had been so good to her that she just loved sharing her enthusiasm and felt it was kind of a repayment for those that worked in her lab. And she knew from experience, the best way to get an undergraduate to open up was to talk about what they thought of the classes they had taken.

"Well I took Fish 250, Fish 350, Fish 351, Natural History of Marine Bio, Foundations of Marine Phys plus the core requirements for the biology department like

Principles of Taxonomy, and stuff."

"Which did you like the most?"

"I'd have to say Foundations of Marine Physiology..."

"What did you like the least?"

After a moment's hesitation, Carol said, "That would definitely have to be Bio 300 with Dr. Hafferty. It was kind of dry and had a lot of straight memorization. If I had my choice, I would have taken Foundation of Marine Physiology first so I would have known what the body parts and permutations of physiology were, and then taxonomy would have made more sense. The one thing that I do remember from Dr. Hafferty's class was when we were studying sharks. Dr. Hafferty brought in a tooth of a huge megalodon and compared it to the tooth of a great white shark. I remember when he did that last quarter; we had just gotten the first of the salmon sharks. I started thinking just how close these sharks must be to a megalodon with them both being in the same family. They say that species within the same family are capable of mating, so there couldn't be that much difference between the salmon sharks and a megalodon. With megalodon having gone extinct only ten or eleven thousand years ago, who's to say how close the salmon sharks are to megalodon? It's not like anybody has done a genetic study on megalodon."

That's what Christina just loved about undergraduate students; they were unconfined in their thinking. They were able to see the obvious when experts saw problems to inquiry. Their perceptions were unclouded and unrestricted by schools of thought, scientific research procedures, peer reviewed publications, or their mentor's points of view.

"Just how would you do genetic studies on species that has been extinct for eleven thousand years?" Christina asked, fully engaged by this undergraduate student's stream of consciousness.

"Well on all those crime scene and science shows, they can match DNA extracted from a skeleton's teeth to identify somebody," Carol stated confidently. "Why not just take DNA out of a megalodon tooth like Dr. Hafferty brought to class. I mean, if we already know what most of the DNA looks like -- like what we've done for the salmon shark -- all we would have to know is just what is different from a megalodon, wouldn't we?"

"If only it was that easy," began an amused Christina. "For starters, the newest DNA we could extract from megalodon teeth would be a minimum of eleven thousand years old if we were lucky to find a tooth from one of the last living megalodons. Even then, DNA breaks down with age and exposure to the elements. All we would be able to get is a bunch of bits and pieces, and we wouldn't know what order it would all go in. It would be like doing a puzzle with a hundred million pieces and no picture on the box to give you a direction. There would be no way of knowing just what exactly the few chromosomal changes were that separate a megalodon from salmon shark."

"Even though megalodon teeth are encased in enamel?" Carol asked somewhat deflated. "Wouldn't that protect the DNA?"

"Well, yes it would. But it's the bony, lower part of the

tooth that anchors into the jaw that's the problem. That part of the tooth has no enamel on it. You see, bone is porous, and a shark tooth exposed to sea water would be filled with microorganisms that entered the bone matrix and mingled their DNA with that of the megalodon, making it virtually impossible to determine which bits of DNA are shark and which are from some flagellate."

"Oh," said Carol, now fully deflated. "Well, it would have been cool."

"And, besides, from my perspective," Christina continued, "I'm not sure of what value it would be to understand an extinct shark when there is so much to learn about living sharks that might help keep them from becoming extinct."

"Well, that makes sense." Carol reached down to pull the plug on the sink of suds, having rinsed the last bowl while finishing her conversation with Christina.

"It's getting kind of late, so why don't we lock up and walk out together?" Christina offered brightly, hoping to take some of the sting out of Carol's disappointment.

"That sounds great; just give me a sec to wipe my hands and I'll be right with you," said Carol, perking up at the offered camaraderie and turning on her beautiful smile.

5

Later that night, Christina was on her back porch at her home on Queen Anne Hill having a glass of merlot from a vineyard in the Yakima Valley. It was a beautiful summer night with a full breeze coming from the ocean. Christina had bought the refurbished bungalow, not for the Craftsmen Style design and woodwork throughout the house, but for the spectacular view of Lake Union, which nestled below the University of Washington. Her home, on the northwestern side of Queen Anne Hill, was far enough away and around the hill from the business district, the Space Needle left over from the 1962 Seattle World's Fair site, and the international restaurant district to be accessible, but out of sight; during the day it had a spectacular view of the Cascade Mountain Range, weather permitting. But tonight the lights and lakes below her couldn't hold her attention as her mind kept coming back to the conversation she'd had with Carol in the laboratory. Everything that she'd told Carol was true. But Christina's subconscious kept returning to the matter, trying to solve the problem of re-sequencing fragmented DNA. The more Christina thought about it, the more it became a logistical problem and not a theoretical impossibility. In her mind, the problem was really one of computing power. The best way to attack this problem wasn't to try to put the pieces of the puzzle together from fragmented DNA of a megalodon, but to establish the base DNA construct for the mackerel sharks.   Then she would only have to determine the locations within the DNA sequence that gave the megalodon its distinct characteristics.

The best way to accomplish this was to determine what sequences within a species varied from fish to fish and then compare that to the two target species. At that point, she could have a good understanding of the variability within a species and between species. If she worked from two very close relatives of the *Carcharodon megalodon*, like *Carcharodon caracharias*, the great white shark or maybe the salmon shark, she could really narrow the search down to a very small set of DNA locations. The biggest difference between the great white and the megalodon was believed to be primarily size. The biggest difference between the salmon shark and megalodon presumably would be size, body temperature regulation, and tooth configuration. That would narrow down the alleles sequence sites. She knew that this was a simplistic approach. But as a first pass, it might lead the way to more complex and real DNA restoration.   Best not to complicate the trial run by overreaching and adding too many variables to manage, she concluded. In the first pass, she would only attempt to approximate the body characteristics of megalodon.   In subsequent attempts, she would address behavioral and the other alleles.

'But how to get DNA of a megalodon?'   As she thought about this, she came to believe that it wouldn't be an

insurmountable problem. Recently, scientists had recovered soft tissue including connective tissue, blood vessels, and cells containing nuclei by de-mineralizing forty-five million-year-old dinosaur bones. There were several things in her favor. Megalodon first appeared only sixteen million years ago, so even the oldest megalodon teeth would be one-third the age of bone that the process had already been proven successful upon. Even if she obtained teeth one to two million years old when many scientists believe megalodon actually went extinct, she had a much higher probability of obtaining usable DNA.

Shark teeth, or in this case megalodon teeth, were already mineralized by calcium to a much denser level than bone. Jaws and dentition were the hardest structures of the animal kingdom, which is why they were found in greater frequency than any other bone types. She theorized that the denser mineralization of the teeth would retard the fossilization process because teeth were less porous than bone, due to the enamel that covered seventy percent of the teeth, and the existing high density of calcium would further slow the process. This theoretically meant that the probability of finding megalodon DNA was certainly looking very real, if not inevitable.

Where to get megalodon DNA would be a simple matter: the internet. All she needed to do was peruse the internet for sites that sold megalodon teeth. But she would have to be very particular in her purchases. If megalodon had been extinct for about eleven thousand years, as other scientists suspected, less than the blink of an eye in terms of world history, the trick would be to identify the youngest megalodon teeth and the locations that were yielding them. She wasn't an archeologist, nor an expert in artifact-dating methods. To get someone who was would be expensive and time-consuming. Since she was taking a flyer, departing from her normal research and its protocols, she concluded that she was just going to have to trust to appearances.

Christina wandered inside her house to a bedroom she'd converted into an office and sat down at her computer. After a few hours of research, she'd determined that megalodon teeth had been found on just about every continent and well inland, like Patagonia in South America. Megalodon teeth coming out of rock matrixes wouldn't be viable candidates because, not only would there be the known issue of cross DNA pollution from microbes in the soil, but also mineralization due to the fossilization process. The best candidates would have to come from sea beds, Christina reasoned, because they would be the newest detritus of all life's cycles that collected on top of the earth's crust. Further, the most ideal candidates would hopefully come from deep water. Microbial life dropped off drastically with depth away from the sun. A tooth from three to four hundred feet or better would be ideal. To further her chances of finding the least fragmented DNA, the enamel of the teeth would have to be wholly intact.

Further research showed Christina that the few deep-water recovered megalodon teeth wouldn't be research possibilities. The few that were known to exist were in the hands of academics. And in order to get DNA extraction from the core of the tooth, which would have the least probability of DNA cross-pollution, she would have to use a very invasive and destructive process, sure to destroy the artifact value of the tooth. To ask to perform such a procedure would surely be met with academic scorn. No, the best way to procure samples would be to buy them from the purveyors of shark teeth and novelties. There were plenty of sites if you were willing to shell out two to twenty thousand dollars. There were even divers who specialized in diving and digging for fossil sharks teeth from the seabed. You could even buy them on eBay. Christina decided for her purposes, since there was no way to date much of what was for sale on the open market, that the best possible route would be to not focus on the size of the tooth, but the color and condition. She reasoned that a newer tooth would have had less time for discoloration to set in and thus less possibility for DNA cross-pollution.

After some initial research into shark tooth divers' websites, she chose some promising operations which Christina contacted by email with a description of what she wanted.

She also decided that she would use her own personal credit cards to pay. That way no one at the laboratory would know or have any clue of her dalliance in the phantasmagoria. One part of her was fascinated, while another was horrified with the idea of DNA sequencing an extinct species. This was decidedly not an exercise in conservative research methodology; quite the opposite. It was a flier into pop culture. *'How many "mad scientist meddling with nature" movies had been made,'* she wondered. And how would she know that whatever sequence she came up with would actually be correct? On paper, it would look legitimate and plausible, but what if there were other differences that she didn't know about or couldn't identify? In the end, who was to say she wouldn't just sequence a big salmon shark with enlarged great white shark teeth?

'But if it could be done, the possibilities were tremendous,' Christina thought. If she could do it with a simple fish, like sharks, then recently extinct species might be resurrected if she could develop a process. The Dodo and Tasmanian Wolf were a few of the better known, but as a marine biologist, she knew there were thousands of lesser known species that disappeared every decade. Maybe these had a chance of being reincarnated from the abyss of extinction? Her mind flashed to images of specimen trays in the back storages of museums. She'd read an article long ago that explained that during the eighteenth and nineteenth century it had been fashionable for English nobles and the nouveau rich dilettantes of American Society and Europe to commune with nature and preserve it in their private collections. It had been kind of a snob's competition, each vying for the most exotic location from which to collect. This eventually fell out of favor with the wealthy and the collections had been donated to museums which, in many cases, were overloaded with donated collections. Usually the museum just placed them in some back store room, unexamined, or inventoried. Now, after

a hundred or more years after the collections were donated, they were being inventoried by eager graduate students looking for work – and the results were incredible. They were finding hundreds of species that had gone extinct before modern taxonomists had created their catalogues. Maybe these extinct creatures could be resurrected if she could just figure out a process to re-sequence extinct DNA.

At least that's how she justified it to herself.

'Besides, there was some scientific merit, just to see technically if disparate tidbits of DNA could be organized into a cohesive codex of chromosomes,' she argued to herself. And further, it would determine just how close a relative species' DNA blueprint overlay would need to be to produce viable results.

Christina thought how she just happened to be the right person, at the right place, at the right time ,to try this. It all lined up. The fact that her lab was fully funded to the point that she could take the time to even attempt this and hide the trail in the budget of other programs was way outside the norm and probability curves. The fact that she had a target species that had a relatively small and uncomplicated DNA structure relative to the more complex terrestrial phylum of amphibians, reptiles, birds and mammals also moved the expectation of success into the realm of possibility. In addition, she already had DNA from close relative species in the salmon and great white sharks, sampled and sequenced; this readily available material base moved the experiment closer to likely success. Finally, she was at a major research university that allowed her access to expertise and equipment she would need, but didn't have in her laboratory, furthered the reasonableness of conducting such research. The confluence of her circumstances and the fact that she lived and researched at a time when the technology was developed enough to make this even a remote possibility, merely gave further credence to her reasoning.

She mused for the moment that this attempt at fossil species reconstitution was really the legacy of the juncture of AIDS research and the Human Genome Project. Both these medical endeavors into the human condition developed the groundwork in tools, techniques and methodology of DNA sequencing. Just ten years ago, the best science could do was to track and test for a couple handful of genetic markers. Now, they played with the whole DNA sequences with a good understanding of what was protein construction instructions and what was triggers, modifiers and junk sequences. And all of these tools were available to her because she'd chosen the right university years ago and a native American tribe in Alaska that had a pile of money with an itch.

All she needed now was the right tooth.

After a few weeks a box arrived at Christina's house from a diver working off the coast of Baja, Mexico. Inside was a megalodon tooth that looked remarkable. The tooth was almost six and a half inches across at the widest part of the tooth root and nearly seven inches in length. It was almost white with very little discoloration, the enamel fully intact. Even the serrations on the edge of the teeth, usually the first part of ancient teeth to wear off, were fully expressed.   Except for just the slightest hint of discoloration, this tooth looked like it might have fallen out of the jaw of a shark just a few years ago.

Christina was giddy with excitement as she examined these specimens. She knew that it had DNA in it; she could just feel it by the weight in her hand. The price for this remarkable specimen: twenty thousand dollars. Christina didn't even blink; she knew that she could shift funds from the lab's materials budget to cover the cost.

'What I'm about to try is worth far more than I've already spent,' her mind whispered.

With the tooth moved to the lab, Christina had determined that it would be prudent to do a trial run to see if what was conceivable in her mind, possible on paper, and feasible in theory, was indeed something more than a whimsical flight of fantasy. Besides, what she learned from this first rough pass would help her tease out the weakness of her assumptions going in, and allow her to shape a serious inquiry next time around. No sense in possibly losing some of her hard-earned reputation and scientific currency by announcing to the world what she was doing, when she fully expected this first pass to fail miserably in reconstructing an extinct animal's genome. She didn't even know yet what she needed to know in order to create a working protocol.

In a way, it was exhilarating working outside scientific protocol.   Just doing and seeing, without the careful measurements, record keeping, hypothesis formulation and conservative analysis. Christina had long ago realized that scientific publication was nothing more than sales of a different stripe. The conclusion was the product, the experimentation methodology was the packaging, the journal of publication was the distribution channel, the target market was marine biologists, and the currency was acceptance and reputation. Christina envisioned herself blasting down the highway of investigation on her motorcycle with the winds of discovery blowing through her hair, without a care for the sales cycle afterward.

After shaking herself back to the present and letting the thrill of discovery fade, Christina got down to the serious business of processing the tooth for DNA. She set out sterile collection paper sheets on a sanitized granite lab counter top, upon which she laid the tooth. Using a high speed rotary tool with a very small cobalt drill bit, she made a series of parallel vertical bore holes from the top of the tooth's root towards the tooth's interior, but was careful not to penetrate too deeply into the tooth. The high speed rotor tool created a lot of heat at the bits point and this heat could destroy DNA. This area of the root enamel was most likely to be contaminated by other organisms' DNA, so she wasn't too concerned about heat damage.

Next she switched to a slow speed rotary awl that worked at a much lower speed, essentially scraping out a bore hole. She was careful to stop every centimeter of penetration into the tooth and collect the fine white powder scraping ejected from the bore hole. This material was placed into little plastic vials with snap-on lids and pointed bottoms used in DNA extraction processes. After the tooth looked like Swiss cheese, she replaced the drill bit with a larger rotary burr and ground the material out from in between the holes following the same pattern: discarding, collecting, and labeling.

After several hours of work, she'd several trays of vials of more than six ounces of material. When you are looking for molecular structures, the proverbial needle, six ounces of material to search through was more than just a haystack. Her mind was reeling with orders of magnitude trying to calculate just how impossible this task could be. Yet the intuitive side of her brain kept telling her that the computers would do all the mundane, repetitive work sifting through vast quantities of data. All she needed to do was focus on the key aspects and her regular work load.

Over the next weeks, Christina worked well into the wee morning hours preparing mass batches of her samples. She tried various methods of reducing or eliminating the calcium and magnesium that had concentrated in the tooth using various dilutions of acids. The product of these procedures was then sent through a series of processes to amplify any DNA segments. In turn, these batches were then fed into DNA sequencing machines, to capture any sequences that existed in the batches.

Most batches were blanks, but occasionally, a paucity of organic molecular structures were captured. Slowly, a mass of DNA snippet sequences started to emerge. After six weeks of intensive sequencing activity, Christina started her DNA reconstruction program.

At first nothing appeared in the output runs; then small

sequence segments started to assemble. The process accelerated as larger and larger chunks were connected together. The computer and its programs rushed to a conclusion... and a conundrum.

The computer finally signaled that it had compiled a DNA sequence out of the input data. But did that mean it was really the true sequence of the animal in question? Was it a matter of garbage in - garbage out? Were there any flaws in the sequence? Surely there were. Even in nature, every time a DNA sequence was split in cell reproduction, errors in replication could and did occur. Scientists had a nice little word for nature's mistakes: they called it mutation. What kind of mutations had she introduced to this sequence by the way she'd constructed her sequencing program?

The only way to tell was to compare her generated sequence to the DNA sequence of a known species: enter the great white and the salmon shark. Only then would she be able to tell whether her efforts had produced garbage or the DNA record of an extinct animal. And even then, there was still plenty of room to go wrong; even if her megalodon DNA was a distant cousin of the great white and the salmon shark, the distance in species and its accompanying DNA evolution might be too big a gap to bridge.

It all depended on the megalodon's family tree.

Christina now turned to her comparative programs to evaluate her generated megalodon DNA sequences to that of her two known baseline species. This process was the opposite of the generation sequence which was additive:

trying to add together, piece together, sequences. The comparative was subtractive in nature, identifying shared sequences and deleting them to end up with only the differences.

It was fall when the comparative runs were completed. Christina ended up with three hundred forty-three differences in alleles between the salmon shark and the megalodon and one hundred sixty-nine differences between the great white. The ratio made sense to her, confirming what she'd assumed in the great white was much closer in ancestry. *'But now what'*, she wondered?

"Great, on paper I've got it all nailed down. Except I have no way of knowing whether I've got a handful of horseshit or the real thing," she said to herself after her third examination of the comparative reports.

Frustrated, she decided to take a walk along The Cut, the waterway between Lake Union and Lake Washington, to seek some clarity. It was a warm Indian Summer night in the Pacific Northwest as she started her walk or, more accurately, her march. With her head down and a skull full of conflicting ideas and emotions ricocheting inside, she plowed ahead west into the sunset. She always knew this moment would come. Since she started this escapade, she'd always understood that at some point she would have to leave the warm and fuzzy turf of academic theory to test whether she'd actually developed a workable methodology to reincarnate the dead. The next step, the next leap, was into an abyss that she'd been dreading. The only true proof of concept would be to move to live subject testing.

She'd come to the end of the university's campus at the end of The Cut where it joined Lake Union. A dock jutted out into the lake with several boats tied alongside. Christina, on impulse, decided to sit on the end of the dock and watch the sun set over Queen Anne Hill. She found a piling to sit on and stared at the day's last rays reflecting off the shimmering waters. *'If I moved on to live subject testing by genetically altering a living embryo, it would be a huge academic risk from which there was no return,'* she reasoned. She knew creating Frankensteins was something her reputation would never recover from if she failed and it came to light. *'But it was the only way to prove my DNA recovery methods. Even a near miss would prove I was successful, like a fully developed fetus stillborn,'* she countered. At least then, she would have a good base from which to fine-tune her process. Her gaze had fallen to the waters right below her seat on the piling as she was pondering. Out of the corner of her eye, a movement in the water grabbed her attention in time to catch sight of a beautiful fourteen-inch rainbow trout rise to snatch an insect as it alighted on top of the water. At that moment, her mind was made up. *'Hell, at the end of the day, all I'm worrying about isn't anything more than a fish. It's not like it was a human fetus,'* she observed. *'If it doesn't conclude well, I can just throw out the evidence wrapped in yesterday's newspaper.'*

6

The timing for her decision was driven by the gestation study for the salmon shark funded by the Tlingit. Her plan was to harvest a fertilized zygote from one of the females they planned on impregnating, and to insert new DNA sequences via a molecularly engineered virus into the zygote, and re-implant it back into the shark host. She'd pioneered many of these processes and she felt confident she could get it done.

The next day, Christina made an announcement to her lab staff that they would impregnate all three of the salmon shark females but only monitor females one and two. Female three would only be generally monitored. Its purpose was to produce a late term shark fetus for dissection. What she didn't tell them was that shark number three would be implanted with an in-vitro embryo made to the specifications of her research into the megalodon's genetic makeup.

That was eight months ago. All had gone well with the fertilization and pregnancy of all three female salmon sharks. The nine-month gestation period was close to a successful conclusion. Many shark species were known to have in-uterine cannibalism among developing shark pups. Christina made sure only one zygote, her genetically altered version, was allowed to grow in female number three. It was a good hunch because the gestation study revealed that salmon sharks should be added to the list of shark species whose young ate each other in the womb.

It was a cold, late spring overcast night, the clouds low and heavy that threatened rain when Christina arrived home early from the lab. She really wasn't feeling well, having caught a cold the day before. She'd been keeping the cold at bay by heavily dosing herself with over-the-counter cold remedies, but they had made her drowsy and cotton-headed all day. Her plan was to turn in before seven, take a double dose of some sickly sweet, cherry-red nighttime medicine and let it knock her out for a good night's sleep.

It felt like she'd just crawled into bed when the ring of the phone ripped her from her dreamless slumber. She jerked her head upright, not really sure where she was, taking several seconds to recognize her own room. She clumsily thrashed about her nightstand searching for the phone, her hands clumsy from the medicine which had taken full effect.

She finally found the phone and brought it to her head, "Hello," she breathed heavily into the receiver.

"Hi, Dr. Katzburg, this is Charles…"

It took Christina a moment to connect the voice on the phone to one of her prized graduate students who worked in her lab.

"Oh, hi, Charles," she said huskily.

"Listen I don't want to alarm you too much but I noticed that female number three in the salmon shark pen appeared to have some convulsions a few minutes ago.

She just kind of shuddered a couple times and lay motionless for a few seconds before resuming normal behavior."

Christina was shot with adrenalin at these words and became awake instantly. "Oh, thank you for letting me know so quickly. What time is it anyhow?" she asked at the same time realizing that she'd a digital clock sitting on the nightstand that read eight thirty something. "Never mind, I got it," she corrected herself. "I'll be right down."

Christina hastily re-donned the clothes that she'd shed on her way to bed and headed for the front door. She popped the front open to look at the street. She wanted to get to the lab as quickly as possible, and her motorcycle was by far the better choice for speed. "Good, no rain," she murmured to herself, "I'll take my bike." She grabbed her bike keys and bolted out the door. The bike fired on the first turn of the starter, and Christina pulled a little heavily on the throttle as she headed out her driveway. She hadn't gone more than a block when a gentle rain started to spatter her as she sped towards her lab.

It had not rained for quite a while by Seattle standards. A layer of engine and exhaust oil had accumulated upon the surfaces of Seattle's streets, along with other fine debris. This added a level of slipperiness to the roads that Christina could have cared less about at the moment. Her mind, preoccupied with possible scenarios about female number three, her senses slowed and dulled by the medicine she'd taken, and her need for haste all led to the inexorable catastrophe of physics that followed.

Christina was making her way through the residential neighborhoods heading for an arterial. She was charging and laying her bike in on every corner, heavy on the power, digging out of each turn until about six blocks from her home when she was too deep and fast into a hard right hand turn before seeing the pothole she was going to cut right through. Given the conditions, she knew she was already using all the traction available to her machine's front and rear wheels leaving her no braking or maneuvering options. Her only option was to try and hold on to control going through the pothole. When her front tire became airborne from the pothole, the back tire couldn't pick up the excess demand and lost all traction in the sudden shift of cornering forces. The rear end spun out of the turn as the bike laid down on the pavement for a split second, sliding the tire first on its right side until both the front and rear tires simultaneously found traction a split second later and whipped the machine onto its left side. This had the effect of first laying down Christina to the right and then whipsaw-catapulting her high into the air as the bike flipped. In her haste, Christina hadn't fastened the chinstrap of her helmet, and the forces of being catapulted ripped the helmet from her head.

Had there been any witnesses to the accident, they would have seen Christina's body sail sixty feet through the air before her legs hit the back end of a mid-size sedan parked on the street opposite of the corner she'd tried to take. The impact started to cartwheel her body as it came into contact with the street, each somersault brutally smashing whatever was at the contact point until her momentum, as well as her body, was finally broken by the curb that she came to rest upon.

The raindrops fell from the night sky straight into Dr. Christina Katzburg's eyes, each one seemed intent upon landing on her face. They formed somewhere high in the darkened sky in gray, low scudding clouds unseen above. As the raindrops squeezed from the clouds, gravity's gentle tug started them earthwards. Gradually they traveled earthwards at first, gaining mass by colliding as fine mist droplets within the cloud to form larger drops before reaching terminal velocity and crashing straight at her head. Or so it seemed, as the drops entered the halo of the street light above her on the pole just a few feet from where her broken body lay. Right for her face they came. She was powerless to stop them. She could feel the cold rivulet of rain running in the gutter her body lay across and partially dammed. She could feel warm blood leaking from her shattered leg, imagining it mingling with the night's rains to make a red streamlet meandering down the gutter to the sewer. She could hear the rhythmic pop and fizzle as rain drops hit the hot cylinder head and exhaust of her motorcycle that lay on its side, piled up somewhere outside the circle of the street lamp's light.

And voices.

Excited voices -- but vague, mixed with the sound of gentle patter of rain joining with the world around her. *'I'm going to die here,'* the sudden thought popped into her head with finality and surprising gentleness.

7

Dr. Christina Katzburg lost consciousness shortly after being loaded onto the ambulance and never regained it. She was pronounced dead forty-five minutes later at, fittingly, the University of Washington Hospital's emergency room. A lovely funeral was held on a Thursday, eight days later, for the very honorable Dr. Christina Katzburg, attended by a myriad of family, friends, colleagues, staff and admirers, at a cemetery in north Seattle.

Still dressed in his funeral finery, Dr. Hendles stopped by Christina's lab to check on the progress of dismantling it. It had fallen to him, as the department head, to dismantle and return the property that had accumulated in the lab to the proper parties. Most of Christina's grants for research had been awarded to her personally, not to the university. So upon her death, all of her grants and research had come to a sudden halt. This had a terrible impact on many of the graduate students whose doctoral theses were being funded in part or whole by Dr. Katzburg's grant funds. They now had to write off their work and hoped to start over somewhere else. Many never would and their Ph.D. dreams died with Dr. Katzburg. One of the first things that Dr. Hendles had to do was to arrange for the release of all Dr. Katzburg's live test subjects. With the loss of the main source of funding and organization of the lab, feeding the population of large sharks quickly fell into disarray. The last thing the university wanted was any accusation of cruelty to animals, or fish for that matter, in its research labs. He'd arranged transportation and release for the warm water sharks that were due to be shipped out tomorrow. As for the salmon sharks, Dr. Hendles had contracted a local fishing boat, in its off-season now, to take the sharks out to the Strait of Juan De Fuca between Vancouver Island, Canada, and Washington State, and released them two days before.

As Dr. Hendles was surveying the collection of tradesman, technicians and students who volunteered to help break down the lab, when Charles, one of Dr. Katzburg's doctoral candidates, hurriedly approached him with a blue-bound lab journal in his hands.

"Dr. Hendles, I'm glad I caught you. I've got something that you need to see," he said thrusting the journal into Dr. Hendles' hands. "I've been cleaning out Dr. Katzburg's office and as I was cleaning out her desk, I came across that. She'd gotten a little secretive and touchy about some of her work in the last year, and well... I was a little curious to see what she was working on. So I started to glance through her lab journal to see what she was doing." His face reflected a mixture of doubt and pain. "I'm not sure what to do with this."

Dr. Hendles turned his attention to the book he now held, flipping it open to the beginning to begin reading. At first, it was clear that Dr. Hendles was speed skimming the contents, but then with a notable jerk, his eyes became riveted upon the journal and his body stiffened. With each passing moment he read, more color drained from his face, until he snapped the book closed. "Jesus H., Mother of God..." He stated loudly to himself, his face ashen. He startled back to his senses to find Charles searching his face.

"Where is your burn barrel?" he asked the young lab assistant standing before him.

8

Back to present day…

Blue sky tumbled with green water, and time seemed to slow to a crawl.

Eric flailed his arms and pumped his legs wildly as the apogee of arc was reached and he started his descent. Ten feet above the water, his safety tether line attached to the boat paid out and jerked him into a flip. Eric hit the water at an odd angle, having never found purchase in the air to right himself. It was probably a combination of hitting the water in an uncontrolled belly flop and the bone chilling temperature of the water that knocked the wind from his lungs. He found himself ten feet under the water trying to figure out which way was the surface and praying his lungs would work if he got there. He clawed frantically to make it to daylight.

He broke the surface and mercifully his lungs regained their rhythm as he gulped in lungful after lungful of air. Spinning in the water he tried to find his boat. After a moment's panic, he spotted the boat twenty yards away, upside down, the propeller thrust at the sky like an accusing finger. All he could see was the outboard and the stern of the craft, but it was sitting at a funny angle.

He swam to the boat still dazed and confused, reached the outboard motor, and used that for handholds and a step to climb over the stern, before flopping onto what was left of the boat's hull bottom.   He was shocked to see that the front portion of the boat was seriously damaged.

He was going to need to flip the boat over to see if any of his gear survived the event. He carefully crawled to the one side of the boat and stuck his hand in the water searching for the rope used to tie up the boat to docks. His hand found the line suspended in water and hauled the rope up to his position.   Once the rope was gathered, he slowly inched his way to the opposite side of the boat, rope in hand. From his knees, he slowly leveraged himself over the hull using the rope and his weight to lift the boat's opposite side from the water. Yet the boat wouldn't flip; the weight of the motor forced the boat into the water instead of flipping. It was unavoidable. If he was going to flip the boat he was going to have to sacrifice his body and go back in the water again. The boat wobbled as he got to his feet, inching out on the rope and leaning further and further over the side until his body's counterweight and leverage of the rope finally flipped the boat.   As it started to spin in the water, his feet lost their purchase on the steep angle of the wet slippery rubber and he tumbled back into the water.

Swimming to the rear of the boat, once again he used the outboard motor as step and climbed back into the wrecked boat. The sight of the shambles where the front half of his boat had been utterly confounded Eric as he tumbled into the rear section. Rolling to his knees in three inches of water that filled the stern section, Eric saw that the front half of the fiberglass inner hull was gone, its sides and bottom ragged and shattered. The front two air compartments on each side was shredded and floating just below the surface; all of his gear where he'd been sitting just moments ago, gone. The only thing keeping the boat afloat was the last two stern air compartments on either side of the shattered carcass of what was left of his boat.

"What the hell just happened?" he wondered aloud, half in plea to the roiling white froth that still surrounded the boat, and half in question to himself to make sure that he wasn't dead. He tried to come up with an explanation as to what had just happened, each scenario more improbable than the last. He finally settled on two explanations: he was attacked by a sperm whale or been struck by a meteor. The problem was he didn't believe either one of these possibilities. But it was a better explanation than being struck by blue ice from a high flying airline, the Air Force misplaced a rocket, sudden volcanic activity on the sea floor below, a long lost mine from WWII, or aliens.

Many moments he sat there trying to gather his thoughts; slowly the miasma of shock started to wear off and the chill of being wet set in. He started to take stock of his surroundings and determine his next move.

******

The hungry eyes slowly cruised away from the scene of the commotion it had created in search of some real food, bits of rubberized canvas gently flapping in its slipstream, caught in the fish's teeth.

******

The 'Beach Kit', as he called his survival gear, was still lashed to the port side in the rear compartment. It was a three-foot-long tubular bag with a flat bottom, two straps sewn in the seam of the bottom and into the sides so that it could be carried like a backpack that was tightly folded at the top, the folds held by a clip to make it waterproof. In addition, his cooler, lashed by a bungee cord to the starboard hull, and the fuel tank under the rear seat were still in place. *Was the boat capable of travel?* He knew the answer before he even asked it. This boat was supposed to be unsinkable, and so far given the extensive devastation, it had lived up to the manufacturer's claims. But there was no way this boat was going anywhere. Even if the motor started, it was the one thing that looked undamaged compared to the mutilated hulk of the inflation tubes, the shattered rigid fiberglass inner hull was an open shovel that would just scoop up the sea until the nose plowed under and flipped the outboard over the front. Given his predicament, the last thing that he wanted to have happen again was to be uncontrollably introduced to the water, especially with a heavy outboard motor with a spinning propeller in the mix.

His next idea was to see if he could put the motor in gear and try to reverse the boat to shore, hoping if he went slow enough and used his body and remaining equipment as counterweights for the damaged and missing boat front, he might be able to work his way ashore. Eric tried to start the motor, but the electric starter just cranked the motor in vain. *'The immersion in the water must have flooded the carburetor'*,Eric thought. He unlatched the motor's cover and set it aside. Everything looked in place and there was nothing obviously askew, so Eric tried cranking the motor again.

Nothing.

Clearly the water had penetrated some vital system of the engine, but without tools, there was no way for him to disassemble the engine to sort it out. Reaching a dead end with the motor, Eric replaced the engine cover and started to examine his other options.

His CB radio that had been in the Beach Kit would be of little use in this bay. The radio was only good for about two miles normally, four miles maybe with good line of sight bouncing off the water. But in this bay, the towering hills would block his signal. He could sit here and hope that his batteries held out long enough that his radio signal would reach the outer channel through the bay mouth and that some passing fisherman would catch his SOS. It was salmon season now, but he didn't keep track of the fishing openings.   The Alaska Department of Fish and Game monitored the salmon harvest every week and determined where and how many days, called openings, the following week fisherman would be allowed to harvest fish.   At this time of year, they were usually allowed two to four days a week. So potentially he could sit here for up to five days before there would be any fisherman passing by to catch his call.

If his batteries held...if a fisherman was listening... too many ifs, he decided.

Not to mention that he only had the food he packed for

today plus some dehydrated trail foods in his Beach Kit:
maybe enough food for two days.

Besides, he would have to deal with tides and currents;
there was no telling where he would drift. But he knew
that sooner or later his smashed boat would end up on the
beach. He also would have to deal with weather. The
bottom of his boat was flooded, he was wet and, if he
stayed with the boat, he would always be wet. The days
were not warm enough to survive in a wet boat. After no
more than two nights with the boat he would be so
hypothermic he'd be nonfunctional and death would soon
follow. And that was if it didn't rain during the two days.
That wasn't a realistic expectation either.

No, the only way he was going to survive was to get
ashore.

'Alright,' he thought, 'once I'm ashore, what's the plan
then?' For the first time he really looked hard at the bay's
terrain. Green, heavy foliage covered steep, very steep
hills that rose to two thousand feet on either side of him.
The beaches were relatively clear and he could walk them.
But there was a hitch there too. Most of the bigger islands
like this one had heavy populations of bears. Not the big
brown bears on the mainland, but the smaller black bears,
and one of their favorite haunts was to scavenge the beach
for food. So if he stayed on the beach, sooner or later he
was going to have a run in with bears. And sooner or
later, he would meet a sow with cubs; it was almost a
certainty. He might be able to spook off a male, but a sow
with cubs would attack first, ask questions later. And
where would he go once on the beach? He could walk out

to a beach facing the channel and hope to signal a passing fisherman. But most of them traveled at night to get to their fishing spots by morning, so he would have to stay up day and night, maybe for days, to keep an eye out. Again, that didn't have a high probability for success.

Then he recalled that he'd seen a small set of buildings in the next bay over. He remembered it as some sort of small permanent encampment. He didn't know what it was, but he'd seen evidence of people there three or so weeks ago when he'd followed some whales into that bay. The encampment was on the side closest to the shore next to him so all he would have to do is cut over the top of the ridge, drop down onto the beach, and follow it until he found the encampment; probably five miles as the crow flies, up and down two or three thousand feet -- a piece of cake...

The grim reality of his situation really started to set in for Eric; he now understood that his only salvation was a hard and dangerous hike over rugged, hostile terrain. He sat in boats all day; he was lean but not in shape. This was going to test his will and skills and if he didn't pass the test, he could very well die in the next day or two.

At least he'd been brilliantly lucky in getting shipwrecked in this particular bay that was within hiking distance of an encampment. The Alexander Archipelago was over five hundred miles long; the same distance of the Oregon and Washington coast combined. There were only seventy-two thousand people inhabiting this stretch of American coast, seventy thousand of which lived in four cities, leaving only a couple thousand people living in small villages among the tens of thousands of miles of coastline. With those kind of odds, if someone wanted to disappear off the face of the earth and leave no trace of their passing, very few places were better than this deserted stretch of continental America. Yes, he mused, he'd been unbelievably lucky to get marooned on an island that might be inhabited.

And the people that lived here -- now they were true pioneers. You could live in Southeastern Alaskan and go as long as you wanted without seeing another human being in this vast wilderness. It took a different constitution to live here year round, surrounded by nothing more than nature at its rawest. Eric knew just working up here less than half the year, even with frequent trips to town, he felt the desolation tug at his soul. By research season's end, he was always extremely eager to return to humanity.

Having set his course of action, he now set about the problem of getting to shore. He took out the soda cans, water , then re-lashed it to the boat's side with a bungee cord, hoping to come back to salvage the motor and other things he was about to leave behind once he got back to Ketchikan. He opened the waterproof bag and added the items from the cooler. He thought for a moment whether he really needed toilet paper for what he was about to partake. It was a necessity on a small boat with no bathroom; he just relieved himself over the side. There were bound to be leaves and grasses for that sort of thing on shore. He decided that the real value of the toilet paper would be as fire starting tinder.

With his pack in order, Eric took a last look about the boat to salvage anything else he could use. He thought of the coil of bow rope that had been in the nose of the boat. He could see the bow ring on the nose of the boat under the water with a piece of rope still tied to it. Reaching into the water, he pulled in the tattered, deflated front third of the boat slowly towards him; it was heavy, having filled with water, so he'd to be careful not to swamp the already precarious floating portion or end up pulling himself into the water until he was ready. Slowly the shredded and tattered rubber yielded to his tugs as he inched his way around the right side to the bow ring. He came to a shredded section very close to the front and had to gingerly work his way through it so as not to drop it and have to start all over. As he was working his way through the shredded section, he caught sight of something white imbedded in the rubber of the boat. It was a good ten inches from his path to the rope. He wanted to see what it was, but he was afraid he would drop the boat edge if he tried to work with one hand. So he continued on to the bow ring, determined to use the bow rope to tie off the front so he could work with two hands to get whatever was imbedded in the rubber.

After reaching the bow ring, he pulled in the rope, coiling it in his lap. He tied off the bow rope to the outboard and then started to haul up the rubber nose onto the shattered fiberglass floor. After a few moment's work he'd landed the section in which he spotted the white object earlier. It appeared to be a piece of gleaming white bone with two horns that protruded at the corners. He

instantly knew what he was looking at. This was the root
of a tooth! "Holy cow," he muttered, "what have I got
here?" the curiosity mixed with incredulity. This was
unlike any whale tooth he'd ever seen, and only a whale
was big enough to destroy his eleven-foot boat.

What a monster though; it had to be at least six inches
across the top, from horn to horn. Eric pulled out his
multi-tool from his belt holder and selecting the straight
blade began to cut the tooth out of the rubber tubing.
After a minute or two's work cutting the tough rubberized
canvas of the boat, he had the tooth free. In his hand was a
triangular shaped tooth that flared out two thirds of the
way down the serrated, enameled portion to join with the
root brow ending in the two root horns he'd initially seen.
It was probably seven or eight inches long and an inch-
and-a-half thick where the enamel met the root brow.

This was impossible! This was a shark tooth. But there
was no species big enough to fit this tooth.

WHAT HAD ATTACKED HIS BOAT?!

A hundred questions flooded his mind. He let them
roll over one another in his mind, just trying to catalogue
them, not ever trying to answer. The one thing that he
finally concluded was that he didn't know enough and
this was an important marine artifact. He carefully
inspected the rest of the rubber of he inflation tubes to see
if there was another tooth imbedded. There were no
more.

He replaced his multi-tool into its holder and carefully
packed the tooth into the waterproof bag along with the
rope he'd taken from the bow and tied the bag to the end

of his boat safety line. He took one more look at the distance to the shore, steeled himself against what he was about to do. He dropped the waterproof bag in the water and watched it settle, riding deep in the water, its back barely breaking the surface before he threw the line in to the side so that he wouldn't get tangled in it and slid into the green water.

It was every bit as cold as he remembered from earlier; he started in an overhand crawl stroke that was strong, smooth with deep pulls. The waterproof bag trailed behind him on its tether, just slightly buoyant; neither floating nor sinking, it created a lot of extra drag. He reminded himself to breathe every other stroke; this was going to be a marathon and not a sprint. Eric had grown up around the water in an upper middle class neighborhood in Florence, California; most of his friends had pools. Subsequently, his mother drug him to all sorts of swimming classes just so she could be assured that when he was out of sight swimming at the neighbors, she wouldn't need to be worried.

He'd been so preoccupied on trying to breathe and fight the panic that the cold, cold water of the Pacific would sap his strength before he made it to shore, that he was late in reacting. He'd not gone more than forty yards when he hit his first jellyfish; on the downward pull his right hand hit a big blob of Jello-like substance that was the bell of a jellyfish. His hand cleaved through the firm mass of the jellyfish's body. He reflexively pulled the stroke short and away from the jellyfish, but too late. His hand passed through into the stinging tentacles that draped his entire hand in slimy, stringy filaments of stinging cells. Dog paddling for a moment, Eric shook his hand this way and that under water, trying to clear his hand of the slimy blob of goo that he knew was attacking his skin with poison.

Eric had felt the sting of jellyfish before, when he was hauling up his sound gear from the water; the cord might pass through the drifting tentacles pulling them off the jellyfish and wrapping the strings of stinging cell around the cord. He would have to scrape off the stingers before it got on the cord reel; sometimes the sound heads would get entangled with a jelly fish, fouling the gear so badly that he would have to rinse the head with splashed water to clean it while scrapping away jellyfish slime with his multi tool.

His hand cleared of the tentacles, Eric started to swim again for the shore. His right hand started to tingle from the venom that had been injected by billions of stinging cells. Slowly the sensation increased from a tingle until his entire hand and wrist felt like it was on fire, and no amount of water could put out the blaze.

It was getting difficult to remember to breathe with the pain in his hand threatening to take all of his focus away from the shore. It was getting harder to swim because his hand burnt so badly; he was tending to stroke less fully with his right while his left hand carried more of the work. This in turn made Eric start to swim in a left hand arc. He had to constantly correct his course, which was slowing him down, increasingly drawing down his strength.

Eric didn't know how far he'd gone from the first

jellyfish, when he hit another. This time he'd taken a breath under his right armpit and was turning his face back into the water when he hit a jellyfish full on with his face. The body of jellyfish didn't fracture this time, but was pushed under and slid across his face to his armpit and side. Instinctively he rolled to his left away for the jellyfish. In the commotion of his emergency maneuver, he whipped some of the stinging tentacle up into his face; instinctively he clawed with both hands to wipe the gooey strands from his face.

This was the worst thing he could have done.

By trying to wipe the tentacles from his face, he merely smeared the stinging cells broadly over his forehead, eyelids, face and neck, rubbing them in to his skin. Within moments, his face, with its much thinner skin than his left hand that he'd used to wipe the tentacles away, were a blaze with the fire of pain.

Nearly blinded and in agony, he oriented himself to the shore again. He'd almost covered nearly half the distance to his goal. The thick kelp bed stalks calmly floated on the surface, now only twenty yards away, beckoning him. It was an ebb tide and the level of the bay had lowered with the departing tide. The kelp, built by mother nature to float, had less distance to cover to the surface from the seabed so, consequently, there was a larger portion of each kelp stalk floating on the surface, making the kelp bed a thick mattress of tentacles.

His smooth and powerful stroke was now a series of choppy shallow flails when he plunged into the kelp bed. At first Eric was soothed by the gentle slimy feel of the kelp on his burning skin. But the kelp started to grip his body in its gentle embrace. He was struggling to move a few feet at a time. As he kicked, the kelp wrapped itself around his legs, feeling like it was threatening to pull him down. The waterproof bag that had caused relatively little drag in open water now tugged at his safety harness like an anchor.

The fear that he felt from the jellyfish stinging turned to a sense of panic. Fueled by the pain of the jellyfish stings, combined with the sense that the kelp would drag him down to his death, Eric was no longer able to control rational thought. The panic built into a full-on animal instinct to flee, to get way. He struggled and struggled against the thick kelp mat until he was exhausted. He flipped to his back and lie there gulping great lungfuls of air. Strength eventually returned to his limbs along with the animal desire to extricate himself. He rolled back into the kelp and struggled until he was exhausted again and had to rest. With each stop his overall panic lowered as the exhaustion and cold numbed his limbs and his mind.

Through his panic and desperation, Eric had not been able to catch the signs of hypothermia which was starting to manifest its symptoms. As he struggled against the kelp his body was in motion yet, when he needed to rest, uncontrollable shivers racked his body. Every time he oriented himself to the shore he didn't notice the edges of his peripheral vision were shrinking into a tunnel. The jellyfish stinging started to fade, as his body's warmth was slowly sucked from him and first his skin and then his limbs started to go numb.

The cycle of struggle, exhaustion and rest repeated itself until Eric lost track of the number of times he'd rested. The only thing that was driving him now through kelp bead was pure instinct to survive. He no longer had the strength or energy for fear, panic, or calculation.

So it came as a great surprise to Eric when he broke free of the kelp bed twenty yards from the shore and a great big, beautiful beach covered in football sized, rounded gray rocks opened up before him. His heart leaped and he surged the last of his energy in one last frantic surge at the beach. But he wasn't going anywhere and the beach remained out of reach. The waterproof bag was still in tow and entangled in the kelp. This had an even worse affect upon Eric, now that he was so close to safety. Ironically the kelp that he struggled against was actually giving him traction to pull the waterproof bag through the kelp bed. He was now being staked to the kelp bed, killed by his Beach Kit that he would need to survive if he could cover the next ten yards. At this point, he broke mentally. His efforts subsided as the last of his energy drained. He let loose an anguished gasp that came from the depth of his soul as he struggled weakly against his leash.

His strength, his will, were now gone; and with it hypothermia's seductive grip of sleep tightened as his core temperature crossed a threshold. Eric started to sink. He sank about five feet until he bumped into the gently sloping bottom. It didn't register upon Eric that he was resting on the bottom. Time had seemed to stop for Eric. Then with a searing jolt of recognition, he realized where he was and some little corner of his mind was screaming

"STAND UP!" With that understanding, his over taxed adrenal glands released the last molecules of adrenaline that his body possessed into his blood stream and Eric jolted to a standing position, his head broke the surface with his feet planted on the seabed. He stood there breathing, numb, the stinging in his face and arms registered upon his psyche for a moment but it seemed that it was happening to some other body. Happy to standing again, even if not on dry land, he stood there for many moments just enjoying the thought that he was alive and the he'd made it ashore.

Eric didn't know what broke his reverie, but he realized that he'd to get out of the water. He turned to face the kelp bed, grabbed as best he could with numb hands the tether rope and leaned away into rope, dragging the bag out of the kelp as he backed his way up the beach inch by inch to the water line. The bag finally broke free into open water with Eric in waist deep water. Eric turned and staggered over jumbled, slim covered, slippery boulders and cast himself face first on the boulder beach just above the water line.

He lay there for no more than a few seconds before the large amounts of seawater he'd swallowed roiled in his stomach. Literally heaving himself to his knees, he ejected all that was in his stomach. When he was spent, Eric rolled to his back away from the pile of stomach contents. There is a fine line between sleep and unconsciousness. It was hard to say which side of the line Eric slipped into.

9

When Eric eased back into consciousness, his senses, his face, and body ached from the cold and pressure points of the boulders that he'd been lying upon. That it was still daylight registered upon his slowly reviving senses; he brought his left hand up over his face as he lay upon his back to see the time. It was a quarter past five. How long had he lain here, he wondered? It had been about eleven o'clock when he went into the water the first time. But he'd not glanced at his watch since then. He'd no idea how long he spent on the boat before abandoning it, or how long it had taken to swim to shore. Then his mind flashed to the horrific swim to get on this point. He reached both hands to rub his face. His hands and face felt normal as if the agony of the jellyfish stings had never happened or was just a bad dream. But he knew the bad dream was just beginning and he'd better get started on trying to survive and get his little behind over the mountain ridges that lay between him and his succor.

He rolled over to his knees in the direction away from his vomit; he felt like someone had beaten his entire body with a baseball bat before switching to rubber hoses. His clothes had partially dried on top from gravity and the sun, but for the most part he was still wet, which made the clothes clingy and difficult to move in. He struggled to his feet in his straitjacket shirt and pants, and felt his shoes fill with saltwater that gravity was pulling out of his clothes. As he turned to face toward the hill behind him, he was overwhelmed with the bloody, crappy mess that he was in.   The brush looked impenetrable, the mountain impossibly steep.   A wave of despair washed over him and took with it his newfound energy for survival. He felt like crying.   Slowly he realized that it was just the exhaustion that wasn't allowing him to keep his emotions in check.

With a concerted effort, he slowly willed himself back into the here and now. *'Better keep your shit in one sock, boy,'* he told himself, *'cause out here, if you don't hold it together, you might as well kiss your ass goodbye. And nobody will ever find your body.   Hell, they won't even know where to look. Even if they find the tattered boat on some beach, they will have no way of knowing if you came ashore on this island or if your boat just washed up from somewhere else.'*

'Gotta keep a positive mental attitude, that's your only ticket out of here. That's the only way you're going to survive.'

He figured that there was another two and half hours of good sunlight left, and that was plenty of time to set up a camp for the night. It felt good to put some sort of measure and metrics on his position. All he could see was uncontrolled nature all around him. Just the little thought of the manmade measurement of time in the wilderness gave him the illusion that he needed: that he could impose his will upon nature and survive.

With the certainty born of desperation, exhaustion, and the instinct to survive, he set out to get situated for the night.   The first thing that he did was to pull in his waterproof bag that had settled in the surf line. Once out of the water, he picked it up with the coil of towline and headed up to where the rock beach hit the forest and a one-foot high berm of exposed earth held together by the roots of the grasses and plants along the edge. The vegetation made a natural seat. He found a tuft of grass, sat down, setting the waterproof bag next to him. First, he untied his shoes, struggling with the still wet laces of his athletic training shoes that he wore when he was going to be onboard boats all day, pulled his shoes from his feet, and dumped the water from them. Next he wrestled off his socks and wrung them out. He set both socks and shoe in the grass beside him, hoping that this would help to dry them out a little before he would have put them on again. Next he pulled the waterproof bag over and set it upon the ground between his feet, bracing it with both his knees. Taking the clip off that clamped the folds together to make the bag watertight, he casually unrolled the remaining bag until the end appeared, which he opened into a circle. To make it easier to empty the waterproof bag of its contents, Eric folded and reversed the excess bag material back on itself like a sleeve being rolled up. The first thing that came out of the bag was the coil of bowline, which he set behind him in the grass. Next came the tooth, set in the grass to his left. He pulled the soda cans, water bottles, food, and toilet paper out next and set them aside. Now he rummaged in earnest for what he really wanted from the bag. His hands pawed through plastic wrappers and small items that he couldn't identify until his hands wrapped around cold steel. "Come to pappa, beautiful,"

Eric crooned to his new-found possesion. A long thin cylindrical object made of black plastic and blued steel emerged from that bag. It was a pump twelve gauge shotgun with a shortened barrel, plastic checkered fore grip and folding stock with a light canvas shot shell belt wrapped around it, holding fifteen shells plugged into elastic loops.

Laying the gun in his lap, he gently unwrapped the ammo belt until he could lay it across his thighs, careful not to get any dirt or vegetation on the shells. His thumb found the release of the stock's hinge mechanism and folded the stock backwards until it locked into position. He then folded down the butt plate of the collapsible stock to create a secure surface to brace into his shoulder when he fired the weapon. Next, starting at the end on the left hand side so as to not disturb the careful sequence in which the belt was organized, he took the first shell with an "B" written on the side of it in felt pen, and loaded it into aperture. The pivoting latch in the bottom of the receiver to hold shells into the tubular magazine of the gun flicked back into position as the shell passed into the weapon's gullet. With the first shell in, he racked the slide with a satisfying 'shick-shich', first back and then pushed forward as the shot shell was loaded into the chamber and the firing pin was automatically cocked. He loaded one more "B" shot shell to replace the one just loaded from the magazine. He flicked the safety to "ON" which was a little button on the trigger housing just in front of the trigger. Eric could unsafe the weapon with just a touch of his trigger finger before he curled it around the trigger. It was all designed for speed. Pump shotguns were the fastest firing non-automatic weapons available. By design, bird hunters, for whom shotguns were primarily designed, had only snap split seconds to shoulder their weapons, find their small fleeting targets with the sights, get off a shot, reload, reacquire and fire again. A good shot gunner could get off three shots before the bird was out of range. A good shooter needed but one shot to bring down a bird. Eric's gun was meant for slightly different work. The magazine had the plug removed, which had limited the magazine to the legal bird hunting limit of two shells in the magazine and one in the chamber when hunting birds, so that he could store four shells in the magazine and one in the chamber. The barrel had been shortened, no choke, and only a simple small round brass bead imbedded in top of the barrel's end for a sight. A shorter barrel was easier to swing through an arc to find a target, but a shorter barrel also was less accurate at longer ranges, allowing the lead pellets to diverge more widely over the target. Accuracy and concentration of pellets were not a major concern, nor were small fleeting targets. Eric's shotgun had been configured to deal with bears.

This was actually the gun of choice for most Alaskan Guides to put down a bear when confronted in the bush. If you had to fire the weapon it would be at close range with the target charging. And bears were amazingly quick. To defend yourself successfully, it was more a matter of firepower than accuracy. The more shots you could get off the better your chances of survival. When hunting bears, hunters preferred a rifle, counting on the placement of one good shot to bring down their quarry at a distance of their choosing, usually the farther away the better. Even with one good shot that totally destroyed the heart and lungs of a bear, they were still incredibly resilient. With the lungs and heart turned to jelly and sucked out the exit wound by the vacuum of a high powered rifle bullet, a bear still had over a minute's worth of oxygen in its blood stream, and that was plenty of time to cover a good distance to maul its attacker.

One bullet was all that a hunter wanted to use because the hunter wanted the bear's carcass in a good as shape as possible, whether it be for the pelt, meat or both. A trophy bear was no good to the taxidermist if it had been punched full of entry holes and massive exit wounds. But that was a planned approach where the hunter snuck upon a bear and took careful aim. If Eric encountered a bear it would be as far from that scenario as one could get. In the heavy brush, you would be lucky if you could see the bear from forty yards out. And a bear could cover that in a second or two. There was little or no presence of man on the coastal island, so bears were the apex predators. With no natural enemies, bears would throw caution to the wind and charge anything they determined not to be another bear in expectation of an easy meal.

Of course, there was also a good chance that being an apex predator would work in Eric's favor too. Bears were nearsighted as hell. But unless the bear had scented whatever it was thinking of charging, it was very likely that it would circle upwind to identify its next meal before it did anything rash. Every experience in the bear's past would have been that of a prey turning to flee before the bear, trying to escape its crushing jaws and ripping claws. Like most bullies, a bear would get confused when something stood its ground or turned the tables by getting aggressive with it. The bear's simple brain could make the simple calculation: if it wants to mess with me, then maybe I do not want to mess with it.

The idea was to keep a bear's mind from slipping into predator mode. Predator's minds were hardwired to make the calculations of whether the potential prey could be obtained without more expenditure of effort than it was worth; and it had to be obtained without grievous injury to the predator while bringing down the prey. Most animals solved that problem for the bear by turning to flee. Instinctively, a bear knows that it is impossible to fight while running away so its chances of grievous injury are minimized. However, something that is willing to engage in battle is something that is willing to inflict grievous harm to the bear, will trigger the instinct of self preservation, to move on, and find more compliant prey. Fight or flight impulses could be made to work in Eric's favor. Scare or confuse the bear and it would scuttle away at high speed. As long as he didn't overdo the threatening posture and force the bear's brain to conclude that imminent danger was about to befall it and its best option was to stand and fight.

Alaskan Bushmen had developed a brutal strategy for these confrontations. Shotguns were loaded with a special mix of shells to reap destruction upon the flesh of a bear to bring about a swift conclusion to any confrontation. The first three shells out of the shotgun contained buckshot. A total of nine, thirty-two caliber lead balls would be hurled out to the barrel with each shot; the intent was to destroy the bear's nose, eyes and ears. All of the sensory organs with which the bear wanted to find you. Even a blinded, deaf bear with a destroyed nose still has claws to kill a man, so the next two shells in the pattern of shells were massive hollow point slugs designed to break the bones of a bear's shoulders, neck and arms from close range so that it would be immobilized, pinned to the ground.

The best spot to aim for was to put the sight bead on the bears face. Usually, a bear would charge with head slightly down in the center of the bear's mass. If Eric aimed for the bear's face, where all the sensory organs he wanted to destroy were located and he was high, low, left or right, he would still disable some aspect of the bear. He didn't need to kill the bear, just make it go away.

Eric loaded three more shells labeled B, S, and S in that order- S for slug, B for buckshot. As he loaded the last shell into the shotgun, he started a mantra that he would mutter countless times in the days ahead "Shoot the head, shoot the head, shoot the head…"

Now, Eric had a faint sense of security about him. He knew there was still plenty that could go wrong, though. The gun could jam, a bear could be on him before he could get the gun to his shoulder and draw down, he could panic and run, and worst of all he could miss or just wound the bear and further infuriate it. Even so, the cold blued steel still felt mighty reassuring. He set the gun on its black plastic butt stock and propped up the barrel in a sapling behind him within quick reach.

But what to do with the cartridge belt though? In a flash encounter with a bear it was going to be settled with whatever was loaded in the gun. It would be over, one way or another, before he would get a chance to reload the weapon. The chances of him surviving a bear attack were fifty/fifty. He'd enough shells for three encounters, and he was pretty sure that if he'd to put down three bears, one of them was bound to get him, or just enough of him so that he would die from some complication of major wound trauma before he reached his destination and safety.

He decided to arrange the shells by type and use it as a belt to hang other gear in dry bag upon. Having settled upon that, he proceeded to empty the bag of its remaining contents to take inventory. Actually, he was really stalling for time. He was fuzzy-headed from the exhaustive swim and overdoses of adrenaline. He felt rooted where he sat, his legs just not up to the burden of movement now that his butt was installed on a nice cushy patch of grass. He kidded himself by trying to sell himself on the notion that he really needed to dry out a little more before he went on the move. At a subconscious level, he understood that he was drawing sustenance for his courage by seeing and feeling the gems of modern man's manufacturing prowess that were emerging from the innards of the bag.

The next items to come out were the handheld CB radio; a waterproof container full of strike anywhere matches for making fire, plus a flint and steel striker as a backup; a big survival knife in a scabbard; a hatchet with a curved handle, leather grip, and head cover; some packets of vacuum-packed trail mix of nuts, raisins, candy and four packs of instant meals that just needed water added to eat, two of stew and two of chicken with gravy and rice; a water purifying straw; space blanket and a ten by twelve foot silver tarp with a fifty-foot coil of three-eighths inch yellow nylon rope. The hatchet and survival knife he decided would go on the ammo belt around his waist; the rest would be packed and carried in the dry bag on his back.

Looking at the CB radio, even though he knew it would be futile, he turned it on and tuned it to channel 9, the emergency frequency, and held down the button "Mayday, mayday, mayday. Anyone on this channel, anyone on this channel -- this is Eric McCallister. I've been beached, my boat has been destroyed. I need assistance. Please respond." Nothing but static returned his ethereal pleas. He tried again with the same results. He tried all the channels. Nothing. *'Better save the batteries,'* he concluded, turning it off and relaying it in on the bank next to him.

After heaving his guts on the beach and seeing the water bottles, he suddenly realized how thirsty he was, so he twisted off the lid on a bottle of water and drank it in one pull. The water soothed his irritated throat from the earlier vomiting. He decided to keep the bottle so that he could fill it from a stream later.

It was funny; it occurred to Eric that when he was ordering the survival supplies, he never really envisioned using them. It had been an esoteric exercise of survival needs guessing. As he looked at his little piles of treasures laid about him, he realized that he never had thought through how he was actually going to use this stuff. Everything had been considered from disjointed, fragmentary thoughts of imagined survival scenarios. *'A tarp could be made to make a tent or a poncho. I'll need fire...'* But now that he was actually on the beach, it all looked pitifully inadequate. He could think of a hundred things that he would need. More food, a bigger water purifier, and a backup in case his little purifying straw crapped out before he got to safety. Rain gear, first aid kit... a spoon.

'Best not to dwell on the negative,' he told himself. *'I've got to stay positive.'*

He repacked his dry bag with the items placed in order of what he thought that he would need first. He resealed the bag with the clip and turned to his shoes. He struggled to get the wet socks back on his feet and the wet shoes over the socks. All he needed to do was to get up, put his ammo belt on, hoist the dry sack to his back, grab his gun, and go.

Yet he remained seated.

He sat there hoping for a miracle... that someone would just trip on by and rescue him. What he really wanted to do was continue to keep his back to the monster behind him and the monumental task before him, for which he knew he was ill-prepared.

With a final bit of mental exertion he rocked forward. That little inertia seemed to break the chains that had anchored him to his seat, and up he stood. He turned to gather his things and adjusted them to his body as best he could. "What is that old saw?" He said with some forced bon homme to no one in particular. "A journey of a thousand miles starts with the first step. Yeah, well, la-di-dah."

With that he stepped off into the island wilderness.

The initial slogging was tough going. The vegetation was thick and heavy with moisture. Heavy plantings of ground willows made it difficult for Eric to squeeze his body between branches, especially with the dry sack on his back. The ground was covered in decaying leaves that were slimy from the morning dew that never burned off. This made if impossible for Eric's flimsy athletic shoes to find footing. His feet just slipped out from under him. The hill facing him was near a fifty-degree incline, so that he'd to pull himself up using his hands more than anything. Within forty yards of travel up the hill he was totally winded and soaked again from his elbows to his toes. As he sat there resting, gasping for air, he tried to scan up the hill for the best path to skirt around obstacles. He'd envisioned himself sneaking quietly up the hill so as not to attract any unwarranted attention from the bears in the neighborhood, but his gasps for air sounded like a foghorn in his own ears. God only knows, he imagined, what all the noise he was making sounded like as it reverberated through the surrounding woods. After his breathing returned to something resembling normal, he took a few moments to rest on his feet before pushing on for another forty years.

This cycle repeated itself several times before he broke out into a small clearing where the incline reduced to something close to forty-five degrees.

The clearing was modest, if not miniscule by forest standards; approximately seventy yards by twenty. But it was enough for Eric. He'd pushed himself as far as he could go. Night was starting to approach, and in a large bowl of the bay that he was in, the walls of that bowl would shut out the daylight much quicker than if he was on the open sea. He found a place along the edge of the clearing where a small bench in the terrain had formed and dropped his pack after propping his shot gun up against a nearby tree.

First order of business was to make some shelter for the night. He took his hatchet and survival knife and set about gathering stout poles to make a shelter frame. Materials were abundant and it didn't take him long: a couple four-foot poles with forks at the end, which he set into the ground and buttressed with rocks; a long ridge pole to go between the two set in the forks. Next, Eric leaned poles along the ridgepole at a steep angle. He then started gathering armfuls of pine and cedar bows for the low-hanging branches, cutting them off with his survival knife. The longer bows were stacked over the frame of his on-sided lean-to, interweaving them with the poles and each other to give the structure a little more rigidity. When he finish he took a moment to admire his work; "Not waterproof," he mused aloud, "but it shouldn't blow over if the wind came up during the night."

He laid half of the remaining pine bows under the lean-to form a bed foundation, with a pile at one end to make a pillow. Next, he extracted the tarp from the sack and

folded it into thirds and folded one end over. He placed
the tarp over the bed he'd made. He next scraped armfuls
of pine needles, which were distributed over the tarp and
then topped it off with the remaining pine bows. The
whole idea was to create as many air pockets against the
tarp for insulation. Given the matrix of pine needles and
bows, he felt that he would survive in good order and stay
dry from the dew. The weather forecast thankfully called
for fair weather like today's for the next day or so before a
weather front moved in, as far as he could recall.

Next, he set about getting tinder and as much dry
firewood as he could carry or drag over to the campsite.
Finally, before attempting to start a fire, he built a little
enclosure in front of his lean-to which he lined with rocks
from around the clearing. This would create a windbreak
from the convection currents of the morning and evening
temperature swings, plus it would capture the heat of the
fire and radiate the heat back into the lean-to, even long
after the fire expired.

With every thing in place, lighting the fire using the
toilet paper and matches was easy. Soon there was a very
brisk fire burning and the heat felt luxurious to Eric. The
last thing he needed to accomplish was to eat some food
before he went to sleep. He rummaged around in the bag
until he found the two sandwiches he'd made for lunch.
They were turkey with mayonnaise and mustard. Eric
suddenly was concerned about the mayonnaise. Had it
been out of the cooler too long and gone bad? He
envisioned himself running from the lean-to, awoken from
sound sleep to throw up yet again, or endless diarrhea

from food poisoning. After mulling over the possible consequences, he was too tired and hungry to say no to the food in his hands. Since the food was questionable, it made no sense to eat one sandwich now and leave the other for breakfast. In for a penny, in for a pound he reasoned. He ravenously wolfed down both sandwiches and polished off another bottle of water. In the morning he would find a stream and fill both water bottles. But he knew for now, that he'd seriously depleted his body's reserves with all his exertions, and it was better to load up now rather than to start what may be a long and arduous journey with a deficit of body.

He'd been fine as long as he'd been in motion, but as Eric had sat there finishing his sandwiches, aches and pains started to erupt from the entirety of his body. With pains and aches stacked on top of each other, he crawled to the head of his makeshift bed, took off his shoes and set them under the lean-to next to his bed, and placed the shotgun beside him within easy reach before he wiggled down into the tarp layers. From inside the folds of his cocoon, he folded the edges of the tarp up over his head and sealed himself away from the mountain he was scaling and the wilderness that was on the other side of the rubberized cloth.

His mind was a jumble of thoughts about tomorrow and the day's events. But the last thought that he had was to drift back to the moment today when all his troubles began, when he found himself sailing through the air and wondering what kind of animal could have done this to him.

10

Pete Sondergrass was a third generation fisherman. Like all longtime fisherman, he knew the superstition about leaving harbor on a Friday. He knew it was silly and a bunch of gibberish. But it didn't always matter what he thought. If other boat captains thought that you were bad luck, then they would start to act inconsistent around you; and when you are piloting sixty-three foot boats, often in close quarters, that can be a bad thing. Crews were even more susceptible to superstitions. Breakdowns in equipment were inevitable, no matter how good your maintenance. But leave on a Friday, and the first little thing to break down automatically is attributed to jinx because of a Friday departure. So Pete had the *Linda Bea* tied up to the cannery wharf at the south end of Ketchikan with the main diesel warming and one of its two generators making power. It was a twelve-hour run to where he wanted to fish so he could have elected to push off tomorrow mid-morning. Instead he choose to push off the Saturday morning, twelve o' one a.m., rather than after daylight, because he knew the crew would be tempted to get in all the last minute revelry that a Friday night in town could afford them. Fishermen will be fishermen, and Pete didn't hold it against them. He just didn't want to put up with an ill-tempered, hungover crew that may not be paying attention to running the boat.

Experience had taught him it was better to show up early with a refreshed crew.

Pete was a High-Liner among salmon purse-seiners and the *Linda Bea* showed it. Naming it the "Linda Bea" had been a tribute to his mother, who gave him life; and to the sea, which sustained his life with its bounty. The *Linda Bea* was a new sixty-three foot, the legal length at the water line, fiberglass purse-seiner with top-of-the-line gear and systems. Of course the boat was actually several feet longer when she was fishing. The way Pete got around that regulation was that the boat only had to be measured once to be pronounced fit and in regulation for commercial fishing. So, before inspection, Pete made sure all the holds were empty, the fuel, water and lube tanks had little or nothing in them, and no supplies were on board. What gear he required to have on board for inspection was piled at the stern so that the bow would be rocked up. The *Linda Bea* rode like a cork in the water and the steep rake of her bow floated the intersection of the waterline much closer to the keel than normal. This was as light and tall in the water that the *Linda Bea* would ever ride in her working life. When fully loaded, with the brine chiller center hold full, the *Linda Bea* was closer to sixty-six feet.

High-Liners were the top ten percent of moneymakers in the fishing fleet; consequently, Pete had his pick of crew replacements. This year again, he'd a top-notch crew; all five were milling about on the deck, waiting for orders to cast off. A few of them were playing with Corky, his female Border collie mix that was the unofficial mascot of the boat. As a puppy, she loved to chew on the plastic floats of the purse-seine net that keep it from sinking. In the old days fisherman had used hollow-cored floats of cork to do this task. But tradition dies hard among fishermen and, even though true cork floats disappeared long ago, the nomenclature still stuck. Pete had originally named her something else, but the crew continued to call her Corky after her favorite pastime and the name just stuck. All the gear and supplies for the four day fishing opening, starting Sunday, were stowed and lashed down for the run out to the fishing grounds off the outside of Noyes Island where he wanted to work.

At twelve o' five a.m. he gave the orders to cast off the stern line while he used the main propeller and rudder to pivot the stern out towards the channel, using the spring line as a fulcrum pivot point. Once the stern had sufficient angle to back into the channel, he ordered the spring line and then the bowline cast off. It was a matter of a dozen minutes or less to exit the channel and set the boat on a southwesterly course. Most of the crew had already turned into their bunks in the fo'c's'le, except for his engineer/first mate who he always trusted with the first wheel watch out of town. Each of the crewmembers would spend two hours steering the boat on wheel watches. It was mainly an exercise of staying awake, since the boat was on autopilot. The main activities were to check the radar for other ships and to use as a cross reference to the Global Positioning System, and charting their position. Occasionally a course change or correction was needed but that was usually just dialed into Iron

Mike, as the crew called the autopilot. The real task was to stay awake and not run the boat onto rocks or the beach. That, and to look for deadheads. These were logs that floated vertically in the water which could punch up into the boat's hull bottom.

The fo'c's'le, pronounced "folk-sill" was a bastardized form of the old English word for forecastle. In the days of galleons, boats were built with elaborate, high structures at both the stern and bow of the boat to help the boat sail into and with the waves, with the middle deck of the ship much lower to the waterline and horizontal pivotal axis. Ships sail forward and usually the bow is the first part of the boat to meet the waves, lifting the boat and pivoting it on an axis somewhere in the second half of the boat. The best ride in most boats is towards the rear, which is why ship captain's cabins are always in the rear. The ship's cargo had the second highest priority in shipbuilders' minds and so the holds were always amidships and low, to ensure that the cargo was subjected to the least punishing rides as possible. The crew was given the lowest priority of all and their berthing was in the forecastle, with its rough ride. Over time the word for forward crew berthing had been truncated to its current pronouncement, as the tradition of giving crew the harshest riding part of the ship for their quarters continued.

Pete switched the radar from standby to the ten-mile radius search pattern after he was well clear of town and the other boats' radars. After he was satisfied that the clutter adjustment was set, he turned the boat over to the engineer and headed for his stateroom on the main deck. He called Corky, who knew the nightly drill. She trotted into the Captain's stateroom to her rug on the floor, scratched the rug, did her normal three turns, lay down, tucked her nose under her tail, and went to sleep. Pete shucked out of his clothes, flopped into bed, felt the boat running smoothly and straight, and slid into a comfortable night's sleep.

The next morning, Pete was awakened to the sound of the crew rummaging around in the galley and to the smell of bacon, eggs and coffee. After a good breakfast and some lighthearted give-and-take with the crew, Pete anchored up the *Linda Bea* in a bay a half-hour away from where he intended to fish the next day. After an hour's worth of work by the crew to get the boat and skiff ready to fish, the crew was released to goof off the rest of the day, while the engineer serviced and lubed the skiff's engine and running gear. After he finished with the skiff, he went to the engine room and set various valves and pumps to flood the main hold. The Captain liked to run the boat empty when traveling to the fishing grounds, because it took less fuel than when she wasn't tanked. The *Linda Bea* sank into the water as she took on water in the main hold and settled with less than a foot of free board of deck above the water. Once filled, the brine chiller that refrigerated seawater to near freezing was turned on. This would act as a big refrigerator to preserve the salmon they would catch in the next days so they didn't have to leave the fishing grounds to get their catch to a tender boat or cannery before it spoiled. That was one of the ways High-

Liners stayed a High-Liner. With a chill brine system, they could stay out on the fishing grounds much longer when their competition, who didn't have chill brine systems, had to run to a tender, causing them to spend time and fuel running to and fro to unload daily. The crew loved it because, rather than spending their nights waiting their turn to unload at the tender, they could get a good night's rest.

It was a nice day and the crew took turns jigging for halibut off the side of the boat. Occasionally, they actually caught something and it was a welcomed addition to the trip's cuisine. Pete spent the day watching videos, while Corky roamed the boat in search of an idle hand of a crewmember to pet and scratch her. The youngest deck hand had 'Corky Duty.' His job was to keep an eye on a spot of the deck where Corky always did her duty and to grab a hose and spray refuse overboard through the scuppers. He took a lot of razzing for the task, but he really couldn't hold it against Corky because she always seemed to know that he was getting teased because of her, and singled him out for extra licks and kisses.

The next day they were up before light and were first in line on the point they wanted to work. The opening specified no nets in the water until eight a.m. At eight o one, the *Linda Bea*'s net was set in the water. The fishing was light to moderate. The first four sets were routine and getting the fisherman four to five hundred fish, mostly pinks with a few money fish, like chums and silvers in the mix.

In the early afternoon they were making their fifth set

of the day. Everything went normally; the *Linda Bea* made a headlong rush at a point and at the last instant made a turn to shear off. At that moment a crewman on the back deck yanked on a large ring attached to the pelican release that held the skiff to the back of *Linda Bea*, releasing it to continue the charge to the point, while dragging the net off the back of the *Linda Bea*'s deck. The skiff driver butted the rubber pads and quarter tire sections on the bow, up against the point's rocky outcropping and throttled back the little boat's huge diesel power plant. The twelve-foot boat's twenty-eight inch prop kept it on station without being rubbed up and down against the rocks by the waves.

While the skiff anchored one end of the net close to the rocky point, the *Linda Bea* raced away in the opposition direction as the net frantically escaped over the stern. The net was made up of several discrete components: cork line to float the whole assembly; lead line which weighted the bottom of the net so that it would hang vertically in the water; three-inch web netting in between to corral the salmon; and the purse line, running through rings tied to leaders off the lead line that acted as a cinch to close the bottom of the net. Once the net was set, both the *Linda Bea* and the skiff would turn their bows into the prevailing current and keep the net suspended in relatively the same spot for a half-hour to forty-five minutes. When salmon were migrating they swam in the top five feet of the water. The net acted as a deterrent to the fish, but if left too long, the fish would just swim along the net until they found an opening at either end or underneath.

The *Linda Bea* had let her net soak for about thirty-five minutes, and Pete was just about to call down into the galley to tell the crew to gear up to pull in the nets, when he noticed there was a great roiling of the water about mid-net, with a lot of salmon leaping clear of the water. Pete stepped onto the upper deck behind the bridge to take a better look. '*Crap,*' thought Pete, '*We've got a seal chasing the salmon along the net again.*' He started to turn to muster the crew to get what they could from this set before the seal chased the salmon out, when he caught sight of a five-foot dorsal fin clear the water out of the corner of his eye. He turned to inspect, but it was gone. This was new; he'd never had a killer whale run his net before. He'd heard stories of it happening before, but had never seen it. At that moment, he caught sight of two harbor seals porpoise out of the water along the net in a headlong sprint at the *Linda Bea*.

The water was roiling and fish *en masse* were rapidly moving towards the *Linda Bea*'s end of the net in a way he'd never seen before. Worried, Pete signaled to the skiff to return to the *Linda Bea* and then hurried onto the bridge to move the *Linda Bea* up current and circle in to meet the skiff. The crew heard the change in pitch of the engine as Pete advanced the throttle and felt the boat start to change direction. Most were out the door and onto the deck shrugging on rain gear to work the net before Pete had a chance to yell down the stairs for them to get ready.

As Pete looked back at the net, he realized that the situation was actually much worse than he thought and that things were moving too fast for him to control. A roiling knot of water and leaping salmon were headed for the *Linda Bea* and would be on him in a matter of seconds. The crew had noticed the commotion, too. Even Corky, who was standing with her front paws on the railing of the wing deck behind the bridge, was barking at all the commotion in the water.

The roil engulfed the *Linda Bea*. Crewmen on the back deck were astonished to see salmon leaping over the gunwale and on to the deck. Laughing like children, the crew started corralling the flopping fish when the *Linda Bea* was violently rocked as it was struck by something immense below the water line. Pete had to grab onto the bridge's dash to keep from going down. Crewmen on the back deck struggled and whipsawed; two slipped and hit the deck. Nobody saw Corky being launched through the air or landing face first in the roiling mass of salmon. Nor did anybody see the enormous gray-black shape rise in a flash, swallow Corky whole before she could even rise to the surface and then disappear into the disturbed, frothy water.

When Pete jerked himself upright as the boat righted itself, he started to turn to the starboard windows to see what had struck his boat when a bright red light lit on the control panel, followed in quick succession by two more and a warning buzzer erupted.

'The bilge alarms!'

The warning lights were telling him that he had a breach in the hull and that water was starting to accumulate in the engine room, fo'c's'le, and the section over the steering gear at the stern of the boat called the lazarette.

Pete's mind went into overdrive.

'*I need sea room!*'

He ran back to the wheel and put it hard over to port as he slammed the throttles forward. At the time of the collision, he'd been heading towards the beach and shallower water to meet the skiff. Deeper water was needed to buy time if he was in trouble. As soon as he got the boat headed in the right direction, away from land, he ran out on the wing deck and waved off his skiff driver, Steve Hannah, signaling him to cut loose the net and return to the boat.

Steve acknowledged back with a concerned, puzzled look on his face, oblivious to the collision with the underwater object. He was too far away and preoccupied with maneuvering his end of the net and hadn't seen what had transpired. Pete could see the confusion in his eyes at his new orders and the *Linda Bea*'s abrupt change in course. Pete didn't have time to explain. He needed the skiff now in case whatever he struck was flooding his engine room or, worse, killed the main diesel that ran all the boat's pumps.

Pete didn't have time to make sure the skiff driver cut loose the net either. In the back of his mind he knew if Steve wasn't quick, the faster *Linda Bea* would rapidly run out the slack in the net and could end up dragging the skiff, capsizing it, making it an anchor that could hang up the *Linda Bea*, pinning her to the sea bed and possibly her death.

Meanwhile, the crew had watched Pete's frantic signals

to Steve from the back deck with a rising sense of dread. When he was through communicating with Steve, Pete turned to his crew on the deck, "Men, we've got a problem," he stated without preamble. "We're going to dump the set and get that net on board in record time. It doesn't have to be pretty, just get it on board, now!" Pete then singled out the crewman responsible for separating and coiling the net's webbing which normally would be piled over the lazerette hatch with special directions, "Webs, *do not* cover the lazerette hatch, we need to get in there. Now get going!"

Pete ran back into the wheelhouse and cut the main engine back to idle, but left the prop engaged. He wanted to keep the boat moving forward, just a little to keep the net from fouling the prop, which could turn the situation from bad to catastrophic. He hit the engage button on the autopilot and jumped feet-first down the steep stairs at the rear of the wheelhouse that lead to the main deck, dropping just as quickly down the hatch that lead to the engine room.

He expected to see water overflowing the bilge and coming out of the floor gratings and boards that made up the engine room floor.

'What the hell?'

Everything looked normal.

Pete pulled up some deck boards to peer down into the bilge. The oily black water that was always present in bilge looked normal, a little high, but normal. The panels in the fo'c's'le at the bow revealed more of the same.

Back in the engine room, Pete went to the control panel

that housed the switches for the bilge pumps and activated the pumps to empty the fo'c's'le and engine room bilges.

On the back deck, the last of the net was coming off the power block, which was the big hourglassed-shaped, hydraulically operated drum suspended from a stout boom from the ship's mast. The crew quickly gathered up the net and secured it. Pete stepped onto the deck, T-handle in hand for the lazarette as the last five feet of net was spun off the power block and then fell to the deck.

As Pete walked quickly to the aluminum lazarette hatch cover, the crew fell in behind him. He was feeling more assured that the situation wasn't critical. The lazarette hatch cover was an aluminum oval hatch, eighteen by thirty-six inches in measurement, which was set flush to the deck to provide access to a dry compartment that housed the steering gear over the rudder. Pete set the T-handled key into the center of the hatch cove's receptacle and started to spin the handle. As Pete lifted the now unlocked hatch cover clear and peered in, all appeared to be normal.

'Boy, that was lucky.'

Whatever had hit them, didn't appear to have damaged the boat. The crew had been watching him intently. By this time, the skiff had made it back and was tied up amid starboard of the boat. Steve, as the boat's engineer, had joined them on the back deck and anxiously looked at his captain for instructions. "Boys, it looks like we really lucked out. Whatever we hit didn't do any damage… that I can see." With those words the pallor in the faces of his crew receded, "Looks like it just hit us hard enough to sluice the bilge water up to trip the bilge alarms. That's why I dumped the set and ran for open water. Everything looks normal in the engine room and lazarette." He could see the tension ease in the faces of the crew, even as he felt it ease from him like balloon that had lost its knot.   But given what had just happened, he figured they could all use a break before they set the net again.

"Lets take a quick break for some sandwiches before we start up again, OK?" he said to collective nods.

It was only as the crew shrugged off their gear and made their way to the galley for sandwiches, someone noticed that Corky, who never missed a meal, was absent.

A frantic search ensued for the next hour, but of course, Corky was nowhere to be found.

11

Eric woke up the next morning in blackness and confusion. It was probably more appropriate to say that Eric oozed into consciousness. It was a long and painful journey, as he first became aware of his breathing echoing and reflecting back into his face, which he pondered for quite some time with what few wits that had shown up for the occasion. Slowly, more synaptic junctions joined the part, bringing messages of pain, exhaustion, cramps and soreness with his growing awareness. Slowly he corralled, then beat back, the screaming messages of his body until he was able to ponder just where he was. With an effort from his protesting body, he flipped off the folded flap of tarp that covered his face. As he did so, he was greeted with brilliant sunshine that hurt his eyes, adding more pain to his miserable existence.

'Great,' he said to himself, '*my eyeballs were the only things that hadn't been hurting, and now I've gone and pissed them off too.*'

Winking and alternating his eyes shut to try to reduce the pain, he slowly scanned his surroundings.

There was a wisp of smoke rising from the fire pit, and yet somehow the trees looked different from last night, as though crisper, in greater relief.

Stirring himself, Eric flopped and squirmed his way out

of his survival sleeping sandwich and crawled out of the improvised lean-to. As he stood on the flap of tarp that had covered his head, his body was caressed by the cold convection wind that was blowing up the mountain. The sun heated the air faster over land than the sea below which created a convection air current pulling the cooler ocean air up the mountain over Eric. The mechanics of nature's heat distribution system was totally lost on Eric; all he knew was the warmth that his makeshift bed had infused in his body was now readily being pulled from it by the chill morning wind.

His shoes, which had never had an opportunity to dry from yesterday's trudge through the soggy underbrush, had not dried any more overnight. He grunted and mentally cursed as he fought to pull on the cold wet shoes over his warm feet and tie the stiff, unwieldy wet laces. Standing, Eric wandered several feet into the woods to relieve himself, his stomach the whole time reminding him of its need for attention, too. As he made his way back to the camp, he decided to try one of the freeze-dried meals; stew was sounding especially good this morning. A little water on the included chemical heating pack of the stew and a few minutes was all that was needed for a hot meal in the middle of nowhere.

'Might as well get started at breaking camp,' he decided as he waited for the food to warm.

All that really meant was retrieving the tarp and shotgun. After stowing the tarp in his waterproof bag, his meal was ready, so he sat on his bed and savored every bite of what would have been normally considered a tasteless meal.

Having always been very conscience of the Green, Save-the-World, Eco-Friendly movement, he suddenly found himself considering what to do with the stew's pouch. He was loath to just throw it to the ground, and mar the beauty of his little sanctuary. The cannons of eco-friendliness, which had been pounded into the collective consciousness of modern living and the academe which he consider himself one, dictated he should pack out what he'd brought in and leave the wilderness as he found it. His aches and fatigue caused his anger to flare suddenly at this line of thought.

"Like I found it?! Yeah right," he said with sarcasm. "I haven't 'found' shit. This shit has found me, it's not like I'm on a voluntary nature walk here. And I'm supposed to respect you?" he glared at the trees around his campsite.

Yet, he still couldn't bear to throw this simple little piece of foil pouch to the ground. He tried to rationalize and project whether an empty pouch would be of any use to him in the upcoming travails.

'The pouch would smell like food and attract bears,' he reasoned. *'Did the usefulness of the pouch outweigh the possible jeopardy that it might bring?'*

His mind, still slowed by exhaustion, was stumbling over such minor decisions. He knew this was a bad sign, but couldn't seem to overcome the mental ineptitude he recognized in himself. In the end he decided to keep the pouch by promising himself to clean it at the first pool of water he came across to reduce, if not rid himself of the scent trail. At least, that's what he *told* himself. Deep down inside he really knew that he was keeping it because every little reminder of man's technology he carried was like armor that protected him from the wilderness; he didn't want to give up his talisman.

He could feel himself putting off his departure, perhaps chewing each tasteless bite a little longer than necessary, scraping the sides of the food pouch with exaggerated concentration. The lean-to put together in a matter of minutes had given him the illusion of security and safety, like a drowning man, as he almost had been, clinging to a branch that couldn't support his weight. It was hard to let go of this branch.

'*How odd…*' he philosophized, '*that I'm in the middle of a wilderness that I don't want to be in, while trying to cross the unknown to reach an outpost of civilization, that all of sudden I'm attached to this particular patch of wilderness that I don't want to leave. But I've got to. I've got to get up. Staying here, means dying here.*'

With great mental effort he broke himself of the false security of his little camp and forced himself into motion. All his possessions were securely re-stowed in the dry bag which went upon his back, and with his shotgun slung over a shoulder, his belt with ammo, knife and hatchet about his waist, he started up the hill once more.

The slope stayed the same, but the terrain varied. At times there were dense stands of pine and spruce saplings, young trees with little underbrush. At other times, he would hit patches where the trees were more spaced out with heavy underbrush. Each presented its own obstacles.

The stands of thick young trees required Eric to twist and turn to squeeze through the small openings in tightly packed trees, which was difficult and strenuous with his shotgun and pack on his back.   At times he was forced to take off the dry sack and gun to squeeze through the smallest of openings.   Occasionally, the brush was just too impenetrable so he was forced to move laterally across the mountain's face, rather than wrestle through the tangles, deadfall and other obstacles like rock outcroppings.   These thickets were fast depleting his reserves with massive amounts of energy needed as he twisted, turned, ducked and sidestepped his way through.

When not squirming his way through thickets of ground alder or patches of dead fall, the forest opened up with areas where the trees were spaced wider apart. Here the open spaces lent themselves to thick vegetation. Sometimes he could bull right through it. Other times, he would find himself halfway through the chest level vegetation before he would have to retreat to take another approach to punching through a thicket. The leaves and branches were covered with the morning's dew, which never seemed to evaporate or dry out. So Eric was always soaked. His shoes and socks, which were never meant for heavy hiking in wet conditions, started to each work against him, tenderizing his feet by blistering his soggy wrinkled skin on both feet.

The heavy exertion, weight on his back, steep slope, not to mention his soft muscles, all conspired to limit his travel to ten-yard intervals before he'd to catch his breath. He did this, ten paces at a time, over and over again. While his over-extended lungs worked hungrily to catch up to the demands his muscles were making on his body, he'd use the time to scout out the best path through the next ten yards of terrain and set a goal for the spot he would need to reach before he rested again. He didn't always make it, but it was good to have a plan.

With each move up the hill, the squirrels seemed hell bent on annoying him. As he made his way up the mountainside, he passed from one squirrel's territory to another's. In turn, each owner would scamper branch to branch above Eric and constantly scold him with the staccato chittering and tail waiving of a disgruntled rodent. At first Eric was afraid that this scolding by the squirrels would act as a beacon to some hungry bear that could mark his progress and pinpoint his location by the constant barrage of verbal abuse directed his way by the squirrels. He fantasized about letting his shotgun have the last word with one of these overly self-important rats with bushy tails. But ultimately, he knew it wouldn't do any good because twenty or thirty yards up the hill, another squirrel would take its place. His fears of attracting a bear slowly diminished as he heard other squirrels making similar sounds in the forest around him and decided that all squirrels must live lives of constant agitation and displeasure. But what became even more angering to him was he was afraid that the constant chatter of the squirrels would mask the approach of a bear until it was too late.

The sky above Eric, at least the small portion that he could see through the trees directly overhead, remained blue and cloudless. In Southeastern Alaska though, a storm front came off the north Pacific every three to five days. Eric couldn't see the horizon in the middle of the forest, so he'd no way of knowing what might be blowing in. The weather forecast that he could recall from yesterday -- constantly broadcast and updated from the Coast Guard UHF Weather Channel out of Ketchikan -- indicated that a low pressure storm front was expected to make landfall in the next day. Sure, these things could change rapidly Eric knew, since weather fronts could veer, accelerate, stop, or reverse course. It was just another fact of life for Eric to worry about. Sooner or later, this fine Southeastern Alaska weather that he had been enjoying would come to a close.

'Christ,' he moaned, *'I'm soaked all day because of the dew that never goes away. I don't even want to think about how miserable I'm going to be if it starts to rain. And I know it will eventually.'* Involuntarily, he shuddered at this line of thought. *'Gotta stay positive. Gotta stay positive, if I'm going to get out of this,'* he reminded himself and forced the thoughts of rain from his mind.

Ten yards stop and rest.

Eric had made a pact with himself not to start up the hill for his next goal until he repeated his mantra, "Shoot the head." He'd read of instances where people had frozen-up when confronted with a bear leading them to do something stupid, like run or just stand there. And he was painfully aware that with each stop it was taking longer and longer for him to recover. He didn't know if it was from the lactic acid buildup in his over-exerted muscles, the increased altitude, or probably both, he guessed. He did know he was getting sloppier as his exhaustion grew. And that this was when people made stupid mistakes. But he'd an antidote for the situation. While catching his breath, he would practice rapidly slinging the shotgun from his shoulder onto a random target. He did this over and over, forging muscle memory into his tired limbs. He repeated his mantra so he wouldn't freeze or forget what he was supposed to do.

He'd no way of knowing just how high he was up the hill or how to gauge his progress. The woods were too thick to get a good visual reference from the surrounding bay, so there was no way to judge his elevation or how close he may be getting to the summit.

He was getting very thirsty, too. He'd half expected to find a stream to fill his water bottles shortly after he left camp, but it hadn't happened. He'd finished his water early in the day, fully expecting that water wasn't going to be a problem in such a wet environment. But the higher he'd climbed, the dryer it had gotten and the terrain had become sparser in vegetation. The daily convection winds had finally dried up even the cursed dew from the plants. He was starting to get the little dry patches in the back of his throat that no amount of swallowing could coat. Mentally, he chastised himself for not being disciplined and consuming all his water so early in the day.

'How quickly things change here,' he chuckled aloud, as the irony struck him. 'Yesterday, I almost drowned. This morning I was miserably cold from always being wet, and now I'm dying for a drop to drink, which I can't find anywhere.'

In his exhaustion, at moments he was almost driven to

tears with frustration, but he didn't have the hydration in his body to produce any; other times he just wanted to laugh out maniacally, but it hurt his parched throat.

He tried to fight back his emotions as he climbed. *'Gotta stay positive, gotta stay positive,'* is what he told himself each time he felt the vapors of negativism starting to cloud his mind. He'd heard somewhere way back, where he couldn't remember, that the difference between those who lived through ordeals and those who didn't was the will to live bolstered by a positive attitude. He could now see why this was true. With each step, his exhaustion grew, slowly dulling his senses and making it harder and harder to fight the demons of negativity that were circling closer and closer in his mind.

'Gotta stay positive; where's my next goal; shoot the head.' Rest – a cycle that seemed to go on without end.

With little fanfare, the trees suddenly thinned and the summit ridgeline came into view not more than thirty yards ahead. The incline rapidly transitioned from steep to gradual to flat. Eric's thighs were burning as he pushed himself hard to gain the flat ridge where he could stand on both legs to catch his breath without having to stand on one leg or on his toes as he had to on the steep slope on the way up. Winded, he sat on the ridge's flat for a good long time enjoying the satisfaction of knowing that the hardest part was over; the rest was downhill from here. Long after the sting had left his thighs he finally roused himself.

'First, I should be able to see or guess where that cabin will be once I get a good look at the bay,' as he moved to find an

opening between the trees. When he found one, the view stopped him dead in his tracks.

'Oh, for the love of Pete!'

Below him lay a valley below, and another ridge of equal height on the other side.

Crestfallen, anger surged through him. He'd been so sure that the bay would be on the other side of the ridge. The parch in his throat that had disappeared when he reached the summit, suddenly roared back into existence.

He put his hands on his knees and breathed deeply until he'd calmed himself, before ambling to a position to get a better look at the valley below him.

'Maybe it's not as bad as I originally thought. It's only down a thousand feet to the valley floor and another thousand feet to the far ridge. I'm sure the hillside I just came up was two-and-a-half, maybe three thousand. It should only take me half a day to do the other side. AND I'M SURE, the bay is on the other side of that. So what, maybe two hours to the bottom, another six to eight to climb to the top of the ridge, and maybe another three hours to get to the bottom? I could be on the beach by tomorrow night. Yeah, I can do this.'

And the best part to his parched palate was that it was all downhill to water.

'OK,' Eric thought, *'No problem...remember, shoot the head.'* With that he stepped off down the hill.

With gravity finally working for him, he made great time and was able to continuously walk downhill at a relatively easy pace. That didn't mean that it was easygoing, or safe. In fact his tension grew tremendously. When he'd been going uphill, he'd only covered distances that he'd surveyed for many minutes, while catching his breath. In this fashion he was able to listen and get the pulse of the woods around him. Now, on the move down, he was making noise because each step came crashing down with his full weight plus gear. But more importantly, when on the move he couldn't hear anything moving around him. His footfalls were constant and they drowned out the forest's sounds around him, plus, he wasn't stopping to listen while he caught his breath. In essence, he was walking blindly and could stumble into any curious animal in the vicinity before he had a chance to draw his weapon.

'At this rate, I could easily stumble into a mother sow and her cubs before I know it.'

This tension made Eric's parched throat ache even more.

'There was no getting around it, if I'm going to survive and get out of this, chances are going to have to be taken.'

Within an hour-and-a-half, Eric found himself emerging onto the flat valley floor. And, shortly, he was able to hear the low level rumble of a swift moving mountain stream in the distance. As he approached the stream, the vegetation got thicker, and wetter. He found himself working his way over slimy, wet boulders and blow-downs, and back to squirming between aspen ground-trees again, this time driven by the siren's call of fast moving water, just out of sight and his reach.

It was like Mother Nature had a plan to deny him, by throwing all these obstacles between him and that which would ease his pain and give him succor. He abandoned all pretense of caution and restraint as he found new energy to bull his way through the dense undergrowth to get at that water.

Finally, with startling abruptness, Eric found himself at the edge of an eight-foot-wide torrent of a mountain stream. It took all of his control not to just plant his face in the cool water and suck until his heart's content, but instead he un-slung the shotgun and dry bag from his back and opened it as quickly as possible, really not taking care where he dropped the fastening clip.

'Dammit, where's that purification straw? I know I left it right on top!'

But it wasn't.

Due to all the shifting, jostling and wild arcs the pack had been subjected to, the water purification straw had slipped off the top to some place lower in the bag. Bent over the bag, Eric cursed as he pulled item after item from the bag and dropped them without thought to the ground, his focus singular on finding the water purification straw and ending his torture. Finally his hand felt the straw in the black recesses, and he pulled it triumphantly from that bag.

Two strides and he was at the water. Eric, straw, and water blissfully connected. It didn't matter to Eric that the water came in small, laborious pulls. He drank until his belly was stretched tight. Even then his thirst wasn't slaked nor his torture finished. In one of the ironies of the human condition, a stomach could be full to the point of bursting with water and still be thirsty because the water in your stomach had not yet been absorbed into your body's system. All the while, the body still flooded the brain with signals of distress due to under hydration. It took another twenty minutes before his thirst finally abated. Even then, he still didn't leave the water, he just hovered above it for several minutes while his body slowly absorbed the water that it so desperately craved. The crisis now passed, he returned to the bag and rummaged through the contents until he found the empty water bottles, which were taken to the stream and filled. With a clearer mind, he eyed the mess he'd made. Eric returned to the bag and its former contents scattered haphazardly around the bag's base and carefully reloaded it. Along the way, he found last night's dinner pouch and cleaned it in the stream before repacking it as he promised he'd do.

It was a little after midday, so Eric decided to sit and rest for an hour or so, and eat one of his packets of trail mix for lunch. So, he set about eating and getting comfortable. He found a tree and a stretch of ground that was dry and in the sunlight, propped the bag against a tree, and then wedged himself against the bag as a cushion, shotgun across his lap, and tore into the trail mix. He closed his eyes in a spate of pleasure as the salt of the peanuts and sweet of the candy and raisins hit his tongue with satisfaction of a huge slab of medium rare prime rib. Oh, and to top it all off, he finally found a use for that food pouch; it was filled with water at his side with the purification straw to go with his meal.

When he was done, he topped off his stomach and water bottles with fresh water from the stream before repacking the bag one more time before propping his back against it in a patch of sunshine.

Eric closed his eyes and let the waves of contentment roll over him as he enjoyed the sunshine's warmth until his exhaustion crept up on him, tugging him gently into an undisturbed slumber.

12

The core of killer whale society was the mother/daughter relationship. These relationships, like everywhere else in the world, dominated the social architecture of the Northern Clan of the Three Clans Tribes of killer whales.

A small pod of orcas, a splinter pod off the Northern Clan, had chased a school of herring into a long bay, when the leader of the pod detected an odd-looking craft floating on the surface of the bay.

He was very protective and very cautious when it came to his newly-formed pod. The Pod Leader had been part of his mother's larger pod of thirty whales that formed the core of the Northern Clan for most of his life. Occasionally, he'd briefly left the pod to roam with a few other solitary males in a bachelor pod, but had always returned, missing the chatter of females and close relatives. Orcas were social animals. They hunted and socialized as one; always together, always communicating, always hearing others talk. It just wasn't the same when he was with the bachelors group. These groups tended to be quieter. It just had not felt the same.

The Three Clans tribe of killer whales roamed a home range in the protected inland waters of the western coast of North America from Vancouver Island on the south to the Alexander Archipelago on the northern border and preyed mostly upon fish. In the summer, about this time each year, all three clans of the Three Clans Tribe, the South, the Middle and the Northern, would gather to form a super pod of several hundred killer whales for a brief period. At the gathering, old relationships were renewed, new relationships were kindled, and brief but intense courtships were pursued and consummated. During these gatherings, those not involved in the raucous play of procreation, socialized and swapped stories.

It was during these times that the Pod Leader first heard the stories of the other tribes of killer whales. There was a tribe that roamed the deep waters off the coast known as the Ocean Travelers. The Pod Leader had some experience with this tribe garnered in his youth. While on a youthful jaunt in a bachelor pod of Three Clans tribe orcas, he had ventured further out to sea where they had encountered the Ocean Travelers. He learned firsthand that their differences weren't just physical. Although the same size and general configuration, this other tribe had different markings and dorsal fins. But the most striking difference to the Pod Leader was their completely different culture. These other killer whales were more savage and aggressive; and although they spoke much less often, when they did, they used the similar vocalizations of whistles, grunts, and clicks as the Three Clans Tribe. They spoke much less because they were a hunter culture; the prey they hunted knew the sounds of killer whales on the hunt and fled when they heard the dreaded sound in the water. So they were always in stealth mode, speaking only when necessary. The language that they spoke, however, was different and very difficult for the Pod Leader to follow. They were not interested in eating fish, preferring the taste of mammal blood and attempted to get the bachelors to work with them in hunting seals, dolphins and other whales. Ultimately these brief interactions between the tribes dissipated amiably due to a difference in tastes for food, difficulty in conversing, and cultural differences too deep to overcome.

This encounter could have ended badly. The bachelor pod, which was composed of younger adult males from the pods of the Three Clans tribe, were fueled by bravado and testosterone. The dare and thrill of roaming beyond the tribe's range into another's territory was part and parcel of being a young and semi-mature male killer whale associating with others in a similar affliction. However, the Ocean Travelers Tribe of killer whales encountered were just as curious about them as they were of this foreign tribe. They were curious as to why the bachelors of the Three Clans Tribes breathed so often when they generally took deeper breaths and held it longer. They were also curious as to why they were so chatty when, from the Ocean Travelers' view, all that excess communication did was to alert and panic their food sources to relocate. After both groups' curiosities were satisfied, they drifted apart in search of their favorite foods and the comfort of their own ways.

There were even stories told during the summer super pod gathering of a tribe of killer whales that lived beyond the Ocean Travelers called the Open Water Tribe, who were said to be the most savage and fearless hunters of all the tribes of killer whales.

Yet, despite all the companionship found in the Northern Clan, he didn't want to follow his mother's pod or always go where they wanted to go. He was a strong-willed son, learning from his mother's side, observing, as she controlled, corrected and disciplined behaviors in him as well as other members in the pod. It might have been because his mother was the matriarch of the pod, and all things about the pod's activities flowed from her, that the Pod Leader couldn't be a strong Pod Leader that she had raised him to be while he stayed in his mother's pod. The Pod Leader really couldn't pinpoint his emotions that drove his actions. But the last time that he'd returned to his mother's pod, he felt differently and took a different approach. In the course of time, he pair bonded with a female of a different matriline. She'd already come of age and had a male calf.

Since mothers and daughters, no matter what their age, never left one another until death parted them, his life-mate wouldn't leave until her mother was free to move. So in the spring when his life-mate's grandmother died, the Pod Leader was able to convince his life-mate and her mother to bring their children to form a new, breakaway pod with him.

The Pod Leader was very content now. He had the company that he craved and the freedom to take his family where he pleased; it was a tale of male domestication as old as Y chromosomes. At the same time his paternal instincts were fully aroused by the juvenile daughter of his life-mate's mother and the infant male of her daughter, his life-mate. At her age, this would be his life-mate's mother's last offspring.

So now, when encountering this silent, odd craft upon entering the bay, the Pod Leader decide to spy-hop to get a better look at what was floating on the surface while the rest of his pod continued to chase and corral the school of herring further back in the bay. The Pod Leader stood on his tail and thrust himself out of the water, raising his eye level so that he could better see his surroundings. From this vantage point, his eyes were six or so feet out of the water and he was able to get a much better view of the boat floating several hundred yards away. This one was different because it had two bodies that were connected at the top. He'd seen enough of objects in his life to know that it wasn't an animal, but some sort of object that rode upon the water and sometimes had strange creatures that rode upon its back. He'd always been curious about the creatures that rode upon these objects, but the cautious nature of his breed kept him and most orcas from exploring these strange objects and their passengers.

Normally, these objects made loud noises that made it difficult for the orcas to use their sensitive hearing. This one however was silent, and still, both of which were unusual. And this roused the Pod Leader's curiosity, yet he was cautious, despite being the ocean's top predator, in investigating this unusual craft.

However cautious killer whales were in their daily lives, this would be completely abandoned if their offspring were imperiled. All bets were off, all calculations bypassed. Anger and confidence, coming from being at the top of the food chain, replaced thought. And restraint, what little they possessed towards other species, if any, was replaced with a savage glow of one of nature's basic pleasures: destruction.

Since no orca had ever tasted the creatures that rode upon the backs and innards of these strange objects that floated upon the water, the essential calculation of tastiness versus risk had never been consummated. Besides, the seas were abundant with other delicacies that came with little or no risk in taking.

Satisfied that the two-bodied object upon the water posed no risk to his pod, the Pod Leader slid vertically back into the water and turned to join the pod who had corralled the school of herring mid-bay.

The pod circled below the herring and was slowly forcing the school to the surface of the water by rolling over to flash their white underbellies at the school of fish. The killer whales, with their black-with-gray saddle patch just behind their dorsal fins, blended into the mottled hues of the deep green Pacific waters when seen from above. The herring could detect the killer whales indistinctly when viewed from the top, aware that the killer whales were present, but just not sure exactly where. When the killer whales abruptly rolled to their backs and flashed their white underbellies, the patch of white would panic them to flee in the opposite direction, up.

As the school of herring was condensed and driven against the surface, the pod of killer whales readied for the next phase. The whales individually made their way to the surface, took extra large gulps of air before reassembling, circling below the herring school. When all was ready, the Pod Leader signaled with a double click and the killer whales simultaneously release air through their blow holes as they circle, creating a curtain of bubbles. The reason for the bubble curtain was to further distract and frighten the herring into a much tighter ball. The glint of light wildly reflected off of the bubbles' surfaces creating thousands upon thousands of points of light totally obliterating the herrings' ability to see beyond the little sphere inside the curtain. The killer whales now circle in closer for the feast. One of the females charged through the curtain of air bubbles and slapped her powerful tail against the ball of herring, stunning hundreds and outright killing dozens that floated listlessly in the water. Then other adult females charged right behind her through the curtain and whacked the ball again with the same results.

Meanwhile, the two immature killer whales continued to get breaths of air and maintain the curtain of bubbles while the Pod Leader prepared his run at the ball of herring.

With all their focus on the ball of herring forced to the surface of the water, none of the five killer whales detected the large blue-gray shark below that had been attracted by all the commotion. And why would they? As lords of the ocean, killer whales were never concerned about keeping an eye over their dorsal fin for enemies, because they had none.

Until this moment.

With the adult killer whales alternating their attacks

and the young whales left to keep up the curtain, none of them saw the lightening swift vertical attack on the youngest male killer whale as it approached the surface for another lungful of air.

The massive shark showed an incredible burst of speed and hit the young male twenty feet below surface. The shark bit the whale just in front of the pectoral fins and removed most of its head with the first bite. The young killer whale died noisily, without ever knowing what had killed it.

The young whale's mother, however, saw everything.

With a horrifying shrieking whistle she launched herself at the massive Shark that was almost double her size. The Giant Shark's impact with the now dead juvenile killer whale had halted its climb to the surface; it was now swimming horizontally, trying to position the killer whale's head in its maw before finally gobbling it down. The Giant Shark sensed the quartering attack from its right side through its lateral lines and executed an incredibly tight turn for an animal its size to face the attacker.

When the young mother saw the Giant Shark turn to face her attacker, she was instinctively confused by this move; everything in the seas ran from attacking killer whales. Nothing ever turned into an attack, so she veered to the left to break off the assault. It was a fatal error.

The Giant Shark now was in a position to attack her. Belying its size, with blindly quick strokes of its caudal fin, the Giant Shark closed the gap and thrust its jaws forward, extending the five-foot ring of serrated, stout, razor-sharp teeth, snapping down on the side of the Pod Leader's mate. The Giant Shark's eyes rolled back in its head as it scooped out a massive ball of flesh and blubber, including portions of her ribs and her right lung. A cloud of blood released instantaneously from the bite into the water was exploded into a pink froth by the escaping air that had been held in her lungs. The explosive decompression of her air supply lead immediately to the collapse of both lungs, which flattened like popped balloons under the water pressure of even this shallow depth and invaded her chest cavity once it had been breached. The Pod Leader's life-mate, nearly paralyzed by searing pain of mortal injuries, rolled to her side and jerked spasmodically as she quickly suffocated and bled to death.

The mother of the Pod Leader's life-mate and her daughter were already in a headlong charge at the Giant Shark when she saw the fate of her daughter and her agonizing death. The Giant Shark, still sensing danger from an attack, continued to move forward to fight rather than flee. The older female turned to her left at full speed to make it difficult for the Giant Shark to turn towards her and vectored her away from the Giant Shark's jaws. Simultaneously, she sent a call of help to the Pod Leader on the other side of the herring ball. Unfortunately, her juvenile daughter was following on her left side and couldn't see the Giant Shark, masked by her mother's body and so caught up in her mother's sudden aggressive behavior, she didn't see her mother change direction until it was too late. The immature female ran nearly head-on into the Giant Shark's jaws; she tried to twist out of the way, but the Giant Shark's powerful jaws crushed down on her back. She released a tremendous squeal of pain as the Giant Shark's teeth sliced into her soft skin and struck her backbone. The Giant Shark shook the young killer whale with little effort as it tried to rip a giant bite out of the tender young whale. As the Giant Shark shook, its teeth drug along killer whale's vertebrae until the point of one tooth found the soft connective tissues of muscle and ligaments holding together the protective spinal column, easily parting two vertebras and severing the spinal cord two feet behind her dorsal fin. The shark released the paralyzed whale in a cloud of its own blood.

The paralyzed killer whale couldn't move its fluke to propel itself, but hung in the water thirty feet below the surface in an ever-expanding cloud of red water, crying for her mother, who was circling nearby. The paralyzed killer whale had taken an extra large breath to continue the bubble curtain for the herring. But the sudden exertion of following her mother's actions followed by the terror of the attack and panic at being unable to move had drawn most of the oxygen out of the air in her lungs. She frantically waved her pectoral fins, trying to claw her way to the surface to breathe. Her mother saw her daughter's distress and moved in to assist her daughter by nudging her from below toward the surface. A mere three feet from the surface, the young whale, panicked by her impending death by asphyxia, exhaled. However, fear, panic and pain had caused her to misjudge her rate of ascendancy and the young whale filled her lungs with seawater before she breached. She reached the surface only to convulse for a few moments before she finally drown.

By this time, the Pod Leader had brought himself into a position from which he could survey the scene with his sonar and took in a scene of devastation to his small pod and the Giant Shark that was swimming amongst the still corpses of his pod. He hurled inquiries at all the lifelessly suspended bodies as he swam towards them, but no one responded. All he could hear was the soothing light squeals of the one remaining female as it tried to comfort her adolescent daughter, now dead, floating on the surface. He was in shock; a moment ago they had been operating as a pack of well-trained hunters, and the next moment, most were horribly mutilated and dead. And the culprit swam heedlessly through the carnage from one corpse to the next, trying to measure which would be the most succulent to start its feast upon. And the Giant Shark it beheld was like nothing the Pod Leader had ever encountered. It was much larger than him in size and weight. As the Pod Leader measured up the assailant through the cloud of carnage that it had reaped in mere moments, fear and intimidation clouded the Pod Leader's mind stunning him into inaction.

As the shark returned to the adolescent female it had just killed, her mother did something very rash, stupid, and motherly. The female saw the shark returning to maul her daughter's body and charged the Giant Shark in a blind rage, intent only upon hurting it, inflicting pain and delivering the wrath of a grief-crazed mother. But the mother had learned nothing from the attacks on the others. Killer whales were used to the movements of the

only other animals of that size, whales.   Whales'
movements were graceful, ponderous... deliberate; this
shark moved with the swiftness of a much smaller fish.
She charged headlong to bring her powerful jaws to bear
upon her expected victim. But the Giant Shark saw the
attack unfolding and parried her thrust, turning sideways
while keeping its nose to the killer whale, letting its
momentum carry it past. As the killer whale slid by, the
Giant Shark latched down on the right flipper as it passed
by its mouth. The powerful jaws of interlacing, serrated
teeth easily sliced through the flipper's flesh and bone,
and two quick tugs, combined with the killer whale's
momentum, amputated most of the flipper, leaving only a
stump of five or six inches and a stream of blood ejecting
into the killer whale 's slipstream.

Overwhelming pain seared through the female killer
whale.   The pain overrode all thoughts of her dead
daughter and the carnage about her, and her only thought
was to escape to the surface to get her breath and then flee,
flee, flee!

All of this happened in front of the Pod Leader's eyes,
as he watched the last of his pod get viciously mauled.
The last act brought a savage, blinding rage over him. He
shifted to a head down position and let burst a cry that
came from his inner recesses.

TTTTHHHROOOOM   click-click-click-click,
TTTTHHHROOOOM   click-click-click-click,
TTTTHHHROOOOM click-click-click-click.

It was a cry that had not been heard for eleven
thousand years.

The Pod Leader left the scene of death and quickly found the wounded female heading out of the bay into the channel, swimming as best as she could. The pain of her wound and the pain of her loss drove her in a blind run to where she knew not, nor cared. When the Pod Leader caught up to her, she was already in advanced shock. He tried to comfort the deteriorating female, but despite his tender entreaties and efforts, his life-mate's mother died two hours later of blood loss and shock.

13

Eric woke gently, the warmth of the sun on his face as he slowly roused himself from a pleasant, deep nap. He stretched himself into a sitting position and was immediately notified of his body's protest. For two days now, he'd heavily taxed and tested the limits of his endurance. Every muscle, it seemed, was trying to out-scream every other muscle to be given a longer reprieve before commencing the torture again. The brief nap was all the delay he could afford right now, the small voice in the back of his head was warning him to keep moving.

Slowly he stood, groaning as he did, to attempt to smooth the wrinkles form his limbs with a few light stretches before saddling up again. After policing up his gear and re-stowing it in the dry bag, he took stock of the situation.

As if hitting him for the first time, Eric noticed that there was a good sized mountain stream of freezing cold water that he now had to cross.

The stream was filled with large boulders and ranged anywhere from eight to twelve feet across as far as he could see. The water was too deep to guarantee successfully negotiating it by wading it without getting swept away. The boulder tops sticking out of the water were wet and mostly covered with moss or slime ensuring the impossibility of a safe crossing. A vision of him slipping, arms flailing, as he tried to nimble his way across the stream by running ended with those same slippery rock tops slamming into his rib cage and breaking bones. Involuntarily, he shuddered.

'Nope, no way that was going to work,' he thought.

He decided he would just have to follow the stream until he found a downed tree across the stream.

'But which way? Upstream or downstream?'

With a mental coin toss, Eric chose upstream and started clambering over boulders and weaving among the trees and brush further up the bank. After a half hour's searching, he finally found a spot that looked good enough to risk his life.

The fallen tree trunk lay at a slight angle across the stream, the root ball pulled from the earth, jagged roots pointed at the sky, ten yards from the stream's edge. The tree was three feet in diameter, had probably been down for a year or two across the stream. Most of the bark had been washed away and the branches broken off leaving one to three foot stubs pointing in all angles. The tree was barren of limbs on Eric's side of the bank up to about halfway across the stream and was sitting about six feet above the water on his side, inclined upwards towards the other bank.

'All I have to do is get on top *of a log sitting six feet in the air, shinny across the wet, slippery, bare tree trunk that's sloping downhill, step around, over and through a maze of branch stumps while carrying a heavy bag and shotgun on my*

back, without falling into a raging, ice cold mountain stream or impaling myself on one of the branch stumps,' he said to himself, a sarcastic grin spreading across his face. '*Yeah, I think that nicely explains it.*'

Eric stared at the scene for several more minutes.

"Good to go," he said to the log by way of mental preparation, as he attempted to leap and pull himself to the top of the log.

Unfortunately, the weight of the dry bag and the shotgun on his back made him too heavy to pull himself up on the log. Every time he tried, the weight on his back tipped him over backwards when his hands couldn't hold on the log's surface.

'*Time to go to Plan B,'* he recognized.

Off came the shotgun and bag, which he set on the ground just under the tree trunk before extracting the towrope and safety harness from the bag. Using the rope, he tied the shotgun's shoulder strap and bag together and attached the other end of the rope to his safety harness. Without the extra weight, after two attempts, he was able to scramble to the top of the log. Standing on the narrow, slippery log top, Eric hauled up the bag and shotgun carefully. This made him extremely nervous. The barrel of the shotgun was pointed at his face the whole time and he knew that the gun was loaded and cocked. He made damn sure the shotgun didn't bang against the log to flick off the gun's safety button or snag the trigger. After several perilous moments the gun and bag arrived on the top log without incident. Weighing his options, he decided that it would be easier to just keep the harness on, his position much too precarious for any extraneous movement. The next problem was to transfer the pack, which was now sitting in front of him, to his back. Normally this would have been nothing for him and wouldn't have given him a second thought; however now he was six feet above a creek bank, standing on a very narrow, slippery surface.

Slowly, very slowly, like some Cirque du Soleil performer executing feats of balance and strength, Eric got the bag to his back while holding the shotgun pinched between his legs. Once the pack was on his back, it was relatively easy to get the shotgun to his shoulder. He'd already made the decision to cross the open stretch of the log standing up. It would have been safer to cross on his hands and knees, but moving with the bag and shotgun on his back, neither designed to be worn horizontally, and either of which could suddenly slip, it was better to cross upright to minimize any shifts of his gear. Of course, that was just an illusion. If he lost his footing and had to make a quick movement to regain his balance, he was just as likely to be pulled off the log as his load shifted. But this way, he wouldn't be forced to transition from hands and knees to his feet halfway down the log when he hit the tree branches.

With a deep inhalation through his nose, followed by a forceful blow from his mouth he psyched himself up for the next step before he announced to the log and stream, "Let's get this show on the road."

Slowly he inched his way down the log, transferring his weight, heel-toe, heel-toe with each footstep. Only twice did he have to weave and flap his arms to regain his balance.

After what seemed like forty-five minutes, but in reality was only three or four, he arrived at the first branch that projected just slightly off center on the right. His concentration was so focused on the moment that it was somewhat a surprise when he arrived at the first obstacle. As Murphy's Law would have it, he arrived at this first juncture with his left foot forward. If he'd arrived with his right foot forward, it would have been a piece of cake to stand his right foot and swing his left foot out and around the protruding branch. Further complicating the delicate negotiation, the log had narrowed as he traveled towards the tree's top. His poor, overmatched tennis shoe had no lateral support forcing his ankle muscle to constantly compensate, rolling from side to side. He was starting to feel the burn in his calf muscles.

His leg muscles told him he didn't have time to dilly-dally, they were starting to give the signs of faltering and he still had the hardest part of the log to traverse. Quickly surveying his options, a plan came together in his head; and if the plan didn't work out, Plan B was to grab for the jutting branch stumps that were impeding his progress and pray that he caught one before he tumbled into the river. He even thought for a moment of bending over and using the branch stub projections as a hand hold, but subconsciously knew that this was a mistake because, in that position, the dry bag would shift, throwing him off balance and into the creek. His calves and ankles were really starting to burn from the exertion now.

With his left foot solidly planted, Eric lifted his right leg until his thigh was brought parallel and calf hung at a right angle. His left ankle worked furiously, rocking left and right, compensating for his shifting positions. Slowly he lowered his leg as far as he could over the top of the jutting branch. But due to the declining slope of the log, he wasn't able to settle his foot before transferring his weight. He stood there for a moment trying to figure out what to do. Finally, he realized that there wasn't a thing he could do, so he lunged forward, hoping that his foot wouldn't slip when his sole hit the log's wet surface.

Contact! And traction.

'Yeah, baby!'

Frantically he weaved and waggled to gain his balance on his right foot. After a few furious moments he was able to settle and straighten up. Realizing he'd been holding his breath, he sighed and took a deep breath, enjoying the relief for a moment before the burning in his calves reminded him that time was running out.

Taking a moment, he counted how many more of the obstacles he was going to have to overcome. It looked like three more limbs were going to require leaps of faith.

After negotiating several more feet of the trunk in his heel-toe dance, he came to the next branch that blocked his path. This time, the limb protruded in a manner that he was able to swing his leg around with only a very minor leap. Which was good, considering that the tree had now narrowed to that point that it was getting very hard to stay balanced over one foot.

The ankle muscles in his calves were beyond burning now from the concentrated exertion on that muscle group. He hoped that his calves would hold until he reached the bank.

A few more moves...heel- toe, heel-toe.

The far bank of the stream was now just a few feet in front of him. Even if he was sure of his footing, there were protruding branches that stopped him from just jumping the last few feet. He would have to pass at least two more branches before he could make that jump. Unfortunately, the last two branches were packed right together, both pointed to the right, close enough that he couldn't plant his entire foot between them. It was too big of a stride to try to cover both in one step. He had no option other than to stand on his toes and try to quickly limp over the trouble spot.

The pain in his calves demanded it was now or never.

With an air of desperation, Eric took a second to line up his thrust, and with a touch of panic, jabbed his right foot at the opening between the two branches while leaping forward with his left leg.

His right foot hit the spot right where he had aimed, and his weight shifted smoothly and quickly as his center of gravity passed over his toes between the obstacle limbs. His eyes acquired the target patch beyond the limbs where his left foot needed to land.

As he leaned forward in anticipation of centering up on his left foot, things went terribly wrong.

His right foot lost traction and his ankle muscles failed simultaneously, rolling the ankle awkwardly. His foot pronated inwardly, spraining the ligaments and tendons along the outside of the right ankle. His weight had not yet been shifted off when his right leg collapsed; reflexes took over, throwing his weight forward. His aim for his left foot was affected and hit just left of his target on the side of the tree just enough for him to change his forward momentum to the left.

He realized that he wasn't going to fully make the bank and he was going down.

He flung himself into a full dive, hoping to catch just enough of the bank so he didn't end up in the stream. In mid-tumble, the shotgun slung from his shoulder and he instinctively threw it up the bank to prevent it from falling into the creek. The throw didn't allow him to brace for the crash that was to be his landing or to break his fall as he landed heavily on some small rounded boulder with his left ribs.

A loud "Wooomppf," was driven from his lungs by the uncontrolled impact, his left side seared with the fire of pain.

But he made it.

His body lay awkwardly, partially on the bank while his jaw gaped, like a landed fish, trying to pump air into his stunned lungs. After what seemed an eternity of pain from his ribs and ankle, his diaphragm started functioning, pulling air into his lungs.

He lay there for many moments just breathing, trying to sort out what had just happened. Once winded, he slowly crawled his way up on the bank of the creek and rolled to an upright sitting position. The roll to sit made his two ribs burn with agony. He needed to inspect the damage and he couldn't do so from his sitting position with the dry bag on his back. Through much grunting due to the pain, he stood on his good foot while steadying himself with his bad right ankle while he shucked off the dry bag. Wiggling out of his shirt and then his t-shirt required even more gritted teeth and grunting to subdue the pain.

After poking and prodding his damaged ribs, it was clear they were heavily bruised, but it didn't feel like they were broken. He could breathe OK, and he was sure if they were broken, each breath would be agony. As it was, it only really hurt when he moved his arms or twisted. Bruised, not broken, was his conclusion. Now for his ankle: it hurt, but the pain had dissipated over the last several minutes. Again sprained but not busted.

'Best to do what my coaches in football had always told me and walk it off,' he told himself.

He hobbled for a few steps. The odd contortion of his gate made his ribs grumble in protest. After few more hobbles, his ankle seemed to loosen up, encouraging him to take longer and longer strides until the ankle was functioning near normal again.

With the extent of his injuries inventoried, he re-donned his shirts, loaded his dry bag and gathered his shotgun from where he'd thrown it up the bank and inspected it for damage. The inspection showed only a slight scuff of the gun's bluing of the receiver. With his mantra of "shoot the head" repeated, he set off across a relatively narrow piece of thick creek bottom vegetation before starting up the last slope he hoped he would have to climb.

As he moved away from the stream, the vegetation thinned a little but he still had to bull his way through much of the chest-high bushes and thick stands of birch bushes.

He started up the slope, his legs tired, and again he was into his pattern of ten yards advancement followed by rest stops to catch his breath. Only this time, every deep draw of oxygen caused a wave of pain from his ribs.

The pain and exhaustion robbed him of his concentration. Slowly his mind drifted to the subject that he had instinctively been avoiding as he trudged up the hill. He'd told himself that he'd been too exhausted to truly deal with what really had happened rationally. And now, after a relatively good night's rests, he was ready to confront what was lurking in the back of his mind, what had happened getting to shore. It wasn't the jellyfish or the clinging kelp that had induced panic as he was wrapped in its cold, slimy embrace. No, it was the finish when he'd given up that he had to confront. He'd given up on life, given up on himself, and he had been ready to die. Sure, an ember of life had flickered and then flamed across his fading consciousness, allowing him to regain his grip on life, plant his feet, and surge to the surface. So he could argue that he really hadn't given up, but it was an argument that he knew in his heart that he would lose. At that moment, death had reached out its hand to him and he'd accepted it. He had let go as he had begun sinking to the bottom to drown, and he'd quietly, blissfully accepted it. He'd no idea that he was only in less than six feet of water. Had not the shallow bottom disturbed his embrace of death, he would have faded from life and made himself a bountiful meal for the crabs. With that visual, of himself washed up at the tide line, his carcass being consumed by maggots, crabs, and the odd bear that had wandered down to tear off an arm or leg to carry up on to the hillside for a meal of partially rotted flesh, his stomach lurched in protest. Why had he chosen death? The question haunted him now. He'd always prided himself on being a fighter, a competitor that always got the job done. But he'd quit, quit, quit. And the thing that now frightened him the most was that it had been easy, very easy. He feared now that he'd a taste of just how easy it was to quit. The next time he was faced with the question of life or death, would he be that much quicker to choose the easier option?

He realized that he'd been taken beyond his breaking point. And now, by definition, he was a broken man, somehow defective. It was unsettling to now consider himself 'defective'.

Now, as his psyche was being peeled back by his analysis and reflection, he became aware of the glaring fissure of his inner being. He wondered whether this fracture would mend in time or would it corrode and enlarge? If it did mend, would the weld be stronger than the original material or weaker and unstable, predisposed to snap at an unknown stress load? At the bottom of it all was the question of whether he could trust himself and whether he would seek to find the answer or run from situations so that he would never be forced to find out.

It was odd, he thought as he was lying in the pitch-blackness of his little tarp sleeping structure in the middle of the wilderness tonight, that he would be seeking life's truths.   He wasn't really sure what to make of his newfound self-awareness. He felt altered, but was unsure how. He was startled out of his reverie when he heard a loud "wooof" ahead and the sound of heavy twigs on the ground being broken by a heavy body. He snapped his head up to find himself in a section of light woods with knee high grass and he new instantly what it meant.

He fumbled to get the shotgun unslung and to his shoulder, safety off.

Adrenaline shot into his system as he searched ahead for the bear that knew where he was.

He scanned the landscape in front of him over the bead front sight of the shotgun.   The bear was somewhere uphill from him. He'd not been keeping track of the wind direction, so he'd no way of knowing if the bear had scented or heard him. It was very doubtful that the bear had seen Eric for, if it had, it either would have approached to investigate or attacked. The more he stood there, the more certain he was that the bear had probably been startled by him and it was out in the woods, waiting for him to make a sound, he reasoned. Or maybe again, it was circling quietly to get behind him to attack. At this thought, he flicked his eyes away from the front of the gun, trying to get a look to his sides.

It was a bad decision.

While he had been searching to his sides, the bear had slipped noiselessly out from behind some bushes thirty yards in front of him. Eric was standing stock-still and the lack of movement prevented the bear from immediately identifying him as prey.

Eric shifted his eyes back to his front gun sight, perhaps because he'd caught a glimpse of movement out of the corner of his eye, to find it perfectly centered on the shoulder of a large black bear quartering towards him from the right. Another shot of adrenaline slammed into his system as he reacted primitively, instinctively to the powerful predator standing before him. He must have moved or reacted physically because the bear straightened and raised its head, its eyes boring in on Eric with an intensity that made his innards quiver and his whole psyche screamed "RUN!!"

Yet he held his ground, his brain's rational side overriding his emotions, as he waited for the bear to make his move. In the blink of an eye, he calculated that at this distance, he could get two, even possibly three shots, off before the bear hit him if it charged. He also reasoned that the bear now knew where he was, so standing there and acting like a deer trying to hide in plain sight would eventually invite attack.

So would running.

That left one option for him: attack. Maybe he could bluff the bear into retreating.

"HEY!!! HEY!!!" Eric shouted with all the bravado and threat he could muster, "GO AWAY!!!" "YOU BIG PIG, I'LL BLOW YOU AWAY!!"

The near panic in his brain and the adrenaline made it difficult for his to think of threatening bluster to hurl at the bruin coldly eyeing him.

NOTHING.   The bear's focus and intensity didn't change.

"HEY, I'M TALKING TO YOU!!"   "YOU WANT TO DIE!!!?"

The bear was motionless as a rock. Eric could see the tiny cogs of its brain churning, trying to make sense out of the picture presented by this motionless, loud, oddly smelling thing before it that was willing to stand its ground and shout aggressively.

Eric cycled through the only threats he could think of once more:

"YOU BIG PIG, I'LL BLOW YOU AWAY!!"   "HEY, I'M TALKING TO YOU!!"   "YOU WANT TO DIE!!!?"

Still the bear stood stock-still.

'This isn't working.'

It seemed like an eternity to Eric as this confrontation wore on.

'Wait a second,' it dawned on Eric, *'this bear isn't moving because he doesn't know what I am. Surely he's scented me by now, I know I'm ripe after two days of hiking, so he probably has no idea what a human is. That makes sense; I mean no one walks in these woods so it may not have ever seen human before or have any idea if I'm edible.'*

At that moment Eric had an idea.

'Maybe I need to up my game, go big or get eaten. I need more intimidation.'

He looked for something to thrash or rattle, but found nothing handy and he didn't want to break a stride to the nearest brush a few feet away, which might trigger a bluff or real charge from the bear.

Then he looked up and saw a low hanging branch overhead.

'Perfect.'

But the branch was too far over head for him to reach with his hand.

'Shit. Shit! SHIT! I'm going to have to use my shotgun to grab or rattle that branch. Do I want to un-target the shotgun? I've got to if I want to break this stalemate. Why don't I just shoot bastard and be done with this?'

But he knew the answer.

'Because dipstick, if I don't kill it with my first shots, I will be dealing with an injured, pissed bear. Even if I blow its heart to smithereens it will live for another minute, which will be the longest and last minute of my life as it rips my body into agonizingly, gory little bits, that's why. OK, it's the branch. I'm betting the ranch that that I can gun back on 'em to knock him down if comes."

Eric never took his eyes off the bear, as he lifted the shotgun straight up with his right hand and waved it around over his head until he hit a branch with the barrel of the gun. He felt the gun catch on the branches above and gave a little yank down, while shouting another round of threats at the bear. In the periphery of his vision, he saw the foliage on the branch tips wave wildly.

This was enough for the bear. With startling swiftness, the bear wheeled one hundred eighty degrees and took off at a three quarter run. He was happy to see that the bear must have decided that anything that could reach higher than it could, looked as bulky as he did with the dry sack on his back and was willing to stand its ground wasn't an easy meal. The sound of it crashing through the brush diminished until the woods were quiet again.

And just like that the confrontation was over.

He dropped the shotgun to his side, and stood there for several minutes gathering his wits, although at the moment, as his body tried to flush out the adrenaline that had coursed through his arteries moments earlier, his mind was completely blank. He was happy to stand there and just drink in the noises of the forest, to which he'd already grown accustomed.

Slowly he gathered his thoughts, before setting his feet into motion again. This time before he pushed off up the hill, he repeated his mantra "shoot the head" with a new found earnestness.

He was happy to be in motion again, even if it was up a steep hill. The exertion helped him work off the feeling of helplessness that he was now feeling over the confrontation with bear and the sense of stupidity towards himself that had washed over him. He knew it was irrational, but he couldn't shake the feeling.

'That was stupid, stupid, stupid...letting that bear getting the drop on me like that. How did I let down my guard like that? I knew it was out there, I knew it was up hill from me. I started to second guess myself is what I did and looked away. That shit will get you killed, Eric-boy.'

Recriminations continued to wash over him as he reviewed the confrontation in his head while he plodded up the hill in ten-yard increments.

'What was I thinking, taking the gun sites off the bear! What if the bear had charged and the gun had gotten hung up in the

branch? Where would you have been then? Dead, dead, dead.
I'll never do that again!'

'And what about those threats -- how lame was that? "You
big pig, I'll blow you away." It's a good thing that it couldn't
understand English, otherwise it would have charged me for
being a lame idiot savant of threats.'

But most of all, the one thing that scared him the most,
was how close to total mental lock-up he'd come. When
he needed his wits the most he'd nearly frozen.

'I couldn't even come up with good taunts to yell at a bear for
Christ's sake! And getting the shotgun off my shoulder and
aimed had been haphazard at best.'

As he thought about this disturbing dimension, he
realized that next time he wouldn't have time or the ability
to think his way through a situation. Next time, if he was
going to survive another encounter, he needed to have a
game plan in place, practiced again and again until it was
reflex. With that now settled in his mind, he made a
practice drawing his weapon to his shoulder, sighting and
flicking the safety off every time he thought of it, which
was often. He also came up with the plan to tap his
survival knife on his hatchet's head to create a metal on
metal sound, reasoning that if bears relied so heavily on
their hearing in the heavy brush, they would be spooked
and flee before an un-natural clicking sound in the woods.

The long shadows of the late afternoon found him high
up the slope. His goal was to make the ridge crest before
night, but he wasn't sure that he was going to make it.
He'd tried to gauge his progress by watching the only
thing he could see, the opposing slope that he'd come

down that morning. He knew the hill he was on was slightly lower, but how much lower he had no real way of telling.

He wanted to reach his goal for the day, and hopefully look out on the bay where he hoped to end this blasted hiking trip. But if he pushed it too much further, he wouldn't have enough light to properly set up camp. The skies were starting to cloud, which meant a storm front was on its way. Tonight, in all probability, he was going to get rained on, all the more reason to make sure he had a proper camp and plenty of firewood.

He was starting to feel the pressure that he'd pushed too hard for the ridge and waited too long before making camp when the hill suddenly flared out before him into a gentle round top ridge that was heavily wooded with little underbrush. The trees were small, spindly pines tightly spaced together. The upper foliage of the downhill slope trees blocked any view of the bay, if it was even out there. Eric's disappointment hung in his throat like a giant horse pill that couldn't be swallowed.

Hard pressed for time to put up a camp before it got dark, Eric concentrated on gathering all the raw materials he could quickly compile, afraid that he might easily walk past his campsite in the dark of the gathering dusk. He quickly amassed a large pile of fir boughs, which he found to be softer to sleep upon. He next cut down some pine bows from the nearby trees with his hatchet for his shelter. Then he set about gathering firewood. There were lots of deadfall pines that were just a few inches around. They were already dry so the branches broke off easily with the lightest swing from his hatchet; most still had their bark still attached.

There really was no time to pick an ideal piece of ground, so he chose two trees close by to string one of his downed pine trees between as a ridge pole. Tonight, he was expecting rain according to the last weather report he heard on his boat before he left, so he hung the ridgepole low between two trees to make an A-frame shelter using half the tarp before leaning the pine boughs along one side. He draped the tarp over the boughs and anchored it into place with rocks on one side and placed a dead fall across the other side to secure it. The other half of the tarp would be used to make his sleeping fold-over pocket that worked so well the night before. The floor under all the pines was a heavy layer of pine needles so he felt confident that that any water would drain away underneath his makeshift bed.

It was now very dark, so he hurriedly shoveled the pile of fir boughs onto the floor of his tent before flipping the folded tarp over it. He folded the foot well of his makeshift sleeping bag so that when he shifted at night the warm air wouldn't escape. After that, the pile of pine boughs was thrown on top to complete the insulation package.

The clouds looked angry and pregnant with rain in the gathering gloom of the dusk, prompting him to make fire the next priority. There was no telling how long the rain would hold off and if it would drown any fire he started. He wanted to feel warm for at least a few moments on this bruising day and he fantasized about a warm meal.

Quickly he cleared the forest floor mulch from near the mouth of the lean-to and started assembling his pile of tender, twigs, sticks and small tree trunks he had gathered earlier. In near darkness, he organized them into a starter fire pile before retrieving a match from the waterproof bag. One quick strike on the side of the box and the match flared in the dusk, giving him light to gingerly maneuver the flickering flame into the heart of the pile. A small puff of smoke emanated from the moss and shavings tinder, and hung over the little brown pile, obscuring whether a flame had taken root. The flame of the match burned his finger and thumb forcing him to flick the match away into the darkness aided by the reflex of the pain of flame on his skin. He was reaching for a second match when a yellow flame flickered and cast a slight glow from the bowels of the fire pile. Eric got down on his knees, face to the ground and blew gently until he had bellowed the flames that were hungrily licking the entire pile.

Now his fantasy of a warm meal looked more like a done deal. Gathering a few small stones, he rubbed all the dirt he could from them before piling them in the fires edge with a stick. While the stones heated, he prepared tonight's meal. He poured water into last night's meal pouch then used a pair of forked sticks to start placing the heated stones in the water. After the third stone, the water started to boil. The boiling water was slightly brown due to the dirt on the heated rocks.

'What the heck, it's boiled ,right? So it can't have any germs on it.'

Eric shrugged, as he added the boiling water to the

chicken gravy and rice and waited for it to rehydrate.

As he waited, he thought about Melanie, his girlfriend back in Ketchikan. She too was a researcher who worked out of Ketchikan during the summers, cataloging and studying geological samples that came in from field teams. It was a happy medium for her. She'd hurt her knee two years ago and was no longer up for the rigors of field collections as a geologist, yet she could still be in the thick of things from the relative comfort of the civilization that Ketchikan offered. The real bonus to her situation was that she got to talk to Eric almost every night.

It was good for his morale, too. It could get a little lonely, even though he loved what he was doing. The arrangement between Melanie and Eric was to wait twenty-four hours after he was overdue before reporting him to the Coast Guard and the Institute as missing. He'd checked in the night before his skiff was attacked, so he wasn't technically due to report in again until tonight. It wouldn't be until tomorrow night that Melanie would report him missing. But he knew that she was already worrying, because he never missed talking to her more than one night at a time.

A lump raised in his throat because he knew she was going to be upset and worried. He had told her many times that there were a million and one technical glitches that could make the radio communications impossible and that when that happened, he would head for Ketchikan. She had sailed with him several times in the islands of Southeastern Alaska and knew that from just about anywhere he was working, he could make it back to port in twenty-four hours, which is why he had made her agree to twenty-four hour delay before reporting the missed contact to the Coast Guard.

He pictured her beautiful green eyes that hinted of Asian influence framed by classical high cheekbones and heart shaped face that was the gift of her Irish father and Eskimo mother. Strikingly stunning without makeup, her feminine curves couldn't be fully hidden by the flannel shirts and jeans she normally wore. He smiled as he recalled her rough and calloused hands. She loved the feel of stone in her hands, which left them calloused and a bit rougher than most women's hands. He often joked with her that she would never make it as a hands model. But he didn't care one iota. She was kind and direct in an earthy way that was perfect for life in the outdoors of Alaska and perfect for him. He really didn't realize how much he missed her until just now. She'd always been there, a thread woven into his life without him even realizing how imbedded she'd become until the fabric of his life ended up here, on the wilderness hillside of an island archipelago.

They had been seeing each other for five years and slowly, almost unnoticed, the gyrations of their lives and careers had harmonized. The freedom to pursue careers that took them to remote places was anchored in the knowledge that the other would be there, waiting patiently. He began to feel neglectful that he hadn't explained to her how deeply his feelings ran for her; he'd just assumed that she knew. But right now, here on this mountain, that just didn't seem good enough.

'I promise to let you know how I feel about you when I get out of this,' he said as he stared into the fire with dreamy eyes.

His food was ready and he'd to put his musing aside for the more practical matter of fueling his body. By the light of a small, steady fire and a dying day, he finished his meal in a pouch and then prepared for another night in the wilderness snuggled in his makeshift sleeping bag. On cue, as he flipped the flap tarp over his face, he heard the first soft patters of rain hitting the tarp. Tomorrow was going to be one wet, miserable day.

As he settled in to his primitive sleeping arrangement, his thoughts were drawn back to the day's confrontation with the bear. It could have gone either way. The bear could have charged and he could just as easily have been killed, killed in the middle of wildness, his body never to be found. A cold, wet, lonesome death.

The rain pattering overhead on the tarp now started to beat with some verve. The sound of the rain drew him back in time to the first time he'd seen death up close. It was on a cold, wet night like this one. His family had relocated from California to Washington state and had settled on Seattle's Queen Anne Hill's exclusive neighborhood of quaint, well-maintained bungalows and yards of impeccable grooming. One night, he'd been watching T.V. in the living room when the screams of police and ambulance sirens at the end of his block drew his attention. Curious, he'd put on a jacket and had gone out into the drizzling rain to see what all the commotion was about. At the end of the block, his neighbors had gathered around the flashing blue and red lights of the first responders. Making his way to the back of the crowd, he jumped and craned his neck to see what was happening. Not able to get a good look he spotted Thomas, a kid from the block, craning his neck to peer through the crowd a few feet away.

"What's happening?" he asked as he came along side.

"It's that doctor chick from up the hill a couple of blocks. She crashed. She's all messed up. Check out her bike over by the streetlight," he said while gesturing in a direction beyond the police cars.

Eric knew exactly who he'd meant. Every male kid in the neighborhood knew who she was. It wasn't very often they saw women with a smoking-hot body drive up and down the street on a motor cycle in this neighborhood. She was supposed to be some sort of hotshot professor at the university. Of course, that really hadn't impressed the hormonally challenged youth in the neighborhood as much as the way she looked on her motorcycle as she drove on by.

Eric continued to try to get a better view of the happenings, until he'd finally found a crack in the crowd to look through. The people in front of him parted just in time for him to see the paramedics lift her listless body, strapped to a yellow backboard, onto the gurney. Her once awesome body, the rage of discussion among the boys, now lay at odd, twisted angles between the stainless steel rails as the paramedics pumped furiously on her chest. Eric could see blood oozing from several tears in her clothing, her wet hair plastered to her head, her skin pale and lifeless, washed of its humanity by the harsh glow of the streetlight. At that moment, he'd had been struck by how fragile and toy-like she looked as she was loaded into the back of the ambulance. She'd always seemed bigger than life as she whizzed on by on her motorcycle, capturing the imagination of all the boys on the block. Now she looked...she looked...dead. The crowd's murmur quieted for a moment as the ambulance doors were shut, and he remembered that he could hear the rain sizzling off her still hot motorcycle in the near distance.

It was odd that he would think of that, here, now... after all these years. He wondered what had ever become of her and what her life had meant. And God, he hoped that he didn't end up looking like her in death, meeting such a pointless and ignoble end. At least her passing hadn't gone unnoticed or unattended, which was more than he could say if he were to die in this wilderness.

14

Melanie Heaton arrived home after an average day of work to her apartment in Ketchikan at her usual time of six thirty in the evening. She thoroughly enjoyed her work of sorting and cataloguing geological samples that were being sent in from field teams from the Alaska Department of Natural Resources scattered throughout South East Alaska. Most people in the U.S., all but the tiny thimble-full that had been to Alaska, didn't realize how big, vast and plentiful Alaska really was. It comprised close to forty percent of all the land in the U.S. and had more coastlines in this one state alone than the entire west coast of the lower forty-eight. She considered it a privilege to be part of the team that was constantly exploring and cataloging its vast natural resources. In her mind, she romanticized that her activities were that of a banker keeping tallying of America's mineral riches for a time when her country might need them. And the DNR had only just scratched the surface, literally.

The one thing that she always had trouble getting used to every summer when she came to Alaska was the daylight. It was six thirty at night and in her and Eric's hometown of Portland, Oregon, the day at this point would be giving way to obvious signs of aging and hinting of night's approaching appointment. Here, however, due to the high northern latitude and the tilt of the Earth's axis, the sun wouldn't set until well after nine and rise before four-thirty a.m. She almost felt like she was cheating her research because so much of the day's light was spent in bed or doing other things. But if she really pushed it, her bad knee would remind her in a painful way that her body couldn't compete with the sun, like it was doing tonight. For some reason, her knee had started hurting yesterday morning around eleven.

It was funny, she mused, that it would be her leg that was the greatest source of trouble with her body. Melanie wasn't totally focused on looks and glamour as much as the rest of womanhood in America was; nor was she oblivious to it. She enjoyed coming to Alaska to let her hair down so to speak. The standards for feminine appearance were certainly much laxer in Alaska than in the lower forty-eight. Here, men tended to outnumber women by a significant margin, so the competition for the attention of females, attached, married or otherwise, was pretty intense. She'd often joked with Eric that all a women needed to do to dress up in Alaska was to tuck in her flannel shirt. It didn't take much effort on her part, certainly less effort than she would put into her appearance when she was back working as a professor at Portland State University, to set herself apart from the rest of the females. A little attention to her eyes - eyeliner, shadow, mascara, a touch of blush and - voila! She'd been blessed with near perfect skin, thanks to her mother's heritage, so it required none of the bases and foundations that cosmetic companies hawked without shame along with claims of anti-aging. But the best part of her body in her opinion had always been her legs, long by most standards, but athletic. Her choice of profession kept her hiking in rugged terrain, which really had made her legs firm and fit. When she was feeling a bit coquettish, she would wear a tight-fitting skirt with a hem well above the knee and revel in the impact that it had on the men around her; their surreptitious glances to peek at her legs as an unspoken compliment. And now the source of her personal pride, her gams, or more specifically, her left knee kept her from fully pursuing her passion for unraveling the Earth's geological history. Sometimes, the irony was just too much to contemplate.

She fixed herself dinner, heavy on frozen vegetables and instant meals from boxed ingredients. The cost of living in Alaska was one of the highest in America. Fresh food and vegetables were prohibitively expensive, especially on a government salary. Ketchikan was located on a headland on the southwest corner of Revillagigedo Island in the Songass National Forest. It was totally cut off from the rest of Alaska by road. The town existed on a tiny strip of flat land between two near vertical peaks with Ketchikan Lake to the rear, and the sea to the front. The town over the years had tried to grow up the hill but it was too steep to make much progress, so its growth had followed the coast, becoming one big waterfront strip. The only access to Ketchikan was from the air and sea. Air transportation, the most costly, was reserved for people, emergency medical supplies and machinery parts. In reality, most things arrived by sea to Ketchikan. Ketchikan International Airport wasn't even in Ketchikan or on Revillagigedo Island. It was on Gravina Island, just across Tongass Narrows that separated the two islands. So anything that landed at the airport had to be ferried across the Narrows. Even the bush pilots who served as one of the prime means of transportation landed in Tongass Narrows before taxiing to the docks that lined Ketchikan's waterfront. Airlines regularly flew in fresh vegetables and meat to savvy entrepreneurs who sold to the well healed and the finer restaurants. The rest the population had to settle for vittles brought in by supply ship; and the things that traveled best, aside from dry goods, were frozen vegetables and instant meals in a box.

After cleaning the dinner dishes, she flipped on the satellite television to find out what was happening in the rest of the world while she waited for the eight o'clock hour when Eric usually called. She was a little disappointed that he hadn't called last night; he rarely missed calling her. And when he did, he usually called the next night breathless with a "tail" of a whale encounter that happened late in the day that kept him out on the water till late into the summer day, returning too late to call. It was a private joke between Eric and her, calling his nightly updates on the running saga of the life and times among his pods of whales Eric tracked. The joke was in the "tails" because that was one of the primary ways that he identified different individuals. She actually enjoyed hearing about the lives and relationships of the whales that Eric followed. Eric's favorite company was a new small pod of killer whales that had broken away from the larger pod of killer whales that ranged in the southern part of Southeastern Alaska.

The eight o'clock hour came and went without a call from Eric. With each sweep of the clock's second hand her concern grew. The protocol that they had agreed upon was that Eric would call every other night, and if he failed to meet that schedule, she would wait for twenty-four hours before notifying the Coast Guard that he was overdue. It would be another day before she would declare him overdue and missing. The reason for the delay was to decrease the risk of false alarms. While Eric's boat had many redundant systems, life on the sea and aboard ship were hard on equipment. Occasionally, things broke. And if it was bad enough that Eric couldn't report in, he would be headed in to Ketchikan to get it fixed anyhow. Eric was an able seaman and was generally within twenty-four hours of sailing or steaming to Ketchikan. His boat had a transponder that could be pinged at anytime to find the exact location of his boat, if one had the transponder number. That transponder would automatically signal if the boat sank. The transponder had not sounded. She knew this because no one from the Institute, who tracked such things, had called her. So she was sure his boat was afloat. What wasn't clear was whether Eric was safe and on board. She worried sometimes because she knew that he spent great amounts of time in his little rigid inflatable chasing whales and had no such signaling devices to identify his location while in it.

Eric had only failed to report in one other time. An electrical short had fried a section of co-axial cable between his satellite communications equipment and the antennae. He had spare connectors to fashion a new cable but not enough length of spare co-axial cable to make a repair. He'd told her that he could have cut cable from other equipment, but in the long run it would have caused more problems than it solved so he'd just opted to return to port to get it fixed. She was hoping that this was just another one of those situations.

She headed to bed that night just as the sun was fully set, a little before ten p.m., knowing that her worries wouldn't give her a solid night's rest. Tomorrow would be worse.

15

The Pod Leader had hovered near the body of the deceased female for an hour after her last breath, not wanting to let go of the last vestige of the family life he'd built with his new pod. Eventually, the shock of the attack and deaths of all his charges before his eyes wore thin enough for the reality of the situation to set in. The Pod Leader realized that it was all gone and he was floating beside a corpse. With that realization, he turned his fluke to the bobbing body and with steady, powerful, purposeful strokes, he distanced himself from the scene of devastation that clung to his mind like a jag of searing pain. He swam at a steady, swift-moving pace of speed-swimming that allowed him to effortlessly cover twenty miles or more of ocean an hour by launching himself completely from the water when he needed a breath and re-entering the water without a splash.

He was in search of his mother's pod. It was the only home left for him now. With each mile, his hate for the Giant Shark that had killed his pod festered and grew. He would find his mother's pod and together, they would hunt this fish down and kill it. The members of his small pod that had broken from his mother's to be with him were known and loved by all the members of the Clan. They wouldn't let this stand; they too, would want revenge. Or at least that is what his fevered mind fixated upon. As he swam, he listened for the telltale sounds of his mother's pod. He'd a good idea of where to find them.

At this time of summer, his mother's pod, the Northern Clan, would swim north into one of the main inside passages between certain islands and join with the Middle and Northern Clans of the tribe to make a super pod at the rendezvous. Killer whales formed strong bonds that lasted a lifetime. When young females meet and cavort with young male killer whales at this annual rendezvous, sparks tended to fly among the unattached, while older, mated relatives living in different pods caught up with one another. At the end of the rendezvous, it was common for there to be some shuffling of the constituency of the various pods based upon the romantic bonds formed. Usually the males of the newly-formed bond pairs would follow the pod of his mate, but not always. In this way, unwittingly, killer whales had kept their gene pool from becoming inbred. But love wasn't on the mind of the Pod Leader, revenge was. It should not be very difficult to hear the sounds of one hundred fifty plus killer whales having a social gabfest.

After swimming for several hours, the light began to dim as the day's interval began to melt into the island ridges above. Swimming in the dark wasn't a problem for the Pod Leader. When he was traveling hard and fast, he relied heavily on his echolocation senses to see what the ocean and sea bottom looked like around him. This sense worked just as well at night as it did during the day. However, he was a mammal, and all mammals require rest and sleep. He was beginning to feel the exertion of the steady speed swimming for hours without having eaten today. Taking the last few minutes of the day, he grabbed as many of the salmon, which were thick in the waters as they made the final journey to their birth streams to spawn and die, before finding a place to hole up in for the night. Quickly, he ran down and consumed a half-dozen six-pound salmon before the edge of hunger in his stomach had been knocked off. It took him another half hour or so to gobble down another dozen before his hunger abated.

The fatigue that crept through his body had more to do with his emotional losses of the day than with his hard traveling. It was also clouding his thoughts, so choose to sleep right where he was at in the main channel tonight. Normally, he and his pod would find a nice bay to sleep in every night because the tide actions were a lot more muted than in the open channels. Having had his clan attacked in the relative shallows and safety of a bay of this morning, he'd suddenly developed an aversion to the closed confined areas. Tonight, he would sleep in the wide-open space of a main channel with plenty of room to sense any thing that may try and sneak up on him. He settled in for the night, floated near the surface of the main channel he'd been traveling. Every other minute or so he would methodically rise to the surface and take breath; eventually he settled into a fitful sleep.

******

The Pod Leader awoke tired and edgy in the dawn's light. He'd startled awake several times during the night, unsure whether the nightmares of the slaughter of his pod had jolted him awake or that his senses had detected the Giant Shark circling below him, preparing to attack. The tides had moved him several miles north during the night and now were reversing. He was starting to drift away from the direction of his advances. He was immediately aware of the absence of his pod mates. In the short time they had been together, he'd formed very deep bonds and he missed the reassuring sounds of the two mothers of his pod, checking on the whereabouts of their children in the morning.

Hunger was the first order of business this morning. The dim light of the dawn would keep the salmon from starting the annual migration. Although guided by the earth's magnetic field on their migration and their sense of smell to find their exact birth stream, they were a visual fish and needed the light to see where they were swimming. When migrating, salmon swam in the top three feet of the water because it was the warmest for their cold-blooded exertions and the most lighted for them to see obstacles and dangers. There was an added benefit to this strategy too. They were able to cover vast distances with little expenditure of energy. When conditions were right, the salmon would tuck themselves into crests of waves headed in the direction of their travel and let the energy of the wave carry them along, surfing the interior kinetic forces of wave propagation. But these were inside waters; the main feature was the total lack of waves and often glass-like surface of the ocean as the shores of the outer islands absorbed all of the Pacific's wave energy leaving calm on the leeward side. The Pod Leader knew all this from years of hunting his favorite meal which also meant that he was going to have to wait for his meal before he could resume his search. The delay frustrated him.

To counter his frustration, he stretched himself lazily and took time again to review yesterday's horrors in his mind. This just served to fire him with anger. *How dare this shark attack his pod? They were killer whales, and all creatures of the sea ran before them when they were hunting; they were the Kings and Queens of the Oceans. Did this Giant Shark not know that it was in the Coastal Realm of the Kingdom of the Tribe of Three Clans of the killer whales, their private hunting grounds, where they determined what lived and died, the place where the killer whales' children were sacred and heirs to the Kingdom?*

He'd heard the lore of the Clan told at the annual rendezvous of his youth, the stories of a large shark, the size of a near-mature female that resided to the south. Even this shark fled before the killer whales when the pack was hunting. *Who was this interloper who thought it could kill members of the Clan with impunity?*

As he struggled with these concepts, the Pod Leader also was dealing with a new feeling that he'd not known since he was a very young calf: fear. For the first time in his adult life, he now knew fear, not so much a fear for himself, for he was a male in the Southern Clan of the Tribe of Three Clans of the killer whales, a leader of a pod. He was a warrior. No, what he was afraid of now was the safety of the Clan's young. And that thought alone made him even more determined to find and kill this thing that would bring terror to the young whales of the clans.

The light was now sufficient for him to find this morning's sustenance. The salmon were on the move again and plentiful this morning. He spent the next hour gorging himself on the fattened fish. He wanted to push hard; he should be able to find the rendezvous late that afternoon, and he didn't want to stop again for food before then.

Having feasted, he set out again at his best distance chewing speed-swimming pace. The hours and miles passed until he arrived late in the afternoon in the general area of the rendezvous. He dropped out of his speed swimming to cruise at a more sedate speed so that he might listen better to the currents of the ocean.

He alternated between speed-swimming and casual cruising, listening as he continued to move north until he caught the faint sound of his dialect upon the ocean's currents. He swam in a semicircle to confirm that the sound's direction didn't change regardless of his bearing, and when he was certain, he headed west up another large main channel between two islands. As he speed-swam, he was unable to hear well; as the water flowed over his skin at this speed it created tiny vibrations, noise, that prevented him from hearing anything remotely faint. As he got closer to the expected rendezvous location, he would have to drift and listen.

Again, the hours and miles melted away. The tide that he swam against in one phase of the tides would assist him in the next phase. After navigating around several islands, he finally arrived at his general goal area in mid-afternoon and started listening drifts.   And after eight hours of hard swimming, he needed to rest anyway.

A leisurely swim around the western half of an island and three listening drifts later, he finally heard the faint echo-clicks of a large group of whales to the west, down another large intersecting channel. At the sound of voices, clan voices, he suddenly felt the gloom that had been clinging to him partially lift. It had been a lonely trek for the Pod Leader, and not a little scary having seen what the Giant Shark had done. He'd kept an eye to his rear and below, but now with voices nearby, he felt a little inkling of safety.

He grabbed a large breath and sprinted toward the voices; his tired muscles finding new strength.

After ten minutes of hard sprinting, the voices were becoming louder and clearer; he could hear them distinctly now, even over the turbulence his headlong sprint created around his body. He cleared a rocky point, which opened onto a large bay five miles wide to his left, and the volume zoomed to a din of overlapping voices. The super pod had found a bay to hole-up in and was into their preparations to rest for the night.

The Pod Leader banked as hard as he could into a left turn and dived thirty feet to get room to launch into a breach. At a full sprint, he angled sharply for the surface; the momentum of his nine-ton mass launching at near thirty-five miles-an-hour carried him all the way out of the water and twenty feet in the air. He pirouetted in the air to crash almost horizontally on his left side, all the while grabbing a lungful of air. Huge walls of water shot upward to the left and right of his body as his slick, smooth skin parted the water under him, gravity ushering him back to his natural realm.   As soon as he was immersed, he dove again to thirty feet and then launched himself into another spectacular breach; massive gouts of water again parted as his body pounded the glass smooth surface of the bay. The gouts crested at the top of its arc before frothing and splintering into thousands of drops that pelted the surface to creating a second reverberation to the pounding his body had made upon the surface.

As he re-immersed, he headed straight for the center of the pod at full speed along the surface, slowing only enough to roll sharply to his right to slap his big dorsal fin on the water's surface. Moments later, he repeated the slap.

The young killer whales, which had been playing on the perimeter of the pod, had taken little notice of the breaching male at the mouth of the bay. The adults of the super pod reacted quite differently. With the large number of young and juvenile whales playing about, all the adults on the pod were highly vigilant, even those without young. Many had focused their attention on the Pod Leader after the first breach, more after the second. Anyone who wasn't aware of the on-rushing large male was instantly focused upon him with the first dorsal fin slap, a universal signal of danger. Almost in unison, the adults of the super pod turned towards the fast approaching stranger and sent dozens of underwater echolocation clicks in his direction to identify this strange-acting interloper who may himself be a danger to the young. With so many whales emitting echolocation clicks simultaneously, the return signal and identification of the charging male was confused and muddled, which only seemed to heighten the tension among the adults. Several large males pushed aside females and started to aggressively rush to meet the charging unidentified male. The young and juvenile whales that had been playing blissfully unaware were now alerted to the unfolding drama by the massive echolocation clicks, the likes of which they'd never heard.

The assemblage of killer whales hurled dozens upon dozens of echolocation impulses aimed at the Pod Leader. His senses were temporarily overwhelmed by the intense sonic energy. The intense focus of the transmitted energy aimed at him momentarily blinded his echolocation sense and he wasn't yet in visual range. He couldn't see the dozen large males that were now charging him.

The dozen large males sent more echolocation impulses as they continued to charge, which continued to keep the Pod Leader blinded and confused.

The charging males and the Pod Leader rapidly converged; the pack of males intent upon battle, the Pod Leader only filled with relief.

The Pod Leader saw a dozen large, full-sized males materialize from the green waters of the bay and instantly took in their hostile posture and intent. He immediately peeled left into a hard left banking dive, exposing his vulnerable flank to his attackers. By doing so, he assumed a non-threatening posture, the equivalent of surrendering, which also displayed the unique pattern of his gray patch astride his back just behind his dorsal fin as well as his full body pattern of black and white markings.

Three of the charging males, members of his mother's pod, instantly recognized the Pod Leader and broke off their charge, changing their course in three different directions. This break in ranks confused the other charging males, and delayed their attack just a fraction.

The Pod Leader immediately started shouting greetings, sensing the impending attack.

This was enough to break the charge of the remaining nine killer whale males as they immediately recognized the dialect of the single adult male as that of a member of the Tribe. Unfortunately, eleven massive whale bodies had been converging on the same spot at full speed, a closing speed of roughly seventy miles-an-hour, and one of them had turned broadside in front of the other on-rushers. The convergence point had been near the surface, which further reduced maneuvering space to prevent a collision that could prove deadly to the recipient. While a killer whale's shape is extremely hydrodynamic, allowing it to swim effortlessly and efficiently through water, it wasn't designed to move sideways through the thick medium of water that produced tremendous resistance to objects with large surface areas, like the side of a killer whale. A killer whale's anatomy, while very robust as a keystone predator, was designed to deliver punishment, not absorb it. Due to the weightless nature of buoyant life in the sea, a whale's skeleton was very susceptible to the lateral forces of being rammed. If one of the on-rushing whales hit the Pod Leader while it was broadside, the water opposite the direction of the strike wouldn't give much, forcing the Pod Leader's internal organs, bones and ligaments to absorb the energy of the punishing blow.

With agility not expected of a sixteen thousand pound animal, the remaining nine charging killer whales canted their huge paddle-like pectoral fins, biting deep into the water, grunting against the strain, arching their backs and twisting their bodies to avoid collision. Whale bodies flew everywhere. Some were able to breach over the Pod Leader, some were able to dive below him, others rubbed over his back or shot behind him.

One whale in the middle of the charging pack had no place to go, all his escape vectors occupied by whale bodies. His only option was to pull himself into a parallel dive of the Pod Leader. But he was unable to check his forward momentum. His inertia carried him into the Pod Leader, slamming into the broadside whale. Fortunately, much of the charging male's kinetic energy had been bled off into the whale's emergency turn, and only caused the Pod Leader to grunt, no vital damage was done to either whale.

To the on-looking pod, who saw the dozen males rush to attack the approaching male killer whale, the jailbreak melee at the point of interception looked like a full-fledged attack. Many were still sending echolocation clicks into the melee, trying to see what was happening. With so much sonic energy in the water being returned from all the different bodies and bay floor, nobody was able to see anything. So they waited anxiously for some sign of what was happening in the throat of the bay.

The Pod Leader was now spent. The impact of the other whale had jolted him, causing him to exhale the captured air in his lungs. The sudden adrenaline rush of having narrowly turned the attacking whales from setting upon him, on top of his sprint to join the pod after two days of speed swimming, left him exhausted. He barely made it to the surface to take a breath. Once there, he slowly gathered himself as the male killer whales, who moments ago aimed to rend his flesh, now gathered around him in curiosity.

Questions from his observers pelted him. Those males who knew him demanded to know where the rest of his pod was, and with all the energy he'd left, he responded: Dead, all dead.

This quieted the pack about him. It was incomprehensible to them for an entire pod of killer whales to die. They could also see that he was clearly spent.

After a few moments of silence, allowing him to suck several large breaths through his blowhole, the questions started again.

How? Where? When?

The Pod Leader answered in short, clipped bursts: Giant Shark, yesterday, over a day of hard swimming due south.

This confused the gathering even more. The only sharks they knew were the salmon sharks and basking sharks, neither of which posed a concern to killer whales except for their newborns. He surely couldn't mean the tiny dogfish sharks. None of those could kill a healthy whale, unless there were many, many sharks. But all the sharks that they knew were solitary. There was lore within the Clan of a Giant White Shark that lived in the waters to the south, but no one had seen one in his or her lifetime. But even so, it was said that this shark was only the size of a juvenile killer whale, and would be no match for a single killer whale, let alone kill an entire pod.

This killer whale just wasn't making sense.

The group of adult males slowly steered the Pod Leader to the center of the super pod. His mother recognized her son and the exhausted condition he was in. She quickly organized her daughters and grandchildren to go gather salmon for the new arrival to help revive him. The curious drifted by to ask questions, the rumors of a giant shark that could kill a pod of killer whales were already ricocheting around the super pod. Too tired to answer, the Pod Leader just tried to rest on the surface.

Soon, salmon offerings started to appear in the jaws of his sisters and nieces, which he gratefully accepted. Shortly he was full, and could no longer stay awake. Sleep overtook the Pod Leader, oblivious to the fervor that his arrival and terse account was causing about him.

******

In the morning, he awoke late. Most of the pod had moved out into the main channel outside the mouth of the bay to feed on the running salmon. There were a few of his sisters still hovering about him, keeping an eye on him until he awoke, but once assured that he was properly functioning, they all moved out into the channel to feed.

It was very soothing to be surrounded by his sisters and their children. It eased his ache for his mate that had been killed two days ago.

The Pod Leader was filled with a series of emotions that just recycled through his head. He needed to warn the tribe of the impending danger of the Giant Shark, he grieved for his lost life-mate and the others of his small pod and he burned with the need to hunt down and kill the Giant Shark. The need to explain the threat to the Clan would have to wait. The rhythm of the rendezvous was to spend the mornings in smaller groups eating and to congregate in the late morning until it was time for the mid-afternoon feeding session. He would wait until all the clan had come together before detailing his warning.

With so many killer whales in such a confined area, even the salmon that were normally abundant had been thinned, so the Pod Leader had to travel far afield to find sufficient schools of salmon to fill his stomach. The long distance travel to find food plus his late start brought him back to the midmorning clan gathering very late.

When he arrived at the gathering, he made his way into the center of the pack and rolled to his side twice so that his dorsal fin slapped the water.

Rapidly, the head females in each of the matriarch lines of all the pods assembled and the oldest males soon surrounded him for council.

Questions pelted him as soon as whales started to arrive.

What is wrong?

What is the danger?

Why are you signaling a threat?

He waited until all of the Council of the Tribe had assembled, including his mother, before answering their questions. He did so by giving a short narrative of what had occurred, only to be bombarded with more questions.

What did this killer shark look like?

He responded by telling them it was like the small gray shark that fed on the salmon we all know, but bigger by a head and then some. It was the size of a large gray whale or sei whale.

Many were skeptical of a shark big enough to threaten adult killer whales. But those that knew him and those that feared the possibility of what he said to be true held sway in the court of opinions. After some debate, it was agreed that there would be no harm in sending five pairs of adult males, already life-bonded, to accompany the Pod Leader to seek out and destroy the killer Giant Shark. It was roundly agreed that eleven adult male killer whales should be more than enough to deal with any threat in the sea. The tribe would hold the rendezvous until the new moon, giving them nine days to find, kill, and return.

Ten large males volunteered from the assembly. With that, the council meeting of the tribe dispersed, and the ten volunteers went off to say goodbye to their mates.

The Pod Leader had not properly said hello to his mother or thanked her for organizing his succor the day prior. He found her near the middle of the bay surrounded by two generations of her daughters, nieces, and nephews. After stroking him with her fin, she asked about his mate and her mother, whom she'd known all of their lives, and let him know she was saddened by their deaths. His sisters, nieces, and nephews gathered around and asked to hear about the Giant Shark that could kill an adult killer whale that the tribe was buzzing about, and as he started to tell them, other whales who didn't attend the council came close to listen to his replies. His responses left the audience clearly shaken. As he relayed the events, he was reminded of his own family that had been slaughtered just days before and just how vulnerable his extended family was still.

He didn't tell his mother of the painful way in which his pod-mates died. In the water there was no such thing as a whisper due to the density of water and the way it propagated sound; anything he said would be carried to many ears. He didn't want to relive his mate's and her family's deaths for public consumption; he was still too distraught.

With that emotional note, he knew it was time to say good-bye to his kin and set about the business of killing the Giant Shark that threatened them before they returned to their home range in the south.

The Pod Leader made his way to the bay's mouth. Several of the volunteers were already waiting for him. Soon all were present and accounted. Some of the volunteers were from his mother's pod and knew the territory well. For most, it would be their first time in another Clan's range. After a brief discussion, they decided upon a pace that would allow all to conserve energy yet still cover ground rapidly. With that agreement, they headed out of the bay, eleven of the largest male killer whales of the Tribe of the Three Clans, arrayed abreast, determined to find and destroy the interloper that would dare to wage war on their young and females.

16

Eric awoke to the same darkness and loud echoing sound of his breathing on the tarp as the day before. Again it took a few moments of confusion to shake the cobwebs from his consciousness and place himself on a mountainside wilderness on an island in Southeastern Alaska.

What in the hell am I doing here?

The events of being catapulted from his boat, the imbedded tooth in the tattered rubber of the boat, and the near-death experience swim flooded back to him, followed by the more pressing biological needs of hunger and a bladder that needed emptying.

Eric flipped back the covering flap to find a forest heavy with moisture from the night's rainstorm being timidly courted by the first morning rays of the sun filtered by heavy clouds that still lingered in the sky. He reached a hand out and found his damp tennis shoes which had dried little overnight. Struggling, his semi-dry socks seemed to fight him from entering the still cold, wet shoes as he wrestled them onto his feet, the laces followed suit.

Striding across camp to empty his bladder allowed the wet shoes to sop his socks in just a few steps. He also noticed all his fire fuel was soaked and he doubted that he would find anything dry enough to burn. His stomach rumbled as he grumbled to himself, "Looks like no fire this morning means no hot food."

He was down to his last meal package. He debated about holding it in reserve until he absolutely needed food. The Tlingit had two sayings that came to his mind: "Only an idiot could starve in Southeastern Alaska," and "When the tide is out, the table is set." Eric knew that food wouldn't be an issue once he got back to the shore. It may not be tasty, but he could find enough food in the tidal zone to get the necessary calories to keep him going, if need be. So he decided upon a compromise: he would rehydrate the food and put it under his shirt where his body could warm it and eat a half an hour after he started out down the hill.

His curiosity and desire to see what lay beyond the hill made him anxiously glance every few minutes at the curtain of pine trees screening the answer. Was it another valley or was the bay below him? He felt sure that this time it had to be the bay below. The sooner he got on the way, the sooner the answer would unfold.

A wave of optimism swept over him as he set about breaking down his little camp.

'Yes', he thought, '*today is the day I make it to the cabin on the shore of the bay.*'

While his mind was reflecting on the upcoming events of the day, his hands had been busy packing his belongings into his dry bag and preparing for another day of cross country hiking in a rugged terrain for which he was so il-prepared. He set off in the general direction of last night's travel, leaving the crest of the ridge, and soon was on a steep downhill slope.

The waist-high bushes were full of the night's rain. Water clung to each leaf, and in turn, to Eric as he brushed by. Within minutes of leaving camp, he was soaked to his underwear. He thought about some way of making the tarp into a skirt, poncho or whatever, but finally concluded that it was too late, he was already soaked; besides, he didn't want to cut up the tarp just yet. It was too valuable as a shelter at night. Also, he had to admit, he was a little concerned about the noise the tarp might make; first, in attracting a bear's interest, and secondly, it might also mask the sound of a bear's approach. But the going was easy, and he had a sense that he was almost at his journey's end, so his mind started to wander.

He could see it in his mind's eye, the little cabin with a stone chimney set in the tree line above the shore, smoke wafting out of the chimney, a hut set three quarters of the way up the rock beach, set on stilts. A dock ran alongside it, also on stilts, with a ladder at the end that led to a floating dock, where he'd seen a small aluminum gill netting boat tied alongside. As he viewed the scene in his mind, he'd a sudden, awful realization. What if the occupants of the cabin were actually out in their boat, gill netting? They could be gone for a day or two and delay his getting back to his boat, his life...Melanie. He hoped that he didn't need to break in and rummage around to find a radio, if no one was there. The thought of rummaging around in someone else's home to find a radio or how to make it work didn't settle well with him. He just hated the thought of messing around with some else's property and violating their space, even though he was in desperate straits.

'*Best not dwell on what might not happen,*' he cautioned himself.

Besides, he knew Alaskans were a different breed of people, not materially dominated by their possessions or their space like city dwellers that fenced in their suburban yards, clearly saying, "This is mine! Don't touch." Here company and human contact were scarce and accepted warmly when encountered, whatever the circumstances. Outback Alaskans would be more concerned about a person's welfare than the loss of some easily replaced possessions; they would just be genuinely happy to help someone in need because living in the wilderness, they too might one day find themselves having to rely on the kindness of a stranger to help them out of a jam.

'*Funny,*' Eric thought, '*how the pressures on people couldn't be more polarized between living in the wilderness of Southeast Alaska and the city. When I live in the city most of the year, I try all day long to carve out my own personal space, starting the moment I open my eyes in the morning. Our room is full of things Melanie and I picked to make our home unique, defining our space to our shared vision. My toothpaste has to meet my requirements for flavor, brighteners, fluoride, and breath freshness, not to mention that is has to have fancy stripes or sparkles. I put on clothes that are uniquely me, yet it performs the same exact function as everyone else's. But I've been told I have to set myself aside from the crowd by making a fashion statement - trading comfort over fashion, or his case,*' he chuckled to himself, '*the ability to do both at the same time.*

'My breakfast is selected from eigtty thousand different items at the mega mart to my specifications. I know the odds are astronomical between two different people going into a store and putting the same one hundred items in the basket. Or for that matter, what were the chances of two homes in America having the same items in the cupboard. I bet I would have a better chance with lottery tickets.

'Even when I get in my car to go to work, I get in a car I picked to set me apart and made to show everyone I'm an individual. Even as I zoom in and out of traffic, I can feel the unseen but always present pressure of other people intruding into my space:

'Don't crowd the lane.'

'Nice turn signal buddy.'

'Red light-you go; green light-now it's my turn.'

'Get in line to turn here.'

'Who's right-of-way is it?'

'All of those unseen and unknown people crowding into my thoughts, putting psychological pressure on my personal space. So what do I do? I flip on the radio to distract me from the demands of other drivers. I get to listen to my stations, selectively allowing which radio DJs I like to tell me about what's going on in the world: the weather, the news, local events…the time.

'Until I get to work and set about doing my research, which I do because I love it, but also because it sets me apart in the world of science and other researchers as a man of expertise and knowledge.

'All my life spent trying to isolate myself from the masses, now it was ironic that all I want is for there to be another human being out there at the endof this sojourn.'

Eric felt stripped of all his humanity, the one thing he was craving, counting on was the kindness and tolerance of a stranger he was yet to meet at a home he prayed was occupied.

Living in Alaska, he learned, put the opposite psychological pressure on a person. Except for a handful of cities, most people lived lives of isolation. The extreme weather of winter isolated people, too, even in the cities. It kept most people indoors most of the time, making daily outings a luxury beyond what was needed to secure one's living. Satellite television had come a long way, including even the most remote village in the events of the day. But it was all a distant, remote drama to which they couldn't contribute nor influence. Human contact was limited to those in your village, that is, if you lived in one. Life was hard, the elements brutal, the distances staggering in Alaska. All this played upon the mind of even the heartiest souls. So when the opportunity came to make a new acquaintance, the thirst for interaction with a live, responsive human knew little bounds. Often, what lower forty-eight denizens would consider a casual acquaintance had a much more significant meaning to the inhabitants of Alaska. Even a brief acquaintance made while visiting or passing through the remoter pockets of civilization took root. It wasn't uncommon to be invited home, served a proper meal, and given the keys to a car, truck, snowmobile for as long as you were in town, because people living in isolation with limited opportunities for friendship made the most of it. Friendships and relationships were the real currency in the remote wilderness of Alaska. They were treated like precious gems on long, cold winter nights when they are taken out of the corners of the mind to re-examine, polish, and to treasure previous conversations, laughs shared and a meaningful smile extended from a kind heart. Even the briefest encounter was of great value.

Not like the throwaway society of the lower forty-eight where one could afford to piss-off the person behind the counter serving you for the perceived infraction of not meeting an undisclosed standard or expectation. After all, there will be dozens, if not more, of the same ilk that will be encountered by week's end. People in the lower forty-eight have only so much time and energy in a day and almost unlimited opportunities for investment into relationships. So they can afford to be picky about whom and where to invest.

His tennis shoes had a full half-inch of water sloshing around in the bottom by now. Although the bushes were only belt-high, the water they had imparted to Eric's clothes had managed to wick its way up to cover most of his chest. The one area not sopped by the bushes was his shoulders. That area was reserved for the raindrops falling from the pine needles above, drenching him at a slightly slower rate. He was chilled by all the cold water being transferred to him; he knew that there would be no stopping today, for if he did, he would soon start shivering uncontrollably.

After a hundred yards he hit an especially thick patch of bushes on a steep portion of the hill. Trying to keep his activity level high to stay warm, he plowed into the patch at his steady pace. As he stepped on the thin, pliable wet stalks of a bush, they folded downhill under his weight, forming a slick skid on which his shoe found no traction. His feet flew out from under him, his butt hitting hard on the ground, the weight of the dry sack on his back pulling him over backwards. His backside under the dry bag, the one spot that had been relatively dry, was now dampened by the wet grass that grew under the bushes. The shotgun flew from his shoulder and rolled in the wet grass.

He was miserable. And he just couldn't contain it any longer. As his anger boiled over he let fly with every curse and invective he could think of and when he was finished, he went through the batting order again looking for new combinations to express and ease his misery. After a third round, he realized that no amount of verbal tongue lashing to his surroundings was going to improve his situation or intimidate the bushes to become less slippery. Pushing himself to his elbow and rolling to his side, he gathered his feet beneath him and replaced the shotgun on his shoulder. This time, he eased himself down the slope by sidestepping while holding onto the bushes. Unfortunately, this slowed his progress tremendously, and it wasn't totally effective. He still ended up on his backside frequently; however, the crashes were a lot less forceful, more like hard sit-downs.

As he was getting up again from the third fall, he glanced out through the trees and caught a glimpse of something foreign. It took a moment for the slice of panorama that he could see between the trees to register on his brain: a body of water and a distant shore came into view. It was the bay! He'd been so busy looking for hand holds and foot placements, that his attention had been wholly diverted from looking to see what lay below him. He was going home! He was going to be warm and dry by the end of the day. He was going to eat hot food!

This new discovery made all his misery vanish. He could put up with anything now that he knew he was close to his sojourn's end. He took a few moments' time to eat the food that he had under his shirt. When he was done he licked his fingers and with an air of distain he threw the empty foil package to his side, happy to not even look where it landed. With a bit of jump in his step, he got up and navigated the rest of the wet, steep brushy patch, checking his progress against the slowly changing view of bits and pieces of the bay below him every other minute.

Slowly, hour after hour, he wended his way off the mountainside.

He was now low enough to see water features on the bay below him as he crawled over downed trees, slipped and slid on the wet vegetation, muck and mud. His clothes were now covered in mud, but it didn't matter because he was getting close - he could feel it, even though it was still hard to see through the tree canopy.

Steam was rising off his head as his exertions raised his body temperature, burning off the water from his head and upper body. A wind suddenly blew across the forest and shook water from the limbs above as the trees were suddenly swayed by the emphatic shove of the wind. After a few minute's bluster the wind seemed to die out.

'*A second more powerful front must be moving in behind the weak one that passed through last night,*' Eric thought.

As the sound of the wind died in the tree limbs, a new sound came to Eric's ears, one he could just barely make out. It was the sound of a dog barking, below and to his right.

'*The wind must have blown my scent to the dog below, alerting it to my presence*', he reasoned, '*I must be close to the cabin. Finally, my luck must be changing.*'

As the dog continued to bark its warning at Eric, he tried to triangulate its position. He couldn't make out anything other than its general direction, but that was all he needed. He'd been worrying over which way to turn once he hit the water. As cold and miserable as he was, the thought of walking a half hour or more in the wrong direction had been more than his mind wanted to contemplate.

Now he had a beacon to guide him home in the dog's bark. Relief flooded through him.

Eric abandoned any pretense of stealth and caution and loped down the hill at his best speed, angling when he could in the direction of the dog's barking. The barking was getting louder and clearer as he charged down the hill busting brush. The closer he got, the more urgent the dog's bark became.

After what seemed an eternity, Eric glimpsed the shore fifty yards below. At a near sprint, he literally ran the rest of the way off the steep hill, the dog's barking now extremely close. As he cleared the last of the trees at the shore's tree line, his momentum carried him to the middle of a beach of smooth, black rock boulders and sand. By the time he was able to pull up, without twisting an ankle, he could hear the dog directly to his right.

As he turned to greet his barking savior, he took in a scene completely different than what he'd expected. In an instant, he understood what was really happening.

Between him and the dog, seventy yards down the beach stood a huge black bear that had to be close to four hundred pounds. The dog had not been barking at Eric, but at the bear. He'd stumbled into their confrontation.

Shit!

The black bear heard the commotion behind him as it confronted the barking dog and whirled to see his new antagonist. In the blink of an eye, the bear, now bracketed by adversaries, calculated that the newcomer was acting less aggressively than the barking dog and would be the best one to attack to break up this trap. The bear whirled and charged Eric with amazing speed.

Without thought, he smoothly whipped the muddy shotgun to his shoulder and stepped into the attack. All the practice at his rest stops of the previous days guided the gun to his shoulder in a firing stance. His finger instinctively found the safety and flicked it off. The phrase "shoot the head," flashed through his mind as he brought the front bead sight to bear on to the bear's head and squeezed the trigger. Eric was vaguely aware of the thundering explosion of his shotgun as the recoil rocked him backwards and the barrel skyward.

He'd practiced this so many times in his mind over the last several days that without thinking, he jacked the next round into the chamber. The recoil had temporarily taken his eyes from his target; had it not, he might have seen that his first shot was high, going straight over the bear's back and sending up a great gout of shattered rock and sand on the beach behind the charging bruin.

But Eric's full focus was on emptying his shotgun completely into the approaching killer. As the barrel and sight bead dropped onto the bear's head from the arc of the first shot, he pulled the trigger again. Another muted roar and heavy recoil, as Eric furiously jacked another round into the chamber.

This time, nine thirty-two caliber lead pellets in an eight inch diameter pattern tore into the upper left part of the bear's head, half the pellets eviscerating its left ear, the rest taking a massive divot out of his left shoulder.

The bear twitched to his left as that bolt of pain coursed through its head, but continued its charge.

Eric was working furiously to pump shells into the bear. With the next thunderous round, one pellet tore into the bear's left eye orb of its skull, exploding the eye in a shower of bone fragments. The other pellets seared into the bear's right shoulder.

With that jolt of searing pain, the bear seemed to pull up slightly as its vision picture changed from stereoscopic to mono. The black bear took a half second to reacquire Eric, and as it did it let out a low, deep-throated growl to give voice to its pain and its desire to rip and shred the stinging attacker in front of it.

The bear had covered over half the distance between Eric and now was only twenty yards away.

Eric desperately jacked another shell into the chamber and settled the weapon on the bear again. From twenty yards away, the bear loomed large in his sight picture, too close to miss. The question was would he hit something vital? The bear's powerful muscles threw it forward again as it resumed its charge as Eric pulled the trigger again.

A lead slug the size of Eric's thumb tore through the bear's left shoulder, shattering its left scapula. The bear staggered and slewed to its left side, the left front paw unable to accept any weight. The bear howled, now convinced that the only way to survive this attack was to kill this creature standing before it. Blind in one eye, blood pouring off its head where its left ear used to be, the bear was totally taken over by the fight or flight reflex. Its brain was totally focused on rage with all the brutal savageness it possessed.

Picking itself up from a stagger, the bear resumed his charge on three legs, its head pulled high, mouth open exposing its huge white daggers of teeth, in anticipation of the powerful bone-crunching bite it intended to deliver.

In less than a second, Eric had the last round chambered, but it was too late. The bear was just feet away from him, still on its feet; it would have him in its jaws in less than half a second.

Without a conscious effort, Eric's last act before he met the death in the bear's jaws was to just point the gun at the bear and shoot.

With magnificent, uncanny blind luck, the slug hit dead center in the bear's spine just behind the last cervical vertebrae, obliterating the bone and severing the spine, paralyzing the bear from the chest backwards. The bear's legs lost all control instantly as its body obeyed the laws of gravity and collapsed to the ground. However, its headlong charge still gave the bear's body forward impetus. The bear's body bounced off the rocky beach surface in a tumbling, rolling mass of fur and muscle. Eric reacted instinctively and tried to jump over the black bowling ball of fur headed for his knees. In the few tenths of a second that the bear's body needed to close the distance, Eric had only enough time to get his feet an inch off the ground before the bear brutally impacted into his knees.

The bear was paralyzed, but not dead. It still had control of its neck muscles and jaws. The bear felt no pain behind its neck where its spine was severed; it just ceased to have control of that portion of its body. While its non-responsive body bounced and rolled uncontrollably, the bear was still focused on delivering a killer bite. It swung its neck and head at Eric's leg as best it could, clamping down with crushing force as it saw and felt Eric's leg in its mouth.

Time seemed to be in ultra slow motion as Eric mentally prepared himself for the highlight reel as his life flashed before his eyes.

Had Eric stayed rooted to where he was, the impact of a four hundred pound bear into his legs would have surely broken bones and ruined his knee joints. However, the laws of physics worked in his favor today. Slight as it was, the little push off from the ground he'd in the tenths of seconds before impact shifted his center of gravity upward. The bear's body swept his legs, uncoupled from terra firma, out from underneath him; he started to spin around his center of gravity, somewhere above his naval. Just as he was violently starting to spin, his legs at nearly a forty-five degree angle behind him, he felt himself being drug back towards the bear, which was now directly underneath him. The sharp tug on his leg lasted only for a fraction of a second as the bear's body passed underneath him and rolling past. Eric continued his pinwheel spin in the air, his shotgun and dry bag flung from his body by the centrifugal force took two separate arcs of flight.   In slow motion he watched as his face and shoulders rushed to meet the stones of the beach, while his feet continued in a slow curve over his body. The impact of his face on the rocks stunned Eric momentarily, a flash of white light follow by black. His legs slammed into the beach, the right taking the brunt of the impact, but Eric never felt the waves of pain shoot through him – he was already unconscious.

17

Nearly senseless, his body tried to reconnect the jarred circuits of his brain and the first to come back online was his hearing, sort of. After five thunderous shotgun blasts, his ears were ringing and deadened. The next sense to blink on was pain from his legs as the damage from being slammed into the beach was communicated to his brain on every open pathway. As his eyes finally began to focus, he saw a man's feet approach and stop in front of his face.

A gun butt was set on the stones and two feet pivoted as a hand appeared in his field of vision, disappearing before he felt it grasp his shoulder. The impact had knocked the wind from him, and at this moment his diaphragm decided to kick in, allowing him to take a painful giant gulp of air just as the hand rolled him to his back.

He looked up into the aged, weathered face of a clean-shaven man in his fifties wearing a red-and-black plaid wool jacket

"Are you badly hurt there, partner?" he asked in a gentle voice. "You went for a helluva spin."

"Shit," Eric croaked with his barely functioning diaphragm. "I think my right leg is broken. It hurts like hell."

"You just hold still, I've got to take care of something," the older man said and his face disappeared from over

Eric's view, leaving him looking at a gray, heavy cast sky. He heard the man's steps move a few feet away before hearing the unmistakable sound of a rifle bolt being cycled and an expended cartridge hitting rocks, followed by the explosion of a high-powered rifle going off at close range.

Eric levered himself up to his elbow and saw the man standing over the bear's head with the muzzle inches away.

"I just had to make sure that bear wasn't going to give us any more problems. Here, let me give you a hand getting up," said the man as he extended his hand down.

Eric reached up to grab his and was surprised by how his hand seemed to get lost in the stranger's big, heavy-callused hands, which pulled him easily to his feet. His right leg hurt like the blazes on his shin, but it took weight, which was a good thing, so it must not have been broken.

"Can you stand?" Eric's benefactor asked.

"Yeah, I can stand," Eric said through gritted teeth, wobbling a bit as he tried not to put too much weight on his damaged leg. His lip was starting to fatten from the impact of the beach rocks, making his speech a little indistinct.

The stranger strode over to his dry sack and easily shouldered it in a way Eric never could and then walked over to pick up his shotgun from where it had landed. Having retrieved his possessions, the stranger walked back over to Eric cradling two guns in the crook of his arm, looped his free arm under Eric's right shoulder and said: "Here let me give you a hand getting back to the cabin. Come, Bullet!" he tossed over his shoulder at the dog that was sniffing the carcass of the bear.

The dog, which looked to be a cross between a Malamute and a German Shepherd, wheeled at the man's command and fell in behind the procession as they hobbled together the hundred yards up the beach to the man's cabin. Eric needed help getting up the stairs, but once he hit the level ground of the porch, he was able to manage on his own getting into the cabin.

The interior of the cabin was crowded with supplies but well organized; the furniture about the place was worn but well cared for, which gave the place a feel of hominess. Eric saw a table and chairs and headed straight for the chair which he dropped himself into with little formality.

Spinning in his seat, he turned to face his benefactor to find him intently studying him. He looked down at his clothes to see them wet, covered in mud, and now sand.

"It looks like you've been doing some hard travelling," the man said before turning away. He walked to the fire, which was burning pleasantly and threw on two big logs then wordlessly disappeared through a door in the main room and returned a few seconds later with a blanket.

"Here," he said while setting the blanket next to Eric on the table, "you need to get out of those clothes and get warm by the fire. With the two logs I just put on, this room should be hot as Billy Blue Blazes shortly. If you want, you can go in the next room to get out of those clothes. Just toss them to me, and I'll rinse them off outside for you."

"Thanks," muttered Eric through clenched teeth, already starting to shiver uncontrollably. Eric grabbed the blanket and limped into the room that he'd seen the stranger go into early to find a cozy, little single bed, neatly made with a little nightstand orderly arrayed with a windup clock and a small battery-powered book light. An oil lantern hung from a metal hook over the middle of the bed.

Minutes later, Eric emerged from the room with the blanket wrapped around him and a wad of his clothes in one hand.

"Here, let me take that from you," the man said as he grabbed the clothes in both hands and headed for the front door. He had no more than walked out the door before he returned again and headed to a big, old-fashioned wood stove in the corner of the room. On his way, he swiped a big thick handled coffee mug off a shelf on the wall and filled it with steaming black coffee from a coffee pot on one of the burners.

Eric had settled into the worn, stuffed cloth chair closest to the fire, shivering a little less now; getting the wet clothes off had helped, but he was still cold. He watched the big man cross the room and shoved the mug into his hand.

"I reheated this morning's coffee while you were changing into something more comfortable," he said with a twinkle in his eye and the hint of a smile at the corners of his mouth. "This should help with the thawing."

Eric tried to nod his head in his acknowledgement of the man's kindness, but the shivers he was still experiencing made it look like a neck muscle spasm.

The man bustled out the front door and soon Eric could hear water being sprayed on his clothes. After a few minutes the spraying sound ceased and was replaced by the sound of a generator being fired up followed by the chug-chug sound of a washing machine agitating clothes.

When he re-entered, he swiped another mug from the shelf before filling it from the coffee pot and settling into a chair opposite Eric. Placing his mug on a little table beside the chair, he reached into his pocket, extracting a red and white pack of cigarettes and an old-fashioned Ronson lighter. After lighting up his unfiltered cigarette and taking a big drag, he reached his hand out to Eric, "I am Dutch Pederson. But you can forget the Pederson part and just call me Dutch."

Eric took the man's big paw. "Eric McCallister. Thank you for helping me," was all he could find to say.

Dutch took a big sip of coffee from his mug before his whisky and cigarette baritone voice ambled into conversation.

"It was a good thing I was in the cabin today. Normally this time of year, I'm out fishing most of the week. But there's a couple of storm fronts s'posed to be passing through starting last night. If it were just one front, I would have fished, but when they're stacked up like the weather reports says, there's just no money in bucking Mother Nature."

Dutch took another sip of coffee before picking up on his conversational thread, "It surprised the hell out of me to see you come running out behind that bear, though."

Wrapping his hands around his mug to warm them, he settled them into his lap before he finished his thought. "It was a good thing I was keeping on eye on that bear. Bullet," he said waving his mug at the dog that had settled in the corner near the fire, "lets me know when one's around. Usually they don't take kindly to Bullet's barking and move on right quick, but this one wasn't so bothered by Bullet. If he barks more than a few minutes, I usually grab my gun and go out on the front porch to make sure Bullet doesn't get hurt. He knows better than to tangle with a bear, but you can never tell what they're going to do. Normally, all I have to do is clank some pans and wave my arms, and they get the picture and move off. I was just getting ready to clang some pans when you popped out, so I was only able to get off two shots at that bear before he was on you."

"You fired twice?" Eric ask, stunned by this bit of news. He'd heard nothing but the thunderous report of his own gun the whole time.

"Yep. Not sure where I broke him, though. Couldn't see the head 'cause he was running away, so I was trying to blow out his lungs and heart. Knew it wouldn't stop him before he was on you, but it was all I had to work with. I was just hoping that brush-buster of yours was going to plant him. As he was closing on you, I didn't have much of a shot without hitting you. It was a crappy shot, but nothing I could do about it. Glad it worked out OK, though," he said taking another drag from his cigarette.

"I musta got lucky with the last shot and hit the head or

spine the way he just dumped like that," Eric speculated.

"You hit him in the spine at the neck junction. He was still flopping his head about when I got to you, had to put him down. Had a big piece of your jeans in his mouth still. He came mighty close to taking a chunk out of you. When I was spraying off your clothes, I saw where he took that hunk out of the shins on your jeans. Lucky for you all he got was cloth; otherwise we'd be sitting here praying the Life Bird out of Ketchikan would make it here before you bled out."

The mention of Ketchikan jerked Eric upright as he remembered he needed to call Melanie to let her know that he was all right so she didn't call the Coast Guard and start a search for him now that he'd been 'found.' "Listen, I'm about to be reported overdue if I don't contact my person in Ketchikan today. Do you have anything that we can contact Ketchikan on here?"

"I use short wave radio," he said pointing a meaty finger at a set of radios on a shelf in the kitchen. "Best give 'em a call now, since I got the generator running," he said as he got up and moved to the kitchen. As he flicked switches on a big radio transceiver, lights and meters sprang to life. When he was satisfied, he picked up the desktop microphone and squeezed the transmit button, "This is TANGO-ZEBRA-ECHO-LIMA-SEVEN-FIVE-ONE-NINER calling Ketchikan Alaska Coast Guard Station on one oh nine point three megahertz, over." and released the talk button to listen for a response.

After a couple of moments, over the speaker he heard a tinny voice respond, "This is SIERRA-LIMA-MIKE-MIKE-

SIX-EIGHT-FOUR-TWO U.S. Coast Guard Station Ketchikan to party calling Ketchikan Alaska Coast Guard Station, please say again, over."

Dutch keyed the mike again, "This is TANGO-ZEBRA-ECHO-LIMA-SEVEN-FIVE-ONE-NINER calling Ketchikan, Alaska Coast Guard Station on one-oh-nine-point- three megahertz, over."

This time the voice came back and said, "Roger, TANGO-ZEBRA-ECHO-LIMA-SEVEN-FIVE-ONE-NINER, this is Coast Guard Station Ketchikan, how can we help you today?"

Dutch paused a moment, glanced at Eric and waived the microphone in his hand, indicating Eric should talk to them.

Eric shuffled over to the radio set in his blanket and took the microphone from Dutch, keyed the button and spoke into the round-screened disc in his hand, "This is Eric McCallister, I missed a scheduled communication contact due to technical difficulties and my onshore contact in Ketchikan should be reporting me overdue sometime today. Could you call my contact and let her know my status and that I'm returning Ketchikan and will contact her when I can with more information? Over."

"Roger," said the Coast Guardsman on the other end of the radio, "we're always happy to avert false alarms. I need contact information. Over."

Eric gave the operator Melanie's name and phone numbers before thanking the operator and handing the microphone back to Dutch.

"TANGO-ZEBRA-ECHO-LIMA-SEVEN-FIVE-ONE-

NINER, over and out," Dutch finished, setting down the microphone and flipping off the switches to kill the radio. With a wry smile, he turned to Eric and said, "I believe that a man's business is his own. But from what I've seen, you've had more than a little 'technical difficulty.' Maybe you ought to tell me how you ended up on my beach."

"Oh that…that was my girlfriend that I had them call. I know she's probably worried sick about me by now. I just wanted to relieve her worry and keep the message short. If I'd told the Coast Guard tell her that my skiff sank, she'd worry even more, even knowing that I was okay now. I just didn't want her to worry any more was all."

"Does she make you happy?"

"Beg your pardon?" Eric asked, taken aback by such a direct query from a stranger.

"Does she make you happy?"

"Well,…yeah."

"Let me give you some advice. Too many young people are afraid to commit to marriage because they are dying to experience bliss; day by day, dying as the sands of their life run out. They're dying because the likes of Hollywood sell bliss and rapture like they can bottle it. People forget that bliss and rapture stand on the shoulders of happiness. Find someone who makes you happy. Bliss will come along sooner or later if you do.

"My philosophy," he continued, "has always been: Anyone can piss you off. That's easy. But how many people can make you happy? When you find one that can, that's a keeper for life. If it's a man, befriend him; if it's a woman, marry her.

"Do you need a refill on your coffee or something to eat?" Dutch offered, abruptly changing the direction of the conversation again.

"Yeah to both."

"Well why don't you pull a chair up at the table while I fire up the stove, and tell me what's going on? Maybe we can figure out a plan to get you back where you need to be."

"Sounds good to me," Eric replied, shuffling over to the table and chairs in his improvised blanket kimono.

Dutch gathered two mugs, refilling both at the stove. Then he produced a fifth of whisky and put a generous splash in his mug before raising an eyebrow and gesturing with the bottle to Eric, "A little hair of the dog for you?"

"That sounds just kickin' to me," Eric told him with a nod.

After the fortified brew was delivered to Eric's hands and then lips, he started in on his saga while Dutch started fixing food, his cigarette dangling from the corner of his mouth.

"My boat is anchored up at Fillmore Island on the south side. I use my skiff to follow whales and make my recordings of the communications. Two days ago, I followed some whales into Nagat Inlet."

Here was the part he'd thought about for the last two days: what to say and who to say it to. He'd decided that it was better to not be generous with the facts, and a small lie would be best until he understood better what had happened.

"Near the mouth, I hit an underwater obstacle which

punched holes in my rigid hull and tore the bottom out of the inflatable section. The boat was un-seaworthy so I had to abandon it and swam for shore. It took me two days to hike overland to get here." He shrugged his shoulder as if to say 'what else was there to say.'

On cue, at the end of Eric's story, Dutch turned around with a steaming plate of Spam, hash browns, powdered eggs - scrambled - and a fork, all of which he placed before Eric. Normally, Eric eschewed the mystery meat Spam, but he was so suddenly hungry, that he gobbled up everything on the plate, hardly chewing each mouthful.

As Eric was wiping up the last of the crumbs of hash browns from his plate, Dutch had been watching him patiently. Finally, Dutch asked, "Where exactly at the mouth of Nagat Inlet were you when you hit bottom?"

'Uh-ooh', Eric thought, 'he's not buying it.'

"Oh, probably a couple of hundred yards in on the west side of the Inlet."

Dutch rubbed his whiskery chin with one hand and said. "That's odd. I've fished up and down that area of the Inlet and my nets had never snagged on anything. It's one of my favorite places to quick drift a net."

Eric was caught in a lie. He knew local gill-net fisherman like Dutch dropped lightweight drift nets made of green monofilament held afloat by oval floats at the top and a weighted rope on the bottom that set relatively shallow. Gill-nets weren't cheap and the fishermen knew all the spots where they might snag and lose their expensive gear. But how else was he supposed to explain the sinking and loss of his boat, which was supposed to be nearly unsinkable. There was no way he was going to tell Dutch about the tooth or what he suspected. *'Time to send this conversation in another direction,'* Eric thought.

"Did I hear a washing machine going? You've got all the amenities here. Got a dryer too?"

"I was never much for laundry, but I'm even less fond of wearing crusty smelly clothes. So I got one of those old agitating pot washers, light enough to get up the dock and damn near indestructible. Perfect for out here in the bush. No dryer though; we'll have to hang them on a line over the fireplace. Dries out clothes real quick if you stoke up the fire; speaking of which, your clothes should be done. I'll go check."

Dutch headed for the door, returning with Eric's clothes in his arms. A thin line hung from a hook on one wall; Dutch ran the line to a hook on the opposite wall and hung Eric's clothes close to the fire. After accomplishing that, he turned to Eric.

"Now let's figure out what to do with you," he said, pulling out a rolled up oceanographic chart from the pile and placing on the table. He used salt and pepper shakers to hold down the corners and peered over it. "We're here," he said tapping the map at the cabin's location. "Where exactly are you anchored?" he asked over his shoulder at Eric.

Eric came over and tapped the map. Dutch grabbed a small set of navigational dividers from a box near the maps, and after calibrating them to the map's legend, started to walk the dividers out the bay and up the channel to Eric's boat.

"I figure about twenty one miles, give or take. That's about three hours running with my boat. It's too late in the day to make the run now, but if you wait 'til morning, I can run you out then and grab some line sets on the way back in. Or I can call a bush pilot friend of mine out of Ketchikan. If he's not out on a run, he could be here in an hour and pop you over to your boat. There should be plenty of light to get up and down after he drops you off. But I'd be real surprised if he's just sitting around, though. We could probably find a pilot out of Ketchikan if we called around. I have frequencies for four or five of them. It's your call."

Eric was torn, he needed to get back to his boat and his world, but he didn't want to bother Dutch any more than needed. "Let's give them a call-out and see if any pilots are available."

Dutch went back to the shortwave radio, fidgeted with some dials and switches, and started making broadcasts.

Eric had settled back into the chair by the fireplace. Between the fortified coffee, his full stomach, his fatigue, and the warmth of the fire, he was fast asleep within minutes.

******

A gentle shake of his shoulder brought Eric around. He noticed the hand on his shoulder had maroon smears of blood on it.

"Well," Dutch began, "unless it's a life and death emergency, the bush pilots I got ahold of said that they could get you out tomorrow. So it looks like you're stuck here for the night."

Eric rubbed his face, stalling for time so that he could fully wake up. After a few moments hesitation, Eric replied, "That doesn't surprise me. If I can't get airlifted out until tomorrow, I might as well have you run me out to my boat. It would be the same amount of time. That is, if it's not that much of a bother to you. I'd gladly pay you for your fuel and time."

"That sounds fair," agreed Dutch. "We'll get a good jump on the morning and get out of here an hour before sun up."

"What happened to your hand?" Eric asked, nodding towards Dutch's bloodstained hand.

"Huh? Oh, you mean the blood," he said examining his hands now. "I had to do something about that bear you killed. If I'd left it on the beach, I have more damn bears down here eating it so I field dressed it. Better to do it while the corpse is still warm, much easier to skin that way. I have a meat cache up in a tree away from camp. I'll let it hang for a few days to age and then carve it up for stew meat and freeze it. Say, you want the skin for a rug?" he asked with an amused gleam in his eye. "You killed it, it's yours."

"Nah, I'll just keep the nightmares of my little encounter as my only souvenir."

With business concluded, Eric and Dutch spent a lazy afternoon and evening swapping stories and opinions and turned in early after a large dinner. Eric slept on the floor in front of the fireplace and slept like a lamb until Dutch stirred him the next morning.

"Morning," Dutch's baritone called out from across the

cabin.

Since Eric had no toiletries, he didn't need to bother with his morning routine. It was a simple matter of throwing on his clothes, and he was ready to roll out. His pants were now dry, and for the first time, he was able to examine the huge hole that had been ripped from his jeans near the right ankle as the bear collided with him. He fingered the edges of the tear, not yet sure how to process that event in his life.

Dutch served a plate piled with breakfast: bacon, powdered eggs, toast and hash browns. Bullet got his bowl of dog food, and all three were soon happily downing their grub. After a quick clean of the kitchen, Dutch disappeared out the front door to check the oil and lubricants on the boat before topping off the fuel and firing up the diesel engine and radar. While the engine and electronics warmed, Dutch was back to the cabin to fill a couple of thermoses and water bottles, and pack some sandwiches. Eric was familiar with this routine, and headed out to the outhouse to clear his bilges before they got on boat. Dutch did likewise and soon all three of them were headed out to the dock.

Without ceremony, Bullet jumped on board while Dutch used the ladder to board *The Stalwart*, which was riding high with the tide. Eric handed him the food, beverages, Eric's dry bag, and shotgun from where they had deposited them on the dock before he boarded.

The Stalwart was a thirty-foot all aluminum bow picker gill-netter with a square barge-like bow topped with a set of vertical rollers that looked like a field goal post. A hydraulically rotated drum loaded with the gill-net sat midship, and a wheelhouse festooned with radar and antennae sat at the stern of the boat. Buoys with flagpoles lined the stern gunwale of the boat. A rotating, winched boom was mounted on the port side gunnel for transferring heavy loads of fish or cargo just aft of the net reel. Normally worked by two people, Eric could see that Dutch had modified the boat by moving and adding controls so that it could be worked single-handed. The cabin's heater had warmed up the cabin and after stowing their supplies, Eric headed back on deck to cast off the lines.

By the light of The Stalwart's deck lights, Eric untied the stern line and tossed it into the boat while Dutch spun the nose of the boat towards the dock, pivoting on the spring line with a gentle touch of forward thrust and some rudder. Quickly, Eric ran down the dock untying the spring line and the bowline, tossing the ropes back into the boat, before he jumped down into the boat himself.

Dutch backed the boat out away from the dock until he'd enough room to turn the boat around and head for the bay's mouth, steering by radar before extinguishing all of the external lights except for the running lights. Once clear of the bay, Dutch set the boat on a compass heading to steer clear of the first of many headlands he would have to steer around and turned 'Iron Mike,' the autopilot, on. The water was smooth as glass with nary a breeze, which was great because Dutch would be able to get very precise radar returns since he didn't have to adjust the clutter controls to compensate for waves. Both men settled in for the journey, content to soak in their thoughts in the pre-dawn darkness.

Shortly after sunrise, they started to run past Nagat Inlet, were Eric had been forced to swim for it when Dutch seemed to grow very serious and intent upon the radar. He fidgeted with dials and was squinting at something off the starboard bow. He grabbed the binoculars that were sitting on the control panel of the boat and started scanning the waters in front of the boat. "Well what do you know..." he murmured, his voice trailing off as he handed the binoculars to Eric. "Look about ten degrees off the starboard bow," he directed.

Eric scanned the water for several seconds before his eye caught sight of something low in the water three quarters of a mile out. It was the remains of his boat. The tide had pulled it out of the bay and into Pearse Canal, which they were now transiting.

"We might as well salvage your outboard," Dutch said as he steered the boat a few points to starboard. "I bet you thought that was long gone."

As Eric stood there looking at the remains of his boat, he really didn't know what to feel yet about finding his boat, primarily because he didn't quite yet have enough information to create a reasonable hypothesis and didn't know what to make of what had happened.

******

The Giant Shark circled below the flotsam on the surface of the channel. He'd come to the surface to inspect the object that was actually fairly large, and bumped it with its side several times. The shark's electrical sensors were picking up the slight currents being passed by the bi-metal construction of the outboard motors construction interacting with salt water. It wasn't until he mouthed and tasted the tattered rubber remnants of the boat did it remember what it was and the bad taste it had left in his mouth a couple of days before. It looked and sounded much different this time. The low pulsing of an approaching motor registered on its senses and the Giant Shark flicked its tail and submerged.

******

Dutch eased the throttle down as they approached the remains of Eric's rigid-hull inflatable. He put the wreckage of the port side of the boat where his winched boom was located. He had to back down ever so slightly to stop the forward momentum of the boat. Dutch had done this approach thousands and thousands of times picking up his net and made it look easy. Eric stood ready with a gaffing hook to grab the boat, but in the end, he didn't need it because Dutch had so expertly positioned the boom over the part of the boat that was still inflated. As Dutch came out of the wheelhouse, he reached inside a waterproof cover mounted on the front of the wheelhouse to turn on the hydraulic system; immediately, there was a slight drop in the idle of the diesel and the whine of hydraulic pumps could be heard.

Dutch went over to the boom and rotated it out over the side of the boat and eased the control lever on the hydraulic winch to pay out enough line so he could unhook the end of the cable from the catch-ring welded on to the boom. With cable in hand, he turned to Eric and stated, "Over the side you go," motioning for him to take the cable. "I'll hold you alongside with the gaff pole, and if you go in the water, it'll give you something to hold onto," he finished with a crooked smile.

"And I was just getting used to this staying dry thing, too," Eric groused. It had been a stroke of luck to find the boat with its motor still intact, especially since the two storm fronts had moved through the area. He didn't feel so lucky at the moment, though, because he knew he was about to get wet, really wet, again.

"Ready?" Dutch called as he secured the skiff to the boat.

"Ready." Eric called back, as he hoisted himself over the gunnel, cable firmly in hand. He eased himself into the stern of his mangled skiff. There wasn't much room to work with since only a small portion of the boat was still holding air in its flotation chambers. The back section was filled with an inch of water from the rain that instantly soaked Eric's feet again. This all seemed nightmarishly familiar to Eric.

A low whistle came from Dutch, hanging over the edge of his boat. This was the first time he really had an opportunity to examine the wreckage. "Well, I'd say this qualifies as a 'technical difficulty,'" Dutch said in semi-mocking voice as a smile crossed his face and he winked at Eric. "When you told me that you hit something that ended up wrecking your boat, I thought you were full of shit. These boats are made to take abuse without sinking; I can't even think of anything that would do this to a boat. The damage doesn't look like anything I've ever seen before. This rubber is hard to puncture, but just look at how shredded it is! And the fiberglass hull has just been sheared away..."

Eric had seen it before and was intent upon disconnecting the fuel-line from the motor. He hooked the end of the cable to the handle of the fuel tank and wrapped the fuel line around the cable. "Ok, take it up," Eric directed. Dutch put the pole down on the deck and moved to hit the winch uptake lever. Once the tank was above the boat's side he rotated the boom inboard and deposited the tank on the deck. He rotated the boom out again and dropped the cable down to Eric.

"I'm going to need some rope to wrap around the motor," Eric said up to Dutch. "I don't want this cable to scratch up the paint, plus this cable isn't flexible enough. Can you give me about five or six feet of three-eighths nylon?"

"Sure, I'll be right back," Dutch said as he disappeared from the side.

The next step would require him to kneel in the boat's bottom to loosen the turn screws that were holding the outboard to the rigid hull inflatable's transom. He was in no hurry for that. While Eric was standing in the boat holding on to the rail and watching Dutch cut a hunk of rope from a coil on top of the wheelhouse, the skiff gave a little lurch under his feet. Eric caught himself and mentally chastised himself, *'Better pay attention or more than my pants would get wet.'*

Dutch reappeared and rope in hand, giving it to Eric, who quickly formed a noose with a loop on the free end.

He passed the noose over the engine and snugged it tight where the engine housing met the down shaft housing. He slipped the cable hook over the loop and had Dutch take out the slack just enough to put a little tension on his sling.   Eric's feet were soaked the second he'd hit the boat, and now it was time to go all the way. He knelt down in the cold seawater collected in the boat's bottom and started to loosen the two turn screws holding the motor to the transom. Soon the motor was free, and Eric was back on his feet to help guide the motor. As the weight came off the transom, the boat under Eric's feet became squirrelly, sliding this way and that. It was all Eric could do to stay upright in the boat, let alone guide the motor up. He walked the rigid hull hulk down the side of the boat with his hands to move out from under the engine's arc, not wanting to be crushed by it if it slipped.

Dutch set the motor on the deck and came over to help haul Eric over the side. In the cool morning's air, Eric looked miserable.

"Why don't you go inside by the heater and get warmed up," Dutch suggested. "I just need to secure the deck and then we'll be back on our way."

Eric was back in the wheelhouse with the heater cranked full on in less than ten seconds. He watched as Dutch put a pin in the boom to prevent it from rotating and took a little more slack out of the cable before coming over to the switch on the wheelhouse to turn off the hydraulic system. Eric watched as Dutch pulled a multi-tool from a pouch on his belt and folded out a blade.

Knife in hand, Dutch turned and went to the side of the boat where the wreckage of the skiff had been and hung over the rail. Eric could see Dutch's body shake as he worked on whatever he was doing.

Suddenly, Dutch's legs flew up to parallel with the deck and his whole body was drug forward. Eric could see something was jerking on Dutch. Eric became alarmed.

'What the hell?'

Dutch's whole body jerked spasmodically for a second or two before going limp and his legs crashed back to the deck. Eric came flying out of the wheelhouse charging to where Dutch's body lay slumped over the rail.

"Dutch! Dutch! Are you alright!?"

As he skidded to a stop next to Dutch's body, Dutch straightened and stood up. Hearing Eric's rapid approach, Dutch, turned to Eric and said with his typical directness while jabbing his knife in the direction of the water, "That son of a bitch nearly dragged me under when she went."

Eric looked over the rail to see that the carcass of his boat was five feet underwater and sinking rapidly.

"What were you doing?"

"Didn't want to leave a navigation hazard on the water. That rubber was hard enough to puncture - it would play hell if it got caught up in mine or somebody's prop," Dutch said laconically. "Time to get this show on the road again."

Both headed into the wheelhouse, settled into their chairs and soon the boat was back in motion. The next couple of hours were spent in the dull routine of scanning the water for deadheads, making course corrections when needed and in light conversation.

Finally, after coming around a final point, Eric's boat, the *Pacific Chanteuse*, came into view, a white forty-eight foot catamaran lying up at anchor. She was a Chris White design 48 Atlantic catamaran with a central cockpit, cabin aft extending to nearly the end of the hulls, a net stretched between the front two hulls for the first third of the boat, giving excellent sight while sailing the boat from the cockpit or cabin. A large salon stretched above the two hulls behind the central cockpit. The salon had an inside steering station, chart table, and electronics bay that housed all of Eric radios, satellite communications, computers and sound gear. There was also a generous table in one corner and a casual living space in the other corner with a sofa and seats. A big flat screen TV was bolted to the wall above the couch to which Eric could send computer images or entertainment. From his electronics bay, he could hook into any communications satellite or pull up whatever was playing on HBO. In each of the two hulls, the boat had a queen bed berth, a twin cabin berth, and bathrooms with showers. The port side housed a work area and the starboard galley. The engine compartments of each hull were accessed through deck hatches and each housed a diesel main engine and a generator as the last compartment aft in each hull. The boat was designed for long distance cruising and was quite suited for intercontinental sailing. It was a fast sailing ship with main and jib sails capable of seventeen knots under sail in prime conditions and cruising at eleven knots under power. But the most important fact of all was that it was a Chris White boat, known for its stoutness and stable rides, even in the roughest storms. It was designed to sail the north Atlantic in comfort and safety, so she could easily take what the North Pacific could throw at her when taken to outside waters.

Eric had Dutch maneuver his boat's landing platforms at the rear because accesses to the boat's deck was easiest through steps built into the hull at the aft of each hull section.

After tying up Dutch's boat to the end of each hull, Eric stepped into the salon to the steering station and fired up both engines to charge the batteries and in preparation of raising the anchor, while Dutch prepared to transfer the outboard to Eric's boat.

Assured that both engines were idling smoothly, Eric went down the starboard hull steps. On the back wall of the salon cabin were two davits where Eric's now demolished rigid hull inflatable skiff could be raised and lowered to the water by small electric winches. Eric had decided that he would lift and secure the outboard motor to one of the davits and store the red plastic fuel tank that feed it in one of the forward storage hatches in front of the cockpit.

Raising the outboard motor was a tricky little procedure that required Dutch to hoist the motor and attach the *Pacific Chanteuse*'s winch cable, then swing it outboard into the space between the two hulls. As Eric's winch took up the slack, Dutch paid out line until the catamaran's winch had the full strain before Eric disconnected Dutch's line. After which, both men set about securing their decks for travel.

As Dutch prepared to hand over Eric's dry bag and his shotgun, he said, "This is a nice boat - you live here all by yourself?"

"Yep. Would you like a tour?"

"Don't mind if I do. Here you go. Grab this, will you?" he commanded, handing the dry bag and then the shotgun over to Eric, who placed them up on the main deck. He then returned and grabbed the fuel tank and hose as Dutch swung them over the rail.

Eric grabbed the tank and walked up the steps and along the port deck turning right toward the port locker in front of the cockpit beside the main mast. Meanwhile, Dutch had joined him on deck carrying his dry bag and gun, watching him store the tank in the port forward locker.

"Come on," Eric said to him as he stepped down on the seat cushions of the benches that lined both sides of the sunken cockpit, and then onto the cockpit's floor.

"Now I know why you had on tennis shoes in the forest," Dutch panned as he eyed his fishing boots and the nice seat cushion he'd have to step on to get inside the boat.

Eric swung around the steering console and wheel in the center of the cockpit, and with a flourish, he opened the salon door with a sweeping bow, saying, "I hope my humble abode isn't too fancy for you." He'd gotten to know Dutch pretty well over the last twenty-four hours. In some measure, he owed him his life; however, Dutch had strongly disagreed. He'd come to enjoy teasing the gruff, direct frontiersman. As Dutch stepped inside, Eric dashed down the five steps to the galley while Dutch piled his gear on the salon table. Out of a cupboard he grabbed two cups and a bottle of Rumple Minze Schnapps and climbed back up the steps.

As he set the bottle and cups on the table, he said, "First, let me give you a little 'house warming shot', so to speak." Eric poured a generous mug for both of them before handing Dutch his cup. "Here's to your hospitality to strays and strangers," Eric said lifting his mug in salute to Dutch. Dutch, Eric had learned, was no stranger to the world of spirits, plying him with whiskey in various guises yesterday. When Eric had first met Dutch, he'd assumed that his red-rimmed eyes were just a result of the outdoor life he lived on the sea and frontier. Now he suspected that they might have more to do with his taste for liquor than windburn. This man seriously liked to tip a bottle.

"Well, Eric, you are a gentleman and a scholar. And obviously schooled in the finer customs of chivalry despite what your higher education and tree-hugger upbringing might indicate," Dutch replied, saluting Eric in return before slugging down the mug of one hundred proof Schnapps. Eric had learned Dutch considered any scientist or researcher a tree-hugger, so he didn't take Dutch's comment personally.

"Let me show you around," invited Eric. After a quick tour of the boat, they returned to the salon. Dutch stepped over to the navigation and electronics center, examined the equipment, and asked curiously, "So this is where you talk to the animals, I presume, Dr. Doolittle?" He mocked Eric with a little twinkle in his eye, whether from mischievousness or from the Schnapps, it was hard to tell.

"Yeah, this is where I analyze and store my data every night when I come in from tracking all day or when the weather doesn't allow me out for the day. When I'm out in my skiff, my main goal is to just capture data and log identities of the subjects. There's no way for me to carry the computing power and acoustic reproduction electronics with me. In fact, on the bottom of the boat is the large scale TTACS system I was telling you about at the cabin. It is slaved to the video camera outside, so if anything happens while I'm out, it'll capture all the action acoustically and on video."

"And what do the whales tell you when you talk to them?" Dutch asked with his gentle ribbing.

"We don't *talk* actually. I just listen and learn mostly. No one has really been able to talk to them yet in their own language. In zoos and aquariums, they've learned to respond to human commands and hand gestures, but that is only because humans control the food. No one has been able to interact directly with them in the wild, yet. Out here, they can get their own food. We're getting close though. We know enough of their vocabulary, syntax, and range of inflections that we should be able to talk to them, but I guess it's a matter of trust and necessity. They're very pragmatic creatures – I don't think they see any benefit to talking to a man in a boat, or more from their perspective, a boat that's attempting to talk to them with a man on its back. I'm not sure they make the connection that it's the human initiating the conversation and not the boat. Maybe in their culture, it's bad form to have conversations with inanimate objects, too. Besides, it's not like I can tell them where a herring school is or where a school of salmon are swimming. No, I think that until man has something useful to offer Cetaceans other than a harpoon in the back, they will continue to ignore us.

"It's kind of like being a voyeur, though, but with the observee's consent or a Peeping Tom that's ignored at the dinner table. I'd hate to think that I'm nothing more to them than a yapping Chihuahua is to us. Who knows, maybe they tell their children to just ignore me and I'll go away. Which is true. At the end of the day, I always have to leave and it's hard to find the same pod of whales day after day. So for all we know, maybe we're talking, but only one of us is listening for the moment."

A moment's silence fell over the salon as Dutch's mental mill ground that grist before refocusing on Eric. "Well, I best let you get back to your work." He said, climbing to his feet, "No fish are going to jump in my boat tied up behind yours either."

Eric followed Dutch outside and down to the steps to Dutch's boat. After scrambling over the rail to his deck, Dutch turned to Eric and offered his hand. "It's been a pleasure, Eric. I wish you the best of luck in your research."

"Thanks Dutch, I owe you a lot," Eric said, taking Dutch's hand in a crushing handshake. "Now that I know your VHF and UHF frequencies, I'll give you a hail now and again. And don't hesitate to call me if you need something. Who knows, I just might be heading into town and can run it out to you. I've got to work off my debt somehow."

Both men eyed each other warmly, then Dutch reached out and grabbed Eric's elbow as if to deepen the handshake. His powerful paw clamped down Eric's elbow and drew him closer. In an instant, Dutch became very serious, his eyes boring in on Eric's. "You've seen it, haven't you? The giant shark. There's no way you could do that to your skiff by running it aground. The giant shark did that to you, didn't it?"

Eric was completely taken aback by this sudden change in tone and demeanor. It was all he could do to stammer, "I haven't seen anything, Dutch, really." Which was true, Eric had never actually seen anything. He knew enough to know that the giant tooth he'd in the dry bag was most definitely shark, but to his conservative researcher nature, one tusk didn't make an elephant. Eric at first thought that Dutch was trying to accuse him of something or interrogate him. But as Dutch's eyes continued to search Eric's face, he saw that what Dutch was looking for was confirmation, and that by putting his question out there in front of Eric, he'd made himself vulnerable and liable to ridicule for believing in mermaids, sea serpents, and a giant shark that could eat a small boats in a single gulp but couldn't possibly exist. Anyone who said so would be labeled a loon.

"Honestly, I never saw what I ran into Dutch," Eric said half-convincingly. At that point, he saw a flicker of recognition in Dutch's face as he realized that Eric might not be telling him the whole truth – and why he was equivocating - which was a confirmation in itself.

With that, Dutch released his grip on Eric and said as if nothing had happened, "Well, take care now and have a safe trip back to town. Untie me, will you?"

Eric obliged him, casting off his lines, still a little unsettled by the rapid change in direction of their conversation. With a wave, Dutch throttled away, and Eric could see him lighting up another of his ever present cigarettes.

18

"Well, first things first," Eric said to himself as he tried to re-orient himself away from the last disturbing moments of Dutch's companionship. "I need a shower, shave, and to brush my teeth."

Eric went back into the salon and turned on the cabin heaters before descending down into the starboard hull to his cabin beyond the galley. He quickly stripped off his clothes and tossed them in the clothes hamper in a lower cabinet, then headed towards the head that was the next compartment forward. There, stripped in front of the mirror, he was able to see for the first time the complete damage to his body: his feet were riddled with blisters; his chest was covered in bruises from his creek crossing; his right thigh was bruised from his run-in with the bear; he was going to have a little shiner from where his face hit the beach. In fact, there wasn't a limb on his body that wasn't bruised and battered. And he was still bone tired from his over-land excursion.

After taking a full inventory of his wounds, he shaved and brushed his teeth, giving the main engines time to heat the water in the hot water tank. After completing his normal morning ritual of cleansing, he leisurely strolled to the shower in the port hull. The hot water system wasn't limitless, nor was his on-hand fresh water supply, but he luxuriated in the shower for fifteen minutes before the hot water gave out, using the time to figure out his next moves.

First, he needed to get the boat moving towards Ketchikan. As soon as he had maneuvering room, he'd turn on the autopilot and use the boat's satellite communications to call Melanie. He desperately wanted to talk to her. After that, he would call the PKMI and apprise them of what had happened and to request a new skiff and supplies to be sent him, as well as a new and revised list of survival gear to stock his boat with. They could probably have most of that on the Alaskan ferry out of Bellingham, Washington by tomorrow, so he could pick it up at the Ketchikan terminal in two or three days if he got a move on.

But for now, he'd to get the boat moving. After raising the anchor and lashing it down to its stanchion, he used his diesels to maneuver out into the Pierce Canal. The prevailing winds were coming out of the southwest from the Pacific Ocean. He didn't want to waste a lot of time tacking back and forth into the wind in such narrow quarters so he elected to power out into the Inside Passage and sail north into Revillagigedo Channel then follow Tongass Narrows into Ketchikan.

He figured that he'd about a hundred twenty miles to cover. If he was lucky he might be able to cover half of that with a following wind or quartering wind to his stern. The *Pacific Chanteuse* would quickly convert the wind into miles covered. Even with the late sunlight hours of the northern latitude, it was going to be nip and tuck as to whether he would be able to make Ketchikan tonight. It depended on the winds and how much tacking he would have to do. If he got close enough, he could motor in at night. At night, he wasn't willing to sail under canvas because he just wouldn't be able to see what his sails were doing relative to the wind.

If he didn't cover enough ground, he would just have to lay up on anchor overnight and make it in tomorrow morning.

There was one other thing he'd to be mindful of; he was still exhausted and injured. He was in no shape to push his luck, unless he wanted to fall asleep at the wheel and run his boat onto the rocks for real. Eric knew the rule of good seamanship was there were times that one might have to take chances or push it, but one never does it voluntarily. The sea was an unforgiving mistress. In fact, she could be a downright life-sucking bitch if you pushed her too far. It was always better to take it close enough to be within sight of your limit, and then back off. If he lost the gamble, he would end up in the water again. If he went in the water in this wilderness, void of humans, he could just go ahead and count himself dead. If he were real lucky, someone might snatch him from death. But he knew not to count on it. Out here, he knew your only prayer was your radio, and hopefully he could get off a May Day with his position before the boat went down. But there was no guarantee that radios, electronics, and antenna would survive an impact with an immovable object. Especially with a fast boat like the *Pacific Chanteuse*.

As Eric took a quick mental inventory of his person and boat, he realized that he had to play it safe. His fatigue and injuries would prevent him from being mentally sharp over an extended time and might force him to make a bad decision in a crisis. His boat's supply of survival gear was exhausted, his skiff destroyed. The *Pacific Chanteuse* was equipped with a ten person life raft attached to the back of the salon, above the skiff davits, that would automatically deploy if the boat sank. But that was intended for open sea survival and really wasn't suited for emergencies in inland waters where the winds and tides were happy to smash such a flimsy craft on her jagged, rocky shores.

He'd been lucky when he'd ended up on a rock beach a couple of days ago. The vast majority of the coast of Southeastern Alaska was rocky outcroppings. There were thousands and thousands of miles of shoreline that had no human habitation. The odds that he had landed on an island with habitation and one that he knew were at a million to one, or better. And if being that lucky left him this battered, bruised, sore, fatigued, cut and abraded, he sure as hell didn't want to see unlucky, ever.

'*And not to put too fine a point on rushing headlong into town and screwing the pooch along the way was the fact that I've tremendous scientific discovery sitting in a bag on my salon table,*' he told himself.

No, cautious was the only way he was going to play his cards.

As he made his way into the main channel of the Inside Passage, he put on a waterproof windbreaker and a safety chest harness with built-in life-preserver, air horn and safety line and went into the cockpit, where he clipped a safety line onto the D ring mounted to the cockpit.

From the cockpit control consol, he turned off the autopilot, shut down the engines and folded the propellers to streamline his underwater profile. Next, he lowered his dagger boards with a set of switches on the console. Then, he set about un-securing the main sailing lines and travelers before unfurling the sail. The *Pacific Chanteuse* was designed to be sailed by one person from the cockpit. All the rigging was designed to be operated on the strength of one human, but given his soreness, raising the main sail's haul line taxed his stiff muscles.

The winds were coming out of the southwest at about fourteen miles per hour, which put him on a reach, when the winds are broadside to the boat. This is when a sailboat really comes into its own; the seas only had a little chop and if he managed the sails right, he might be able to eke-out sixteen knots from the *Pacific Chanteuse.*

Once the sails were set, the *Pacific Chanteuse* was perking right along at fourteen knots. He was just too tired to work the sails and boat any harder and settled for what she was giving him. As soon as she left the sheltered water of Pierce Canal, the *Pacific Chanteuse* entered the unsheltered waters of the Pacific, gently rocking in two foot swells that were well spaced apart.

Eric made himself busy with phone calls now that the boat needed little attention. His phone call to Melanie was brief and sweet. The line sizzled with emotions on both sides, but neither wanted to say much over the phone, each just wanting to savor the sound of the other person's voice. Next came the call to his boss, Sid Wenslow, at the

Pacific Ketterman Marine Institute. He'd been gravely concerned when Eric had started to tell him about his "mishap." But Sid knew immediately that Eric's little episode on the beach was far more serious than Eric was letting on. Eric had made the determination that he was going to need the assistance of all the Institute's resources in trying to determine the significance of the tooth to the scientific community. He didn't feel, in good conscience, that he could or should keep this type of scientific information from his employer.

'*No matter how crazy it makes me seem,*' he told himself.

So after explaining the travails of his journey to shore and over land, Eric took a brief pause in the conversation to ease into this delicate subject.

"Sid, there is one other aspect to this that I need to make you aware of. Prior to abandoning the skiff and swimming to shore, I found something imbedded in the rubber of the inflatable hull. I found a tooth that is Selachimorphica in nature."

"You mean a shark? Well that makes sense Eric. You were probably hit by a great white that had swum way north of its known Pacific range. From what it sounds like, you were drifting along emitting whale audio emission that confused a great white into an attack. This is very exciting news, if we have evidence of great whites in Southeastern Alaska, it's going to change all the modeling of great white distributions and populations, not to mention the impact on ecosystems," Sid said breathlessly from the excitement.

"Sid, I'm afraid it's going to be a little more ticklish

than that. It may very well have been a great white. Sharks aren't exactly my area of expertise. But I have seen great white teeth before and this is most certainly *not* like any great white tooth I've ever seen."

"What do you mean, Eric?"

"The tooth that I have is enormous, Sid. It's a full seven inches across at the bottom and six inches tall."

After a long pause, "That would be equivalent to some of the largest Megalodon recorded. Are you saying that great whites are being super-sized in Southeast Alaska?"

"Actually, I am being careful not to say *anything* until we have further data. The tooth is the only evidence, and we can't be sure of what we're looking at until we've run DNA tests and had it examined by experts. Until we have more evidence, all we have is an anomaly, one that would be rightfully treated with skepticism by the scientific community. And I do *not* want to be the darling of the cryptozoology world by saying I saw a sea serpent."

"You're right, Eric. I got a little ahead of myself there. You've obviously had time to think about this, so what would you like to do, and how can I help?"

"I'd like to send you pictures of the tooth right away, so you can have shark experts tell us what we might be looking for. I need you to have a rush DNA sample analyzed on the tooth that I'll overnight to you Monday when I get in port. I'm going to hold on to the tooth over the weekend for the moment; there's a friend of my mine that lives up here I want to take a look at it. Also, I'm going to need some tracking gear, something that we can shoot at the fish to track its location and swimming habits.

Preferably it should do it in real time. Next, I want LIDAR for the *Pacific Chanteuse*. If I can find whatever left us the tooth again, I might be able to get enough LIDAR images to thoroughly catalogue what it is we found.

"And lastly, I need the Institute to pay for a rush fitting of that gear here in Ketchikan," Eric said finishing his mental shopping list.

"All right, that all sounds reasonable," Sid said without hesitation. "You know that at some time, we'll need to have a body of the fish for proof of existence," he said without emotion.

Eric was conflicted on this point. He knew very well that what Sid was saying was true, but his research and philosophy were built around observation and study of *live* specimens. His only saving grace was that he knew he wasn't equipped for that task on the *Pacific Chanteuse*. "My first thought is to find it if we can. If I find it and can tag it, then we can make that decision later on. But finding it will be extremely difficult - this is a huge seascape we are talking about and when I encountered it, I was very close to the Canadian border. For all we know, it may already have moved into their waters. They won't have a problem letting me search in their waters since my research is supported internationally, but I'm not real sure that they'll allow us to kill it if it's in their territorial waters. There's just a whole bunch of ifs too far down the road to deal with at this point. Let's just see if we can find it first. I think that alone is a tall order, considering we know absolutely zero about this creature."

"Agreed," Sid said, obviously trying to digest all that

Eric had said. "But from everything that you've said, this is a very important zoological find, and we need to take every step possible to conclusively bring it to the marine biology community's attention."

He knew exactly what Sid meant. This was 'management speak' for money. While the Pacific Ketterman Institute was founded and originally funded by Jason Ketterman, a new age industrialist who made hundreds and hundreds of millions in software products during the computer boom of the eighties and nineties in the Pacific Northwest, the Institute still needed to supplement the Ketterman Endowment with grant money and donations from wealthy benefactors. The Institute, if it was responsible for the discovery of a new keystone species, could throw endless wine and cheese galas to separate the new wealthy from their checkbooks to ease their symptoms of affluenza, the sudden onset of guilt that rapid wealth accumulation evokes. It was a case of Sid doing the right thing for the wrong reason. In any case, it was still what he was hoping to hear, and it only annoyed him a little bit that it was for the wrong reason.

"How long before you can get that out to me?" Eric probed, wanting to get the conversation steered away from the politics of the Institute.

"I don't know. Some of the stuff you are asking for, like the LIDAR and tracking gear, we will have to get from other research facilities or buy. I will start making calls and keep you apprised so that you can coordinate installation up there."

They concluded their conversation with the agreement

to stay in close contact over the next several days.

   'Game on,' Eric challenged the unknown creature in his mind that had so changed his life.

19

The pack of killer whales accompanying the Pod Leader had made good time and covered the distance in two days. They were in good shape, well fed and relatively rested after their journey from the northern rendezvous. As the pack approached the area of the attack they spread out to form a picket line across the channel. With the killer whales, ability to search the water in front of them with their echolocation sense, each whale could cover a mile or better swath before it, depending on water conditions, especially considering the size of the creature for which they were searching. It would only take two or three killer whales to search the main channels, which were usually free of major rock formations at the bottom that could hide or mask their quarry. What would be time-consuming would be checking all the bays and inlets. They devised a plan that the three or four whales in the main channel would be used as position of rest and observation to see if any of the scouting whales flushed anything out from their sweeps in the bays or inlets. This would prevent the shark from backtracking or slipping behind their search picket to escape. If any of the whales found the Giant Shark, it was to give out a war cry to signal the others. The job of the scouts was to search all the bays and outlets as rapidly as they could. This should place four scouts on each end of the picket line.

As each whale encountered food, it would grab a meal on the run. There would be no collective fish hunting until the Giant Shark had been cornered and destroyed.

The search went on this way for two and a half days. The strain of constant hunting and meals on the fly was starting to take a toll on them. But more than anything, they missed their mates and the society of their pods. For while they were collectively hunting the shark as a coordinated group, the fact of the matter was that each whale was alone with his activities all day long. Each could hear the next in the distance, but that wasn't the same as the interacting, talking, touching and general lollygagging that passed for pod life. This collective solitude was beginning to show itself in small ways among the group. Tempers and aggressiveness to each other started to intrude when the whales traded positions or if someone didn't respond right away when called.

Normally, the cohesion of the pod was solidified by the females. The males were bonded to their mates, and their mates were bonded to their mothers, sisters and offspring. Age generally determined the alpha female, because the pod valued the experience stored in her memory. By default, the alpha female's mate was considered the alpha male by association. There was no need to fight to prove who was the top male for breeding rights, because of their monogamous relationships. Without their mates, the group of males really had no desire or incentive to congregate outside of the common goal of finding and killing this threat to their families. It was an uneasy alliance that was starting to fray around the edges.

On the journey south, the mood had been jocular, as one might expect of a group males. Each killer whale, aside from the Pod Leader who had seen the Giant Shark and what it could do, secretly harbored the idea that in the end, the Giant Shark wouldn't be as big or as dangerous as foretold. None of them had ever met their match in the seas; none of them could image it happening now. This bred a certain recklessness. Each told the group how they would single-handedly kill the Giant Shark; that it couldn't stand up to the attack that he would rain down upon the probably old and toothless basking shark that it would turn out to be. Each one would top the other's boast with claims of their ferocity, power and strength. Every once in a while the Pod Leader almost started to believe them.

That was, until he remembered how quickly his small pod had been wiped out while he watched. At first, he tried to remind them of these facts. But each time he did, he was met with bravado and bluster. Soon, every time he attempted to share the voice of experience with them, they would deride him, questioning his decision to run from his last encounter to help his slain mate's mother, rather than hold his position and fight. So the Pod Leader quit trying to center the group on the challenge they faced and listened in silence as he heard them convince each other of their invincibility.

The mindset became 'how dare this interloper hide itself and not come forth to be slain so we can go home.' So assured were they of their ability to reign over the seas, that when the hunt didn't go as they had convinced themselves it would, the bravado began to turn to frustration. And that frustration began to lead to the first rays of doubt.

It was in this emotional stew of creeping doubt that the first war cry sounded.

Four scouts were searching separate bays on the western end of the search picket, while the scouts on the eastern end were similarly engaged. The channel picket line whales were resting and trying to catch salmon to fuel their bodies as they swept south and the Pod Leader was searching the rearmost bay on the western side of the channel.

The second lead scouting whale on the western side had just entered a medium-sized bay that was roughly three miles around and was taking his first look using his echolocation senses when he sensed a large whale towards the back and left of the bay swimming by itself. It was an oddly shaped whale, one with which the scout wasn't familiar. This alone would have given it reason to go inspect the mystery animal. But whales were social animals and were almost always seen in the company of others of their species. Swimming completely alone was odd behavior for a whale.

The scout killer whale rapidly approached the whale, still scouring the rest of the bay looking for other accompanying whales. As the killer whale drew nearer, it became more confused about this whale. Its body shape wasn't like a whale's. Whales usually had some sort of bulky forehead or protrusion called a melon that concentrated echolocations clicks. This whale had no such feature. It also had an enormous dorsal fin, proportionally just slightly smaller than his fin. And the fluke orientation and movement was all wrong.   Whales propelled themselves with their powerful back muscles on the upstroke; the down stroke was less powerful and was more of a recovery stroke. This whale's tail moved from side to side like a fish. But by sheer size alone, it had to be a whale; no fish, shark or otherwise, approached the size of whales in the northern Pacific.   Maybe this was the mystery Giant Shark for which they were looking...the only way to tell for sure, though, was to visually inspect the mystery swimmer.

The scout killer whale maneuvered directly at his target at a quick closing speed.

                              ******

The Giant Shark was ravenous again. It had entered this bay in search of porpoise, seal or small whale only to find it empty of any large size animal. The sandy bottom had yielded no dining opportunities.   Not that there wasn't food on the bottom - just that he couldn't catch the halibut that swam on the muddy flats.   It had found several six-and-a-half and seven foot halibut close to three hundred pounds swimming along just a few inches off the bottom. Every time he made a grab for one, though, it would dart away in a cloud of mud on a new tangent. For the Giant Shark, it was like trying to bite a moving wall. As its jaws were automatically extended from its head, making it easier to grasp its prey, its eyes rolled back into its head for protection. The Giant Shark had no eyelids or nictating membrane to protect its eyes when it was in such close proximity to its prey as it violently shook, using its body for leverage to pull out great chunks of flesh. So when the Giant Shark tried to bite the halibut, it was blind, eyes rolled back in its head and it had to rely on its other senses, like its ampullae of Lorenzini, to detect electrical impulses and steer it on to the prey. But by luck or instinct the halibut, when attacked, kicked up great clouds of mud and silt with their tail fins, creating a curtain of fine particulate matter in the water. As each one of the fine particles of sand collided with each other, they rubbed off electrons to each other. The net affect was that the silt cloud set up a faint but opaque curtain that shielded the halibut from the Giant Shark's senses. In addition, the Giant Shark's jaws were best suited to prey it could grasp with both sides of its jaws; the flat halibut couldn't be grasped on their backs. The only way the shark could get a grasp on the halibut was edgewise, and the halibut weren't cooperating.

The shark was getting ready to meander out of the bay when it sensed the approach of the oncoming killer whale. This was better, how nice for food to come to it for a change.

******

The killer whale approached to within forty yards of the shark. It was at a depth where plenty of surface light made it easy to determine that this was the killer Giant Shark that they had been seeking. It gave out the mighty war cry of the Clan, TTTTHHHROOOOM click-click-click-click,   TTTTHHHROOOOM   click-click-click-click,

TTTTHHHROOOOM click-click-click-click, and charged the shark.

However, since the killer whale had been swimming away from the bay's mouth, little of his call reverberated out to his fellow hunters in the channel beyond and was unintelligible. The killer whale on the channel picket line closest to the scout whale that had found the Giant Shark heard a faint sound emanating from one of the forward bays in which a scout had just entered minutes ago. It had sounded like a war cry, but he wasn't sure. No other whale was in the vicinity, so he felt obliged to go see what it was.

The scout killer whale blasted at the Giant Shark, intent on either delivering a nerve and tissue shredding bite or an organ-crushing ram, depending on the Giant Shark's reaction. The Giant Shark was quartering to the whale from left to right. The scout killer whale thought it should be easy to veer left to avoid the jaws and then circle hard right into the fish and deliver its shot. Three powerful stokes of its fluke had the whale at full speed of thirty-six miles per hour. Using his body shape, he deflected his trunk to the left to gain a little separation from the shark and then used his pectoral fins to roll into the shark's back half, losing sight of the Giant Shark's jaws as it lay over for its turn, moving the Giant Shark into the visual quadrant above the whale.

As soon as the Giant Shark saw its meal roll towards it, it moved with blinding speed. It was able to turn in to the whale with one quick flick of its tail fin, jaws extended and eyes rolled back, catching the closest half of the whale's fluke in its mouth and then shook its head violently.

Searing pain tore through the killer whale's fluke just as it was inches from biting into the Giant Shark's side, and then the killer whale was jerked violently backwards and forwards

The whale's tail was made mostly of cartilage and skin. The shark's jaw exerted tremendous crushing force, and the heavy dagger teeth of the Giant Shark easily punched through the cartilage. However, the shark's serrated edges were unable to cut through the cartilage, so the Giant Shark spit out the whale's fluke for the moment.

The scout killer whale knew that it had been hurt badly. As soon as the shark released him, the whale flexed back to look at his tail. The cloud of blood gushed forth as soon as the shark's teeth were retracted out of the horrible wounds it had inflicted on the soft tissues of his fluke. Through the cloud of his own blood, the killer whale could see the near perfect arc of perforations in the left half of his fluke. It was nearly severed and hanging down at a sickening angle, held by only a dozen or so ribbons of flesh and cartilage. Each time he tried to stroke with his fluke, it would merely wave, flop, and fold in the water while the mangled tissue sent waves of shooting pain with each minute movement. He desperately needed to exhale and get a fresh breath; the stress of pain was burning oxygen in his lungs at a tremendous rate that he couldn't sustain much longer. Through the agony of his shattered tail he limped and struggled to the surface and air.

The Giant Shark circled below the struggling whale. The taste of the whale's blood was overpowering to the

Giant Shark. It was totally focused on finishing the wounded prey and the satisfaction the taste of its flesh would bring. It was only waiting for the right moment.

The scout killer whale made it to the surface and released his lung full of expended air while stilling himself to lessen the pain in his tail. It cycled through several deep breaths trying to marshal the uncontrollable pain in its fluke.

The shark saw his victim go still on the surface. This was what he'd waited for; a target with limited dimensions to escape, framed against the surface, lying still in the water. It powered into a vertical attack, its preferred method for attacking the soft underbellies of whales.

The killer whale from the picket had just entered the bay's mouth and emitted a train of clicks to locate the scout killer whale. In horror, it watched as the Giant Shark rose from the depths and ripped the throat out of the scout killer whale in an eruption of blood, froth, and shredded flesh. It was stunned for an instant by the sheer brutality of the attack. How could the scout have gotten so blindsided and let the Giant Shark under his guard undetected. A sudden fury came over the picket whale. But before it dealt with the killer Giant Shark, he turned to the channel and emitted the Tribe War Cry to bring the other killer whales into the fight, the fury of having watched his hunting partner die filling his war cry with determination.

TTTTHHHROOOOM   click-click-click-click,
TTTTHHHROOOOM   click-click-click-click,

TTTTHHHROOOOM click-click-click-click.

And then it charged the Giant Shark that was starting to take a bite out of the dead scout.

The two whales on the picket that heard the call instantly wheeled and charged the bay from which the call had come. Two of the scout whales from the eastern shore also heard the call to arms from their positions in the bays where they were searching and headed across the channel at full sprint. The other scout whales never heard the call due to the acoustic shielding of the bays they were searching.

So the only reinforcements coming to the battle were the four whales streaming across the channel, all widely spaced apart.

The picket whale's call caught the Giant Shark in mid-bite, alerting it to the impending attack of another killer whale. It let go of its meal and descended to a depth of a hundred feet, where there was still plenty of light to see his attacker and enough fighting room to meet the new assailant.

The picket killer whale chose to circle the Giant Shark, counting on the belief that he was quicker and more agile than the shark. His plan of attack was to circle in closer until it was behind the Giant Shark and then attack from the rear. The two antagonists circled two or three times; each time, the killer whale gained the advantage of having a better position. The killer whale's plan had worked to perfection. When he had enough of an angle for an attack from behind, he put on a burst of speed and aimed for the Giant Shark's back.

The Giant Shark had been more concerned about positioning itself close to its food floating in the water rather than engaging the attacker. It sensed the killer whale's sudden burst of speed and put one on itself.

To the killer whale's amazement, the shark easily swam away from its fastest sprint.

The Giant Shark had now been chased from its food and was too hungry to leave. It put on a tremendous burst of speed, swimming ahead of the killer whale only to turn back in a short, high-speed arc towards the killer whale. The two engaged in a game of chicken.

The killer whale had an elemental and instinctive understanding of mass and speed and knew it wouldn't win this contest if the two collided. He calculated that the best plan of attack would be to roll left, go low, and try to rip off the Giant Shark's right pectoral fin. As the two bodies approached at full speed, the killer whale timed his move exquisitely. However, he'd not counted on the aggressiveness of the Giant Shark, nor its quickness as it kept straight while the killer whale veered. As the whale rolled, he put its belly toward the Giant Shark, putting it in a blind spot below his body. Even had he been able to see the Giant Shark, he was so focused on destroying its pectoral fin, that he didn't see the blur of its head and jaws as they snapped down on the soft chest tissues between his pectoral fins, gouging out a huge oval scoop of flesh, cutting and removing the nerves, tendons and muscles that controlled his pectoral fins.

The killer whale willed itself, through the pain in his chest, to close on the Giant Shark's fin as it flashed on by.

But nothing happened as he tried to direct his body towards the fin, and in a blink, the opportunity was gone. All that the killer whale could think of was to escape. Without his pectoral fins working, the whale awkwardly arched his body this way and that while swimming and was able to slowly put himself into an ascending climb to the surface. Once there, he rested on the surface taking deep, sharp breaths. The bolts of pain in his chest had been replaced by a massive stinging type of pain as his chest went slowly numb. He couldn't feel his chest, but could see the cloud of his own blood that he was floating in. He suddenly grew very tired and decided it would be nice just to rest there for a moment until he got his strength back.

As shock from the massive tissue trauma and blood loss set in on the killer whale, vital organ functions began to shut down in his body. Consciousness slowly crept from the big male's body, but not before he noticed that reinforcements had arrived as another killer whale swam through the mouth of the bay. It was comforted by this thought as it continued to focus on its losing battle to breathe.

As the second picket killer whale entered the harbor, it was greeted with a confusing stream of echolocation images. He saw the Giant Shark feeding on one of the attack pod members floating still in the waters while another was motionless on the surface. His echolocation senses were fined-tuned enough to tell the texture of an object at a distance but he couldn't see the cloud of blood around the surfaced whale, and due to the angle, he couldn't detect the gaping hole in its chest.

Regardless, it was his responsibility to kill the Giant Shark. He assumed that the floating killer whale was just waiting for assistance so he called to it, getting only a weak, indistinct response in return. He knew that the last killer whale from the picket line was a mile behind him and coming hard, but he wanted the glory of killing the notorious Giant Shark himself. So he charged.

Meanwhile, first one and then a second scout killer whale emerged from the bays they had been searching on the eastern side of the channel. As was their practice, they first would check with the picket whales before heading further up the coast for the next bay to search. The killer whales were several miles ahead of the picket when they entered their respective bay. When they emerged, they had expected to see the picket had moved closer or past their positions. Instead, what they sensed with their echolocation was two of the picket killer whales sprinting away from them at full speed, about halfway across the channel, heading for a bay opening almost straight across the channel from them. One of the hunting pack must have found their quarry and everyone was joining in on the kill. They both independently charged after the two disappearing picket whales, hoping that the action wouldn't be all over by the time they got there. So now four large killer whales were rushing to join the battle.

******

The Giant Shark became aware of another attacker a hundred yards out and turned to face this new adversary. It was the same size, shape and color as the other two meals. This was turning out to be the most rewarding bay for food that the Giant Shark had ever seen. It would remember this bay and return to it again in the future. The attacker bore straight into the Giant Shark in another game of chicken.

******

The second picket line killer whale was especially brave. He chose to attack the shark head on. He was positive that the Giant Shark would veer because it was a stupid fish, ruled by instinct. And its instinct would command it to turn away to preserve itself. And the killer whale would use that to his advantage; besides, should the killer whale nearby decide to get in the fight, he would have the Giant Shark fully distracted, giving the other killer whale the perfect opportunity to strike.

The Giant Shark accelerated to two-thirds of its best speed to close the distance.

Good, thought the second picket killer whale, the stupid Giant Shark is making it easy to kill it. By attacking him at full speed, the Giant Shark would only intensify its instinct to turn away.

The closing speed between the two swimmers passed seventy miles an hour; in a matter of seconds they would collide.

The killer whale upped the ante. He changed his angle of approach upward ever so slightly so that he would be just slightly above the Giant Shark at impact, giving him the ability to bite downwards as he passed. But more importantly, it would do two things for him. It would put subtle pressure on the Giant Shark to dive below the killer whale, thus limiting its options and giving the edge of controlling the opening salvo to the killer whale. Secondly, by making the shark dive below him, he would eliminate the shark's only weapon, its jaws. He knew from experience that a shark wouldn't swim inverted. It would go into a trance if it was inverted too long, and it didn't take much to induce this state. He'd learned this in his youth by playing with young salmon sharks that populated the waters. The only time a shark inverted itself was if it was trying to twist and tear off a hunk of flesh from a carcass. And then it would only do it briefly while rolling.

Knowing what was about to happen, the killer whale waited and waited for the Giant Shark to make its mistake, fully confident that he was in control.

With twenty yards to impact, the Giant Shark put on its last burst of speed and closed the distance in a fraction of a second.

The killer whale waited and waited and waited too long. The mistake never came. The Giant Shark did something he hadn't expected. It had charged him. And before he could react, he found himself forced headfirst down the Giant Shark's maw. Before the Giant Shark's crushing bite killed him, the last thing that registered on his mind was passing from the light of the sun into sudden darkness. The killer whale actually heard the snap of its neck being broken before all faded to black.

The Giant Shark wasn't really designed by nature to absorb frontal impacts. Sharks usually chase their prey, their jaws structured to keep prey from pulling away, not to be shoved in. Upon impact the shark's gag reflex was triggered first by biting down with all its force. The impact of the two bodies stopped the killer whale before the shark's superior mass and momentum forced it backwards. The two colliding bodies weren't totally centered on the same line however, and following the laws of physics, this slight offset caused the two to spin around the axis of impact. The Giant Shark's initial gag reflex to bite down kept the bodies from flying apart, and they spun in a half circle joined at the head. The second part of the shark's gag reflex was to spit out the object in its mouth, which it did as the two bodies rotated through one hundred forty degrees of their fatal arc.

As the two bodies disengaged, they continued to spin, one lifeless, the other momentarily stunned but trying to right itself out of the sideways spin.

With a powerful flick of its caudal fin, the Giant Shark regained control of its momentum, helped in small part by the small second dorsal and anal fin that provided resistance to the sideways movement through the water. As it was able to gain forward momentum, water began flowing over its gills. Oxygen soon was coursing through its arteries, and the carbon dioxide that had built up in its muscles from the last burst of speed was being released back into the water from its gills. The Giant Shark's jaw was rugged and powerful, but even so, the collision of two big bodies had injured it. It had taken several big bites from the first killer whale it killed and was no longer hungry. Smarting from the collision and full, the Giant Shark now just wanted to escape the bay and the relentless attacks. It located the bay's entrance and headed for it.

It had almost made the entrance when the next killer whale entered the bay. The killer whale announced his charge with the now familiar killer whale's war cry. This time, the Giant Shark turned to try and skirt by the killer whale. But the killer whale would have none of it. In seeing the Giant Shark's eagerness to avoid him, the killer whale took this as weakness and fright. This emboldened the killer whale, which in turn, caused him to overplay his hand.

Oblivious to the carnage left behind by the Giant Shark, the killer whale tried to cut the angle to intercept the fish. The shark sensed the new vector of his antagonist, peeled hard away from the attacker back into the bay where it circled wide, trying to sneak by the other side of the bay's entrance.

This killer whale's instincts, like the others before him, sought to cut off the angle of the Giant Shark's escape, and like before, it brought him within reach of the Giant Shark's sharp serrated teeth. He let the Giant Shark get enough of an angle to bait it into thinking it would get by him, but he was just setting the Giant Shark up for a ramming attack. The killer whale quartered in to ram the Giant Shark just in front of its left pectoral fin, under which the heart lay. But he was unaware to the shark's quickness or flexibility, and as he was about to strike, the Giant Shark suddenly snapped itself into a "C," taking away the killer whale's impact point, as it brought its jaws to bear.

The Giant Shark didn't get a complete bite on the killer

whale, but it was enough. The left half of the shark's jaws sliced into and raked the left side of the killer whale's neck area, starting just behind the white eye patch of the male before the Giant Shark's jaws closed on his left pectoral fin. Its teeth raked flesh off the bone of the appendage, leaving a bone stump protruding from the shredded confetti of what was once a pectoral fin.

The pain and lack of mobility told the killer whale he was gravely injured, and he immediately disengaged from the skirmish to access his wounds where he could breathe.

The Giant Shark was now close to the bay's mouth. But the last attack had delayed it enough so that the first killer whale, that had been scouting the eastern side of the channel, met it in the mouth of the bay. Having just sprinted for several miles to join the fray, this killer whale was winded and surfacing in short intervals to breathe, too winded to sound a battle cry. But he knew that there was a least one scout behind him.

The arriving scout killer whale had witnessed most of the last picket whale's fight and had a good idea what the shark could do. He knew he was too winded to try and take on his opponent alone, so all he wanted to do was stop the Giant Shark from escaping, keeping it bottled up in the bay until the whale behind him caught up. Between the two of them, they should be able to hold the Giant Shark in the bay while the other killer whale caught his breath and they were both ready to press home an attack and dispatch this fish.

The Giant Shark's desire to escape had grown much more urgent now. All it wanted now was to just slip past and to escape to the open waters beyond the bay's mouth.

In the narrow, two hundred yard confines of the bay mouth, it was like a knife fight in a phone booth. The two played cat and mouse, the killer whale mirroring the Giant Shark's movements - first one way, then turning back the other way as they both swam from side-to-side in the bay mouth, one seeking to escape, the other to contain. The shark sped up and slowed down, trying to find an opening. Its superior speed was nullified because the killer whale was able to play the angles and cut off the shark using the bay's sides.

Slowly, the two worked closer and closer with each turn.

The killer whale was still winded though, and slow to react. Plus, its attention was divided between the Giant Shark and gauging the approach of the next scout killer whale. And that was why it was just an instant too late in its reaction to the Giant Shark's move.

The Pod Leader had emerged to sense with its echolocation a scout whale sprinting from the other side heading at the mouth of a bay a couple miles up the coast from him. The Pod Leader called after the sprinting killer whale and all he got back was one squeal.

Shark!

That was all he needed to know. At last they had found the killer of his pod. It was time for revenge! The Pod Leader erupted from the water as he sprinted to get in the fight.

The scout killer whale guarding the bay had banked away steeply, angling to send out a train of clicks to echolocate his back-up's arrival and had left his belly exposed to the Giant Shark, putting it in his visual blind spot for just a moment too long. He was in this position when the Giant Shark tore into his belly.

The shark's eye rolled back in his head, jaws extended as it crushed down on the killer whale's exposed abdomen. The force of the bite at first compressed the killer whale's stomach and intestines in both directions within the sleeve of its body. His stomach and liver slammed against his diaphragm, temporarily stunning the whale's solar plexus. Unable to make a sound, the killer whale hung in the water mute as the shark twisted and rolled, taking a five foot circle of skin, muscle, and guts from the whale's belly.

When the Giant Shark tore free with the whale's belly, the killer whale screamed from pain and blindly headed to the channel. The screams continued once into the channel, but with each contraction of the remaining stomach muscles, he forced more and more of his remaining intestines out the hole in its belly until most of his entrails were trailing in the water alongside him.

This was the sight that greeted both the last scout whale from the eastern side and the Pod Leader, who were converging on the bay's mouth. Right behind the screaming whale was an enormous shark sprinting for the open channel waters. The last scout whale was the closest and tried to cut off the shark but had neither the angle nor the speed to do so. Failing to cut the shark off, he tried to give chase, but was already exhausted from his sprint to get there. Regardless, the Giant Shark easily would have outrun it anyway, and soon the last scout whale was forced to drop his pursuit and watch the shark swim away.

The Pod Leader followed the screaming killer whale. He was overwhelmed to see such a horrific wound to a fellow Tribe member, and the screams unnerved him, but he was driven by the need to give comfort to the tortured whale in what would be its last moments of life. The Pod Leader caught up with the dying killer whale as his screams, speed, energy and life slowly drained from his body. The Pod Leader rubbed up alongside the dying whale, trying to give him as much comfort and skin contact as he could to let him know he wasn't alone. This seemed to help dissipate some of the whale's screams. Through this touch, the Pod Leader felt the tremors of pain racking his dying companion's body. Finally, the whale stopped in the water, rising to surface to gulp air before settling back down in the water to hover in tortured agony. The Pod Leader continued to nuzzle and touch his comrade until it was clear that he was starting to fade. The wounded male was now only semi-conscious of the Pod Leader's presence, so contracted into his own world of pain that he barely noticed and didn't care when the Pod Leader slipped above and in front of him. Nor did he notice or care when the Pod Leader brought his tail crashing down on his wounded comrade's skull, crushing it. Had he noticed, he would have been thankful for the quick deliverance.

The Pod Leader hung next to his dead comrade for a time. A rage was burning inside him; he was getting too good at comforting dying killer whales savaged by the demon shark. The fires of his rage burned higher as images of the last few moments replayed through his mind and combined with the images of the death of his pod.

Slowly the trauma of the moment subsided and the Pod Leader slowly returned to the present. He checked his rage and hatred, tucking it into a corner of his mind as he turned to make his way back to the bay. As he did so, he started calling to any killer whales that might still be in the vicinity but unaware of the battle and the escape of their quarry.

In ones and twos, the remaining whales started to emerge from various coves and bays and hurried to the scene of the battle. All were shocked and horrified by the carnage they came upon. A couple of wounded whales had already succumbed to their wounds. A couple were torpid. The killer whale who had its neck and left pectoral fin shredded was wandering about. The evidence that the Giant Shark had fed upon their comrades infuriated the remaining pack.

As the other killer whales tried to assist the wounded whales, the events of the battle were slowly pieced together. It became crystal clear that the killer whales were no match for the Giant Shark one on one, or two on one. It also became obvious that that their confidence and swagger were sorely misplaced and had contributed to the deaths of the killer whales as they threw themselves piecemeal at an adversary who made a meal of them.

The survivors of the hunting pack decided to return to

the rendezvous and let the Clan know of their losses and to formulate a new plan. They tried to urge their wounded members to start with them back to the north, but the male whose chest had been removed was unable to swim and was going deeper into shock. The pack huddled around him and comforted him until he died of his wounds several hours later.

The remaining pod members had paid their respects and said goodbye to all their dead comrades and were ready to move out. The pod could only go as fast as the slowest member, the whale with wounds to his neck and pectoral fin. One day out, the wounded male's wounds started to show signs of corruption. By the second day, the wounded male was running a high fever and slowed the group even more and they had only covered less than half the distance to the rendezvous. The wounded whale had developed septicemia; angry, black spider veins grew across the white skin patch around his eye. Shortly, afterward he had difficulty breathing and became weak, barely able to push himself to the surface to breath. On the third day, he quit breathing.

The mood of the remaining pack members had been somber while traveling, but after watching the slow and painful death of the wounded male over the last three days, the mood had become morbid. They covered the remaining distance to the rendezvous in a day and a half in near silence, each mulling their own thoughts, a stunning reversal to the mood when they had traveled this very same path just days before.

At first, as they drew close to the rendezvous, the few

killer whales they encountered greeted them triumphantly, until they saw the black mood of the pack and realized that there were only six returning. So they quieted their inquiries and fell in behind the procession until they came upon the bay the Clan was currently gathered in and headed to the center of the super pod.

Those of the Council of Elders that had been skeptical of the existence of the Giant Shark only needed one look at the somber procession and dwindled numbers to now be convinced the threat was real.

20

Eric had good sailing all day due to strong winds from the southwest. The inside waters were always calm, and there was always a good breeze. Sailing was exhilarating. One constantly had to be alert to the wind, the sails and the tides, a fact that always made Eric very aware of his surroundings. This was just one of the things that he just loved about his work: sailing in the majestic waters surrounded by towering mountains and pristine beauty. It was a sailor's paradise.

Melanie loved it, too. Every year she helped him sail the *Pacific Chanteuse* from Portland to Seattle and then up the Inside Passage to Ketchikan. At the end of the season, she would help him retrace their steps home again. They would sail during the day and anchor up at night, taking turns making each other dinner, each trying to outdo the other with gourmet meals and matched wines from the Pacific Northwest, where exquisite vino abounded. The routine was a daily massage to the spirit and a nightly seduction of the senses.

Her nimble mind and keen awareness of nature had made her an excellent sailor and navigator. But more than anything else, they both loved the time together. The trip took about a week and it allowed them to transition from one universe to another. They could relax and talk about things big and small. Eric just felt downright blessed.

What job, other than his, allowed a man to go sailing in incredibly beautiful waters with his significant other, and pay him to do it? It was like having two honeymoons a year. That is, if they were married. It was this time alone together that had probably helped meld his and Melanie's relationship. It had become a love and passion shared by both of them.

It was starting to get dark, and he still had yet to round Annette Island. He'd cut over from Revillagigedo Channel to sail up Felice Strait because it was wide and had less boat traffic to worry about. As best he could figure, he'd about twenty-eight miles yet to cover before docking in Ketchikan. His fuel supply was good, so he decided to push until dark, then lower the sails and motor in. At a ten-knot cruising speed on his twin diesels, he should be tied up at the dock no later that one in the morning.

Normally, he would have anchored up and waited to sail in in the morning, but two factors changed his mind. Firstly, this was Friday night, so traffic out of Ketchikan would be light due to the sailors' superstition about leaving on a Friday. Just about everybody would be tied up until after midnight before leaving if they were headed out of town. This was great because he was running on mental fumes and didn't want to hazard other boats. And secondly, because it was Friday, Melanie didn't have to work tomorrow, and he didn't want to miss a day with her when she could be his all day.

'Wow, that sounds rather possessive, even to me,' he thought, *'but that's just the way I feel about it.'*

Normally he wouldn't come in late at night during the week because he knew Melanie would meet him at the dock and take him home to her place for the night. He didn't want her to stay up late or miss most of a night's sleep on account of him. But tonight was different.

'I really just need to feel her next to me tonight… smell her,' he mentally paused while his mind recalled the smell of her hair and the taste of her lips.

When he rounded the lighthouse on Point Winslow on Mary Island, he dropped his sails, hauled in the dagger boards to reduce his hull resistance and fired up the diesels. It was safer for him to haul in the sails in the waning light of twilight than trying to convert the boat to mechanical power in the dark. The autopilot was set to a new heading, and he retired from the sailing cockpit to the cabin wheelhouse, where he could keep an eye on the radar screen for navigation and traffic. He flipped on the navigation lights: red, like port wine on the port side, and green on the starboard or right side. These lights helped other seaman at night determine the direction of travel and orientation of the *Pacific Chanteuse*. Once satisfied with his settings and sure that he had clear sailing, he popped down to the galley to make himself a pot of coffee and a bite to eat. While sailing this close to Ketchikan he didn't feel that he could be gone from the radar screen more than five minutes before checking on his course and settings. One of the few luxuries he allowed himself here in the wilds of Alaska was the gourmet coffee.

For him, that was coffee from the Blue Mountains of Jamaica. Everybody had a special bean they preferred, but he liked this particular coffee because it reminded him of the first trip he ever took with Melanie. They had been seeing each other for about eighteen months, and they'd decided to go to Jamaica because he had found a killer discount at one of those all-inclusive resorts, where everything was included once you got there, a place they could afford on their salaries.

Blue clear waters, all the adult beverages they could drink, snorkeling, sailing: it was heaven. They found a taxi to take them around the island for a day, which wasn't difficult since everybody on the Island seemed to be working some angle on the side to separate a tourist from his cash. And since the island was small, that covered almost half of the island. The taxi driver took them up into the Blue Mountains at the eastern end of the island to one of the coffee plantations and roasting houses. There, he had the freshest, best tasting coffee from beans that had come out of the roaster just moments before brewing. It was there, overlooking the lush, jagged peaks and sipping the best cup of coffee of his life with Melanie that he really noticed how well everything about her balanced. Her hair wasn't too short or long, too dark or light. Her green eyes were clear and deep but only served to balance her above average features. She was neither short nor tall, muscular nor willowy. Just balanced and well proportioned at everything. Her whimsical side was equally balanced by her intense curiosity of the earth, her generosity balanced by practicality. She just knew how to do the right thing at the right moment; like at this moment sipping his coffee. He was drinking in the beauty of his surroundings only to find that the most beautiful thing in his sight was sitting across the small rusted table from him, smiling quietly at him. He knew that was the real reason that Jamaica coffee was the best in the world to him.

To keep himself awake, he loved to step out on the deck and watch the Aurora Borealis. The solar winds of the sun shot charged ions across the void of space until the earth's magnetic poles slowed then caught them, pulling them into the ionosphere, their high speed diminished but still potent enough to collide and super heat the gases of the earth's outermost atmospheric layer creating the magical show know as the Northern Lights. Tonight's show was spectacular. In fact, it was never less than spectacular. Great curtains of wispy green light highlighted with reds, blues and violets slowly folded and evolved, dispersing and coalescing in a never repeating, never ending display of man's unimportance to the universe.

The *Pacific Chanteuse* sailed on tranquilly, her propellers churning the photo-phosphorous plankton in the water leaving an underwater cone of green light glowing in her wake that rose and dissipated on the surface like a green throw rug.

After an hour and a half, he came in sight of the navigation light at Mountain Point on the southern head of the island that Ketchikan resided upon. He was coming down the home stretch now. Fifteen minutes later, city lights became visible to Eric, twinkling over the water's blackness. The waters and beaches in the Revillagigedo Channel were lined with the wrecks of many a sailor who pushed too hard and lost, waking up only when their boats piled onto the rocks of the beach. He'd made it over the hump; his fears of falling asleep while trying to motor in would remain unrealized. The excitement of being home would be more than enough to keep him going.

Between twelve forty and twelve fifty, he passed three boats coming out of Ketchikan. He reduced the power output of his radar so as not to overpower or cause damage to the sensitive electronics of the oncoming boats' radars. With radar, it was relatively easy to navigate in close quarters with oncoming boats. On the sea, there was no such thing as lane dividers or turn signals. One just had to keep a close eye on the other guy, watch his navigation lights and remember the old sailor's adage: "Red to red, green to green; when in doubt, don't go in between."

Shortly, he was running up the channel beside Pennock Island in front of Ketchikan and the lights of a Friday night in Ketchikan gave partial illumination to the waters of Tongass Narrows. He darted inside to call Melanie to let her know that he was twenty minutes out before he had to disconnect and get back to the wheel. He put the radar to standby and then put out fender buoys from the forward starboard gear locker on the starboard side, tying them off to the boat's handrail. Under decreased power, just barely three knots, he eased the bows of the *Pacific Chanteuse* around the entrance to the city's marina and approached the dock.

And there was Melanie on the dock, waiting for him in shorts, a long sleeved shirt and a fleece vest. *'Always with the shorts,'* he thought, *'always with the legs.'*

"Damn!" Eric said aloud to himself, "She's a sight for sore eyes!" Eric had a hard time docking the boat, his attention drawn to her to the point of distraction, her big green eyes luminescent in the night.

The dock floated up and down on piles driven vertically into the seabed, which allowed the dock to rise and fall with the tides. Like a well-rehearsed ballet, he and Melanie passed and tightened lines until the *Pacific Chanteuse* was secure to the docks. Eric went inside to turn off the boat's lights, electronics, and kill the main engines. He was out the cabin door in thirty seconds, locking it behind him and vaulting to the deck over the rails beside Melanie.

Their bodies crushed in embrace. To Eric, who for the past several days had endured collisions with hard and painful objects, the softness of her breasts against his chest, the gentle encompass of her arms, the soft scent of her body accompanied by the fullness of her lips, served as a stark contrast to his bruised and battered body. Eric totally lost awareness of his surroundings for several moments trying to absorb Melanie's essence.

After several long minutes, Eric gently disengaged from her lips. "Hi, stranger."

"Oh, I've been so worried about you. I've been going nuts waiting to see you. I know you, and when you wouldn't tell me what had happened over the satellite phone, I knew it had to be pretty bad."

"I'm sorry, sweetheart. I just thought if I told you what had happened without being here in front of you, you'd freak out a little bit. I guess I'm just damned if I do, and damned if I don't."

"Of course I would freak out! I love you and I worry about you out there alone all the time. When something bad happens, bad enough that you won't tell me about it until later, then it just makes all my worst fears come true."

"I'd rather not talk about it tonight," he said linking his elbow in hers and steering her down the end of the dock. As they started to walk, he said, "I'll tell you all about it tomorrow. Besides, I have something really big to show you."

Melanie partially turned to him so he could see the playful mirth in her smile and eyes. "Yes, I seem to recall having seen what it is you want to show me before," she told him with a laugh as she tossed her hair back. Still laughing, she said, "Is this where I'm supposed to say, 'Hi, Sailor. You new in town?'"

"Oh crap!" Eric suddenly stopped in his tracks. So preoccupied with seeing Melanie he'd left the tooth in a small bag on the salon table. "I forgot something," he said, taking his arm from hers. He turned to her, pecked her on the cheek with a "I'll be right back" kiss before he turned to dash back to the boat's steps at the stern.

This wasn't the reaction that she'd planned her little joke to have. She stood there a little mystified while she watched Eric run down the dock and then return a few moments later carrying a small gym bag.

She was now even more confused. Eric had duplicate clothes and toiletries at the apartment so he wouldn't have to shuffle things from boat to home when he was town. And the bag was too small for his laundry bag.

"What, you forgot your laundry? It's a little small for that," she said gesturing at the bag. "Did you forget to change clothes while you were out this time?"

"No. This is a little present for you in the morning."

He'd caught up to her, and arm in arm, snuggling against each other they made their way up the ramp to her truck in the parking lot. They rode home in silence. Eric snuggled against Melanie while she drove, like two high school kids, so much so that she was having trouble turning.

******

Eric slept in late, still recovering from his "adventure ashore" as he was starting to call it. He awoke to the smell of coffee, a Blue Mountain blend -- Melanie's favorite, too -- greeting his nose. He could hear her moving things about in the apartment.

Melanie was in the kitchen when Eric emerged from the bedroom in his bathrobe, his hair tousled, and his best morning face on. "Good morning sunshine," she purred, as she poured and handed him a mug of coffee and passed it over to him.

"My, aren't you the perky one…" was all that he could muster, half playfully.

In the morning's light as she was getting out of bed, she could see the parts of Eric's body that were uncovered. He was covered with bruises, scratches and cuts she hadn't seen last night. Maybe Eric had been right to hold back the details, because now she was *really* worried about her man after seeing the punishment he'd taken. It also explained why he'd been so clingy last night. Not that she didn't like clingy, but it was just not Eric's style. She was determined to pamper him today to ease his stiffness and soreness that his gait communicated.

He came forward to grab his cup of coffee and didn't stop his momentum until he was standing against her. "Thanks," he said, waving the cup of coffee slightly. "What's on the agenda for this morning?"

"Well, I was thinking coffee, tea, and then me," she purred again with her biggest smile, looking him square in the eye.

"That can be arranged," he grunted, smiling to himself. "But first let me catch up to you with a shower and shave."

"I can wait...for a while. Do you want breakfast first? You might be busy for a while..." she said, the Cheshire cat's grin on her face as she looked at him with laughing eyes.

"I think that's a splendid idea. I'll get busy on the shower while you cook."

After a wonderful hot shower and a hearty breakfast, Eric and Melanie adjourned back to the bedroom where the first round of passionate love gave way to the tender exploration, playfulness and gentleness of two lovers' intent only on the complete sensual satisfaction of each other.

Afterwards, as each was wrapped in the arms and glow of each other, Eric started to tell Melanie of his "adventure." It emerged slowly at first, in bits and pieces, as he tried to separate his emotions from the events. And then the story came out in a torrent. Melanie gently held him, squeezing him from time to time, or nuzzling to communicate she was listening. He told her everything, except the bit about the tooth.

As he concluded, he rose from the bed and put on his robe before reaching over to give her a playful slap on the thigh of her gorgeous legs and said, "Come on. There's one more thing I have to tell you, but it requires a visual aid."

"Oh, I hope you haven't brought me another rock that you think is interesting," she moaned laughingly. Eric was always bringing her rocks that turned out to be nothing but common stones. She hated telling him that; he always looked so crestfallen afterward. "Remember, you're not very good at it."

Her teasing look froze on her face as Eric pulled the giant tooth from the wadding in the bag. Fossils were no strangers to her as a geologist, and shark's teeth were the most abundant fossils of all. She knew what she was looking at was a fossil. Or was it? This was the best-preserved fossil tooth she'd ever seen. She reached for the tooth to examine it while her eyes shifted to Eric for an explanation. When she took her eyes off the tooth for a second, her hands changed track, and she accidentally jammed a knuckle into the tooth.

"Ouch!" She yipped, jerking her hand back. The

serrated edge had sliced her knuckle and it was starting to trickle blood.

"Sorry! Sorry! I should have warned you," Eric bleated.

Wrapping her finger with a paper towel, Melanie was more fascinated by the tooth to worry about a little boo-boo. "Where did you get that, Eric?"

"I dug it out of my boat before I swam for shore. Whatever hit my boat left this for me."

"Whatever wrecked your boat left you a fossil?"

"There's no sign of fossilization in this tooth. This is a living tooth. This belonged to whatever wrecked my boat."

Melanie was flabbergasted. She reached for the tooth, gingerly this time, and started to examine it.

"You're right; there's no evidence of calcification or mineralization of the bone matrix. This isn't a fossil. But this would have to be one humongous shark to leave a tooth this size, maybe forty or fifty feet. It would have to be the size of a whale!"

"You mean big enough to bite the front half of a rigid hull inflatable off?" Eric asked, raising an eyebrow in question. He watched as Melanie closed the same mental circle that he had in the days hiking over those damn ridges.

"That would mean that there's a monster shark out there that science has never heard of before. That would mean that you've discovered a new species!" she said as she warmed to the possibilities of this discovery.

"Not so fast there," he cautioned. "It may be just a freakishly large shark of a species that we already know about, like a great white or something."

"I didn't think great whites came this far north in the Pacific."

"They don't as far as we know. But the operative words there 'as far as we know.' Sharks aren't my area of expertise. But I have a friend, Chuck Hudson, at the Alaska Department of Fish and Game here in town that I'm going to have take a look at it. He's kind of their shark guru. Maybe he can tell me what this is.

"Now you know why I was a little leery to talk over the phone about this. You just never know who might be listening in on a satellite broadcast. The last thing I need to see is a headline in the *National Inquisitor*: 'Scientist Discovers Monster Shark in Alaska.'"

"Well, isn't that actually what you've done?"

"Well, yeah. Maybe. I just don't have enough data yet to make any announcements. Look, this is going to cause quite a stir when it comes out, and I just want to be sure that I have all my ducks in a row on this, at least as much as is humanly possible. If the evidence is skimpy, the scientific community's critics will eat me alive. It's the difference between 'Whale Researcher Finds Tooth of Giant Shark Imbedded in Boat' versus 'Whale Researcher Claims to Find Tooth of Giant Shark Imbedded in Boa.' If you give them any room to doubt you, then they start to marginalize you by throwing the word 'claims' in front of everything you say. Who knows, they might do it anyway. But I want to give myself a chance to find out as much as possible before I go public. I'm already fighting Sid on it a little. I got him to see it my way and cut me some slack for right now, but I can tell he wants to release this as soon as possible. Which is great for him; if the publicity doesn't go well, he can always blame me to save the reputation of the Institute, while *my* reputation goes down in flames.

"But I know this shark is out there. Remember Dutch, the guy who gave me a ride to the *Pacific Chanteuse*? He grabbed me just before he left and had this weird look in his eye. And then he asked me if I had seen 'the Giant Shark'- which confirms that it's out there. He was trying to convince himself that he wasn't crazy by asking me if I'd seen it, too. I don't want to be the 'Dutch of the Scientific World,' ranting about sea monsters."

Melanie was silent while studying Eric. Then she handed the tooth back to Eric and put a hand on his forearm and squeezing a silent communication of understanding to him before changing the subject.

"So what are you going to do the rest of the day?"

He listed several things he'd to do: go get his laundry, do maintenance on the boat, make arrangements to mount the new equipment to the boat, check his e-mail, box up the tooth in preparation to get it out to the Institute. All in all, it would be several hours of running around. After getting the rest of his clothes on, he borrowed Melanie's truck keys and headed for the door with a promise to pick up where he left off this morning when he came back.

21

At the boat, he checked in with the city dock manager to cover his moorage fees and to let them know that he was only going to be in town this time for a few days. After he pulled his boat a little further down the dock to satisfy the dock manager, he got out a heavy duty power cord and hose from the port forward gear locker and got power and water to the boat. The boat needed to replenish its water supplies and he didn't want to run the generators or drain the batteries. With everything ship-shape he moved indoors to flip valves and breakers for the electrical and water feed he'd just set up.

While that was happening, he got his laundry put together in a duffel bag to take back to the truck. After making a shopping list of food and supplies to restock the boat, he got out his digital camera and put it on the galley table along with a ruler he retrieved from the workbench in the port hull. From the navigation table he retrieved a map which he unfurled face down to use the white backsides as a backdrop to make digital photos of the tooth.

"Not too bad, if I say so myself," he said congratulating himself as he examined his handiwork on the camera's little screen. The two dozen pictures he took showed every aspect of the tooth. After he was done, he replaced the tooth in its bag and returned his ruler to its spot.

Finally he sat down at his computer at the navigation table to send the data to Sid in Portland and to check his emails.

Emails were one of the ways he helped relieve the boredom while out doing his research. He could chat up his friends and stay in contact with the world without running up the satellite phone bill. The funny thing about it was, it cost him the same amount of money to use the satellite on-line services up here in Alaska as it did in Portland. To the satellite company, it didn't matter if the signal bounced off their satellite in Seattle or Saskatoon; it was still the same amount of usage to them.

He powered up his personal computer and the GPS. On his computer, he called up the software that tracked the dish receiver to the satellite housed in a translucent dome on the rear roof of the salon and punched in his latitude and longitude off the GPS. The software took the information and scanned the sky until it located that satellite and locked in on it. The system was designed, once locked on, to track the satellite in the worst of storms. When the signal was acquired, he quickly checked his email to find it was mostly messages from family and friends and the odd spam that made it through the filters. His mailbox had a few messages from work, two from Sid, detailing when and where the equipment he requested would arrive. Everything should arrive tomorrow on the ferry out of Bellingham, Washington.

He was running a little ahead on time, so he thought he'd take the time to check the remotely activated sound system to see if the boat's computers had monitored anything while he was on the beach.

The system showed one event lasting twenty-two minutes.

'*Yeah,*' he thought, glancing at his watch, '*I've got time to run it, at least give it 'the once over.*'

His computer loaded the software that would take the data from the TTACS and build a visual display, labeling individual objects and synchronizing it with the audio track and video camera feed.

The software displayed a simulation with three parts on the screen. The top two-thirds of the screen held the visual simulation from the TTACS, the bottom third was divided in half. The left half showed an oscilloscope style presentation of the sound track that triggered the system. The other half showed the video recording of surface events.

First came the audio and visual displays, as the TTACS didn't have the range of the acoustics system. The lower-lefthand screen showed the voice signatures of four or five killer whales. All the video could show were distant clouds of steamy vapors exhaled as the whales surfaced to breathe and dorsal fins, exactly what one would expect with a pod of killer whales. The pod was moving toward the boat.

Eric had an idea of who this pod might be. To confirm his hunch, he ran a voice identification scan of the soundtrack. The software was the same as that developed for human voice recognition. Scientists had learned to adapt it for whale research once they discovered that each whale's voice was as unique as a human's, and that basic 'words' of whale speech were similar, if not the same, so a baseline for each whale could be established using the same syntax and calls. This had led to some very interesting discoveries. Such as the discovery that whales have puberty similar to humans and a teenage whale's voice cracked, too.

The voice ID came back confirming that this was a recent breakaway pod of the Southern Clan of the super pod inhabiting Southeastern Alaska. Scientists had discovered through linguistic studies that there were two major groups of killer whales related to each other; each with their own distinct ranges. The first major group was made of one pod that ranged from Vancouver Island in Canada to just below the U.S.-Canadian border in Southeastern Alaska. The second major group was composed of three clans of killer whales that divided the Alexander Archipelago of Southeastern Alaska into three ranges: Southern, Middle and Northern. While related, the two major groups never mixed, but from time to time, the three northern clans were noted to congregate into a super pod of one hundred fifty to two hundred whales.

Eric had followed this small pod many times before and had grown to know them quite well. It was comprised of two females, a mother and daughter, their children – a young male and adolescent female - and headed by a by a large male.

He slowly watched as the blow spouts came closer, until the faint images started to appear on the upper two-thirds of the screen; it showed the killer whales chasing a school of herring. The TTACS software had been modified to identify the species and individuals based on the language and calls it could compare in its library. It would then build a visual display with matching icons, labeling species and individuals identified from its library as well as the aspect, depth, yaw, pitch and roll of each whale as it gamboled in the water. The icons were species matched, so if the computer identified the target contacts as killer whales it would show little black and white icons of killer whales on the screen. It was also able to identify males versus females ninety percent of the time based on the turbulent signature of the dorsal fins. The only time the system had trouble was telling a teenage male whose size approached that of a full grown female, but whose dorsal fin had not yet grown to full adult stature.

He watched as the largest of the shapes, the male, came within forty yards of the boat and slowly rose out of the water, spy hopping to get a good look at his boat. "This is one sharp adult male," Eric mused to himself as he watched the whale eye the video camera. He could swear that the whale was looking directly at him through the camera. "He's always super cautious, this one."

In the background he could see that the females and young killer whales had forced the herring into a defensive ball. Their calls were so predictable, he could almost hear them calling out to the young killer whales, telling them what to do.

The TTACS display was somewhat limited in its presentation because as one whale passed behind another or the school of herring, it would disappear from the screen. To compensate, the software labeled each whale with a different number so one could tell which one was in front or behind, relative to the sound head on the ship's bow near the keel.

The male killer whales slid back down into the water and turned to go join the feast of herring. All and all, it was a fairly routine sequence that he could properly catalog next time he was holed up on the boat during a rainy day. Eric was just starting to position the cursor over the close button to shut down the software when the screen suddenly displayed a humpback whale that was swimming towards the killer whales.

"This should be fairly interesting," Eric said excitedly. Rarely, did a researcher get to see the Resident killer whales interact with other whales. It was even rarer for the encounter to be caught on the TTACS system.

Eric watched as the humpback swam towards the pod of killer whales and circled below. The killer whales seemed to be focused on their soon-to-be-meal of herring and paid no heed to the newcomer. It was unusual for a humpback to congregate with killer whales, Eric knew.

'Maybe, the humpback was interested in feeding on the leftovers of herring when the killer whales finished,' he mused.

The killer whales had made no trains of echolocation since they were all within sight of each other and they could see their prey, so they were probably oblivious to the humpback whale.

What struck Eric as odd about this sequence was the humpback had made no vocalizations. They were among the most gregarious cetaceans of the seas. Secondly, there were no other humpbacks that had yet joined the lone individual.   Humpbacks usually swam in very small groups, but not always.

As Eric was pondering these points, he almost missed the humpback icon go ballistic. In fact, he was so startled by what he saw that he'd to back it up to see it again. The humpback blasted to the surface at an incredible speed and looked to go through the ball of herring while breaching. Then the humpback icon disappeared from the screen momentarily during the breach. The adolescent killer whale, which had just disappeared behind the herring ball as the humpback breached, had also disappeared, only it hadn't returned.

'Had the humpback landed on the adolescent killer whale,' he wondered?

Then one of the females appeared to ram the humpback separately, but the humpback seemed to get away, ramming the second young killer whale. Each time the humpback came into contact with one of the killer whales, the icon for the killer whale would shortly fade from the screen. At the end, the last of the females appeared to tangle with the humpback and then left the scene at high speed followed by the big male. Just before the big male left, he gave a new vocalization that Eric had never heard before.

TTTTHHHROOOOM   *click-click-click-click,*
TTTTHHHROOOOM   *click-click-click-click,*
TTTTHHHROOOOM click-click-click-click.

Eric played it several times, running it through several of the voice analyzer's filters.

'This was a new and totally unique vocalization,' Eric

thought excitedly, which added even more intrigue and confusion to this encounter. He catalogued the call into the library and decided to examine it later.

But it made absolutely no sense at all. He watched the TTACS simulation play three times. It was on the third replay that out of the corner of his eye he saw the video camera's feed of the humpback breaching that he realized something was wrong. He enlarged the video feed and played it in slow motion, almost frame by frame, quickly realizing that he wasn't looking at a humpback whale but a giant shark. In an instant, he realized what was wrong with what he was seeing. The video feed of the breaching shark was clear and distinct; however there was nothing in the foreground or background to give it scale. It looked like a great white breaching after a seal. The splash pattern could give relative size but was inconclusive, since the water was perfectly flat, with no to swells of waves to act as a scale.

The TTACS system didn't know what to label the shark. Based on size, it had assigned it a humpback whale icon, which would have made a similar turbulence signature. This had to be the same type of shark that had attacked him.

Now that he understood the mistake in labeling, he went back and could now see the underwater battle for what it was. The killer whales were disappearing from the screen because they were dead. Dead whales created no turbulence for the TTACS to track.

"My God!" Eric exclaimed to the salon. "If this shark is killing killer whales, then everything in the sea is prey."

And he realized just how lucky he'd been with his encounter of this new species. *Species or mutant he wondered? Was it the same shark that I encountered? Or were there more? If it was preying upon cetaceans, the Institute had to know about this. It could radically impact whale populations if they were now prey for his newly discovered shark.* It had rapidly become a priority to find and identify this new type of shark.

But the rational part of his brain urged him to caution. The evidence was still highly subjective. He had a tooth, some video footage that didn't show enough detail or scale to show just how big the shark was, a TTACS simulation that had a measurable error rate and had already misidentified the shark as a whale, and an old rummy fisherman who had seen it but would never admit to it. This wasn't even close to being proof enough of discovery of a new species.

22

Eric shut down the computer, gathered his list and laundry, locked the salon door, and hurried up to the parking lot. Laundry placed in the passenger's seat, he turned right out of the of the marina parking lot onto Waters Street.

Eric had one more stop to make before going back to the apartment. He'd an acquaintance, if you could call him that, who might know if people and fisherman were talking about this shark. He usually hung out in several bars along the waterfront depending on which faction of the waterfront he was working. He'd try the Red Dog Saloon over on the east end of Front Street first; it was a popular spot with the deck hands of purse seiner fleet. If he could find his acquaintance, he would know if anything strange were happening.

The waterfront was a stew of cultures, factions, rivalries and egos. His acquaintance was the rare bird that could travel with and between all the different camps and be welcomed by all as a friend. Because one culture, group, faction or crew always wanted to dish dirt about those not of their clique; this guy was rumor central.

In the twelve minutes it took to cover the four miles to the bar, Eric drove past four canneries, which in turn drove Ketchikan's economy and culture.

The Red Dog Saloon was a hangout for fishermen

between openings. Crew members would hang out, swap stories, and play pool while nursing beers to prolong their buzz and forestall the depletion of their funds. Eric had been there on several occasions. He was unlike the normal academician and researcher who drank coffee from a tiny saucer with pinky raised. He liked to rub elbows with the fishermen; they were the heart and soul of Ketchikan's economy. The fishermen caught it, and the cannery workers put it into tins. But lately, the cannery workers had given way from college students trying to make tuitions for the next year's schooling or kids just looking to make a quick buck for some prized dream possession through long, long hours of work with limited opportunities to blow their money, and to workers from the Philippines and Mexico. They worked harder for less and almost never complained.

There had always been a hierarchy of sorts between the cannery worker and fisherman. The fisherman looked down upon the cannery workers as transients - here today gone tomorrow - as soon as they got their financial grubstake together. So they didn't see much sense in building relationships with the hourly wage crowd. Fishermen saw themselves as professionals. Many returned year after year, working the same boats. But in truth, many of the fishermen who worked the boats were also college students working for next year's tuition. The only difference was that the fisherman subjected themselves to hardship and some level of risk by going to sea. Therefore, they were much braver and worthier as human beings than mere cannery workers, at least in their eyes.

The cannery workers had a different opinion. They worked twelve to sixteen hours every day, and as much overtime as much as they could get. Salmon fishermen were lazy lay-abouts who spent most of their time lounging in bars. They only worked two to four days a week and only when the weather was good. Salmon fishermen never worked in a storm. They were sunshine workers. They could probably not stand the long hours they worked. And working in a cannery wasn't without certain risks. Due to the long hours working around slimy, slippery fish with machines designed to cut, skin, gut, and behead, many cannery workers were seriously injured every year.

Salmon was a seasonal product. The canneries tried to purchase as much salmon as they could and stockpile it in large chill brine tanks to keep their canning lines running all summer long. They were staffed with employees not to meet maximum intake but to process the average summer's intake with the fewest workers over the limited period of time before their stockpiles of fish went bad. Boats rolled in at all hours that needed to be unloaded. First priority went to the fishermen with fish in their holds, but no refrigeration. Next came the tenders. They usually had iced holds or chill brine tanks to hold the fish longer before they spoiled. The fishermen and the tenders would tie up to the piers of the cannery, rafting out seven or eight boats deep in three or four rows along each cannery's waterfront. Every hour or so, outside boats would all untie to let out a boat whose turn it was to unload.

Unless you were the very outside boat that could just pull ahead, most boats had to reverse out of the position in the stack at least enough to get maneuvering room ahead. Skiffs were usually tied snuggly behind the main boats and were towed to the fishing ground or to port. This was fine as long as the boat was going forward. But a purse seiner couldn't back out with a skiff tied to its stern. If it did, the skiff would jackknife, acting as a floppy rudder, trying to steer the boat in whatever direction it bent to as the boat moved backwards. So to back out of the stack, the skiff had to be started, the pelican release pulled to cut it loose, and then it had to back out before the main boat could do the same. The purse seiners would circle briefly to let out the boat headed for the unloading pier, and then circle to reform the raft, while the skiffs would have their own little circles waiting to retie to their purse seiner. It all happened so quickly and routinely, that it only took five minutes to let out a boat that was five deep in the raft.

Of course, that was only if the captain of the boat was onboard. Sometimes a captain would disappear when somebody needed to move. If that happened, boats would circle in the Narrows expecting to see others move. Tempers would flare as captains burned unnecessary diesel and wasted their engine time. The skipper of the boat needing to move would usually be on the CB channel used for that particular cannery castigating the boat that wouldn't move and letting the other captains know who was wasting their fuel. The crew of the stalled boat would then set out on a frantic search of the offices, docks, bathrooms, and adjacent bars in search of their wayward captain. If a boat missed its call to unload, they lost their place in line and were shuffled to the back of the line. Crews would go ballistic because one boat was holding up the whole works and delaying the time until they could finish their work and be off.

And if their catch spoiled before it was unloaded, they wouldn't only lose their profits, they would have to go out to the end of the Tongass Narrows and toss a hold of rotten fish overboard by hand. It wasn't unusual for the captain of the boat whose call it was to unload to appear on the deck next to the stalled boat with a hatchet in hand, threatening and willing to cut the delinquent boat loose if it didn't move promptly. This almost never happened though. The captain usually showed up out of breath or the boat's first mate would move the boat rather than see her cut adrift. That was how grudges started between crews of boats.

One of the other oddities of protocol on the waterfront was that even though gill-netters and purse-seiners unloaded at the same canneries, they never mixed nor tied up to the same pier, or went to the same bar for that matter. It was just an uneasy dislike between the two styles of fishing. Purse-seiners looked upon the gill-netters as trivial. Their gear was lighter, and their boats smaller, as well as their catch. They appeared to the purse seiners to be playing or pretending at catching salmon. But statistically, gill-netters caught forty percent of all the salmon in Alaska, making up for size by sheer number of boats, and made about as much per person if not more than purse seiners.

The cannery workers unloaded the holds of the boats for the fishermen, not so much as a courtesy, but as a financial necessity. After the deck hatch to the hold was removed, three to five cannery workers, depending on the size of the hold, would jump down into the fish that may be eight feet deep or more. After sinking in up to their crotches in salmon, a four-foot round ring, called a brailler with net attached and a cinch drawstring on the bottom, would be lowered on top of the salmon. The supervisor would yell down to the workers which type of fish to load. Salmon soon filled the air, filling the basket. The most abundant were pink salmon called humpbacks, or just humpies for short, by the fisherman. The unloaders would grab humpies from around them and toss them in the basket, until all that remained on the surface were money fish, which they would unload one species at a time. When filled, the brailler would be raised and the scale connecting the basket to the cable would be read for the weight of the fish.

The cardinal rule was for one of the boat's crew to be on hand at all times, first, to watch the unloaders, and second, to keep a running list of all basket weights. If one didn't watch closely, the unloaders would throw in a money fish with the humpies. There are five species of salmon in Alaska, and all of them got caught in the nets. Chinook, known as King salmon, were the biggest, averaging twenty pounds and brought the most money per pound. They actually came in two varieties: red and white. They were identical on the outside but when cut open their flesh was either red or white. The cannery paid the same for either. Next came the Coho, nicknamed Silvers. Averaging twelve pounds, restaurants prized these fish. The next in price were the Sockeye, called dogs by fishermen: a nice size fish at four to six pounds. These were the money fish. And,n bringing up the rear, were Keta, called Chum and the Pinks; only their size differed, as there was very little difference in the texture of their flesh. Depending on the cannery, the price difference between them might only be a penny or two, if any, so they might be loaded in the same basket.

It was a cutthroat business; the unloaders were paid higher wages if they were skilled at slipping King salmon in with the Humpies. Enough of that sort of thing could really boost a cannery's profits. So boat crewmen had to constantly watch what went into the basket and call a halt to pull out the more expensive fish from the basket. It was funny how Humpies never got thrown in the Silvers. A good dock supervisor, supervising the unloaders, would be adept at striking up an entertaining conversation with the watching crewman to distract him from watching the unloading, which is why the High-Liner boats always had at least two crewmen watching at all times.

The boats that already unloaded were usually closest to the pier, so they could shut down without having to worry about reshuffling the raft. On the way into town, the crew scrubbed and cleaned the decks to remove any particles of fish that might start to rot in the balmy sun of the northern latitude. Gear was neatly stowed and lashed. But being unloaded didn't mean an end to the work for the deck hands. After the cannery workers unloaded their catch and the boat was retied into the stack, they had to clean and scrub out their holds of all blood, fish slime, and cast off of thousands of dead fish. The crabs under the cannery docks were said to be the biggest, fattest, best-fed crab anywhere in Alaska.

Once the cleaning was done, fishermen in small groups made their way across the rafted fleet of fishing boats to the cannery's showers. Most purse seiners and certainly none of the gill-netters had showers on their boats. Showers were one of the fringe benefits with which canneries tried to recruit captains to unload their catch with them, rather than a competitor down the waterfront. They constantly vied to have the best and nicest shower facilities for the fishermen.   Captains had their own, separate from the crew's. Of course, the captain's shower facilities were the picture of cleanliness and opulence, while the deckhands' showers would charitably be called spartan. Cannery workers had their own separate shower. So a constant stream of soiled fishermen, with toiletries, towel and town clothes under arm, would constantly stream across the decks of the rafted boats, returning shaved, showered and smelling considerably better.

The culture of the rafted boats was to just walk across any boat you needed without worry of whose boat it might be. It kind of became a little burg of its own on the water. Crewmen would just saunter across decks without any real regard for where they stepped or what they grabbed to help themselves over the gunwales from boat to boat. It was a good idea not to leave anything loose out on the decks if one didn't want it to disappear with all the foot traffic. However, there were rules to be obeyed. One didn't go into a boat unless asked. If a stranger was found inside a boat all alone when a crewman returned, they wouldn't call the police. He would just make the stranger, by any means necessary, turn out his pockets and empty his wallet. If one was stupid enough to break the etiquette and get caught, and compounded the blunder by not complying with any request of the crew, one was guaranteed to 'have an accident' or 'slip on something' that would leave impressions that resembled knuckle marks.

With all the comings and goings, the highly competitive nature of fishing, and the egos of the captains, the boat rafts became a place of fashion statements. Many captains were known to make their crews restack the net on the deck until it was perfectly stacked and displayed within a millimeter of perfection before they got to town. It was a show of seamanship and crew to untie and dock one's boat smartly. Many a crewman had been invited into a closed-door session of the wheelhouse with the captain for instruction if the captain thought the crewman had made him look bad. They may have outlawed cat o' nine tails as a disciplinary method for boat captains, but most captains were adept at flaying a crewman's pride, hide and ego with his tongue.

Each boat had fenders and bumpers tied to their sides, keeping the boats a foot or more apart. Stepping from boat to boat was typically not a big deal because the gunwale tops were usually wide enough for one's foot to

step. That was, of course, if it was light, and you were
sober. Every year, two or three purse seining crewmen
drowned falling between boats, drunk, alone and in the
dark.

Eric's contact bought both from gill-netters and purse
seiners alike, and served not only as the go-between for
the different fishermen, but also the fishermen and the
canneries. And it was this little world along the
waterfront that his acquaintance had his finger on the
pulse.

Eric found a parking spot across from the Red Dog
Saloon and crossed the street to the entrance. The tooth
sat next to him on the front seat in the FedEx box he'd put
it in earlier. Eyeing it, he was torn whether to lock it in the
car or take it with him. In the end, paranoia won out and
he figured this close to shipping it off to the Institute, he
was better off not letting it out of his sight, so he tucked
the box under his arm and slipped out of the truck.

The bar was a nondescript single-story building,
moderate pitched roof and plank siding, painted in gray
that was now long faded. A wooden sign carved in relief
with the bar's name and a sitting dog, head up, howling,
was painted in bright red, sat propped above the door on
the roof. Inside, the walls of the tavern were covered in
cedar plank, not so much as for ambiance, but because
cedar was cheap and plentiful on the island and stood up
well to the salt air. This was common in many of the older
buildings in Ketchikan. Inside, the cedar planks had been
grayed by their long exposure to the air and stained
brown by the constant blue haze of tobacco smoke that

always hovered in the air five feet from the floor. It was a typical bar, with stools made of heavy chrome topped with vinyl seats at the bar, an assortment of square and round wooden tables that filled the floor, and two pool tables in the corner.

'If he's here,' Eric speculated, *'he'll be playing pool.'*

A quick scan of the room proved him right.

"Johnny J!" Eric spotted him standing along the wall with a pool cue in his hand. The man with the cue smiled as he heard his name and recognized his caller.

"Hey dude, how're you?" Johnny smiled at Eric while shaking his hand and pulling him in to touch right shoulders.

Johnny J's name was actually John Jackson. John was a slender six-foot-three-and-a-half with sandy brown hair and the athletic build of a distance runner. He was a tender skipper who made his living by being a friend to all, purse seiners, gill-netters and cannery workers alike. Salmon was salmon as far as he was concerned. It was a competitive business, even among the tenders. Tender captains were a combination street barker and buyer, always looking for an edge over their competition to persuade boat captains to sell their salmon to them. Johnny J had found his niche. He was known to have the best weed around. Any captain that unloaded their catch on Johnny J's boat knew that you would be treated to a great high. It had always been a bit of a split opinion as to whether 'Johnny J' was an abbreviation of his last name or nod at his marketing technique. Alaska was truly the last refuge for the free spirit.

Eric had met John five years ago at one of the bars scattered along the waterfront. Johnny was one of those people who made whatever he said or did seem hip and cool. And he just seemed to invite others to be hip and cool by hanging out with him, by extending any point you made seem reasonable and finding a way to humor everyone, in a way that all could enjoy, no matter how humor-challenged one might be.

Johnny's unique approach to business put him in a position to hear all the latest scuttlebutt among the fishermen and the docks, because each faction always wanted to dish dirt on the others.

"Fine. Can I buy you a beer?"

"Dude, you serious?   Make it some fancy ale from Seattle if you're buying."

Once the beer arrived, Johnny and Eric found a table among the other tables of fishermen. Eric put the box on the table before sitting down.

"Hey, you didn't have to buy me a present, but it sure was thoughtful of you," Johnny said picking up the blue and orange box and shaking it to his cocked ear.

"Very funny," Eric said dryly, grabbing the box away from Johnny and putting it back on the table. "So what's been going on?"

This was all the excuse Johnny needed to launch into regaling Eric with the latest gossip from the fishing world. About halfway through his beer, Eric sensed it was time to ease into the purpose of his trip. "You know, a lot of these guys stay out fishing for days at a time - I bet they get pretty wacky. Do any of them ever claim to see sea monsters or mermaids?"

Despite Johnny's easygoing manner, he was an exceptionally sharp guy and an excellent read of people. The last thing that Eric needed put out on the gossip network was that he was researching sea monsters and whatnot. Then every kook, crank and drunkard would be hitting him up for a free beer while they described their latest delirium tremens-induced vision.

Johnny cocked an eye at Eric and, with a question-raised eyebrow queried, "Why, Doc? Did you find one?"

"Yeah, I discovered an inflatable mermaid on eBay," Eric told him dryly. "She's all blown up down at my boat. You wanna go see her?"

"Nah, not my style. But I had a captain of a gillnetter tell me that it's not a bad way to go with the right lubrication. He also didn't recommend lube grease, unless you were open to a wild weasel next time you go to take a squirt."

Eric laughed loudly at the visual Johnny's words evoked before he shook his head and said, "No, I'm serious. The old sailing ship and clipper crews got so lonely that they turned manatees in Florida into mermaids. Have you ever seen a manatee? Do you know how ugly they are? I just have this professional interest in how sea stories get tuned into myths. I'm sure that you probably hear all sorts of strange things from the people you're doing business with, especially over a roach clip."

"True, true. People do seem to be a bit more sharing while they toke on some bud...I had this one captain tell me a week or two ago that a sperm whale ate his dog. Said that his boat had hit something submerged and when he looked out the bridge window to look down into the water to see what it was, he saw a huge gray shape down in the water swim off. Their dog disappeared right after the incident, so he figured the whale ate it."

"So, how did he know it was as sperm whale? They generally aren't seen in these waters. More likely, it was a humpback whale." Eric said, while taking a swig of his beer to hide his rising excitement of this news. If it was a sperm whale, which he doubted, that would be noteworthy by itself; if it was the shark, he might be able to start piecing together a picture of how it was making its living in Southeastern Alaska.

"He said it had to be a sperm whale because that was the only thing that size that eats meat."

'Not anymore,' thought Eric, his mind briefly touching upon the TTACS simulation on his boat's computer.

"You sure he just wasn't blowing smoke…so to speak," Eric said, as winked at Johnny.

"No, this guy's a straight shooter. Offered him a blunt, but he declined."

"What's this guy's name? I'd like to pick his brain about the whale he saw. Maybe help him identify what species it actually was."

"Yeah, he'd probably like that. He was all torn up about his dog and all. It might help him gain some closure. His name is Pete Sondergrass. He's the captain of the Linda Bea. They're usually tied up at the SamsonCo cannery. But he hangs out at the lounge at the Sheraton downtown; it's a big hangout for all the captains. You know… they can't be seen drinking with the deckhands and all. He's a good dude - you'll like him."

Eric finished his beer and set it on the table. "I think I'll go and look him up. One last question, and then I gotta run - when's the next salmon opening?"

Johnny rolled his eyes in an exaggerated way, like this was knowledge that everybody on the waterfront in Ketchikan should know and not have to ask. "Two days from now. Opens Tuesday, runs for three days."

"Thanks, Johnny. You just earned yourself another beer," he said as he stood up. "I'll catch you later."

"Later," Johnny replied as he saluted with his near empty beer.

Eric swung by the bar and dropped a five on the bartop with instructions to the barkeep to treat his friend to another before he headed to the door with a wave to all.

After getting the truck fired up, he flipped a u-turn and headed back downtown. Front Street turned to Waters Street, which he followed downtown to Jefferson and Second. He parked in the underground parking lot and took the stairs to the first floor lobby. His mind was ablaze with possibilities as he headed to the hotel's lounge.

'Either way, this should be interesting,' Eric thought, in anticipation.

23

It was a typical hotel lounge, hardwood bar and shelving, lots of brass and specialty bottles of liquor, highly lighted with mirrors behind the bottles to make it easier for patrons to find that special request that added two bucks to a shot of liquor that would get watered down with fifteen cents worth of corn syrup and food coloring from the soda gun. There was a built-in couch around the perimeter, with hardwood tables and chairs spaced discreetly apart, filling the floor. Two televisions played lowly in different corners, one tuned to the twenty-four hour news channel, the other to the twenty-four hour sports channel. Several tables were filled with two to three men each, heads bent in conspiratorial conversation. Most were holding drinks with well-melted ice cubes, trying to nurse their drinks long enough to hold off loneliness before they realized that the exotic destination at the end of the plane ride was just another bland hotel with the same faceless, congenial staff the world over.

Eric didn't know which one might be Pete, so he ambled up to the bar and slipped onto a barstool, nodding to the bartender who was preparing drink garnishes for the night shift. Eric had figured that captains were always on the clock and responsible for their boats. The Sheraton was the perfect hangout for that kind of person. It was downtown, far enough away from their boats not to be pestered by their crew, but close to the hotel's taxi stand so that they could be at their boat quickly if an emergency arose.   And boat captains knew that the hotel staff made their tips off of knowing their regular's names and being able to locate them on the premises when they might be needed urgently.

The bartender wore the ubiquitous black pants, vest and tie over a white shirt found in every hotel of the continents that wanted to be perceived as a charter member of the upper crust.

 "Can I help you?"

"Can you tell me if Pete Sondergrass is in the bar?"

"That's him over there," he said nodding at a table with two men sitting at it. "The one facing this way."

"Thanks."

Eric really didn't have a game plan, so he thought the straightforward approach would do, backed up by his credentials as a whale researcher. That and a good dose of congeniality. He wove his way between tables, trying to make eye contact with Pete as he approached.

Eric saw that Sondergrass was watching him out of the corner of his eye and put on smile and his best collegiate airs.

"Hi," he said, "are you Pete Sondergrass?"

"Yes. How can I help you?" It was more of a challenge than an offer of help.

"My name is Eric McCallister. I am a Cetacean researcher for the Pacific Ketterman Marine Institute. I heard you had an incident with a large whale, and I was wondering if I could ask you a few questions about it?"

"Sure, I'll accommodate you," Pete said amiably, as he accepted Eric's outstretched hand. "This is Dean Allen, captain of the *Portland Rose*." Pete told him while giving an introductory wave toward Dean.

"Nice to meet you, Eric," he said getting up. "Here take my chair. I've already heard the tale, and I need to go make some calls."

"Are you sure? I don't want to chase you off or break up your little get together…."

"No, please. You'd be doing me a favor," he said grinning at Pete. "I couldn't bear to hear the demise of ol' Corky one more time and see Pete get all worked up again." Eric saw Dean wink at Pete.

"You chicken shit," Pete lobbed back, a grin on his face, too.

"I'll see you later, Pete." Dean said over his shoulder, and then he was gone.

Eric settled into the chair Dean had just vacated, depositing the FedEx box in the center of the small table.

"Can I buy you a drink?" Eric offered.

"Absolutely."

The bartender was already hovering, anticipating a new round for the newcomer. Drinks were ordered, then Eric focused on Pete and repeated his opening inquiry. "So you had an encounter with a sperm whale - tell me about it," he gently prodded.

Eric could see that rather than answer his question, Pete wanted to ask his own; probably how he knew about his encountered. But, just as quickly as the look came, it changed to another expression, this one of understanding as he mentally answered his own question, knowing that the dock's news networks were as efficient as any in the world at disseminating the incredible, and sperm whale attacks were as good as it got. "Goddamn sperm whale ate my dog, the bastard!" Pete said with sudden heat.

"How long ago did this occur?" Eric asked, his mind screaming, 'Where? When?' at him.

"About a week ago or less."

Boat captains were extremely close-mouth to people they didn't know or trust when it came to discussing where and when they were fishing. They considered that information a trade secret, not to be bandied about with a stranger in a bar, unless the person asking was the Alaska Department of Fish and Game. Eric knew going in that he wouldn't get an exact location. He just hoped that the captain would give him something useful.

"Whereabouts were you? The sperm whale is an open-water whale. It's really unusual for it to come to inside waters."

"I was in the south end of Clarence Straits," was all he would say. Answering 'Alaska' could have been the only thing less descriptive.

"OK," Eric said, thinking it would be better to come back to this topic after he warmed up a little. "Tell me what happened." The bartender arrived with their drinks and Pete shoved aside Eric's box to make room for his drink, which the bartender landed skillfully; Pete waited until Eric had paid for the round and the bartender departed before starting in.

Pete retold the story of the collision and subsequent

emergency actions he'd to take, concluding with the disappearance of his dog, Corky.

"So how did you know it was a sperm whale?" Eric asked when Pete finished.

"Deductive reasoning. When I looked out the window to see what we might have hit, I just barely saw a large gray shape fade away under the roil and froth of all the salmon. It was almost as large as the *Linda Bea*. It was the wrong shape for a humpback whale. It was more streamlined... and it moved completely different. It's the only thing that size that eats meat. Why else would it be chasing salmon in my net and eat Corky, if it wasn't a meat eater?"

"You've got a point there," agreed Eric, knowing full well there was another explanation now. "What did you mean that it moved different?"

"Well," Pete started and paused a moment to try to find the right phrase for what he was seeing in his mind, "Humpbacks swim kind of herky-jerky, kind of bobbing up and down as they swim. This one was real smooth, no up and down bobbing. This just kind of glided away."

This was an interesting bit of information. Eric knew that most sharks wag their head from side to side as they swim, but a few kept their head and torso straight and only wagged their tail like the great white and the salmon shark.

"So tell me, was this just off the shore or were you out in deep water?"

"I had set the net on a point."

That settled it for Eric. It had to be the shark. Sperm

whales did come in to inside waters, but only if the water depth was six hundred fifty feet or more. Only a few of the deepest main channels in Southeastern Alaska came close to running that deep. If they had been on the beach, the deepest the water could have been under the *Linda Bea* was two, two-fifty, max. "Well thank you for your information," Eric said getting up.

Pete looked a little startled at Eric's sudden departure and stood with him. "So was it a sperm whale that ate Corky?" he asked, his eyes searching Eric's, looking for the definitive answer to his pain.

It was Eric's nature and training to deal with the facts in a straightforward manner to arrive at the truth. But this was one of those times that a lie was going to be more palatable than the truth. And besides, Eric really didn't know what the truth was. All he was dealing with were probabilities. It was an extremely low probability that Pete had had an encounter with a sperm whale. He couldn't even begin to calculate the probability of the encounter with an as of yet undiscovered shark type, supported by scant physical evidence and unreliable eyewitness sightings, even though that was what his intuition was telling him. The best he could do was to equivocate.

"It appears that there are certain aspects that would support a sperm whale encounter, though without actually seeing it or any video evidence, I can't really say for sure."

Pete's face showed relief at Eric's seeming confirmation of his guess. "Thanks. It was nice to meet you."

"Pleasure was all mine," Eric said shaking Pete's hand. "I'm sorry about your dog," he said and he meant it.

Back on the street in Melanie's truck, he turned to head for the apartment, absorbed by this new information most of the way back. It wasn't until he pulled into the apartment complex that he realized where he was.

He pulled into the apartment building's parking lot still on autopilot, grabbed his laundry and headed for the apartment. Melanie rushed to the door when she heard it open and met him with a kiss-and-hug combo, super-sized, the kind where she wrapped her leg around his in an effort to totally absorb him. Slowly, he felt all his attention to the new information running around inside his head start to drain through her lips, emptying his brain until the sensation of her body pressed against his and the wet, warm tenderness of her lips became his only universe. After totally disengaging his being from his brain, she released him and turned back toward the kitchen and said casually, "Hi honey."

Eric was left standing at the door dumbfounded, watching her recede to the kitchen. "Uh, hello..." he sputtered after her. And then he found himself again, dropped his laundry bag and boxed tooth, and headed after her to the kitchen. In the kitchen, he was determined to return the favor.

"How was your day?" she asked, standing at the sink, her back toward him.

For an answer, Eric whirled her to face him and bent her over backwards in his arms while smothering her with a well thought-out and executed kiss.

"That good?" she asked rhetorically as she came up for air.

Eric released her and headed for the refrigerator and a beer. "It's been interesting," he said as he popped the cap and took a sip. He sat down at the kitchen table and proceeded to tell her of all he'd seen and learned today. As a geologist, he knew she shared his passion for learning and understanding. Even though this wasn't her area of expertise, these new developments weren't lost on her.

They talked about the ramifications and permutations of what Eric had discovered over dinner and then into a relaxing evening. Slowly the conversation turned to more personal topics of hopes and desires, culminating in a long and loving excursion in the bedroom.

As Pete lay on the bed with Melanie, staring at the ceiling, he was reminded of his decision on the mountainside to move their relationship to a more permanent plateau.

'But how to do it? I want to do it right. This is going to be the most important thing in my life. I've done the 'research' so to speak, and I'm committed to moving it forward. Melanie and I have talked about marriage before. She's been positive about the topic but noncommittal. So had I, for that matter.

'Maybe that was the problem. Two positive noncommittals didn't make a right. Perhaps she was holding back, matching his reticence, knowing that if only one of us was committed to the proposition of marriage, it wouldn't work. But was this the right time to propose? In bed? Shouldn't I be on a bended knee or something? Isn't that what women want? Melanie was a no frills kind of gal, so maybe she isn't into all of that romantic

stuff. But if I'm wrong, this could blow up in my face, badly.'

This was like handling nitroglycerin while someone was tickling your nose with a feather.

Christ, why do women make it so damn hard to get married?' he ask himself. 'OK,' he thought, *'time for a new tack. When in doubt go with the bended knee and ring scene. If it's too much, she might be put off, but wouldn't say no. If it's just right, she'll say yes. That is, if she wants to get married. Maybe she's changed her mind, grown accustomed to the way things are and say no...if she said no, I couldn't live a lie and pretend that nothing had happened. I would have to move my stuff out of the apartment, make totally new arrangements for living and getting around Ketchikan when I came in. And God, what if I ran into her at the grocery store? That would be embarrassing! I'd have to leave.'* His mind raced through the horrors of a broken relationship in a small town.

"Nitroglycerin," he muttered aloud forgetting where he was.

"What was that, sweetheart?" Melanie murmured quietly, nearly asleep as she laid her arm across his chest from the other side of the bed.

"Nothing, angel. Go to sleep. Goodnight."

He heard a cross between a soft moan and a grunt, followed by the sounds of deep, regular breathing coming from her as she drifted off to sleep. It was quite awhile until the demons of the wrong answer slowed enough in his head to let Eric fitfully drop off to sleep.

Sunday morning arrived gray and dull. Eric slept in after a restless night. Melanie, ever the morning person, had been up for a while preparing a Sunday brunch of fruit, scrambled eggs, sausage and English muffins.

Finally, Eric's olfactory could take no more abuse from the smell of delicious food wafting into the bedroom and rolled out of bed.

After throwing on some clothes, a quick brush of his teeth and a shave, he eased into the kitchen to pour a cup of java.

"Good morning, sunshine," Melanie called from the couch in the living room where she was curled up with her big mug of coffee to the apparition that shuffled past her.

He was feeling a lot better this morning, the stiffness and pain from his injuries and exertions almost gone. He grabbed a plate that Melanie had set out for him and piled it with food. As he settled into a seat at the kitchen table, Melanie slipped into the seat across from him with her own plate of food. Eric had already decided that he would go to the JC Penney in town today to buy a ring. He didn't want to get anything fancy; everything was so expensive in Ketchikan. He just wanted to get a placeholder ring, and when they got back to Portland in the fall, they would go out and pick out the right ring together.

"What?! You're looking at me funny," Melanie said from across the table, her face screwed into a question.

"I'm sorry. I was just trying to organize my day in my head, was all."

After a leisurely breakfast and a morning of reading the paper and watching the TV, Eric showered and dressed properly before he headed out for the truck. Melanie wanted to come with him because she 'just wanted to spend some time with him.' Eric had come up with a series of lame excuses trying to put her off, until he was finally forced to use the Big One, he was going to be doing 'man things' that seemed to put an end to the conversation. He was sure he'd hurt her feelings slightly by rebuffing her advances just to be with him.

'*Women! Why did they make it so hard to get married?*' Eric lamented.

In the end, he promised her that the evening would be all hers, at which time he would lavish attention upon her. This seemed to mollify her slightly, but he could still see that she was slightly miffed at not being allowed to go with him today.

He'd two things to accomplish today. He needed to get a ring and he'd made arrangements to go see his friend, Chuck Hudson, from the Department of Fish and Game that afternoon so he could examine the tooth.

First, he needed to swing by the boat to grab some charts to show Chuck where everything had happened.

With the charts tucked into the cab, he headed into uncharted territories as he steered to JC Penney. He'd a strong idea what he was looking for, so it didn't take more than fifteen minutes of looking before he found a very delicate solitaire in a channel setting that was a quarter of a carat. And with JC Penney, as long as he'd the receipt, he could always return it when they went to upgrade to the right ring, or if she said no. To be doubly sure that it was returnable, he put it on his bank credit card.

The little taupe velveteen box was put in his shirt pocket where it stuck out like a tumor begging to be excised. Once back into the truck, he carefully locked it into the glove box. He'd given zero thought to how he was going to get the box into the apartment unnoticed. The jeans he wore would telegraph the anomaly of his anatomy from across the room, so that was out. This was getting more complicated by the minute. Maybe he could wait until she went to the bathroom and then run down to the truck or something. He'd already figured if he could hide it under the couch, then tonight he could maneuver Melanie to sit with him and fish it out when he needed it.

He pondered several refinements to his plans as he drove up the hill to find Chuck's house. The plan gradually came together in his head a block or two before Chuck's house. It wasn't until he started heading up the hill of the residential section of Ketchikan that he was finally able to clear his head and focus on what was coming up.

'Good,' he thought, 'now let's see what an expert can finally tell me about this dad-blasted tooth?'

24

A large residential section of Ketchikan was built into the hillside of Minerva Mountain that sat behind Ketchikan. Land suitable for building was hard to come by and the long-term residents of Ketchikan had built up their community onto the mountain's side. It was a steep hill, but it afforded a great view of the Tongass Narrows between Pennock and Gravina Islands from almost every lot. Eric wound his way up the suburban streets until he found Fairview Avenue and Chuck's house.

Eric had never been to Chuck's house before. Normally, they would shoot the bull in either his office, at his boat, or in a bar downtown. Chuck worked for the fish half of the Alaska Department of Fish and Game. As a state employee, Chuck tried to keep as normal a work week as possible, but during the salmon season, it was nearly impossible. But it was Sunday, and since Eric was in a hurry to have him look at the tooth, he'd invited Eric to his house on the hill.

Fairview Avenue ran horizontally across the slope of Minerva Mountain, and Chuck's house was on the uphill side. It was a nice split-level home that is so suitable for hillside lots. The yard had been terraced with a little front yard that sloped up to the front of the house's lower level, burying half of it in earth to just below the windows set in the walls. A concrete front porch with a railing decorated with potted flowers made an inviting, homey and welcoming entrance to the home. Eric could see that the rest of the lot had been leveled to just under the first story windows all the way around the house to add insulation to the first floor and the back yard had a six foot cedar fence around three-quarters of the house it for privacy.

A middle-aged black man answered the door dressed in jeans, flannel shirt, and hiking shoes. He stood just a little under five eleven with rapidly disappearing black kinky hair that was graying at the temples. His face was round and open, which was at odds with his very dry, droll sense of humor. "Greetings," he said while inviting Eric in by opening the storm door for him. "Come on in," he said dragging it out like he was a game show host.

Eric, box containing the tooth in hand and maps in the other hand, followed Chuck up the stairs into the kitchen.

"You want something to drink?" Chuck offered.

"Does that include beer?"

"Soy-tonly," Chuck said in an imitation of Curly of the Three Stooges. He reached into the fridge and produced two beers, opening one for Eric before opening his own. He indicated to Eric with his beer to sit at the kitchen table.

As they were both seating themselves, Chuck asked, "You've met my wife, Stephanie, before, haven't you?"

"Once. Briefly. She stopped by while we were having a beer downtown on her way home from work. I'd love to say 'Hi' if she's hiding around here somewhere."

"I asked her to take the kids shopping, so we'd have time to talk. She shouldn't be back for another hour or two. She was kind of happy with you, though. She was joking that you should come over more often if it means a directive from the Chief Penny Pincher to go shopping. She was very clear that her absence could be bought."

"That's the McCallister Magic, making points with women, even when I'm not there. What can I say?" The irony of that joke wasn't lost on him, considering his plans for that evening.

"So what's so secret you couldn't talk about it on the phone? To tell you the truth, I figured that if it was so touchy that you didn't want to talk about it over a cell phone, it had to be pretty interesting. I've really been looking forward to you coming up."

Eric reached over to the small bag that he'd set on the table and pulled it toward him. As he started to unzip the bag, he said, "My granddad always told me that when dealing with mules, the first thing that you need to do is get their attention...so here's your two by four upside the head." He pulled the tooth from the box in the bag and placed in on the table in front of Chuck.

Chuck's retort froze on his lips as his eyes locked on the enormous shark's tooth sitting on the table before him. This was so unexpected from anything that he'd imagined Eric wanted to talk to him about. He was stunned by the beautiful specimen of a prehistoric tooth before him. He picked it up and began to examine it. As he did, a cloud of confusion began to build on his face, until he looked up at Eric and said, "I don't understand. This isn't a fossil. Where did you get it?" the questions tumbled out, one on top of the other.

It took Eric the rest of his beer and half of another to bring Chuck up-to-date. "Now that you know what I know, it's your turn. What is this?" he asked, picking up the tooth in his right hand and hefting it.

Chuck took the tooth from him and began to examine it in a more clinical manner. After a pause, he said, "Let's start with the obvious, this is definitely a shark tooth."

"I knew it!" Eric said slapping the table, "I just needed to hear you say it."

Chuck eyed Eric like he would examining a bug, waiting for Eric's exuberant outburst to diminish before continuing with his examination. "It's congruent with the standard confirmation of a Megalodon tooth in most respects, predominantly in size. Typical triangular shape in general, with a change in angularity two-thirds of the way to the root, which terminates in basal cusplets of both ends and a flat interior surface, with slight concavity in the tip-to-root aspect. The well-rounded exterior contour of the tooth's front face surface with the bulk of dentition on the central vertical axis indicates prey of a heavy boned nature. Two well developed heavy root horns to anchor the tooth indicate its ability to withstand heavy lateral forces and the serrated edges also suggests this fish's prey was large and heavily boned, requiring a lot of sawing and cutting to remove bite-size chunks."

"So it's a Megalodon, then?"

"Maybe. Megalodon went extinct about eleven thousand years ago at the end of the last ice age. At least, that's the prevailing theory anyhow. The date of eleven thousand years is based on carbon dating of two Megalodon teeth that were found in shallow water by a couple of Brits, I think about a hundred fifty feet if memory serves me right, off the coast of the Baja Peninsula on the Pacific side. Many in the scientific community felt that the dating analysis results were misinterpreted. Many in the scientific community believe that Megalodon went extinct much earlier based on the preponderance of evidence that Megalodon was an ancient species. Most of the fossils of Megalodon are millions of years old. Megalodon first appears in the fossil record about sixteen million years ago and then suddenly diminishes about one point six million years ago. What fuels the debate is the lack of corresponding evidence of large-scale extinctions at the time of Megalodon's diminishment in the fossil record. The fossil record shows that whale populations, the presumed food source of Megalodon, didn't suddenly die out. No one can explain or come up with a reason why a species would die out when there was plenty of food to be had. That's the current accepted extinction mechanism anyhow, food disruption due to environmental factors.

"I personally don't believe that Megalodon went extinct one and a half million years ago. I'm more in favor of the eleven thousand year peg, myself. The one point six million years ago theory seems to me to be a self-serving argument. Most fossilized Megalodon teeth are found on land, which means they were deposited in the ocean and tectonic plate action slowly conveyed those teeth to land surfaces while fossilizing the teeth.

"If the species went extinct relatively recently, then those teeth are still on the bottom of oceans and, as of yet, haven't been conveyed to the surface. And as far as I know, archeologists are excavating little, if any, of the ocean's floors which, by the way, constitutes the largest terrain surface area of the earth. So essentially, the argument has been 'that based on the fossils found on land, they died out one point six million years ago.

"Now there are some submarine excavations sites, primarily off the coast of the Carolinas, in the lower forty-eight. The data from those sites supports the early extinction date. But my problem with that is this: Megalodon teeth are found on every continent, with the exception of Antarctica, which for obvious reason hasn't been even minimally excavated. So they're one of the most widely dispersed fossils known. Yet all our underwater dating data comes from just a couple of sites. To me, it's far more likely that the dating data coming from the Carolinas is representative of those two geological microcosms, and the dating data has been overly broadened in its extrapolation.

"I think that when a much broader spectrum of data from submarine excavations reflecting the wider distribution is examined, the extinction dates will be closer to the eleven thousand year mark."

"Either way then, it's extinct, right? So what is this from, then?" Eric asked, pointing to the tooth.

"There have been reports," Chuck started, "for decades of remnant populations of Megalodon in the deep waters of the open ocean. It's been popular grist with fiction writers and dime store novelists for decades. But no verifiable evidence has ever been produced of the existence of a remnant population. But on the other hand, deep-sea exploration turns up new species of sharks quite regularly. There are a couple of embarrassing incidents of live or recently dead bodies turning up of sharks long declared extinct by scientists. So it is difficult to say 'never is never.' But the problem goes a little deeper than that."

"I'm not sure I'm following you, Chuck."

"The problem is this: I'm not sure what kind of tooth this is."

Eric looked at Chuck, confusion spreading on his face. "I thought that you said a minute ago that this was 'congruent with the standard confirmation of a Megalodon tooth.' "

"In most regards, remember? Size and general morphology are the most exigent features of this tooth. And Megalodon is the closest known to what is sitting here. But there are some other aspects of this tooth that stop me from conclusively attributing this tooth to a Megalodon." Chuck pulled the tooth towards him and spun the point of the tooth towards Eric. From his seat, he reached up on the counter to grab a ballpoint pen from a cup by the phone to use as a pointer. "See these little points at the gum line where the body of the tooth joins the root dentition? These are called basal cusplets. This is a feature not seen in Megalodon. However, in the fossil record, one of the antecedents and presumed forefathers of Megalodon had this feature. It showed up in the fossil record about twenty five million years ago and then went extinct about sixteen million years ago, just prior to the arrival of Megalodon.

"These cusplets are more reminiscent of the salmon shark. And another thing, the serration pattern is all wrong for Megalodon. The serration pattern on this tooth is more reminiscent of a great white." Chuck suddenly became very ashen and still.

"Are you all right, Chuck?" Eric asked, alarmed by the sudden transformation of his friend.

Chuck took a long time before he answered. "Did I ever tell you how I came to work for the Alaska Department of Fish and Game?"

Eric shook his head no.

"That doesn't surprise me. I rarely tell anybody. Twenty-five years ago I was an aspiring scientist studying *Selachimorphia* - Sharks, if you're not familiar with the Super Order. More specifically, I concentrated on the Order *Lamniformes*, or mackerel sharks, which included fifteen families of sharks: great whites, makos, thresher, basking, nurse, goblin and megamouth, to name a few."

"I didn't know that," said Eric, dumbfounded.

Chuck got up, went to the refrigerator and pulled out two more beers. After popping the two tops, he handed one to Eric and took his to the opposite side of the kitchen where he leaned up against the counter. Deep in thought, Eric could see that he was struggling with how to proceed.

"I was doing my doctoral thesis at the University of Washington under a brilliant scientist named Christina Katzburg. She was just frickin' brilliant and a frickin' train wreck," he said with an edge of bitterness, swigging his beer before continuing. "She'd a huge lab and studied several species, but she specialized in the salmon shark. She got a lot of grant money, most of it from tribes in Alaska, primarily the Sealaska Corporation. She pioneered a lot of research techniques. It was definitely the place to be, and I was thrilled to be selected to do my Ph.D. work under her. Then she got herself killed one rainy night riding her motorcycle after I called her to the lab about and emergency with one of the sharks.

"That was back in the day; I went by my full name, Charles, then. It sounded more important for a scientist, don't you think? Dr. Charles Hudson." After another swig of beer, Chuck continued. "Anyhow, when she died, the grant money dried up and disappeared.

"Me, I was screwed the minute she died. As you know, a doctoral thesis has to be done under the supervision and mentorship of a tenured professor under whom you've studied. She was so far ahead in her field and so specialized, that there were really no other professors I could continue with. I would have had to scrap two years of work on my thesis and start a new thesis favored by a new professor. And that was only if one of the other professors would take me on. The politics in the department were always such that the other professors were jealous of Dr. Katzburg's success. So all of a sudden everyone else was too busy or full with commitments to take on Dr. Katzburg's favorite disciple.

"My other option was to go to another graduate school and do the four years of study again before doing a doctoral thesis. And *that* was highly unlikely. Each doctoral program has its own unique philosophy and approach to the discipline; doctoral candidates are expected to be acolytes and proponents of their mentors' philosophies. I was already branded as a Katzburg disciple, so no quality program was willing to take me on.

"Besides, I was broke, and I couldn't go on living like that for another four years. So I took a job with the Alaska Department of Fish and Game, essentially counting salmon. I always planned to make another run at the Ph. D., but Ketchikan is kind of the armpit of America for Ph.D. studies."

Eric sat silently digesting all this information, wondering what it had to do with the tooth and Chuck's obvious distress.

"Come with me," Chuck commanded as he headed for the stairs outside the kitchen. "I've got something to show you."

"It'll take a few a minutes to find it, but while I'm looking, you can play with the puppies," he said over his shoulder, going down the stairs. "Our dog, Sunchaser, had pups about seven weeks ago; they're just the right age. They're a blast."

At the bottom of the stairs they entered a den that had a TV bookcase, a couple of chairs, and a couch under a large window to the backyard. As soon as they entered the room, the puppies were up pawing and jumping on their pen, making little puppy squeals of joy. "Have a seat on the couch," motioned Chuck. "Here, I'll open the window over it for you - it's a little stuffy down here with the puppies," he said as he swung out the window into the backyard.

Eric sat on the couch while Chuck opened the pen to the puppies. At first they clambered around Chuck's legs until one of them noticed a new victim sitting on the couch. As soon as it started scampering towards Eric, the others took notice and soon a rolling, rollicking, undulating mass of puppies was headed for him.

"I'll be back in a moment," Chuck said as he disappeared through a side door.

The wave of individually colored puppies in black, silver and brown hit the bottom of the couch and Eric's legs. Soon all of them had their paws on the edge of the couch and Eric's knees trying to jump up into his lap. Eric reached down and plucked a black and silver puppy from the adorable mass of little noses and bright eyes. "Hi there, puppy!" Eric spoke in his dog voice and he brought the puppy to his face to nuzzle. His nuzzle was met with a big wet lick of puppy milk breath. "You're so cute, yes, you are," he said dropping the puppy to his lap. The puppy jumped up, put his front paws on Eric's chest while jumping and licking Eric's neck and chin.

This action seemed to spur on the other puppies, and one by one, the other puppies joined their sibling in Eric's lap.

Eric gently pushed the pup down from licking him, but as soon as he did it was replaced by another pup licking his throat. As soon as he pushed that one down, it was replaced by two more. Eric was now giggling like a little boy. The puppies were so animated and cute, their licks tickling his throat.

He felt something soft bump into the back of his head, but was starting to get overwhelmed by all the puppies in his lap and on his chest. He was gently trying to put them down and gain control of the situation. But it was a losing proposition. The puppies found their way back to his chest, their tongues to his neck.

Giggling even harder now, Eric was rolling his head this way and that, trying to elude the tongues of the bouncing, tail wagging balls of love when he felt something soft nudge the back of his head again.

But, Eric was starting to feel a little nauseous from the licking and tickling on his throat. This puppy behavior was a residual behavior from the wild. They would lick their mother's throats to help her regurgitate meat to feed them. It was starting to have that very same affect on him. Eric was starting to panic that he was going to throw up on the couch. He didn't want to stand up, since he knew that some of puppies might get dumped to the floor and hurt. Again, there was a soft bump to the back of his head.

'What was that?' Eric thought, irritated. He dropped his head straight back to see what was annoying him.

His head was resting on the top of the couch before his eyes focused on the inch-and-a-half curved fangs of an Alaskan grey wolf standing over him in the window, the wolf's jaws three inches from his face.

His heart stopped and all awareness of the room left him, as his whole universe became the death grimace of the predator above him. The lips were drawn back, exposing the vicious killing fangs inches from ripping out his throat. The puppies' presence was forgotten.

"Oh look, she likes you. She's smiling,"

Words floated in the room, barely registering on his conscience. Eric was frozen, not breathing as he waited for his throat to be ripped out.

"Come on, Sunchaser, out, out…." Chuck's image came into Eric's peripheral vision as he advanced on the wolf, shooing it out the window. The wolf dutifully backed out the window, leaving Eric's field of vision as Chuck started to grab puppies, two at a time and ferried them back to the pen.

Eric had been so electrified by his near death experience that he sat there numbly while the puppies were cleared from his lap. Ever mindful that there was still a wolf at the back of his neck, as the last pup was lifted, Eric skittered to the end of the couch away from the window. He turned to see the wolf still in the window, her upper lip drawn back, exposing a jaw full of fangs, watching her puppies being put back into the pen.

Eric found his voice now that he realized that he was no longer in danger. "Wolves smile?" was all he could blurt out.

"Sure, just look at her. That's as big a smile as she gets - she must really like you."

'Thank God I was so gentle with those puppies,' he thought. He continued to watch the wolf; the smile never left her face. And he came to realize that the wolf was indeed smiling. Wolves did smile! God, what a smile! It could curdle blood.

"You said that your dog had puppies! For Christ's

sake, you could have told me that it was a wolf," Eric said with the hint of an accusation.

"Wolf…dog…who really pays attention?" Chuck replied with a straight face, his dry sense of humor coming to the fore. "Besides, technically I was right. A wolf is a dog."

Eric had somewhat recovered from his shock, and he understood that his anger now was just a natural response to the fear that he'd experienced just moments ago.

"Alright, alright. But next time give a guy a little warning, will you?" And then another idea hit Eric. "Hey, isn't it illegal to own and keep wolves as pets? Where'd you get Sunchaser anyhow?"

"I got her from one of the game agents that I know. He found her when she was a pup; her mother was killed by a bear. Yah, it might be illegal for *you* to own a wolf, but I like to think of it as one of the perks of the job. And, hey, if you're the law enforcer and you can't bend a few laws here and there, then what fun is it to have a badge?" Chuck lamented dryly.

"Anyways, I found it," Chuck said, drawing Eric's attention away from the wolf and back across the room.

Eric glanced up to see Chuck holding up a plastic gallon zip lock bag that held what appeared to be a lab record book that was burned around the edges.

25

The returning killer whales made their way to the center of the bay where the super-pod was assembled. They were pelted with questions and concerns about the missing whales and the success of their mission.

Those questions were met with stoic silence. Prior to arrival, the remaining members of the search group had decided that it would be best to wait until the Council of Elders had been assembled before they announced the death of another five whales and the details of the failed attack on the Giant Shark.

The tension that the remnants brought to the super-pod was palatable. Rapidly, the eldest pod members were assembled. The survivors started their description of events, telling of their search and subsequent encounter with the Giant Shark. In detail, they related the death of each killer whale based on what they knew or surmised from what they learned from the other killer whales before they died.

As they recounted the deaths, wails and cries of anguish erupted from the family members present of the dead whales and those hovering on the fringe to hear what had happened. Several times, the survivors had to stop, waiting until the family members could recover enough for them to go on or until they were escorted away by other family members who came to comfort them.

When the survivors had finished, an eerie silence fell over the assemblage.   An Elder recommended that they adjourn and reassemble tomorrow to decide their course of action.   This thought was quickly seconded and the group disbanded.

The mourning for the slain whales started in earnest upon adjournment. Five tight little clusters of the family members floated near the surface giving voice to their anguish.   At the center of the grieving whales were the mates of the dead, surrounded by their sisters, mothers and daughters, all rubbing and caressing each other for mutual support and comfort.   Because sound travels so efficiently in water, the entire super-pod became partner to the grieving families.

After a while, the intensity of the bereavement forced many, mostly younger males, from the bay to seek solitude and serenity in the channel beyond the bay.   In twos and threes, the young males mixed and matched, formed and dissolved into conversational groups.   The common theme of their conversation was their desire for revenge and the belief that they could, if given the chance, teach the Giant Shark a lesson.

Late in the afternoon, whales started to filter out into the channel in search of their evening meal, those too affected by grief remained in the bay and family members brought food back for them.

The surviving members of the hunting party had made their way back to their mates and matrilines.   There, exhausted, most chose just to sleep.   After their arduous travel, they were oddly comforted by the sound of distraught whales about them. It reminded them that they were back with their pods and also that others were on guard against the Giant Shark.

Even so, the Pod Leader slept fitfully. His dreams were haunted by visions of the Giant Shark rising out of the depths to disembowel him. Twice he lurched awake from this dream before finally settling down for deep sleep. Toward the evening, his mother, sisters and nieces brought him some meager rations of salmon carried back miles for him to eat. He was tired, but thankful to quiet the rumbling in his stomach, even if partially.

The rendezvous would normally have broken up several days before, but it had been prolonged pending the return of the hunting party. These rendezvous were only possible at the peak of the salmon run. One hundred fifty plus killer whales concentrated in one area wreaked havoc on the ecology of the waters surround the gathering. Even though new salmon swam into the surrounding waters on an hourly basis, the influx wasn't enough to feed the collective predators. They were forced to swim wider and wider afield to find sufficient food. To supplement their diets, the killer whales had eaten every seal and sea otter within ten miles of the rendezvous, and that circle of ecological blight was spreading daily. It now took several hours of travel each way for the members of the rendezvous to find a plentiful feeding ground, and that wasn't counting the necessary hunting time to collect enough food to satisfy their voracious appetites.

It was for this reason that the rendezvous was rotated among the different Clan's territories each year. It took several years for a rendezvous site to recover ecologically.

The salmon runs had already peaked and were now starting to ebb; the swath of lifeless, foodless waters around the rendezvous was growing wider by the day. Yet no one was interested in leaving the Northern Clan's territory. Fear gripped the Clans. The Southern Clan didn't want to return to waters that they knew to be inhabited by the killer whale-devouring Giant Shark. The Middle Clan knew that the Giant Shark could easily migrate into their territory within a few days. They all knew that the only safe place for the moment was the Northern Clan's waters far to the north of the threat.

All were aware that the food stocks were starting to dwindle. The Northern Clan members knew that their territory would recover eventually from the food depletion of this unexpected overstay of their guests, but only if their guests left sooner rather than later. An overstay of too great a length may have a negative impact on the long-term survivability of their territory.

Fear and tension among the Clans was starting to create friction between the clan members. The death of one of their own in the hunting party had brought home the threat to the members of the Northern Clan. Yet it was still seen as a far away threat.

It was in this climate the next day that the Council of Elders formed around midday. Clearly, their existence was threatened, but what to do about it? Just as clearly, they were unprepared to deal with the crisis. Ideas were proposed, and then just as quickly dismissed, until a silence filled the assemblage.

Having seen what the Giant Shark could do, first to his pod and then the hunting party, the Pod Leader felt compelled to give voice to what all had already accepted, at some level: the Tribe of the Three Clans couldn't deal with this threat on their own. They lacked the skills necessary to bring down an adversary as big, fast and powerful as the Giant Shark. They needed help.

This was greeted roundly but reluctantly. The obviousness of that acknowledgement seemed to bring relief to the Council. This was an unprecedented situation. Never before had the Three Clans Tribes ever had a situation that it couldn't resolve. An even thornier issue was from whom to seek help. They were, after all, the Monarchs of the Seas. Again, a silence fell over the Council.

And again it was the Pod Leader who stated the obvious, that this Giant Shark represented a threat to all whales, even the other Tribes of killer whales. It was their help they should seek. Envoys should be sent to the other tribes, the Ocean Travelers Tribe and even to the Open Water Tribe, if they existed. These were tribes that were known or rumored to hunt the Great Whales and would have the knowledge of how to kill this shark.

The boldness of this offering stilled the Council as each pondered its merits and potential for both succor and disaster. The Three Clans Tribe had no formal relationship with the other tribes. Occasionally, random encounters had happened with the Open Water Tribe. And after some brief inquisitiveness was satisfied, both groups had gone their own way. They were disliked because they were different. Could they work with this tribe? Would it spell success or would their differences of culture and language lead to more deaths of Three Clans Tribe members. And what about the Ocean Traveler Tribe? The Ocean Traveler Tribe was nothing more than a myth or fairytale; no one had ever actually seen or met a member of that tribe in their collective memory.

A buzz of dozens of voices broke out as these issues were bandied back and forth until a consensus was reached that there was more merit than peril, and that envoys should be sent to the Ocean Travelers Tribe. It was reasoned that if the Open Water Tribe existed, their neighbors, the Ocean Travelers Tribe, would be the ones to know. And through the Ocean Travelers Tribe's help, perhaps they could find the Open Water Tribe.

The envoys were to explain their peril and the threat to all Orcas, and they should ask the Ocean Travelers to send their best, strongest hunters, for only those had a chance to kill the Giant Shark. Any who were brave enough to hunt the Giant Shark would rendezvous off the second point of land in from the southern entrance to the archipelago in ten days time with another hunting party of the Three Clans Tribe. There, they would make their war plans. And begin the hunt.

The Three Clans Tribe would hold in the territory of the Northern Clan until word was sent of their success or failure.

But first they needed envoys to seek the other tribes. The council called for volunteers who had contact or had swum with the Ocean Travelers Tribe before. Those who volunteered would set out tomorrow after the midday gathering with final instructions from the Council of Elders.

The Council of Elders adjourned to rest before seeking food for the evening feeding session.

The next day, the seven volunteers presented themselves when the Council of Elders reconvened. The Pod Leader was among them. The group of volunteers was a mix of young and old, all were males. He recognized many of the volunteers as part of the bachelor group he'd been with when he'd encountered the Ocean Travelers. The Council of Elders organized the seven volunteers into two groups, being sure that there was a member of the Northern clan in each group to show them the fastest path to the open sea and a member of the Southern Clan to find the rendezvous point at the southern entrance to the archipelago. One group was to proceed north in search of the Open Water Tribe, the other to the south in search. The Pod Leader was selected to go south.

The Council repeated their decisions of the day before so that the volunteers were clear on the when and where of what the envoys would need to convey. When there were no more questions, the entire population of the rendezvous escorted them to the bay's entrance. Once out of the bay, the group headed in a westerly direction under the guidance of two of the volunteers from Northern Clan. Many of the younger and adolescent whales swam alongside them for many miles whistling and squealing encouragement before dropping off and returning.

The envoys swam at their best traveling speed for six hours before taking a few hours before sunset to feed. The salmon were more plentiful here outside the sweep of foraging killer whales from the rendezvous, so it didn't take long to fill their bellies. This trip had a different feel than the outward leg of his last journey. The younger whales had started to boast and brag about their desires to meet and best the Giant Shark, just like the last trip. The envoys were aware that the Pod Leader's pod had been slaughtered by the Giant Shark and that he was one of the survivors of the last hunting group. When he didn't join their banter, which he met with knowing silence, the boasting soon died out.

The following morning, after another productive feeding session, they again made their best speed, taking low angled arcs from the water to breath while cruising around two-thirds their top speed. Time was of the essence if they were to find the other tribes and make the rendezvous in time.

About midmorning, the passage they had been traveling opened upon the Pacific Ocean. At the mouth of the passage, they stopped and took a few minutes to reconfirm their instructions and timetable before splitting into two groups to head in their assigned directions. They bade each other farewell and diverged into their designated directions.

26

Eric followed Chuck upstairs, back to the kitchen. He took a minute to wash the puppy slobber from his face, neck and hands before retaking his seat at the kitchen table with Chuck.

"OK, so what is it that you found?"

"Remember when I said I worked for a brilliant scientist? Well this," Chuck said tapping his finger on the plastic covered book on the table, "is the train wreck."

"I believe the exact words you used were 'frickin' train wreck.'"

"Amen to that."

"Alright, other than a painful trip down memory lane, what does this have to do with large sharks that eat small boats?" Eric asked a little exasperated.

"Oh ye of little faith, I shall enlighten you." Chuck deadpanned. "Dr. Katzburg had Ph.D.s in genetics and marine biology. And as it turned out, she had a God complex, too. Her research into shark reproductivity was, and still is, cutting edge. No one else has been able to put together the type of lab facilities that she had. She'd access to all the University's genetic research facilities and equipment, which she used to sequence several shark species DNA genomes.

"Anyhow, she got this wild idea one day: what would be the difference between sequencing live DNA and extinct DNA. It turns out that she was able to extract and then organize fragment DNA recovered from Megalodon tooth cores. She was able to reconstruct ninety-five percent of the DNA sequence of a Megalodon. But she had a problem. She didn't know if the organized fragments were actually correct and therefore viable. So she used gene splicing techniques, grafting her gene sequences to salmon shark embryos and filled the gaps in the sequences with great white and salmon shark DNA, both of which she'd handy. She was able to create several viable embryos that she implanted into a salmon shark in the lab.

"And then she died," Chuck said abruptly.

Eric sensed a connection emerging, but still didn't see it. His face must have conveyed that, because Chuck resumed.

"She never told a soul what she was doing. When she died, I was cleaning out her desk and found her lab diary." He tapped the burnt book again. "I started reading and was utterly astounded. I was supposed to be one of the graduate students in charge of the day-to-day activities of the lab, and I had no idea that this was going on. I took her lab book to the department head and showed him her diary. The guy turned as white as a ghost when he read what she'd been doing and ordered me to burn the book, which I did promptly, thinking that I could still salvage my career. But I couldn't let her work go up in flames like that, so I pulled this," waving at the book, "out of the fire.

"The apartment head, a real slick operator named

Hendles, probably saw his career go up in flames when he read that book. A famed scientist that he'd some level of responsibility over was building 'Franken-fish,' and nobody knew. If he tried to salvage her work, the grant sponsors would have audited the lab. And the audit would have found a mysteriously pregnant shark without definitive documentation. It would have caused an inquiry, and the whole bloody mess could have derailed his career.

"But here's the real corker, wait for it...the pregnant shark had already been released back into the wild. In Puget Sound around the San Juan Islands. Hard to put that one back in the bottle. So, everything was shut down in a big hurry.

"You know, I always felt that Hendles was behind my not being accepted for my doctoral thesis by the other professors, but I could never prove it. I think it was probably professional jealousy and a little nudge from Hendles. But now, I think he just wanted me gone because I'd read her diary and knew what she'd done. I was just a loose end that needed to be swept away."

"Are you saying that this," Eric began waving at the tooth, "is your doctor's 'Franken-fish'?" Eric was showing disappointment and anger. "Someone's lab 'Oooops'?"

"I don't know. I simply don't know. Even with a DNA test we truly won't know. She kept track of the DNA sequences she used from other sharks somewhere else, probably on her home computer. A lot of her data was encrypted, which makes sense. Researchers are kind of anal about secrecy until they're ready to disclose. The computer file for the sequencing of the DNA she was trying to manipulate would have been huge. Way more than she could put in her lab diary, which is generally used to record methodology and results. And, the university wanted it swept under the rug, so they just probably had the disk reformatted or degaussed. Who knows what happened to her home computer."

"I have already made arrangements for DNA analysis with my boss, Sid, in Portland," Eric said staring at the kitchen wall, trying to assimilate all this new information. "I'll FedEx the tooth to him on Monday. He said he'd run DNA tests as soon as he gets the tooth. The more data we have, the better. Hopefully, we'll have results by the end of the week."

Chuck brought the conversation around again to what they both knew must be done. "We're going to have to find the shark. We may never be able to determine whether this is a man-made species or an ancient remnant species, but the undeniable facts are that it's here now and it's alive. There might be more, so we have to find it and obtain a specimen."

"By 'obtain a specimen' you mean kill it, right? I'm not set up on the *Pacific Chanteuse* to kill something as big as this shark." This was more than just Eric's philosophy of studying live creatures rather than dead specimens coming to the forefront. "Besides, I just don't think that's necessary at this point. I think that we can verify the fish's existence if we can tag it and monitor its movements. If it's tagged and we know where to find it, then we can take any doubting Thomas to it at any point. Proper documentation, recordings and video should suffice in lieu of a corpse. Besides, we have the tooth as physical evidence of its existence. And another thing, there's a whole lot of *we* going on here. What exactly are *we* talking about?"

"I'm going with you to search for this fish. When do we leave?"

'I don't know,' Eric thought, *'this is a mighty risky venture, with a high risk someone might get hurt. But, on the other hand, this will be impossible to do by myself.'*

"Tuesday morning around eight. The *Pacific Chanteuse* is tied up down at the city docks," Eric said, offering his hand to Chuck. "Welcome aboard, matey. Aaaarrgghh," he said with his best smile and pirate imitation accompanying the shake.

Chuck walked Eric to the door and saw him out with a wave, promising to see him at the dock Tuesday morning. All that had happened in the last two hours filled Eric's head as he tried to sort out all of Chuck's revelations. He felt that he was on a slippery slope. Every time something became clear about the tooth, it was instantly obscured by other possibilities. All he still had was a faulty eyewitness, computer simulations, good video images without scale, and a lone tooth that conformed to nothing. He felt like he was trying to catch smoke with a net. Perhaps the only thing to end these ups and downs was going to be obtaining a specimen.

About three-quarters of the way home, he remembered what it was that he'd to do this evening. Now the sensation of the slippery slope really set in. He was going to change everything about his relationship with Melanie. As he thought about it, he realized that he'd been looking at this all wrong.

He was worried that his proposal would change everything between Melanie and him, which it could, if she said no. But really, what his proposal would do is ensure that nothing changed between them. In fact, it would guarantee that it would continue just the way it was now. As he realized that his commitment to marriage was nothing more than the extension of his perfect life with Melanie, a warm glow set in. He smiled all the way home.

After parking at the apartment complex, he realized that he had the perfect way to smuggle in Melanie's ring without her seeing it. All he'd to do was put it in the bag with the tooth. Hiding things in plain sight was always the best... and the most fun.

Eric came into the apartment swinging the tooth bag a little overenthusiastically and whistling to see Melanie preparing dinner. As soon as she saw him, she went to the fridge to pour him a fine glass of Bookwalter Winery chardonnay from little winery in the Yakima Valley of Washington state. One of Melanie and Eric's favorite pass-times was to explore the wineries that lined Washington's Yakima Valley from Walla Walla in the south to The Gap at Yakima in the north. There were probably eighty to a hundred wineries in that area, some making incredibly refined wines while others, like Bookwalter Winery, made high quality wines at a reasonable price that made it affordable to drink corked wine everyday. It was one of the first wineries they had ever visited. It had started as a mom and pop operation, but they soon became a victim of success and had to expand to meet the demand for their products. But the one thing they never outgrew was the mom and pop hominess and their friendly approach to their visitors. It was for this reason that Melanie and Eric snuck off a couple times a year to visit and buy wine. They also brought with them a case every year to Alaska. It was one of their shared little rituals that they both loved.

Melanie delivered the glass of wine with a quick kiss before darting back to the stove, while Eric plopped the tooth bag on the kitchen table. "How'd your visit with Chuck go? Did you learn anything?" Melanie asked with her back to Eric, stirring a pot.

'*Are you kidding*?! *What a loaded question.*' Eric's mind screamed. "Yah, a little…," he replied, making a joke to himself. "I'm joshing you, sweetie," he said gently. "There's so much going on, I hardly know where to start."

"Well start by getting the bag off the kitchen table - dinner is ready and I need you to set the table."

"OK," Eric replied cheerfully, taking the bag and setting it on the coffee table in the living room in front of the sofa.

Over dinner, Eric proceeded to tell Melanie what he learned about Chuck's past, the mad scientist he'd worked for, and Chuck's decision to accompany Eric on the search for the shark. Melanie was intently focused on the flow of information and asked clarifying questions to make sure she was getting it all. He scrupulously avoided telling her about the wolf encounter until they were cleaning up the kitchen, knowing full well that she would become upset with Chuck, and he didn't want to do anything to upset her tonight. He was just as scrupulous about avoiding mention about the tooth's morphology until they had refilled the glasses and adjourned to the couch in the living room.

With Melanie settled into the couch, Eric resumed his narrative. "Chuck went through the tooth's characteristics, explaining them point by point. Let me show you...," he said, getting to his knees in the space between the couch and the coffee table, his back to Melanie. "Wait 'til you see this little gem," he said over his shoulder as he unzipped the tooth bag's zipper. He grabbed the little box sitting on top of the tooth.

'Please say, yes, please say yes...,' Eric prayed.

In one smooth motion, he pivoted to Melanie on one knee opening the little taupe velveteen box to expose the ring inside and presented it to Melanie. "But first, I need to make you a promise. I promise to love and worship you if you'll be my wife. Will you marry me?"

She just starred blankly at Eric. Moments passed like hours.

"*Ooohh shit! She's going to say no!!*" Eric's mind screamed, as he watched her face go blank and an empty stare settle over her face. It was the deer in the headlights look. In a microsecond, Eric evaluated his options: *'I can't go back and retract what I just asked her; I can't hold and sit here on my knee forever. That leaves one option: Charge!! In for a penny in for a pound.'* "I said, will you marry me?"

That seemed to break Melanie's reverie. A flood of joy washed over her face as she smiled from ear to ear while leaning forward, taking Eric's face in her hands. "Yes," was all she said before planting another one of her conscious-sucking, mind-gasket-blowing kisses of hers. She tenderly released him and took the box from his hand to examine the ring.

"I didn't know what size of ring to get you, so we can have that sized this week. In fact, this is just a place-holding until you and I can pick out the right ring when we get back to Portland in the fall." The words just seemed to gush from Eric's mouth.

"Oh, this is just beautiful, Eric," she said taking in the ring, and the meaning behind its symbolism. She reached over and turned up the lamp next to them to better see the ring, while she slipped it on her finger.

Eric got back on the couch and threw an arm around Melanie. She turned quickly to place another kiss, this time on his cheek.

At this point, Eric realized that there was no going back to the topic of the tooth tonight. He leaned forward and zipped shut the tooth's bag, closing his mind too, to that topic. *'It could wait until the morning,'* he thought, *'I have more important things to discuss at the moment.'*

The next morning, Eric awoke to the sounds of Melanie trying to be quiet in the bathroom while she prepared herself for work. He figured he might as well get up because if he wanted to use the truck, he was going to have to take her to work. Besides, it would give her an excuse to use the "F" word. *'Oh, thank you, but I don't need a ride home. My fiancé is picking me up.'* In one smooth move he'd gone from "the boyfriend" to "my fiancé." He was really coming up in the world.

It had been too late last night when the smoke cleared to call her parents. But tonight she planned to have Eric pick her up a little earlier than normal so she could get home and make the calls, which was fine for Eric. He didn't have much to do today. He had to buy groceries and get the boat over to Tongass Boat Works so that the special equipment Sid had sent him could be installed. His new gear and replacement skiff had come in yesterday, and the boatyard had picked it up for him even though it had been Sunday. During salmon season, boatyards and mechanics worked as long and whenever as needed, gladly. They would have all winter to catch up on their reading.

Eric had to admit, he'd enjoyed co-habituating with Melanie over the last couple of years. But in the back of his mind, there was something that had bothered him, the feeling like his life with Melanie, 'living in sin,' was a lark or something. *'What was the old saying…oh, yah. 'Why buy the cow, when you can get the milk for free?'* At first he thought the phrase hit the nail on the head. Obviously, a bachelor and scholar had coined that one, but over time, the connotation that Melanie was a commodity or equivalent to something with four legs started to sour in Eric's mind. His status as 'The Fiancé' brought a new legitimacy to Eric's perception. And he was quite happy with this newfound status of a soon-to-be legitimate domicile partner.

Still lying in bed, eyes closed, Eric heard the bathroom door in the hall open and the pad of Melanie's feet to the bedroom door. A slight rattle of the doorknob was followed by a tiny squeak of the hinges.

"Time to get up, Mister Man-of-Leisure. C'mon, you've got to get up and get going if you're going to give me a ride to work." This was followed by the bedsprings sagging on the edge as Melanie sat, the smell of her fragrant shampoo floating to him before her hair brushed his face, and a kiss landed upon his forehead. Then Melanie was up and gone.

"I'm up," he called after her. Eric, always an early riser, had slept in this morning a little longer than usual, perhaps due to all the nervous energy of last night before proposing, perhaps because a burden of conscience had been lifted by Melanie's "yes," or perhaps because he was now wrapped in a newfound sense of security in the future.

After a quick run through his morning routine, he arrived to the breakfast table to find that Melanie had prepared eggs and bacon for them. He had no more than brought the glass of orange juice to his lips when Melanie started to chide him, "You really know how to blindside a girl."

Eric stopped in mid-swallow, his newfound security evaporating like mist in a strong wind. His mind froze. *'Is she going to change her mind and say 'No' now?'*

"I mean, there you are telling me details of what is one of the most important developments in marine biology, your career, this summer and 'BOOM!' you slip in "Will you marry me?' in between sentences. It was a good thing I decided to marry you a long time ago. Otherwise that little stunt might not have turned out so well."

Eric swallowed.

"You're still going to pick me up after work, aren't you?" Melanie seamlessly continued.

The sensation and feelings returned to Eric's throat as soon as he realized that, Melanie was just giving vent to being so thoroughly surprised. *'I guess I could have telegraphed what was coming a little better,'* Eric thought to himself. *'But wait a second - aren't you supposed to surprise them with the proposal? Now she's telling me that I should have warned her about surprising her? This makes no sense at all! God, why do they make it so hard to marry them?!'*

Eric was one of the very rare men gifted with the sense of when not to say anything to a woman. Maybe it was because he was a little older and established. Regardless, he knew it was in his best interest not to rise to the 'blindsided' comment. "About five o'clock, if that's okay with you."

"Yah, that should be fine," she commented, finishing the last of her meal. The rest of the morning resolved into the standard routine. Eric dropped her off at work, a small single-story building towards the north end of Tongass Narrows about five miles from downtown, before heading to the grocery store to get food and supplies.

He and Chuck planned to go out for two weeks to look for the shark. He wasn't sure if Chuck was a big eater or ate like a bird, but the one thing he was sure of was that he didn't want to come back early because they'd run out of food. So to be on the safe side, Eric bought what he thought two men would eat and then doubled it.

It took two grocery carts to get it all to the truck. The boxboy who was helping Eric, jumped up into the bed of the truck while Eric handed him bags from the carts. With the food secure, Eric headed for the city dock's parking lot.

Luckily, he found a parking spot close to the ramp that lead down to the boat. Eric grabbed the FedEx box containing the tooth he'd packed last night off the seat next to him and tucked it up under one arm. He didn't want to leave his scientific find unattended, if even for a brief second. Closing the door, he grabbed a bag of groceries out of the truck's bed that needed to be refrigerated for the first trip to the boat. Not that they would have spoiled if they sat in the back of the truck for a little while, as it had just barely cracked the sixties, but still it was better to be safe than sorry when it came to spoiled food.

Bag in hand, Eric headed for the dock ramp, organizing the next sequence of events in his head. It was because he was preoccupied that he didn't notice the brown sausage-shaped dog with short legs and thick tail at the bottom of the ramp. When he did notice, he was struck by its odd appearance until he realized that it was a sea otter. Eric stopped. The sea otter glanced up at Eric, sniffed at him, gave him a cursory once over and then went on about his business unconcerned. The otter gave the deck of the dock a quick sniff and then bounded a few feet down the dock to give that spot a quick sniff, its back highly arched. He bounced a few feet to the right, another sniff. This time he'd found a little morsel as his little teeth pried out a nugget from between the boards of the dock.

Sea otters were common in Southeastern Alaska and in the Tongass Narrows. For those brazen enough to come close to the waterfront, a bountiful excess of fish and fish parts could be had from the inevitable cast off and spillage of the millions of fish that passed through the collective boats and canneries. Weighing close to fifty-five pounds and measuring five feet from nose to tail tip, the otter bounded like a slinky over the dock, checking for food morsels that humans so easily cast off.

Eric followed the sea otter down the dock. He saw plenty of otters every year, but never this close and never on land. They had a completely different personality on land it seemed, full of energy and curiosity. And they were just so darned cute and comical. Eric followed the otter closer, thoroughly entertained by its antics. He followed it down the dock, watching it dither here and there, the otter totally unconcerned by his presence.

Unintentionally, Eric crept closer and closer, until finally, after twenty yards of travel, the otter's space had been invaded. The otter whirled on Eric, opened its mouth to show him the teeth imbedded in the light tan fur of his face and hissed menacingly at him.

"I get it, I get it," Eric said to the otter, "I'll back off. Sorry."

Eric took two steps back, and the otter resumed his canvassing of the dock. Eric followed, but this time he made sure not to crowd the otter.

After another twenty yards they arrived at Eric's boat.

Eric had been so enraptured with watching the sea otter that he didn't see the man leaning against his boat two-thirds of the way down the hull until the sea otter bounded over to stand directly in front of the man. On one front paw, the otter bobbed his head up and down twice. The man bent over and said something softly to the otter. The otter bobbed his head twice more and then disappeared over the edge of the dock at the man's feet.

The man stood up and looked into Eric's astonished face. "Hello. My name is George Greenlee. I hear that you've been asking around about strange happenings with a large gray fish."

27

The trio of killer whales had been traveling south for a full day and a half when they heard the faint, brief strains of killer whale calls well off the coastline they had been traveling. Sound waves propagate in odd ways in the ocean. Sound can be reflected off the surface or submarine floor, bent by changes in salinity or temperature. These sounds led to the open ocean.

The trio of whales had lived their whole lives within sight of land in the inside waters of Alexander Archipelago. Even when transiting the open waters of Queen Charlotte Straits, they could still see the large island, Queen Charlotte Island, hulking in the horizon's vapors to the west. Subconsciously, the whales had stuck within visual range of the coast as they searched for the tribe of Ocean Travelers who moved in the deep waters off the coast. It wasn't that they were afraid of deep water. They were killer whales; they were rulers of the oceans and had been raised to fear no creature or thing, at least until now. But every animal has its habits, favorite haunts, and comfort zone. Now the faint calls of the Ocean Traveler killer whale tribe were beckoning them to the open sea, though how far they couldn't tell. They hesitated for a few moments, each trying to get the best bearing on the faint calls. Then the Pod Leader veered hard into the echoes and dared the other two to follow him, which he knew they would. Their families lives depended upon them.

With powerful strokes of their flukes, the killer whale trio speed-swam at the horizon. Alternately leaping from the water in a low arc intended to allow them to exhale and inhale completely before re-entering the water, the trio soon put the sight of land behind them, covering miles of open water quickly.

Although the Pod Leader had lived all his life within sight of land and navigated by land marks, he had no trepidations about leaving it behind. His sense of direction was keen and he could tell, though he knew not how, which direction the sun would come up in and set. His sense was so keen that it could tell when there were anomalies or changes in what his senses told him, actually making those deviations navigational marks in the open sea.

The Ocean Travelers were less vocal a tribe than the Tribe of the Three Clans. It would be difficult to find them in the vast reaches of the open ocean, since they were accustomed to not advertising their presence to their prey. The killer whales' abilities to use echolocation to interpret the seas and their surroundings had its limitations. Larger whales were able to generate larger amounts of sonic energy in their trains, which in turn allowed them to 'see' a larger area around them. Killer whales, one of the largest of the porpoise family, were the size of a medium whale and couldn't cover as much of the seascape as their larger cousins. However, if the trains didn't hit an object, they continued in the ocean until their energy was dissipated. With luck, the trio would be able to get close enough to hear the Ocean Travelers' train and follow them back to their source like a beacon. The trains were directional, their energy projected ahead of the whales. The luck would come in cutting their path ahead of the Ocean Travelers.

After several miles the trio heard a brief series of trains before they were gone. Since sound waves travel five times faster in water than in air, they were able to adjust their course with a level of precision. They were taking a bit of a gamble with the strategy of speed swimming in their search. A whale's skull was a marvel of engineering for underwater acoustics, from a liquid and foam filled inner ear that allowed hearing at crushing at depths, to structures that let them to use their jaw as an antenna to collect sounds and channel them to the ear. But all this engineering could not overcome the problem of the liquid medium of their world, friction. The high rate of speed at which they were traveling caused water to pass over their skin with more friction creating high and low pressure zones, which created sound frequencies that interfered with their ability to hear making it harder to pinpoint the sounds of other whales. The overall effect was that their hearing was diminished somewhat, but they could still hear very effectively. By making sure only one whale at a time was airborne to breathe, the other two could keep survey of the ocean's sounds.

After twenty minutes of travel, the trio heard another series of echolocation trains, this time much closer. The trio was homing in on their goal.

One of the dilemmas the trio faced was how exactly to approach the Ocean Travelers Tribe. They were interlopers in their territory, but they needed their help. They didn't want to anger the Ocean Travelers before they had even had a chance to parlay. If the trio called out blindly, they could spoil a hunt by alerting the Ocean Travelers' prey of the presence of killer whales. If they called out, and the Ocean Travelers didn't want to talk to them, they could merely swim away without even speaking with them. The trio's best idea to approaching was to say nothing and move directly at the pod of Ocean Travelers and then hover within visual distance and let the pod make the first move. It was highly unlikely that the approach of the trio would go unnoticed by the pod's collective echolocation or hearing.

But again, this was all predicated on the belief that the Ocean Travelers' mentality as Kings and Queens of the Sea, common to all killer whales, would make them more curious than distrustful.

As they got closer, they heard echolocation trains being targeted upon them by several individuals. This allowed the trio to now pinpoint the pod's location and move directly at it. In unison, the trio dropped out of speed-swimming a thousand yards from the pod. In the ocean, whales were accustomed to the open space. Things tended to happen slowly, with much inertia and momentum, so it was best to slowly approach the pod.

Whales consider a much larger space about them as their personal space, especially a whale approaching on an intercept course. This cultural norm was based on one very simple fact: They had no muscle group designated to make them stop. They might change directions to bleed off speed or change their angle of attack through the water to increase drag, but to stop they relied primarily on the friction and resistance of their bodies to bring them to a stop. But evolution had spent countless tens of thousands of years streamlining their bodies, reducing their energy needs to move in the heavy medium of water, which compounded the problem of stopping. Whales, as social animals built for effortless forward motion with no brakes, living in vast expanses of open waters without obstructions had their entire culture designed sideways. That is, all social activity happened to their sides and was one of the evolutionary pressures that placed all whales' eyes and earless ear canals on the side of their bodies so they could see and hear those beside them. A polite whale was a whale traveling beside them in full sight and hearing, with enough distance between them to see when the other whales changed direction.

This need for a lateral society also made the whale one of the anomalies of the mammalian world. Most predators had frontally focused eyes to provide binocular vision to aid in prey acquisition and calculation of distance. But since echolocation was every bit as good as binocular vision, if not better, at determining range to objects and prey in front of the whale, evolutionarily speaking, the whale with binocular vision may have had redundant forward sensing abilities, but was socially inept, and unlikely to produce progeny. Perhaps it was for this reason that they found other non-prey mammals, like humans, unsettling. Humans had a face-to-face culture. They had a tendency to come straight at whales, which wasn't socially acceptable, and somewhat threatening. The Pod Leader had been reminded of this when in his exhausted state, he made the bad decision to head directly at the super pod and was greeted by angry whales reacting to a socially uncouth and challenging approach in the presence of young whales.

In the vast expanse of the ocean, they expected that nothing would be in front of them. So only occasionally did they fire out echolocation trains to search the waters in front of them for objects and obstacles. Their senses of sight and sound were always on and targeted sideways where all the social action was, watching and listening for social cues. Perhaps that was why the Three Clans Tribe was so much more vocal than the other tribes - their chosen habitat was more confined and full of obstacles that required more teamwork and vocalizations to keep from injuring themselves.

Unlike sight and sound that were always on, echolocation had to be consciously performed. In their haste and excitement, they had forgotten to echolocate and it had left the killer whales of the first hunting pod vulnerable in their head-on attacks. Those killer whales that had quit echolocating when contact was imminent didn't see the Giant Shark's sudden movements. Because they had attacked from a vector where they couldn't use their always-on senses, they had been blinded at the last second and had paid with their lives for their overconfidence.

The trio circled wide to the left of the pod and came back on a course that had them traveling parallel to the Ocean Travelers pod. They swam for several minutes alongside the pod, allowing the Ocean Travelers to move closer and look them over. Finally, the pod moved to approach the three slow swimming killer whales. As a final act of submission the trio stopped and floated on the water while the seven whales of the Ocean Travelers pod formed a circle around the trio of envoys. Ocean Travelers continued to swim around the envoys slowly, saying nothing, but watching their every move. They weren't threatening, but they wanted to make sure the envoys knew who was in charge.

The Ocean Travelers not only spoke a different dialect, they also differed in appearance. The dorsal fins of the Ocean Travelers were closer to the midpoint of their backs and much more sharply pointed. The females' dorsal fins were much more pronounced in this physical difference.

The envoys were happy for the opportunity to rest. They wanted to be at their best. On their way out to the ocean, the trio had decided to let the Pod Leader start the dialogue and present their needs because he'd spent more time among the Ocean Travelers than either one of them.

Finally, a large male of the Ocean Travelers asked what they were doing in the territory of the Ocean Travelers Clan. The dialect was different from that spoken of the Three Clan Tribe's, but it was similar enough for them to understand. Killer whales used a lot of verbal and non-verbal communications, their minds were also capable of interpreting sound impulses into a three-dimensional understanding of their surroundings. All that interpretive capability allowed them to understand the gist of what was being said.

The Pod Leader responded by telling them that they were in search of the brave hunters of the Ocean Traveler Clan and that the envoys before them came on behalf of the Three Clans Tribe.

This statement was met with silence as they continued to circle. This was unprecedented. No one of either tribe could recall having ever heard of an event where one tribe sought out the other. Again, it was the large male of the Ocean Travelers who asked what business the Tribe of the Three Clans had with them.

The Pod Leader answered his question by telling them that a Giant Shark, big as the largest humpback whale, had invaded the territory of the Tribe of the Three Clans. This Giant Shark had already slaughtered nine killer whales, including females, children, and five of the largest males of the clan sent to hunt it down and kill it.

A female asked why would this concern the Ocean Travelers.

The Pod Leader asked her a question in return: Whose children would the shark eat next once the Three Clans Tribe was gone?

This started a flurry of dialogue among the whales. Some argued that it was none of their concern; others were concerned for their young. Still another asked to clarify what it was that the Three Clans Tribe wanted of the Ocean Travelers. This question seemed to put the discussion on hold for the moment while the question was put to the envoys by one of the females.

The Pod Leader responded that they asked two things of the Ocean Travelers. The Three Clans Tribe was a peaceful tribe used to hunting fish, seal, and the like. They didn't know how to hunt and kill such a large fish. The Tribe of the Three Clans asked that they send their biggest and strongest hunters to help in the hunt and teach them how to kill the big fish.

And the second thing, they asked?

The Pod Leader asked their assistance in finding the Open Water Clan of killer whales to alert them to the new predator that eats killer whales and to ask their help also.

This fired another bout of discussion within the Ocean Traveler pod. The Pod Leader could tell that this new and unprecedented situation clearly had the Ocean Travelers concerned and would certainly explain their presence of the Three Clans Tribe in their territory. The females of the Ocean Traveler Clan felt strongly that the Open Water Clan should be warned of this new development to protect their offspring. The fact that the Tribe of the Three Clans needed their help to show them how to hunt large prey seemed reasonable and was something that they were capable of doing. It was quite a compliment to be asked to show another tribe how to hunt.

In the end, the Ocean Travelers agreed to the Pod Leader's requests. They would send two males to help hunt the Giant Shark.

The Pod Leader told the Ocean Travelers of the rendezvous with thirty of the Clan of Three Tribes' hunters at the southern entrance to their territory in eight days time. Further discussion resolved that two envoys would accompany the hunters of the Ocean Travelers to the rendezvous spot at the appointed time, and one Ocean Travelers' hunter would accompany the Pod Leader in an attempt to find the Open Ocean Tribe that roamed to the east. It was only a two-and-a-half days' swim to the rendezvous point, and the envoys would stay with the Ocean Traveler pod until the return of the Pod Leader and his companion or until it was time to leave for the rendezvous. With that settled, the Ocean Traveler companion and the Pod Leader started south for the waters off the Queen Charlottes Islands where the Open Water tribe could be found during the summer months.

28

After three-and-a-half days of speed-swimming, the pair of killer whales found themselves at the northwest end of the Queen Charlotte Islands on the seaward side. Using the same strategy as before, the two whales cruised well off the coast in hopes of hearing a sound trail. After two days of searching, they heard a cacophony of killer whale chatter offshore.

The Open Water Tribe turned out to be relatively easy to find. The two whales were able to follow the din until they came upon a pod of about fifty killer whales, which were quite vocal and not afraid to advertise their position. The pair of whales approached in the same way in which they had approached the Ocean Traveler Tribe pod. This time the pod was much quicker to meet the newcomers.

In appearance and speech, the Open Water Tribe more closely resembled the whales of the Tribe of the Three Clans. As they approached, they could hear the chatter among the pod members as they speculated about the strange pair of killer whales. The Pod Leader was able to understand much more of what these whales were saying to each other. The pod circled the two so that everyone could get a look at the strangers. This time, instead of silence many greetings were tossed at them that the Pod Leader returned. The Ocean Traveler stayed silent. The Pod Leader could see that the Ocean Traveler wasn't comfortable to being around such a large group of killer whales, especially those circling at his rear.

Questions started to pepper the two: Who are you? What tribe did you come from? Why are you in the water's of the Open Water Tribe? The Ocean Traveler was content to let the Pod Leader do all the talking.

The Pod Leader started by stating he was from the Three Clans Tribe who lived among the islands and inside waters to the northeast, and his companion was from the Ocean Traveler Tribe. He was there to warn them of a new danger and to ask for their help.

This started an excited buzz among the Open Water Tribe, as they posed questions to each other of the type and nature of a threat that would bring an Ocean Traveler and a Three Clans whale to them.

After the hubbub settled down, the Pod Leader began to tell them of The Giant Shark and how it had killed and eaten members of his clan.

The collected pod of killer whales was aghast that there was a creature in the seas that dared to attack a killer whale. Many started to openly doubt that there was such a shark, and the Pod Leader was confused by a great white shark, which was frequently seen in their range and not a bother to the killer whales of the Open Water Tribe.

This all sounded eerily reminiscent of when he initially told his own tribe of the shark. The Pod Leader let this debate go on for several minutes; whale speech tended to be slow and drawn out because of the distances they often communicated at created a norm of slow enunciation. Just like when people shout a conversation at each other from the ends of a football field.

Finally the Pod Leader could take no more of the repetition of mistakes that his Tribe had made and forcefully cut in. He told them that many of his Tribe once thought as they did, that it wasn't a large great white, but something much, much bigger. And that it had taken the deaths of five hunters sent to kill it before all believed that this was a true menace to young and adult alike. He then asked how many of their Tribe were they willing to sacrifice before they would come to believe his warning, a warning that he and the Ocean Traveler had traveled hard and long to bring them. Would the pair, representing Tribes from so far away go to the effort of bringing such a warning if they were merely confused about a great white shark?

This silenced the doubters among the pod. This type of contact among pods was unprecedented. Surely a great threat and a great need had arisen that affected them all.

The question was posed: What help did they need from the Tribe of the Open Water killer whales?

Hunters, the Pod Leader responded, hunters to help hunt down the Giant Shark and to show them how to kill it.

On cue, without a word, the pod broke their circling and swam off a half a mile where they joined into a swimming circle to discuss the Pod Leader's request. The Pod Leader couldn't hear all their deliberations, but he was certain that the females of the clan were leading the discussion.

In the meantime, he took a few minutes to catch salmon

in the waters about him.

After a spirited discussion, the pod broke and swam back to him and the Ocean Traveler where they were milling about in the same area. The Pod Leader saw the returning pod and rejoined his traveling companion. As the pod rejoined their circle, an old female announced they had agreed to send eleven male hunters to kill the Giant Shark.

The Pod Leader told them that they should leave today to meet the gathering tribes of killer whales at the rendezvous point at the south entrance to the territory of the Tribe of the Three Clans.

The circling pod broke into small groups of whales that scattered in several directions. The Pod Leader realized that these were small family groups that were gathering to say goodbye to the hunters that were going to hunt the Giant Shark. Slowly, by ones and twos, eleven adult males filtered back to the Pod Leader and the Ocean Traveler. When all were gathered, the Pod Leader turned to the northeast, leading the gathered killer whales representing three different clans, speaking three different dialects, and comprising various physical, cultura,l and social differences on a common quest to kill an uncommon enemy.

29

If Eric had been astounded by the otter's actions before, the man's statements now doubly astonished him. And it must have shown on his face. He was at a loss for words.

'How did this man know that I've been asking around about strange happenings? I've only spoken to one person about that, and I'm sure I never mentioned anything about a gray fish. And...what had the man said to the otter?'

The man advanced on Eric, his hand outstretched in a handshake. "You must be Eric McCallister. It's nice to meet you."

Eric took the man's hand and dumbly pumped it twice, still trying to find his voice. It came to him as two questions merged into one, "How did you hear about what did you say to the otter?"

"I beg your pardon," George said, dropping Eric's hand with a puzzled look.

"Er...um...I meant to say 'who told you that I've been asking around about a gray fish?'"

"I heard it through the Sealaska Grapevine."

"The Sealaska Grapevine? What's that? I've heard of the Sealaska Corporation owned by the Alaska natives..."

"Yep. That's the one. Heard it through the native grapevine."

"No offense, but I think that your grapevine has got its

wires crossed." Eric wasn't about to blab glibly with a stranger on a dock in downtown Ketchikan about the greatest discovery of his professional career. He was angry that the word was out, that strangers would be accosting him at his boat. "Well, it was nice to meet you, George, but I've got some groceries that need to be put into the freezer," he said waving the bag in his hand. He turned and started to board the *Pacific Chanteuse*.

"If you're going to look for the Great Shark, I can help."

Eric was halfway up the steps built into the back of the *Pacific Chanteuse* with his back to George when he stopped. This guy knew way too much. He pivoted to face George, "How's that?" he said somewhat icily.

George looked Eric in the eye. "You're going after a Spirit Fish. And if you're going to do that, you need me. I'm a shaman of the Tlingit Tribe."

At the mention of "shaman" and "Tlingit," which was pronounce like "klink-it," a klaxon started to go off in Eric's brain. It all made sense: the Sealaska Corporation, Indian grapevine, even talking to the otter...

'*Shit. The last thing that I want to do was to get embroiled in the politics of the local Native Americans and the all powerful Sealaska Corporation.*'

"Why don't you come in and we can talk," Eric offered.

George smiled and headed for the *Pacific Chanteuse*'s stern landing, while Eric unlocked the salon door. Once inside, Eric went down the steps to the galley in the starboard hull with his bag of groceries. "Make yourself comfortable," he shouted up the steps. "I'll be right with you."

As Eric put away the groceries, he had time to study George. He was tall, a little over six feet maybe, close to thirty, brown hair, brown eyes, aquiline nose and light olive complexion. He was wearing a pair of Dockers, a Polo shirt and a comfortable pair of casual dress shoes. All in all, not what Eric would have expected of a Native Alaskan shaman. When he was finished, he went up to the salon, where George was standing, examining the instrumentation of the inside cockpit.

"A very fine boat you have here, Eric," George said, any resentment at Eric's frosty questions gone.

"Thanks. I don't mean to be rude, but I have a whole bunch of groceries up in the bed of my truck that need to be stored before something green and slimy happens to them. Why don't you have a seat until I get that all loaded aboard?"

"I have a better idea. Why don't I help you carry the groceries down?"

"Sure," Eric readily agreed, not one to turn away free labor. Plus it would give him some time to figure out how to handle George.

While both Eric and George ferried the groceries down, they talked about the weather, sailboats and everything but the 'Spirit Fish.' Halfway through the transfer, the groceries were piling up in the galley, so Eric stayed behind to put things away while George finished bringing the rest of the food down to the boat.

When Eric finished, he met George in the salon again. Glancing at the clock on the bulkhead, he saw that he needed to get going to get the boat over to the boatyard. "Listen, George, I need to get the *Pacific Chanteuse* over to the Tongass Boat Works at the north end of the Narrows. Once I get the boat there, I've got several hours of downtime that we could discuss your proposition. Why don't you pick me up there in, let's say, an hour?"

"That's great! I really appreciate you taking the time to sit down with me."

"Perfect. But, before you go, would you mind helping me cast off?" In the water culture of the docks, helping someone cast off lines was an everyday courtesy, like holding open the door for someone.

Eric fired up both diesels from the wheelhouse control panel and let them warm for a minute before going out to the deck to disconnect the shore power and water. George had already disconnected the power and water lines and tossed lines aboard. Eric quickly stowed the lines back in the forward locker before going aft to untie the stern line. George unhooked the line from the dock cleat and tossed the line to Eric. Eric made a quick coil of the line, knowing that he was just going to be tying up to another dock in a few minutes anyway. Returning to the cockpit wheel stanchion, he cranked the wheel all the way to the stops towards the dock and engaged the clutch forward, idling to let the big paddle rudders deflect the thrust of the props at the dock before swinging the stern away. Once the *Pacific Chanteuse*'s stern had almost the angle away from the dock he was looking for, he pushed the clutch to neutral, counting on momentum to carry him the rest of the way. He ran forward and loosed first the spring line and then the bowline. Each time George unhooked the line from the dock cleat, he tossed it up to the boat. Eric just let the line ends lay looped over the boat's railing where George had tossed them knowing that he would be using the lines again shortly. With the *Pacific Chanteuse* drifting in a crowded marina, Eric gave George a quick wave of thanks and then jumped back to the cockpit wheel to maneuver the boat.

One of the nice things about having a boat with duel props was the ease of maneuverability in a crowded marina. Eric expertly moved the sailboat into the middle of the marina channel using nothing but throttle and rudder. Once he felt he'd enough room, he spun the *Pacific Chanteuse* on an axis halfway between the props by putting one in reverse and one in forward. It was actually a little trickier than it seemed at first blush, because the props, having been designed primarily for forward thrust, gave unequal thrust at the same speed when one was in reverse. He'd to trim up the throttle on the reversed engine to get the boat to pivot smartly. He returned both engines to idle, before the bow swung through the direction he wanted to go letting momentum bring the boat around. As the bow lined up in the channel, he nudged both throttle levers forward, kicking the props into forward. The *Pacific Chanteuse* was so light and offered so little water resistance due to its shallow draft that it took little throttle input to make the boat do what Eric wanted it to do. Under idle power, the *Pacific Chanteuse* glided out of the marina and into the channel. There, he steered north, well away from the shore and opened the throttle.

What his trip in at night hadn't revealed to him was the crowded shoreline. Every square foot that was suitable to build a dock was covered with piers and docks of every description. Piers for the canneries, docks for freight delivery, small boats, seaplanes, pleasure craft, marinas, etc. As he powered north, he'd to keep a constant eye out for boat and plane traffic leaving or approaching the shore. Every five or ten minutes, a float plane would land in the middle of Tongass Narrows and taxi to a dock or taxi out into the middle, turn the plane into the wind and give it full throttle. The roar from the plane engines taking off obliterated the ability to talk, leaving hand signals the only communication possible in the din. After about twenty minutes of motoring, Eric came to the docks of the Tongass Boat Works and cut the throttle, floating in front of the dock. Eric went inside the salon and turned on his CB radio, changing the channel to the frequency that they had given him when he made the appointment for work. He hailed the Boat Works twice before someone answered. Eric let them know he was at the doc, ready to deliver the boat. A yard worker soon appeared on the dock to catch lines for Eric and signaled him where to tie up the boat. Fortunately, the yard wanted him to tie up on the same side as where his fenders were already hanging, so Eric didn't have to flip lines and fenders to the other hull.

Five minutes later, he turned off the boat's engines and secured the rest of the boat. The yard foreman met Eric on the dock to discuss the details of the work to be performed. Yard workers were already hooking up power to the boat and delivering pallets of gear by forklift. Eric could see his new rigid hull inflatable being prepared to be brought down to the docks. Eric showed the foremen where he wanted the equipment mounted and in what chase ways cables and power cords should be routed. While much of the scientific equipment on board belonged to the Pacific Ketterman Marine Institute, the *Pacific Chanteuse* belonged to Eric. He knew every seam, joint, bolt, connection, wiring schematic, and more about his boat. And he was very particular about what went where and what it should look like when installed. Eric could tell that the foreman was actually thankful to work with someone who had strong ideas of what work should be done and how. It meant a lot fewer decisions for the foreman and a lot less guessing.

Owning the *Pacific Chanteuse* was a professional and financial windfall for Eric. Because it was used exclusively for research and his work, he was able to deduct all the boat's mortgage, upkeep, supplies, fuel and lubricants, repairs, food and depreciation as business operating costs. While at the same time the PKMI paid for the use of his boat for research which covered all his yearly expenses, including moorage when it was back in Portland in the off-season and a nice researcher stipend. Essentially, the boat cost him nothing to own. In another five years the boat would be paid for. He lived with Melanie in her ranch style home in a nice suburban development in Vancouver, Washington, just over the Columbia River, giving him easy entrée to Portland over the I-5 Bridge when he needed something from the big city. He could be at his boat's mooring in less than fifteen minutes from the house and to the Pacific Ketterman Marine Institute's offices on Front Avenue along the Willamette River near downtown Portland in twelve.

Of course, occasionally the Institute needed Eric to give large contributors a cruise along the Portland waterfront or the windy Columbia River Gorge. The contributors loved that the research boat was sail-powered and thus 'green,' which really seemed to help the Institute loosen up the wallets of their contributors. Eric was happy to oblige the Institute; they had been very good to him, his career, his research, and his passion. Besides, having a boat sit was hard on the mechanical and electrical systems. So what the Institute considered to be scratching their back with benefactors, Eric knew to be necessary for the boat's maintenance anyhow, and he was happy to show it off while building relationships with the upper crust.

The one understanding he had with the Institute was that he wouldn't give any saltwater or coastal cruises in the off-season. It wasn't that Eric abhorred salt water; he spent nearly five months a year on it. The real reason was the Columbia River shoals. Where the Columbia River entered the Pacific Ocean, huge deposits of sands were deposited that constantly shifted. The shifting sands made for a very shallow throat, combining with the tides and wind to create huge waves, waves that could easily flip and pound the *Pacific Chanteuse* into slivers in a minute. It was one of the most treacherous stretches of water in North America. It was so treacherous that the Coast Guard ran only self-righting, fifty-two-foot cutters through the shoals, and even then, they weren't always able to break out into the open seas beyond. It wasn't uncommon for the Coast Guard to roll the vessel trying to rescue floundering vessels in the surf zone of the throat. The large ocean-going vessels bound for the piers of Portland were large enough to take the sea conditions at the mouth, but small vessels had to wait until conditions were optimal to make their run, when winds, tides, and surf were minimal. And even then, it was not trip for the faint of heart. The swells of the open ocean hit the inclining shoals, rising to cresting monsters. It was for these reasons that Eric only took the *Pacific Chanteuse* to the open sea as infrequently as possible when the conditions were nothing less than perfect.

Once he was assured that his baby was in good hands, he headed for the front gate to meet George with the Fed Ex package containing the tooth in his hand.

At the gate, he found George leaning against the front fender of a late-model family sedan. As Eric approached, by way of greeting, George said, "Hop in. There's something I'd like to show you."

Eric got in and set the Fed Ex box on the seat console between them while he buckled in. As George was getting in, his elbow accidentally hit the box, knocking it to the rear seat floor. "Ooops, I'm sorry. I'll get that for you." Still unbuckled, George reached between the seats and groped around once or twice before latching onto the box and handing it back to Eric.

"If we're going anywhere near downtown or near a Fed Ex drop off, I need to get this on its way," Eric said waving the box.

"I know right where one is. And it's close to the way of what I wanted to show you, so we'll make a little detour and get that dropped off for you."

Eric had already determined that he wasn't going to volunteer any more information than George already knew. He wanted to probe George to see what exactly it was that he thought he knew and who he heard it from. The only way to do that was to get George talking about himself and let him make the first move in discussing the shark. "So tell me, George, what exactly does a shaman do?"

"Corporate management mostly and political tribal relations."

"Really?!" Eric was genuinely surprised. George had been one surprise after another. Nothing about this guy was as it appeared.

Sensing Eric's interest, George continued, "I'm on the Board of Directors for the Sealaska Corporation and also represent the Tlingit tribe on the Tlingit and Haida Central Committee here in Ketchikan. That is, when I'm not acting as shaman for my people in The Taant' a Kwáan, or the Sea Lion Tribe. I'm a member of the Dakl' aweidí Kéet Hít, the Killer Whale House. Nowadays, that means being more of a tribal historian of religion, artifact, and ceremony. But lately, there has been a resurgence in the young people of the Tlingit wanting to get more in touch with the heritage and their place in the world. So I am doing a lot more cultural heritage education these days. According to my dad, twenty-five years ago, the young people of our tribe were all about trying to become part of the American mainstream. But with the financial success of the Sealaska Corporation and the access to the Internet via satellite, they no longer feel the pressure to adopt the 'white picket fence' paradigm lifestyle and feel more comfortable exploring their cultural differences rather than focusing on blending."

"You said you belonged to the Sea Lion Tribe, but you also said you belonged to the Tlingit. How does that work?"

"Actually, it breaks down more like this: the Tlingit nation is divided into twenty tribes with traditional territories, and then each tribe is divided into moieties. In my tribe we have two moieties or clans, the Raven and the Wolf/Eagle. The House of Killer Whales belongs to the Wolf/Eagle clan. Within the clans, there are different houses that are ranked in prestige and importance, tribal leaders and warrior houses being higher in rank. It's kind of a caste system, with the exception that, traditionally, women had to marry outside their house. And houses could move up and down in rank depending on the inhabitant's actions. For example, if a low ranking house was exceptionally brave in battle or captured many slaves, their status could improve. Since we no longer make war on other nations and don't take slaves, the pecking order has been frozen for the last hundred sixty years. That has been one of the Nation's biggest objectives in the twentieth century, to redefine the caste system so that all houses were equal. The importance between house is more akin now to that of high school rivalries. Its just one of the ways the Nation has democratized and adapted successfully into integrating to the United States."

"That seems to be a big leap from corporate management," pointed out Eric.

"Not really. No different than you growing up on some block, in a neighborhood, in a subdivision, in a city, in a county, in a state."

"No, what I meant was going from Indian culture to business."

"Again, a little bit of history goes a long ways here. When we were not at war with our neighbors, we had a strong vital trading relationship with them. We have been doing business here in Southeastern Alaska for five thousand years. With the advent of ANCSA, the Nation's business has just gone global, rather than just regional. My tribe and others just felt that I was best suited to represent their interests in the running of Sealaska Corporation." Half jokingly he added, "I'm not sure that's because Ketchikan resides in The Sea Lion Tribe's traditional territory and it's easier for me to get to Juneau for company business or because I have an M.B.A."

"Oh really,...where from?"

"Eastern Washington University. The state of Alaska has agreements in place with Washington State for students from Alaska to get college educations through their universities. I was able to take advantage of some of their programs and scholarships from the Sealaska Corporation."

"So now you're giving back to the Sealaska Corporation?"

"It's not like I'm paying back some faceless corporation. The Sealaska Corporation is privately owned, non-traded and wholly owned by the Indians of Southeastern Alaska. It was one of thirteen corporations formed by ANCSA, the Alaska Native Claims Settlement Act of 1971. For years, all the tribal nations of Alaska had territory claims and disputes with the U.S. government and nothing happened. Then oil was discovered in Prudhoe Bay, and the best way to get the oil out was to build a pipeline across Alaska to Valdez. But the pipeline couldn't be built because it had to go across lands that were tied up by litigation filed by the Native Alaskans. All of a sudden, Congress had to deal with our complaints. The outcome was to abolish all Indian Reservations except for the Tsimshian on Annette Island and to create twelve regional corporations and give each corporation land and money to settle any and all legal claims forever. We, who own the Sealaska Corporation, the Tlingit, Haida and Tsimshian ended up owning two hundred ninety thousand acres of surface lands, double that in mineral rights, including some three hundred plus islands. So I'm looking after my own interests as one of seventeen thousand shareholders of the Sealaska Corporation. The fact that I'm helping all the members of my tribe and others is just icing on the cake."

They were now nearing downtown, and George pulled in front of a Fed Ex storefront. "Here's your drop-off. I'll wait for you here," George said, putting the car in park while letting it idle.

"Thanks, I'll be back in a few minutes," Eric said as he unsnapped his seat belt and slid out his door with the box containing the tooth. Good to his word, Eric was back after a short delay and belted back in. "OK, let's go see whatever it is that you wanted to show me."

George pulled into traffic and started to head up Minerva Mountain to the residential area where Chuck's house was located.

The conversation resumed where it had left off. "So where does the 'political tribal relations' fit in?" inquired Eric.

"There are three Indian tribes lumped together in the Sealaska Corporation and we don't always see things the same way. The Sealaska Corporation's area of coverage, as far as ANCSA is concerned, covers all of Southeastern Alaska and even a small section of coastal Alaska proper.

"Eighty percent of that entire region encompasses the traditional Tlingit nation. Almost all the rest is traditional Haida territory. The problem is that the Haida nation is split between Canada and the U.S., with most of the Haida residing in Canada. In Canada, the government has dealt with and treated the Haida completely different, which sets up a different mindset of how intertribal relationships should be conducted. The Tlingit tend to see the Haida as business partners, and the Haida see the Tlingit as brothers in a cause. This is one reason for the Tlingit Haida Central Committee, which is the political coalition for everything not covered by ANCSA. This Committee has fractured and dissolved more times over political issues than I can count due to this philosophical split. Then on top of that, you have to throw on the Tsimshian tribe and their issues.

"The Tsimshian tribe is from Canada originally. They were being persecuted by the Canadians and their government in the mid-eighteen hundreds. So they applied for and received asylum from the U.S. government, who gave them Annette Island as a reservation. Due to the nature ofthe political asylum and non-native status, ANCSA didn't address or abolish their reservation but they got ownership rights as well into the Sealaska Corporation.

"They have a completely different perspective. One that I sum up this way: They get to have their cake and keep it too. They share in the profits generated by the ancestral lands of the Tlingit and Haida without having to put up the resources of their reservation as collateral or give up their sovereignty as we did. With the Tsimshian, it's all about what's in it for them. They vacillate between 'leave me alone' and 'oh yeah, then come get me on my Federal Lands reservation, where we set the law.'

"Because their reservation, Annette Island, is only a couple miles south of Ketchikan, on the border between traditional Tlingit and Haida territory, the Sea Lion Tribe and me, their representative, get the pleasure of trying to coordinate political activities on a day to day basis."

"It sounds to me," Eric said thoughtfully, "that you guys are still at war with each other. Albeit, a bloodless war."

"At times it does seem to take on that feeling," George confided. "All right, this is what I wanted to show you."

George had pulled the car up in front of a very small park nestled into a residential neighborhood high on the hillside. The park was nothing more than a small patch of well-manicured grass with a sidewalk and some park benches that faced both the spectacular view of Gravina and Annette Islands and the Tongass Narrows to the south, and three magnificent Totem Poles looking out over the scene.

As Eric got out, he saw just how impressive and massive these poles were. Each pole stood fifty feet tall and four feet wide at the bottom. They had carved figures, brightly painted in white, red, black, blue-gray and brown. He'd been in Ketchikan for many summers but had never known of this small park's existence. When he got closer, he could smell the faint aroma of cedar emanating from the totem poles. Framed against the wooded backdrop of the plot and the wispy white clouds of the summer sky, their symbolism felt especially potent and vibrant.

George had walked over to the totem pole furthest on the right and motioned for Eric to join him.   As Eric approached, George started on a narrative.   "Both the Tlingit and Haida believe in the same deities.   There are totem poles here from both nations. The only real difference is in the style of carving. The one in the middle is Haida and the two flanking it are Tlingit. You can see the Tlingit totem poles have distinct demarcations between figures, while the Haida blend theirs together."

Eric studied that totem pole for a moment before nodding as he recognized the distinction in style.

"I'm not going to get into a big dissertation on the symbolism and legend of each pole. But I did want to show you this one here at the bottom of this pole," he said patting a blue-gray carved figure into the base of the totem pole. It was a fish with white tentacles coming from its mouth in the process of devouring a small man below, who could only be seen by the two legs projecting out of the tentacles.

"This is a Devilfish, a sea monster if you will. Our legends tell of a giant shark that devours men, carrying them to the netherworld. The Devilfish has many children that swim in the waters that keep an eye on all Tlingit. And when a Tlingit angers our spirits, the Devilfish will be waiting below for the bad Tlingit to fall from his boat.

"The Tlingit are seafaring people. Traditionally, we built canoes out of single trees. We used them to travel the calm waters of our realm, carrying on trade and war with our neighbors. Infrequently, as we paddled about our little archipelago, a blue-gray fish with large white teeth, sometimes seven feet long, what marine biologists now call the salmon shark, would surface and swim quietly alongside our canoes or follow it for several miles.

"It was this quietness that frightened my people. All other things that size, the whales and porpoises, made sounds that they could hear through the hulls of their boats or when they surfaced to breathe. This fish would just swim alongside and eye the occupants with its cold eyes; this could unnerve even the bravest of our warriors, trying to stare down and be defiant to a fish that never blinks. Of course, we now know that fish couldn't blink because it does not have eyelids, a defining characteristic of that class of sharks, I am told.

"But still, this Spirit Fish has great power in our beliefs.

If you are planning to challenge the keeper of the underworld, you will need me to guide your way and protect you from harm. No one seeks the Devilfish, unless he is seeking death."

George said it with so much sincerity that Eric almost believed him. Or more accurately, Eric was sure that *George* believed what he was saying, but in Eric's world, there was no room for soothsaying and legend.

However, Eric fully understood politics. And from what little he knew of George Greenlee, it was clear that this man was wired in more ways than one to the local and state political structures. The one thing that the Institute couldn't survive was the negative political exposure if he didn't handle the situation delicately. Major scientific discovery or not, Eric's career wouldn't weather an anguished uprising of the local natives crying mistreatment of the embodiment of their spiritual icons. "If you'd like to bless my boat, I'd like that very much," Eric offered.

"I'm afraid that going against such a powerful spirit, you will need far more than a boat blessing. I must accompany you to insure your protection. If you were to die or be injured, I couldn't face my people and tell them that the Great Spirit Fish has arisen and is stalking man. I must be allowed to accompany you."

It suddenly dawned on Eric what George's motivation was with that last little revelation. He was trying to bring his people into the twenty-first century and he didn't want his tribe to get paranoid over a "Spirit Fish' and have them regress in fear of their cultural Armageddon. If nothing happened to them, George could claim it was his shaman actions that carried the day. Or conversely, he could testify to them that their ancient legends had no impact on the outcome, which ever was the most useful to bring his people into the world of the here and now, of corporations and political tribal relations.

"We could be gone for up to two weeks, and once we're out there, there'll be no changing your mind. You'll be in for the duration of the trip, understood?" Eric said raising his eyebrows and inclining his head at George for emphasis.

"I understand."

"Good," said Eric briskly, "I hope your affairs are in order then, because we leave tomorrow morning at eight."

George blanched slightly, and Eric could see that he was tempted to offer an alternative starting time. But, just as quickly Eric saw that George recognized that doing so would definitely not get the expedition off to a good start, and give him a reason to leave without George.

After another moment's reflection, George suggested, "Is there somewhere I can drop you off? If we're leaving tomorrow morning, I need to get busy making some arrangements and rescheduling commitments."

"You can drop me off at the city dock parking lot. I'll just grab my truck. I've got a few things to do myself."

The trip back to the docks was relatively quiet; each was making mental adjustments to the new arrangements interspersed with a few questions from George about things he would need and the accommodations of the boat.

30

George left Eric at his truck with a wave and a promise to meet him back at the dock tomorrow morning. Eric spent the rest of his day finishing what little of his laundry that Melanie hadn't done for him and making phone calls.

He called Sid to give him the FedEx tracking number in case there was a problem and he couldn't be reached, and reviewed the tests and timetables for when he could expect results. He informed Sid of the assistance from the state's Department of Fish and Game and from the Tlingit Nation and how this came to be. Sid was very appreciative of Eric's delicate handling of the Tlingit issue. In fact, Sid saw this new development as an opportunity to court a new and as yet unthought of benefactor for the Institute. He encouraged Eric to "cultivate that relationship."

At a quarter to five, he was off to pick up Melanie. She was especially buoyant when she got in from the first day of sporting her new jewelry and savaged Eric with yet another one of her conscious sucking, all encompassing kisses. Eric didn't mind. Those types of kisses seemed to be coming with a greater rate of frequency since he proposed.

He had Melanie drop him off at the Boat Works to pick up his boat with a promise to come get him in an hour's time at the City Marina's dock. After inspecting the work,

Eric signed off on the bill to be sent to the Institute and backed his boat away from the docks. On the way, he stopped by the fuel docks to top off his tanks before heading to the City Marina. The spot he'd vacated that morning had not been occupied, so he tied up the *Pacific Chanteuse* in the same spot. He made sure that all circuit breakers were off to the batteries, so the batteries would be good to go in the morning without having to hook up shore power. This gave him one less thing to worry about in the morning.

Melanie had waited for him on the docks after helping tie up the boat. After locking the boat up, he made his way to the dock. He took Melanie's hand as they strolled down the dock to her truck, bringing her up-to-date on all that had happened that day. Over dinner, he commented to Melanie on how interesting this trip was going to be. He had companions representing science, government and religion, from marine biologist to Masters of Business Administration, public servant, non-profit employee, and American capitalist.

'That should lead to some lively conversations at the dinner table,' he mused to himself.

The rest of the night he spent trying to focus on Melanie. It was hard to do because he was anxious about leaving her for two more weeks. Somehow, their new level of commitment was making it more difficult for him to leave her, and this anxiety was getting in the way of his ability to enjoy the present with her. It was just a vicious little circle that progressed as the evening did, getting worse the closer he got to his departure.

Eric slept fitfully that night, dreaming Melanie would change her mind if he left her unattended too long because of this outing. He knew that was silly, he had several friends that were salesmen who spent as much time on the road away from their wives and families as he did in the summers doing his research. And he only did that for less than half the year.

In the morning, he arose unrefreshed and cranky. He hated to leave on any sour notes, but he couldn't help himself as he and Melanie worked around each other preparing for their respective days. Finally, the time came that Eric had been dreading all last night. It was time to leave. Eric rode in the cab in silence, unable to think of anything bright or cheery to say.

As Melanie pulled into the parking lot of the Marina and slipped the truck into park, she turned to Eric. "You seem to be a little off your oats this morning. Anything that we need to talk about before I let you go?"

Eric knew that she meant nothing by the phrase "before I let you go." But it fed into his anxiety anyway. He didn't want to tell her of his anxiety of leaving her just now, days after getting engaged, and his struggle to survive after being shipwrecked ashore. But he was afraid to burden her with his silly little fears, which he knew them to be, and decided on a half-truth. "I just wish I had a few more days in port. But everyone wants to get cracking on this search pronto," he said with a little shrug of his shoulder.

"I know, sweetheart," she said taking his face in her hand tenderly, "I know."

Eric looked in her eyes and saw that she, too, desperately wanted more time with him. This bolstered his tired, cranky ego. She understood his angst. She always understood. He didn't need to say any more. Eric kissed her and said goodbye, exiting the truck.

At the top of the ramp to the dock he turned and gave one last wave. This goodbye felt so different, for some reason.

He turned to proceed down the ramp with his laundry bag in hand. As he did, he saw Chuck standing in the center of the dock in near the stern of the *Pacific Chanteuse*. As soon as he was close enough, he hailed Chuck. "Good morning." He added playfully, "You ready for your three hour tour, Gilligan?"

Chuck, who was old enough to understand the allusion, laughed and patted the *Pacific Chanteuse*. "That would make this the *Minnow*, I presume. Remember…. the *Minnow* sinks."

By now, Eric, traveling up the stern steps of the *Pacific Chanteuse*'s right hull, exclaimed, "Shit. We can't let *that* happen. Forget that whole joke thing. How are you this morning?" he asked unlocking the salon door.

"Just fine…ready to get this show on the road."

Chuck had followed him into the salon. "Let me show you were to put your gear. I'm going to put you in the port hull queen bed." Eric led Chuck to his stateroom and showed him all the drawers, cabinets and bins available for him to use. He left Chuck unpacking while he went up to the salon to fire up the diesels and let the radar warm up. With all the circuit breakers on, the engines fired and hummed sweetly. Their exhaust, piped below the water line to let the water act as a muffler, made a little burbling sound at the stern of each hull.

After several minutes, Chuck reappeared. "Ready to get underway?" Chuck asked, starting to head for the deck.

"Hold on, Chuck," Eric called to his back. "We're waiting for another person who will be joining us to show up."

Chuck turned to face Eric, apprehension on his face due to this unexpected addition to the expedition. "And who might that be?"

On cue, George plopped down into the sunken sailing cockpit outside and entered through the door carrying a large bag on a strap over his shoulder. "Good morning. Sorry I'm late."

Eric looked at his watch, ten after eight. *'Not bad,'* he thought. George was actually not as late as Eric had expected him to be. *'Maybe M.B.A. time counteracts reservation time instead of compounding it. Or, who knows, maybe it was vice versa.'*

"Good morning," Eric said while turning to Chuck. "Chuck, this is George Greenlee of the Tlingit Nation. He'll be joining us on this expedition." "George, say hello to Chuck Hudson of the Alaska Department of Fish and Game." Both men shook hands.

"Greenlee...Greenlee," Chuck pondered aloud, "That name sounds familiar to me for some reason. Have we ever worked on any tribal fishing issues?"

"Not with me."

"Oh well. Nice to meet you, George."

"Same."

"Come on George, I'll show you your room. I'm putting you in the single bunk on the other side of my stateroom's bathroom. We'll share a bathroom, like in college. It'll be fun," he said jokingly as he motioned George to go down into the starboard hull. As George went down the step, Eric paused at the top of the steps, spun and faced Chuck.

Chuck raised his shoulders in a shrug and hands, palms up in front of him, asking silently, 'What's this?'

Eric mouthed back wordlessly, 'I'll tell you later,' and turned to accompany George to his room. He was back in a few moments. When he got close enough to Chuck, he spoke quietly, "I had a complication with the local natives. The Tlingit Nation wanted in on the hunt, claims it's a 'Spirit Fish' or some such hooey."

"How'd they find out?" Chuck whispered back.

"I don't know. When I asked, all he would say was 'Sealaska Grapevine'. You'll get the gist of it..." Eric thought he heard George coming through the galley, so he hurriedly said, "We'll talk later."

"All right," Eric addressed his crew, "let's get this show on the road. George, if you handle the lines from the dock; Chuck, you can handle the lines on deck." Everybody headed out onto the deck. From the wheel in the cockpit, Eric called out to cut the stern line loose. He noted that as George slipped the line over the cleat after Chuck had slacked it, he picked the line up and walked in back to the boat, making sure that it didn't get wet.

Nobody liked to handle cold, wet lines when they didn't need to. *'Good,'* Eric thought, *'at least he's spent some time on boats.'*

Next came the spring and bow lines. George was back onboard before Eric pivoted the *Pacific Chanteuse* away from the dock and turned her around in the marina. They headed south out of town as the boat cleared the marina. They passed a gigantic cruise-ship full of tourists tied up to a wharf near downtown. A few of the tourists who were up at that early hour of a cruise ship, waved as the *Pacific Chanteuse* passed, a few of the quicker ones taking pictures. Then Chuck, George and Eric returned the waves, and as the ship passed alongside, each took time to gaze at the passing city as it receded to the rear, each wrapped in his thoughts about the fish they were about to hunt.

31

The Pod Leader and his two traveling companions arrived at the rendezvous point to find that they were the last ones to show up. The envoy group that had gone north had been able to recruit another three whales from another Ocean Traveler pod. This brought their total number to forty-six of the largest killer whales the Pod Leader had ever seen assembled in one spot before.

The only problem so far had been food. Not the lack of it, but the variety. Ocean Travelers preferred warm-blooded food. So they were always off in a different direction than the other killer whales in search of food. The inside waters of the Three Clans Tribe was chock full of seals that had never been hunted by killer whales, the Three Clans Tribe - being fish eaters. Because the seals and sea lions in their range had never been targeted by the Clans, they were much less timid and cautious than the prey stalked by the Tribe of Ocean Travelers, who were amazed by the abundance and ease with which they could catch their favorite food. It had been so plentiful that Ocean Travelers had taken to killing seals for fun.

This had not sat well with the killer whales of the Three Clans. They appreciated the help and the presence of Ocean Travelers, but weren't pleased that the seals of their domain were being killed just for fun. So far, no confrontation had occurred, but friction was building.

The killer whales all returned and collected by mid afternoon, at which time a slow-moving circle of killer whales formed to discuss the hunt for the shark. All the members of foreign tribes had been brought up to speed on everything that was known of the shark as they had traveled to the rendezvous by their respective envoys.

As the caucus of whales started, the first idea to be floated before the group was a mass attack upon the shark. Surely, no creature, no matter how strong or fast, could withstand the assault of so many powerful hunters.

But there was dissent to this idea. Only a few at a time would be able to assault the shark, and this would turn the odds of the battle to the shark's favor. The survivors of the first hunting party guaranteed that a mass attack would kill many of the hunters.

Finally, one of the members of the Ocean Travelers, who had remained quiet during the debate between the Open Water and the Three Clans Tribes, asked what they had done to tire the shark. This question was met with studied confusion. What did the Ocean Traveler mean by tire? Why would they worry about tiring the shark when their objective was to sink their teeth into the shark and kill it?

The Ocean Travelers were the only ones of the assembly that regularly hunted prey that was larger than them. This made their perspective unique among the assembly. They explained in short bursts that the only time that the Ocean Travelers used their teeth on animals larger than themselves was when they'd either drowned their prey or the prey was too tired to defend itself. They explained that they often used more than half a day to chase whales until they were too tired to swim anymore. Those were the only times it was safe to bite into prey that was larger and more powerful. And even then, the objective wasn't to kill the prey, but to bleed it to death. The Ocean Travelers told the assembly, that biting into bigger prey when it was still capable of quick movement was a good way to hurt jaws, damage skulls, lose teeth, or get other members of the pod injured by a fluke lashed out by a jolt of pain due to the bite of another killer whale.

The Ocean Traveler insisted that they wouldn't attack until the shark had tired. But, others questioned, how to tire a fish that could swim faster than they could?

The answer came from one of the Three Clans. When they fed on herring, they corralled them with air bubbles. But instead of air bubbles, they should corral the shark with themselves. This idea was bounced back and forth, refining it into a plan, a plan that wouldn't have been conceived without the input of the three different tribes.

They would use the same hunting technique that found the shark last time. But since they would always be hunting in a channel of some sort, they would use the land to help corral the shark. Instead of one picket line to block the channel with whales sent to search bays and coves before it, they would use two picket lines. The first line's job would be to pass the shark through the line, then contain it between the two pickets. That way the killer whales could swim in relays and in multiples of twos and threes, high and low, to keep the shark near the surface so the killer whales could breathe without losing position.

This way, they would always able to harass the shark to expend its energy without ever losing position of containment. As the shark grew increasingly tired, they would shrink the corral ever tighter, until the killer whales were concentrated and the Giant Shark was too tired to swim. They continued to work on how to kill the Giant Shark once they had it cornered and exhausted it until a workable plan emerged.

When all agreed to the plan, they set out north into the southern entrance of the channel where they had found the shark last time.

32

As soon as the *Pacific Chanteuse* cleared Pennock Island, Eric turned south into Nichols Passage, which ran along the west coast of Annette Island, and prepared to bring the boat under sail power. He chose this route for several reasons. The winds generally came out of the west and southwest off the Pacific in Southeastern Alaska. Coming to Ketchikan, he'd been sailing with wind, so it had been easy to plot the shortest path to town. But now that he was headed south, he would be sailing into the wind. The sails could only generate power when the sail could get enough loft to create the winged sail shape and create horizontal lift. This wasn't possible with winds coming from the front quarters. To overcome this problem, sailboats sailed on diagonal tacks zigzagging their way up the wind stream. The closer the line you could hold to the wind, the more efficient your sailing would be, covering more ocean before having to tack. The challenge to a sailor was that winds constantly shifted in direction, if even by a few degrees. When sailing into the wind this became critical. A shift of wind of just a few degrees could spill the loft and spoil the airfoil effect of the sail, instantly stalling the boat's power. The man at the wheel would have very little time to use the last of the boat's momentum to swing the boat back to an angle that would fill the sails. It was a constant battle between getting the most distance and efficiency versus a cautious a line that wouldn't spill your sails.

The main traffic flow of the Inside Passage went across the north end of Annette Island and down its eastern coast. The heavy traffic of large ships such as cruise ships, the Alaskan Ferries, supply ships; and barges, made it difficult to tack into the oncoming wind. Nichols Passage was much wider and devoid of large ships, making it easier for Eric to sail the *Pacific Chanteuse* south into the wind. This was especially important because Eric wasn't the only one who was going to be sailing the ship. They all would need to take turns on wheel watches. And Eric didn't know how skilled or how much experience Chuck or George had with sailboats, let alone a high performance catamaran like the *Pacific Chanteuse*.

Well it was high time to find out. "Chuck, George! Could you come out here?" he yelled at the two who had settled in the salon, conversing.

Dutifully, both came out and took seats on the cockpit's side benches. "Do either of you have any sailing experience?" Eric asked.

Both paused, before Chuck spoke first. "Sorry, Champ. I've been on boats for years but they always had a throttle to get us to where we were going."

"Me, too," said George.

'That's about what I expected,' Eric mused.

"That's alright," Eric said. "Sailing's not difficult," he started. "You can learn the basics in fifteen minutes. But, learning to sail…well, now that takes years. For this trip, all we need is basic sailing," he said, throttling the boat into neutral. He disappeared into the salon, and both engines' slow burble in the water died as the engines were cut. Eric came back into the cockpit and spent the next fifteen minutes showing them the various lines that controlled the unfurled jib, raised the main sail, moved the traveler, and played out the sails to get the right loft. The boat had been designed so that all these lines led to the cockpit in a logical fashion. Then he showed them how to use the different hand winches at the front of the cockpit to adjust the sails when they were under power. He showed them which switches raised and lowered the dagger boards, where the master switch to the automatic pilot system was, which switches activated and adjusted the system on the rudder wheel stanchion, and which instruments in the cockpit would help them and how to read them.

Lastly, he gave them his spiel on etiquette and safety. "When you're piloting the boat, it's your prerogative when to tack or change course. You have only one responsibility before you take your first action, and that is to *shout* 'Coming About' so that I can hear you asleep in the front berth. That way, everybody can prepare for the change in direction. Movies make it a comedic standard to brush people overboard when a tack change happens. First off, if you go overboard and nobody sees you, it's a death sentence. Secondly, the way this boat is designed, the mainsail boom is at head height. If you're on deck when tacking, the boom can whip from one side to the other with enough force to crush a man's head or face." He paused to let that sink in for effect. "Since you guys are new to sailing, I'm going to insist that at all of us use these at all times." Eric flipped up the cushion on the starboard bench and lifted the lid on the storage bin to produce three harness-like apparatuses. He handed one each to Chuck and George while he donned one himself.

They were inflatable life preservers. A nylon strap ran down the center of the back with a loop at the bottom that held another nylon strap that attached to two nylon rip-stop fabric cover tubes on the chest that were two inches in diameter. Straps at the top of the apparatus went from the top of the tube to meet the back strap behind the neck. Eric showed them how to connect the life preservers across their chest and waist. "You just yank down on this little tab," he said, fondling a plastic tag attached by a lanyard to the right hand tube, "and a little CO2 cartridge will inflate the vest." "This," he said pointing to a little half-sized aerosol can with a red top clipped to the waist strap, "is an air horn. If you go in the water, use this immediately to let everyone know that you're in the drink. Everybody good with that?"

He got nods from both men.

"Alright, swabbies, the first order of business is raising the mainsail. Go ahead."

Eric was a great believer in doing as learning. He instructed Chuck and George through raising the sails. When both sails were set, he took turns putting both on the wheel and had both of them change the angle of attack into the wind, adjusting the sails to the change and recovering after purposefully falling off the wind.

When he was assured they had the basics, he reached

into his pocket and pulled out a quarter. He flipped the coin, catching it in both hands. "Call it," he told George. Eric peeked under his hand.

"Heads."

"Tails. You lose. The first wheel watch is yours. Chuck will relieve you in two hours." Eric took a few minutes to discuss how far he should go before he tacked. "Yell for me if you have any questions."

He left a hyper-alert George at the wheel while he and Chuck retired to the salon. Eric was already enjoying the additions to his boat. Normally, he would sail all day by himself and occasionally sneak inside when he was on a stable tack where he could engage the autopilot long enough to go to the bathroom or get drink and food from the galley. Having additional hands was giving him the luxury of additional time, time he planned on using to familiarize himself with the new equipment installed at the Boat Works.

"Chuck," he said as they entered the salon, "I want to show you something." He went to the navigation table and turned on his computer. After he cued up the episode of the shark attack captured by the TTACS, he sat Chuck in front of the computer and played it for him.

"Wow!" was all Chuck could say as he stared dumbfounded at the screen. "That shark struck and killed with scary efficiency, and that was the ocean's top predator that it wiped out in just seconds. If this isn't the lab fish but a new species, it could totally change the ocean's ecological balance. Wow!"

"It certainly gets your attention, doesn't it? Let me

show you the video on the surface of that first attack." Eric cued the video of the sharks breach on the first attack and played it for Chuck.

Again, "Wow!" was all Chuck could say. Chuck replayed the snippet several times, trying to analyze the footage for anything that might contribute to their knowledge of the shark. After a half hour, a frustrated Chuck turned to Eric, "I can't make out any detail that would allow me to swing identification in one direction or another. The picture quality is OK, but the sheeting action of the water coming off the fish and the splashing makes it impossible to determine any characteristic. The angle of the camera relative to the fish makes it nigh impossible to identify the species."

"Did you just say 'nigh impossible'?" Eric said mockingly, teasing his friend to brighten him from his disappointing scrutiny. "Nobody says 'nigh' anymore."

"What can I tell you, I failed Ebonics at an early age and never recovered," Chuck said smiling back. "But getting back to the video, the only thing that footage confirms is that a large shark from the mackerel shark family took a flying leap."

"The evidence is what it is..." Eric said with a shrug.

"COMING ABOUT," both heard coming from outside.

Moments later, the *Pacific Chanteuse* turned to port and slowed to a stop. Both Eric and Chuck watched as George struggled with his first tack change, yet they watched from different perspectives. Eric watched to see if George did anything that might hurt himself, while Chuck watched to learn from George's mistakes.

George got the sails set for the next tack and as the sails set, the *Pacific Chanteuse* accelerated smartly.

"Not bad," Eric muttered so Chuck could hear.

Eric stepped out into the cockpit to give George some encouragement. "Nicely done. You want anything from the galley?"

"I've got cotton mouth; how 'bout something to drink?"

"You got it," he said over his shoulder while disappearing into the salon door. He returned shortly with a bottle of water. "Here you go," Eric thrust the bottle at George. "Relax - you've just successfully completed the most difficult maneuver there is in sailing." Of course he was lying.

Eric returned to the salon and went to examine the new equipment that had been installed at the Boat Works. A box with a screen had been mounted to the right of the interior steering station, just to the starboard of the salon door to the outside. Eric sat down at the seat in front of the station and turned on the LIDAR.

The LIDAR was a cross between radar and sonar. Instead of radio waves or sound, it used a laser tuned to the blue-green light wave frequency of the water, which allowed it to shoot a focused beam of light out two miles or better depending on water conditions. When the light hit an object, it scattered back the light to a special charged coupling device tuned to the same frequency. The Boat Works had mounted the emitting laser and charged coupling device on the bow of the starboard hull where it flowed into the keel and then transmitted that information into a visual display mounted next to the control box. Eric familiarized himself with the various controls and adjustments until he was sure how to operate it. The LIDAR had two modes. One was a narrow, focused beam that could reach much further out in front of the boat, and a wide beam that swept a much larger area at a shorter distance. The display looked very much like the radar's screen, with the exception that unlike radar, the LIDAR only saw one hundred eighty degrees in front of the boat in a half-spherical field.

The LIDAR could give no details other than the relative size of the object, but that was fine. The shark they were looking for was huge and would give a good return. They should be able to distinguish whale from shark because sooner or later, a whale would have to surface for air. Once on the surface, positive ID could be made. Eric hoped to lure the shark to the surface by using his underwater speakers to broadcast the same whale calls he'd been using when his boat had been attacked.

The control box had automatic sweep mode and a manual mode that allowed Eric to manually focus on an underwater target and then lock the LIDAR onto that target to be tracked automatically. After playing with it for a half hour, Eric was able to use the up/down, left/right controls to find and track objects.

Eric gave Chuck a lesson on the LIDAR and let him play with it until he was proficient.

"My plan," Eric told Chuck, "is for one of us to pilot the boat while one of us will scope the water with binoculars and someone mans the LIDAR. We'll rotate every two hours to keep fresh.

"COMING ABOUT."

Eric felt the *Pacific Chanteuse* turn again, this time the lag until she accelerated on her new heading was a little shorter than last time.

Getting better, he thought.

After two hours, Chuck took his turn at wheel watch. His learning curve was the same as George's.

Eric took some time to show the LIDAR to George after he'd a few minutes to get comfortable. While George played with the LIDAR, Eric took some time to examine the other piece of equipment that Sid had sent him.

On the bench seat at the dining room table was a case that looked very much like a rifle case. It did indeed hold a rifle of sorts. Eric placed the case on the table and flipped off the four latches, flipping the lid up. Inside he found an odd-looking gun with a thick barrel sitting in crate foam cut to the exact outline of the rifle. Also inside the case were three stainless steel cylinders three quarters of an inch wide and six inches long. The cylinders had a little barb on one end attached to a six-inch tether of a thin tough, plastic. These were tracking tags; they had two functions. If they found the shark and got close enough, the idea was to shoot tags at the shark, attaching them so that they could track it and find it at will.

The other function of the cylinder was to deploy a small gas lifting bag. The cylinders could be remotely triggered to release a small bag that would be filled with compressed gas from a small cylinder. The idea behind the system was to track and then recover a specimen when the system's batteries were about to expire. It had been designed to recover much smaller specimens than Eric's intended use. He doubted that all three gas lifting bags together combined would be enough to lift the body of the shark if it was as big as he thought it was. But he'd requested this equipment primarily so that he could tag and track the shark if they found it.

The tracking tags emitted a low frequency sonic pulse and would do so for several months before the battery gave out. The *Pacific Chanteuse* was already fitted with sophisticated, directional underwater microphones for Eric's research. He could use his sound gear to track the shark on the specific frequency of the emitter. This would allow them to build ample evidence on the fish's existence, movements and feeding patterns.

The gun cracked open at the breech to insert a silver tracking cylinder. It turned the tracking cylinder into a projectile by firing it with compressed gases from a larger cylinder attached at the rear of the gun. The gas cylinder had a butt stock attached to it to assist in shouldering the gun. The sights were rudimentary due to the extremely short range of the gun. Eric practiced loading and firing the gun several times until he felt comfortable.

It was getting close to noon, so he and George went into the galley to make lunch for everyone. It was Eric's way of showing George where all the food and supplies were, and, to let him know that he was welcome to anything as long as he left the galley clean and tidy with dishes put away.

When Eric took his turn at the wheel watch it was a beautiful summer day in Southeastern Alaska. The day promised to get into the high sixties. It was on days like this, which made it seem like a crime he was being paid money to sail about in Alaska. After lunch, he settled into his wheel watch. George and Chuck joined him in the cockpit. Sitting on the bench cushions, the three of them discussed Eric's plan to take two hour watch rotations on the wheel, LIDAR and glassing. The three of them refined the plan until all the possible problems were gamed and solved.

Next they decided just what they would do once they found it. All they could do to lure it to the surface was to play whale calls. Eric had thought about trying to chum it in close with ground up herring and bloody fish guts before he left port but had rejected that because the only thing that they did know about the shark was that it preferred whale, having attacked killer whales and Eric when he was mimicking minke calls. Besides, chumming was messy, stinky stuff, and he wasn't really excited about trying it on the *Pacific Chanteuse* during the heat of summer for two weeks without refrigeration for the bait.

They debated about using the much faster and agile skiff as a chase boat to affix a tracking cylinder to the shark. Eric argued that as responsive as the *Pacific Chanteuse* was as a high performance cruising catamaran, she wasn't that nimble compared to the skiff, nor could her speed be controlled under sail power like a vessel under throttle control. But, Chuck felt that it would have a low probability of success. Sharks were attracted to low frequency sounds and vibrations. He felt that the high frequency, high volume motor, and prop noises would overload, disturb or annoy the shark's lateral lines – its audio and vibration sensor organ. The shark would be driven away while it leaned to avoid outboard motor noises. He felt that the best plan would be to use the *Pacific Chanteuse*.

It was relatively noiseless under sail power. The hull was made of non-metallic resins so that the boat presented no major electrical fields to trigger the shark's ampullae of Lorenzini. It wasn't that the *Pacific Chanteuse* could sneak up on the shark; it would know that it was there. But of the options available to them, it would seem the least threatening to the shark.

They would have to approach the shark from directly behind. It they were to make it work, Eric would need to know where the shark was at all times. If they tried to approach from the side and run parallel to the shark, the hulls of the *Pacific Chanteuse* would hide the fish, and Eric would be blind from the boat's cockpit. No, the best way to accomplish the mission would be to straddle the shark between the hulls.

Eric had mixed emotions on this. He agreed that the logic of Chuck's argument was persuasive. In addition, the *Pacific Chanteuse*'s design would lend itself to this kind of operation. The front third of the deck in front of the mast between the hulls was an open span. A spar connected hulls at the front a couple of feet back from the prows. This spar's function was several-fold: it added rigidity to the hulls while giving the front jib sail, anchored in the middle of the spar, a way to transmit the power of the sail to the hull. Another smaller spar projected from the deck in front of the main mast straight out to intersect the cross member spar where the jib sale met the front spar and projected out another four feet in front of the boat. This cross member's function was to add strength to the hull and for its projected tip to provide an anchor point for the guy-wires that held the mast in place and a central point for the boat's anchor to tether the boat to the seabed.

The space between spars and hulls was covered by fish netting stretched tightly to provide a light walking surface. The forward visibility from the cockpit through the netting was excellent. The central spar's projection, four feet in front of the cross member spar would make the perfect perch for a roped-in shooter to tag the shark.

What Eric didn't say, and what he was really worried about, was bringing his boat intentionally so close to such a large creature so they could stick it with a projectile fired from a gun. There was no telling what the shark would do. And it would take very little contact with the shark to seriously damage the *Pacific Chanteuse*. He wasn't sure his insurance would cover the loss of his craft if they knew he'd intentionally chased a large shark with it. He was sure that the fine line between accident and deliberate hazarding of the boat would be crossed if anything bad happened.

In the end, though, Eric had to agree that the best option was to use the *Pacific Chanteuse*. He just hoped nothing happened to her.

They decided on a plan that if they came into contact with the shark, Eric would take the wheel, since he was the best pilot, Chuck would be the shooter and George would grab the video camera to document the shark.

With the important business settled, they passed the rest of the day in pleasant conversation, taking turns at the wheel and practicing with the equipment. George became the unofficial videographer of trip, documenting their preparations plans and the boat for posterity. In late afternoon, they were able to turn east after they had cleared Annette Island.

Around nine that evening, Eric took the helm and piloted the *Pacific Chanteuse* into a little cove on Cat Island, where they anchored up for the evening. Chuck turned out to be whiz in the galley and was able to take the basic staples and whip up a fabulous meal using frozen veal to make his own spaghetti sauce and noodles, complete with salad.

Eric was thankful for the change in diet. Usually, he was too tired at the end of the day to cook anything more complicated than that which required a spin of the dial on the microwave timer for less than two minutes. The meal was set on the table as the anchor was set. Eric ran the port engine to heat water for cleanup and showers while they ate. There were two rules of the sea that were going to be observed on this trip: crews ate well, and the cook never cleaned dishes. George volunteered to be the dish washer so that Eric could do the daily maintenance on the boat's various systems, battery switching and recharging, water purification, etc. All in all, it was an equitable division of labor.

After everyone had a quick shower after dinner, they

sat down at the dining table. Everyone was excited for tomorrow, when they would start their search. As they sat down, Eric produced a bottle of Schnapps, while Chuck produced a bottle of Grand Marnier. When everyone had two fingers of their chosen potion in a small tumbler in front of them, the serious business of discussing sports, politics, and love began.

"So Eric tells me," Chuck started, looking at George, "that you're a shaman of some sort?"

"Yes, of the Sea Lion Tribe of the Tlingit Nation."

"And you have an M.B.A., too?"

"Yes, from Eastern Washington University."

"I just have a hard time reconciling those two things…" Chuck said trailing off.

"It's really not that difficult," George started to explain. "The shamans in our tribes no longer perform incantations to heal the sick or injured. We go to doctors for that. But certain of our rituals can only be performed by a tribe's shaman. So the shaman has become more a spiritual leader and historian nowadays, keeping the stories of our culture tribe's history alive and well. It's a leadership position, no different than the position of a pastor or priest."

"I thought all the Tlingit were Christians?" Chuck countered.

"We are. When the Russians first opened up trade for furs in the Alaskan territory, they brought with them measles and smallpox. The tribe's shamans were unable to stop the decimation of tribes to the diseases, so they fell out of favor. The survivors converted to Russian Greek

Orthodoxy.   Later, when America bought Alaska, they brought with them Protestant missionaries who converted us. A good thing, too - way too much Latin for my tastes, Greek Orthodoxy."

"But how can you be Christians and still believe in your ancestral beliefs?"

"Look, we go to church just like everybody else. And there is no conflict between God and our ancestral beliefs. They are just legend and folklore to us, not religion. How is that so different from you and the tale of Mighty Casey Jones or Paul Bunyon and Babe the Blue Ox? How about the Tooth Fairy, Rumpelstiltskin, Robin Hood, King Arthur and the Knights of the Round Table, the Legend of Sleepy Hollow, Cinderella? Does the fact that you put a quarter under your daughter's pillow every time she loses a tooth make you a pagan?" George said defensively.

"OK, OK. Point well taken, but still it seems to be a bit of an odd couple, historian and M.B.A. One is focused on the past, the other on managing the future. Did you have to study or apprentice to become a shaman?"

"It is a little unorthodox, I'll grant you that. My father was the tribal shaman, so I grew up around all the legends and tales. I watched and helped as my dad prepared to perform ceremonies. He let me help him make ceremonial garbs and things used in rituals. When he died a few years back, I realized, without knowing it, he'd passed on his knowledge to me. The fact that I went to college and understand the utility of money over time, that's just a bonus. And a good thing, too, considering that Sealaska Corporation has nearly gone broke twice now."

"Really? I thought that they were this big, powerful, money-out-the-wazzu company," Eric chimed in.

"Big, yes. Powerful? Now that's a matter of perspective. Money out-the-wazoo…well let's just say that it doesn't matter how much money you have. What matters is *spending* more money than you have. When we first got our settlement money and lands, the Tribal Elders went crazy, spending money on things that didn't provide for the tribe's future. For example, they sent my father down to the University of Washington to have him do a bunch of research on one of our Spirit Fish, Chagatash, the one we are seeking now. They dumped tens of millions of dollars into research that never even got completed, a total waste of money. They invested in some researcher who died before she could produce one cent of return on the investment."

At this revelation, Eric turned to look at Chuck, who had a strange look on his face as he stared back at George.

"But that problem of woeful and wild spending is pretty much in the past. Nowadays, we just hire Harvard and Wharton business school M.B.A.s to handle the business of the corporation. The corporation has focused a concerted effort on finding and promoting people among the stockholders of the company who had aptitudes for higher learning. It used to be that tribal elders were appointed to the Board of Directors. To some extent, it still does. But now it's balanced with people who have an understanding of business practices outside the tribal codex.

"It's gotten pretty complex, really. Sealaska

Corporation owns seven different companies that do everything from selling crushed rock and timber to information management systems and plastic injection molding. The cash flow amounts to several hundred million a year with net profits of around twenty million."

"So, do you do a lot of joint deals with the other native corporations?" Eric asked. "It seems to me that you guys could pool your resources and become major players on any stage you choose to dance. Why not go open a casino in Vegas or something? It sounds as if you've got billions of dollars of assets among you."

"It's not as easy as that," George said, shrugging his shoulders. "The old hatreds die very slowly. Something the almighty dollar has not yet overcome."

This time Chuck said, "I'm not sure I follow you."

"There are four major races of Native Americans in Alaska: Eskimo, Aleut, Athabascan and Tlingit; each different in language, culture, and appearance. The Athabascans are the largest group and generally live in the interior of Alaska and Canada. They're comprised of many different tribes, but typically are known to be a tall, slender race of people. The rest are coastal races. The Eskimo range all over the north and west coast of Alaska down to the Aleutian Islands. The Aleut populate the Aleutian Islands and the southern coast up to the edge of Tlingit territory at Icy Bay."

"I know all this," said Chuck, "but I'm still not sure what your point is."

George was clearly struggling with how to proceed. Finally, he said, "You know that old Alaskan saw, 'you're not a true Alaskan until you've pissed in the Yukon, killed a bear and screwed a klootch'?"

"Yeah," Chuck said.   He was more then a little surprised to hear a Native Alaskan use the word 'klootch.' It was a derogatory word meant to demean the Alaskan Natives and generally it was used to describe the Native Alaskan drunks and winos that populated the bars, streets, and alleys of the major population centers of Alaska.

"Well, the other day, I heard one of the older members of the Board of Directors use a modified version: 'You're not a true Alaskan until you piss in the Yukon, screw a bear, and killed a klootch.'   To him, "klootch" is a term that describes the Aleut.   He was bragging that he was a true Alaskan in every sense of the word, although I don't want to dwell on the 'screw a bear' part...

"The point is, after century upon centuries of warring, the hatred for neighboring races is a part of the cultural fabric.   Each tribe hates the others to the point that no amount of money can overcome their prejudice.   In fact, it would be a point of great honor to enter into a business deal that screwed another race.

"The Tlingit made war and took slaves of the Athabascans and the Aleuts.   Although we have never warred with the Eskimo, the culture of warfare has bred a general disregard and hatred for any race not their own. So getting us to work with other tribes to open a casino, start a bank, whatever, will be impossible until the culture of hatred of other tribes and races is muted."

"Alright," Eric said, "I have a serious question for you."

"Shoot," said George amiably.

"What did you say to the otter?"

"What otter?" a confused Chuck interjected.

Eric quickly told him of his introduction to George on the dock following the otter, finishing with ,"I swear that George had a conversation with the otter."

When he'd finished, George added, "Nothing much, I just thanked him for helping me find you."

"Helping you find me? What, did you send the otter out to find me?"

"No, he was already busy doing his thing. I just asked him to let me know when the owner of the boat showed up."

"And how was an otter to know who owns what boat?" scoffed Eric.

"Simple. The otter told me you and the boat smelled the same." George winked at Eric, downed the rest of his drink and then stood up. "Now, if you'll excuse me, I'm going to turn in."

George left the salon and headed for his berth in the starboard hull, leaving confused looks on both Eric's and Chuck's face.

"What the hell was that all about?" whispered Chuck.

"I don't know. One second he's talking like a corporate executive and the next he's talking to sea otters that whisper back," Eric summarized.

"I don't believe him. I think he was just yanking our crank," Chuck said in hushed tones.

"Yeah, probably," said a not-so-convinced Eric.

"Well, he was right about one thing - it is time to turn

in. Goodnight." Chuck rose with his bottle and headed for the port hull.

Eric shut down all the lights but the white anchor light on top of the main mast, turned off the main engine powering the boat and then headed for bed himself.

As Eric was lying in his bed drifting off to sleep, his mind drifted back to his first meeting with George on the dock. In his mind's eye, he saw the otter at the bottom of the ramp turning to him and … sniffing in his direction. Eric's eyes shot open.

He was now more uncertain then ever.

33

The next morning, Eric was lying in bed, partially awake, when he heard the door to the shared bathroom with George opened and closed quietly. The sound of unshod feet padded across the deck and receded up the steps to the salon. He heard the salon door to the cockpit open and shut quietly. He slowly became aware of a murmuring coming from the deck. Curious, Eric put on his shirt, pants and shoes and went up to the salon to see what was going on.

Peering through the forward windows, he saw George dressed in native costume kneeling on the right hull bow, bowing and rising as he performed a chant. In his right hand was an extended Raven's wing that he raised in supplication before bowing again.

Five minutes later, George finished and rose to his feet, strode back through the cockpit and entered the door to the salon. He was adorned head to foot in brilliant red and black wear. Upon his head was a black hat that rose a good eight inches, canting outwards slightly and more to the front. The designs upon the hat were in brilliant red, depicting the raven in Tlingit motif with silver buttons as eyes on either side of the beak in the front of the hat. Draped about his shoulders was a wrap with brilliant designs of the salmon, bear, wolf and eagle. Upon his chest was a four-sided breastplate, embroidered in gold, black and red that narrowed as it hung to his waist. Underneath were tanned buckskins with frilled tassels along the forearms.

"Morning! Did you sleep well?" George asked with all the bonhomie of a suburbanite in his bathrobe greeting his neighbor, a coffee mug in one hand, over the fence as he strode to pick up the morning newspaper.

"Fine. Busy morning so far?"

"Nah, just getting some essential work out of the way." With that, George disappeared down the stairs with Eric staring after him.

'Well I'm up now,' Eric thought. After getting dressed properly and performing his morning routine, Eric emerged to find Chuck in the galley preparing breakfast. "So what did you think of George's little disclosure of his father's research funding at the university? I was watching you and you got a strange look on your face as he was telling us it."

"I thought his name sounded vaguely familiar when you introduced us but I never made the connection." Chuck said quietly over the snap and sizzle of the bacon he was frying. "I thought it was just because I had heard his name around the office. I met his father several times in Dr. Katzburg's laboratory when he came to check on our progress a couple of times. He was usually surrounded by the school's administrative bigwigs or Dr. Katzburg. All I really did was shake the man's hand and say hello."

"What are you guys talking about?"   George asked conversationally as he emerged from the door at the end of the galley and pulled a T-shirt over his head.

"Oh, we were just talking about some research that may have some bearing on our quest," Eric covered dismissively.

Chuck had finished his cooking and motioned all three to sit down at the dining table as he delivered up breakfast. George ate happily, as if his morning routine always consisted of rituals in ceremonial garb.

Finally, Eric's curiosity got the best of him, "What was that ritual you were performing this morning?" he asked.

"I was seeking protection for us and this boat from the killer whale, the patron spirit of my house in our hunt for the Chagatash."

Chuck listened on in silence, chewing his breakfast. He was able to gather pretty much all he needed to know from the exchange, before he covertly caught Eric's eye and rolled his own.

"Thank you for the consideration," was all that Eric could think to say.

"Gladly," George returned.

"We'll weigh anchor in a half-hour so that the galley can be cleaned and all loose gear can be put away," Eric announced.

And so the first day of their hunt for the shark started, each man rotating every two hours to a different position. The initial excitement of the hunt gave way to routine, and routine gave way to boredom. Occasionally, the boredom broke when a large moving underwater object was spotted, and the excitement built until it was determined to be a whale or misidentified debris. Eric learned that they could shorten the identification cycle if he turned his directional underwater microphone on an object. If it was a whale or a pod of porpoises, he could hear them and identify them much quicker.

This routine went on for days until they settled into a comfortable rhythm. Because the *Pacific Chanteuse* was equipped with satellite communication gear, everyone could stay in touch with their offices and loved ones, or important calls, which happened on Friday, when Sid called Eric with the DNA results.

"So what did you think of the tooth?" Eric asked.

"Very impressive. Very intriguing. I had a couple of marine biologist come up from Oregon State and Oregon to examine the tooth. They weren't able to add any more information than your man Chuck had developed. Of course, they wanted to know where the Institute had obtained such a 'unique' sample."

"What'd you tell them?"

"Only that one of our researchers had recently come into contact with the donor, and that we were trying to identify and verify information on the species."

"That was almost cruel, Sid. I bet those guys--"

"And gals," Sid supplied.

"--about jumped out of their skins at the '...recently came into contact with...'"

"True. Offers to assist in funding your search have started to jump out of my email box in the last twenty-four hours since word of the tooth's existence got out, which is one of the reasons I called you in the middle of your hunt. I wanted to talk to you about these offers before I responded. All of them either want to head the research effort or place people on your team. I can see their point of view, if they're going to pay for research, they want their people present so that their universities can share title to any discoveries made. But I wasn't about to interrupt your efforts to make you rendezvous with someone in the field."

"Look, Sid...I really think we should wait before bringing in other parties and their reputations. I've gathered some information that may indicate that we're dealing with a one-of-a-kind fish and not a new species."

"Could you be a little more specific, please?'

Eric related the story of Chuck's experience in Dr. Katzburg's lab twenty-five years ago to Sid, who remained quiet as the story unfolded.

"That may explain the DNA results on the tooth that I'm emailing you. OK. For now, I will stall any further additions to your search until we need their resources or money."

"Thanks, Sid. I'll keep you updated with progress reports via email, but don't hold your breath. There's a high probability that this fish has left the area, and we may never find it again."

They said their goodbyes and ended the connection. Eric went to his email to retrieve the DNA results, calling Chuck in to help interpret the results. The top two results showed a ninety-nine point six percent correlation to salmon shark DNA, and a ninety nine point two percent correlation to great white shark DNA.

"That's consistent with what you'd expect if this fish

was Dr. Katzburg's Franken-fish," Chuck stated. "But without knowing precisely which DNA sequences she inserted from the fossilized tooth, we'll never be able to confirm it."

"You know," he said after a moment, "those DNA results fall just on the border of the variation one would also expect to see between closely related species," Chuck said rubbing his chin and staring at the salon floor. "I just don't think that this DNA information is going to help us determine what it is. We just come back to the fundamental question: how do you determine a new species from a mutation? Science just doesn't have the answer."

"And that is where religion comes in," said George from the doorway, having slipped in unnoticed from his wheel watch to see what all the interest was about.

Both Chuck and Eric turned to stare at him.

"What?" George asked, mildly defensive. "I'm just saying that it sounds more like a philosophical question than one of empirical interpretation is all." With a shrug of his shoulders, he went back to his wheel watch.

"You know," Chuck contemplated, "he's right. This new data moves us no closer to understanding what this fish is."

Both men went silent for a moment, until Chuck finally broke the reverie. "I guess I'll just check in with my office while I'm in here. Hand me the satellite phone, will ya?"

Eric handed him the phone and went outside to continue his shift of glassing the waters.

Ten minutes later, Chuck emerged with some

interesting news. "My office has gotten reports from fishermen in the area of several killer whale bodies floating in an area not too far from here," he told Eric and George. Both Chuck and Eric, having seen the TTACS data, understood what this information portended. They looked at each other, and then spoke at the same time.

"We should check it out."

"Let's go take a look."

Eric, accompanied by Chuck, went in to look at the navigation charts. They plotted the locations given by Chuck's office, and Eric plotted a course. After Eric discussed the course corrections with George, everybody resumed their posts.

The locations of the killer whale corpses were well to the south. They were sailing into the wind, so it was going to take a lot of tacking, zigzagging, and time to get where they needed to be. And, it might mean that they were approaching the shark.

After several hours of sailing and two rotations, they started to approach the reported locations of the killer whale corpses. Eric was at the wheel, while George glassed the waters.

"Anything on the LIDAR?" Eric yelled back into the salon.

"Nothing."

"I think I have something in the water, ten degrees off the starboard bow," yelled George.

The *Pacific Chanteuse* came right. At the same time, Eric dropped the main sail and furled the jib. He was in a wide enough channel that the boat could drift all day without danger. With the help of Chuck, Eric lowered the skiff from its davits at the stern of the boat and released it. All three piled in as Eric hit the electric starter on the outboard. In seconds, the boat covered the couple hundred yards to the white and black object in the water that George had spotted. Eric idled up to the body then cut the engine.

As they glided closer, it was clear that this was one of the killer whale carcasses that had been reported. It was floating in the middle of the channel with the tides and wind. The water temperature was a cool fifty-four degrees at this latitude, and even though most of the body was submerged, when the skiff approached from downwind, the stench of a rotting body was evident.

Eric started the engine, circled upwind and re-approached the body. It was the body of a full-sized adult male, a full thirty feet long, lying on its side. At first glance, it was clear that there had been some scavenger activity. Large circular hunks of flesh had been removed from the killer whale. Chuck speculated that this was probably due to basking and salmon sharks. As they examined the body, two distinct wounds became prominent. The head had been crushed; the bowels had been eviscerated.

"What do you think killed it?" Eric asked Chuck.

"It's hard to say. Either wound would have finished it. But the head trauma would have killed it instantly. Just look how mashed in it is. The gut wound is huge. The thing that's striking about that wound, aside from its size, is how neat and surgical the cuts are in a semi-circular pattern. If this were an encounter with a boat or prop, we'd normally see a shredded wound with ribbons of flesh showing rupture characteristics. This," he said gesturing at the whale's belly, "is a bite wound."

"That fits with the kind of damage I saw on my skiff when I was attacked," confirmed Eric. "I bet you our shark did this."

"I would agree," concurred Chuck. "Now, the question is: how long ago did this take place? From the scavenger activity and decomposition, whatever happened, it happened several days ago, maybe even a week." The smell of six tons of decomposing flesh was starting to get to Chuck, who had been hanging over the side to better examine the whale, so he sat back down in the boat. "Let's see if we can find some of the other bodies that were reported in the area."

George, who had been quiet up until now, had been taking video pictures of the whale while they had been examining it. Suddenly, he piped up, "Wait!"

Both Chuck and Eric turned to George, who had turned off the camera and set it aside in the boat. "I want to say something over this fallen sea warrior. It is our custom."

Eric could understand his feelings. He watched whales for five months of the year and felt a special affinity for them. He saw them in every stage of their life cycle, young and old. And occasionally he saw them die, which always sadden him. "That would be nice," he said gently to George.

George had perched himself on the bow of the little rigid hull inflatable, facing the whale, he raised his arms to the skies and said a little prayer in the Tlingit tongue. Fortunately, it was a short prayer as the smell of the carcass seemed to intensify.

As soon as George was done and seated back in the boat, Eric kicked the starter and put some distance between the body and themselves.

As they sped back to the *Pacific Chanteuse*, Eric yelled over the motor and wind to George, "What did your prayer say?"

"I asked for the Mother Wind to take the spirit of the warrior whale to the House of Warriors in the sky, because it had fought bravely," he yelled back.

They tied up the skiff to the stern of the starboard hull and resumed sailing to look for more of the reported bodies. They found three more floating as they headed south down the channel. All showed the unmistakable signs of the large shark's bite when they examined the bodies from the skiff. George offered his prayer for each.

They spotted a fourth whale on the beach further south and brought the *Pacific Chanteuse* in close to shore so they could examine it with binoculars. Eric nixed the idea of going ashore to examine the body, pointing out that a smorgasbord that big was sure to attract lots and lots of bears, which they weren't equipped to deal with. He also didn't mention his recent encounter on a beach with a bear, which he'd no desire to repeat. Sure as predicted, as they were glassing the whale's carcass, a large black bear ambled out of the woods behind the body and trudged on down to feast upon it. George had to be content to say his prayer from the safety of the boat.

Chuck had charted all the positions of the bodies they had found that day. "Hey, Eric, take a look at this," he yelled outside. Eric joined him as he hunched over a navigational chart on the navigation bench. "If you assume," he started without preamble, "that the tides, working in both directions cancel out each other as far as drift goes, that would only leave wind to move the bodies around. If we again assume that the winds have been out of a constant quarter, from the southeast, you can see that the locations of the four bodies we found point back to this area," Chuck circled with his finger, "as the place of the attack."

Eric studied the chart and could find no flaw in the reasoning. "Alright, then that means that the shark was in this area somewhere in the last three to seven days. It could be tens of miles away by now, but we'll add this bit of data to its habits." After a few moments of silence, Eric continued. "You know what's really bothering me about the bodies we've found," he paused for effect, "they're all large adult males. The TTACS data shows the shark attacking the smaller killer whales and ignoring the big male on the scene: that makes sense as a predator. There's less jeopardy picking on someone smaller than you.

"So how did four full-size males become the only victims we can find? Did the shark attack a smaller killer whale and the adult males respond with a counter attack? How big was the pod the shark attacked? For this many adult resident killer whales to be present, the pod had to be of significant size. So are there more dead killer whales out there that we don't know about? Does that indicate that the shark was willing to swim into a large pod of killer whales to seek a meal?

"And the million dollar question is, did the killer whales succeed in killing the shark? We might be out here wasting our time. The killer whales may have already torn the shark asunder. I mean, what are the chances of anything tangling with at least four large killer whales and getting away unscathed? My guess is slim to none."

"All good points. Maybe," Chuck responded, pointing to the map again, "This is the area where the shark is sitting on the bottom being eaten by crabs. But all we can do is keep looking. The shark seems to be a messy eater. If it is still alive, the evidence is bound to turn up sooner or later. All I know is that the only thing we can do is keep looking until there's no more evidence suggesting that it's alive."

"Either that, or we run out of time and money," Eric added dryly.

Eric couldn't help but feel that they were already too late. It was clear a terrible battle had been waged, and he felt sure there were victims on both sides.

This feeling deepened over the next four days as their search ground on without results and no more reports of whale bodies came into Chuck's office.

34

The forty-six killer whales were able to search vast swaths of the archipelago quickly and easily. They were also able to eat well. Those whales of the Ocean Travelers and Open Water tribes benefited by having all the bays, coves and inlets searched, which had a tendency to flush any seals out into the channel and into the jaws of the whales of the two picket lines that preferred warm-blooded meals. The whales of the Three Tribes benefited by the shear number of killer whales hunting in the same confined waters. It bounced and spooked salmon into fragmented clusters that tended to run into the open jaws of the hunters with an inclination for cold-blooded meat.

But while this abundance of food had kept the cooperation high and the friction to a minimum, it was clear that the members of the Clan of the Three Tribes were more committed than others from the other Clans. At the end of two days of searching, grumbles of wanting to return home were starting to surface.

This was the state of affairs on the morning of the third day. The Pod Leader was taking a turn as one of the scout whales searching coves and inlets. His next area of search was to be medium-sized by the look of its entrance. His practice was to move from bay to bay and call from the mouth of the bay. If he received a return call telling him that the bay was already occupied and being searched by killer whales, he moved on until he found one unoccupied in the lead of the formation.

The Pod Leader was approaching the mouth of a bay when he noticed by echolocation two thin fin-like protrusions from the surface moving towards the same bay in front of him, on a convergent course. He'd not noticed the objects in the water because the aspect facing him was the knife-edge of the fins and his echolocation streams had to be very close for the thin edge to return enough sonic energy for him to detect.

As the Pod Leader got closer, he saw two shallow hulls indent upon the surface from which the fins were protruding. These were the hulls of the contraptions that humans rode upon. Yet there was no noise, vibration, thrashing prop, or wake of churning bubbles that accompanied all the boats of the humans that he'd ever encountered. Curious, he took a high arch on his next breath so that he could get a better look at this strange vessel. As he cleared the water and it sheeted from his eyes, the Pod Leader saw that this was the same strange twin hulled vessel that had been present when his mate and pod had been wiped out in the first attack of the Giant Shark.

******

"I've got a large fin approaching from the aft," George shouted.

Eric was at the wheel and had been scanning the sea in front of the *Pacific Chanteuse*. The salon's structure blocked his view to the stern, so he engaged the autopilot and grabbed his binoculars, stepping to the port hull to peer around to the rear quarter. Eric's eyes were the best trained at determining the ownership of fins, since he did it all summer long. "I've got it," he said loudly. It took but a second for him to study and determine that it was the dorsal fin of a large male killer whale. He was excited to have something to do for the moment after days of tedium. At least he could possibly get some of his linguistic research done if only in passing. He ran back in to his computer at the navigation center to cancel the minke whale calls that he'd programmed to broadcast in bursts every two minutes. He called up the sound recording and analysis software then trained the directional mike on the whale. It was quiet for a moment, but then the mike picked up a stream of echolocation clicks. A fraction of a second later, a torrent of echolocation streams could be heard. It literally filled the water from every point aft.

"What the heck is this?" asked a momentarily confused Eric. He'd only seen one dorsal fin. Killer whales usually moved close together when traveling. He'd only seen evidence of one killer whale, but the sound gear was picking up at least a dozen echolocation trains.

"What the heck is what?" asked Chuck from his perch.

Chuck had been watching the LIDAR, but it could only scout in front of the boat so he'd not seen the approach of the whale from the rear. He watched with interest from the steering console where the LIDAR was located, first as Eric went to his side of the boat to identify what George had spotted and then as Eric hurried in to the salon to retarget the directional sound gear.

"I've got more fins. Lots more fins!" George shouted from outside.

Eric snatched up the binoculars that he'd brought with him from outside and hurried out to take another look. As he stepped up on the starboard hull and walked to the top of the stairs that led to the waterline platform built into the back of each hull, he focused his binoculars in the direction that George was staring. As he watched, fins started to appear in a line across the channel as far as he could see, spaced out in large intervals. "This is odd," he muttered to himself. All he was seeing were male dorsal fins, no females. And the pod's swimming arrangement was odd.

'It's like they're forming a line abreast...what the heck?' Eric wondered.

He was just about to put down the binoculars when he caught sight of something out of the corner of his eye. An odd-shaped fin disappeared below the surface before he got focused upon it. He watched, waiting, and it reappeared after being submerged for a minute. "That can't be right," he said in disbelief. "I'll be a sonofabitch," he muttered to himself.

"What? What can't be right?" asked an excited George who had moved in close to view the scene with Eric.

"George!" Eric shouted, forgetting that he was standing practically next to him. "Get the video camera!"

"OK. But what's going on?" he asked excitedly.

By now Chuck was out on the deck to see what all the excitement was about. "Eric, what's going on? What are you so excited about?"

Eric took the binoculars from his eyes to glance at Chuck and George, if only to verify that George had not yet gone to get the video camera. "George, quick, go get the camera! I'll explain when you get back. Now go!"

Chuck backed up so George could run for the video recorder. Eric brought up his glasses and continued to scan the approaching line of killer whales.

When George reappeared with the camera he asked, "OK, so what exactly am I supposed to be recording?"

"Start at the right side of the line of killer whales and then pan to your left. Once you get the killer whales recorded, focus on the fifth whale on the line from the right."

"OK," Chuck said as George started recording, "now you're going to tell us why."

"Because, gentlemen, this is the first known incidence of a transient killer whale traveling or being in the company of resident killer whales. If you'll watch closely, you'll see that the top of the fin is different on the fifth whale from the right. It's rounded differently than the others and it is placed farther back on the spine. The transients have diverged physiologically and linguistically so much from the resident whales that the prevailing thought is that it is a distinctly different subspecies, which means they shouldn't be hanging out together. Not only that, the whole formation of the pod is wrong. It's all males, to start with, and they're roughly arrayed in a line abreast. And that is just *not* normal behavior."

As they watched, the line got closer and closer; more whales in the line came into view across the channel.

"If you think that's weird, you're going to love this," George said. His video recorder trained in the direction the line of killer whales had come from. "It appears that another line of killer whales is following this one several miles further back."

Eric reoriented his binoculars in the distance. Sure enough, in the distance a second line was starting to appear out of the haze of water vapor that hovered near the surface on a hot day. The breath spout clouds and fins slowly emerged, spaced out in the same way as the first line. "Well, I'll be. This is just so freakin' unusual. Unprecedented." He'd run out of vocabulary to express his incredulity.

"My prayer has been answered," George said, somewhat incredulous that he had such power. "I asked for the protection of my tribe's patron spirit, the killer whale, and he has assembled all the killer whales in the sea to protect us. The Spirit Shark must be near. Why else would the killer whales be here now?"

The first line of killer whales would be pulling abreast of the *Pacific Chanteuse* in another minute or two. Eric wanted to make sure that the underwater directional sound gear was tracking the line and it was getting all the data. "I'll be right back. I'm going to grab my laptop to follow the sound recordings." Eric pivoted and started to go back into the salon. In all the excitement he saw that he'd lost track of the boat's progress. It was approaching the end of its tack as it was nearing the mouth of a medium-sized bay on the port quarter that looked to be a mile or so wide. He took a detour through the cockpit and dumped both sails and deactivated the autopilot so that the boat would coast and then drift while they focused on the killer whales.

Eric hurried into the salon after he'd secured all the lines to the sails he'd just cut loose and grabbed his laptop computer. He'd a local Wi-Fi network on the boat so his laptop and other devices could work anywhere on the boat or deck. As he walked back to the deck on the starboard hull, he saw that his sound gear was capturing all the vocalizations that the whales were making. As he studied the screen, something even stranger jumped out at him. The display showed vocalization patterns for the resident killer whales and the transient, but now a third distinct pattern of vocalizations appeared on the screen before him. "Holy shit!" he exclaimed as he joined the others on the deck, staring intently at his computer's screen.

"What now?" Chucked asked, caught up in the excitement.

Eric ignored him as his fingers flew from the built-in cursor director to the keyboard with one hand, while his other held the laptop to his chest. He isolated the track that contained the vocalizations of an offshore killer whale. "Everyone be quiet!" Eric commanded. He then played the vocalization track over the speakers of his laptop. First once, then he repeated it three more times, his exquisite hearing confirming what the screen was telling him.

Eric was totally oblivious that Chuck and George didn't fully understand what was happening. Had he looked up he would have seen that they were watching Eric's intensity and facial expressions, and to them, it was clear that something very strange and important was happening.

Finally, Eric uttered: "In-frickin-credible."

Chuck could hold his silence no longer, "All right, spill, will ya? Out with it. What's going on?" he demanded.

Still looking at the computer screen cradled against his chest, Eric started, "Not only are there transient killer whales out there, there are offshore killer whales, too."

Eric looked up from his computer to his companions. Both had excited smiles on their faces , which hid eyes that were blank. Neither said anything to acknowledge they understood the importance of what he had just said. Clearly they were not getting it, so Eric decided to clarify what they were all seeing.

"Let me put it this way: three different types of whales, that are not supposed to mix, let alone cooperate with each other, are swimming in formation like an all-male chorus line."

Both Chuck and George nodded their head in unison of understanding.

Eric broke the spell of the moment, "Chuck, the first line is about to pass -- make sure that the LIDAR is going to capture the line formation of the whales."

"You got it!" as Chuck dashed back into the salon to configure the LIDAR.

Eric watched for several more minutes as the line approached. The *Pacific Chanteuse* had now drifted in front of the bay mouth, and the bows had swung to face the channel when the line of killer whales came abreast. And without notice, the line passed the boat.

Eric watched as the killer whale line receded. And then he'd an idea.

"Hey, Chuck. You up and running yet on the LIDAR?" Eric yelled the question at the deck cabin.

"Yeah, I'm recording."

"I'm going to try something. Let me know if anything happens."

"OK."

Eric went to the vocalization library and called up the mystery call from the TTACS recording of the shark attack it captured. He walked out to the bow of the starboard hull and hit the key to broadcast.

TTTTHHHROOOOM click-click-click-click, TTTTHHHROOOOM click-click-click-click, TTTTHHHROOOOM click-click-click-click.

35

The shark had been prowling for food just inside the mouth of a bay, when it heard the attack call of the pesky patched whales that had attacked it relentlessly. The call came from just outside the bay's mouth. It instantly became nervous. It remembered that the last time it had heard those calls, it had been bottled up in a very similar bay and had to fight its way out to open water before it could escape. It didn't want to get caught again trying to fight its way out. Knowing that there were the patched whales just outside the bay, the shark swam cautiously toward the mouth, looking to escape.

The Pod Leader had drawn to within fifty yards of the boat when the boat emitted the killer whale War Cry. And even stranger, it was his voice making the call. The Pod Leader had intended to pass between the boat and the shore, swimming on by to the bay's mouth. But having heard its own voice emit the war cry from this boat, he decided to circle the boat on the channel side for further inspection. As the Pod Leader circled the boat, he focused echolocation streams at it and the water around the boat. Nothing unusual seemed to be going on with this irregular and silent craft. The Pod Leader had circled halfway around the boat and was facing the mouth of the bay when its echolocation streams reflected the mass of the Giant Shark trying to emerge from the bay's mouth.

******

"I don't know exactly what you did," Chuck called out from the deck cabin, but every killer whale on the screen stopped dead in its tracks and turned towards you

"I'm not sure what I did, either. But I can see that this new call means something mighty important. It seems we've attracted their attention." Eric had noted the scrutiny of a single male killer whale that had come to inspect the *Pacific Chanteuse*. It had circled the boat and drawn even with where Eric stood. "George, please tell me you're getting all this?"

While drifting with her sails flapping and boom swinging in the breeze, the boat had swung nose first into the southeasterly breeze. Chuck was using the manual controls of the LIDAR to focus on the line of killer whales. He didn't see the giant body swim out of the bay into the mouth opening. "Yeah," reported Chuck staring at the LIDAR screen.

Upon seeing the Giant Shark, the Pod Leader was surprised for a second and then let loose with its own war cry: TTTHHHROOOOM click-click-click-click, TTTHHHROOOOM click-click-click-click, TTTHHHROOOOM click-click-click-click. This time, his call was answered by forty-five killer whales with their own war cries acknowledging the hunt was on.

Eric didn't need his sound gear to hear the single male's reply to his broadcasted call, nor the return calls from the other killer whales in the channel. The hull of the *Pacific Chanteuse* acted as an amplifier transferring the calls from sea to air.

******

The Giant Shark found a boat and a killer whale blocking its escape to the sea. It had heard another killer whale's call, so it knew that there was at least one more killer whale blocking its escape. In addition, it could now hear the voices of many, many killer whales in the channel. It decided to retreat back into the bay

******

All the scouting killer whales that had been checking bays on both sides of the channel heard the combined war cries of the hunting party and understood that the Giant Shark had been found. It was now time to run it to ground, so they sprinted from whatever bay or channel they were in to the channel where the hunt would take place.

The Pod Leader saw the Giant Shark retreat back into the bay and knew that he had to go flush the shark from the bay so the trap could be sprung. But first, the Pod Leader wanted to examine more closely the boat that had used his voice when it found the Giant Shark, and alerted the hunting pack. He wanted a better look at the hunting pack's new ally. The Pod Leader aligned himself vertically in the water and with small strokes of its fluke raised its head, flukes and dorsal fin out of the water to get a better look at the boat and its human inhabitants. As he came out of the water, he saw two humans on deck. One stood to the rear and was covering its face with a small object, while another stood on the front of the boat holding a small, flat object. As he rose from the water just feet away from the boat, the human on the front of the boat stepped in his direction. It was speaking to him, although he couldn't understand what it was saying. This must be the human in charge. He focused his attention on the human that had stepped forward to greet him. He noted the colors of the human, the color of its hair and the arrangement of its features. As he examined the human, it raised one of its odd looking flippers and waved it at him, which he took as a greeting.

The Pod Leader pondered this unusual contact with the humans at this time. The boat had been present when his family had been killed. He'd not seen any humans on it that day. Yet, they must have seen the slaughter, because they had just used his war cry to alert the hunting pod and, more importantly, the humans had warned him of the Giant Shark that appeared moments after sounding the alarm. Without that warning, he might have been killed by the Giant Shark in an ambush.

The Pod Leader didn't fully understand the humans and their ways, but he did understand that the humans had been hunting the Giant Shark, too. They seemed intent upon helping him and the hunting pack, probably because they were angry at the killing of his family. He felt a new sense of camaraderie towards them for their desire of revenge for killing his family. He also felt a sudden sense of gratitude towards the humans. And why not? He was hunting today with killer whales of three different tribes. It was going to take the cooperation of many different interested parties to be successful. They all shared the same goal of killing the Giant Shark he concluded as he waved his flipper at the human's leader.

******

As Eric watched the lone killer whale circle the boat, it came to a halt in front of him as he stood near the bow. Slowly, the massive male rose from the water as it spy hopped. His eyes were nearly level with Eric. HE was so fascinated by being approached by this killer whale of the wild that he subconsciously took two steps towards the bow and the killer whale. "Are you getting this, George?" he asked loudly.

"Uh-huh," came George's reply from behind the video recorder.

Eric could think of nothing more to do at this unexpected approach other than to wave at the nice killer whale. He felt foolish for doing it. All his scientific life, Eric had been listening to killer whales, trying to understand what they were saying with the hope that one day he would be able to speak to them. All the while, the killer whales had ignored him in studied silence. Now unexpectedly, out of nowhere, this huge male killer whale wanted to make contact with him, and he was totally dumbstruck and unprepared. He'd his laptop in hand but couldn't think of one vocalization in the computer's library that would be appropriate to play. To make matters worse, the killer whale understood his greeting and was now waving back at him with its flipper. Eric's big chance at establishing interspecies contact in the wild had devolved into waving.

But sometimes in the course of life, it is the simplest gestures that have the greatest impact.

******

The Pod Leader appreciated the help of the humans and it had fixed in his mind the leader of the human boat. But, now it was time to kill the Giant Shark. He slid back into the water and slowly swam at the entrance of the bay, preparing to face the Giant Shark. He proceeded cautiously, sending a constant stream of echolocation clicks until he found the shark swimming three hundred yards beyond the entrance.

36

The lone killer whale slid back into the waters and proceeded to swim to the bay behind them. Eric watched the whale disappear with a sense of disappointment at the opportunity lost. From behind him George asked what he wanted to do. "Let's just stay here for the moment and observe the other killer whales for a while."

George had stopped recording and had resumed watching the killer whales through his binoculars. Eric headed into the salon to watch the whales on the LIDAR with Chuck, figuring that was the best way to see all that was happening. Chuck made room for Eric at the counter and they both watched the screen. "What are they doing?" he asked.

"Nothing. They all seem to be just holding their position and milling about. Here, take a look." Chuck adjusted the laser's sweep to focus just on the whales in the channel.

"I'd normally say that's strange," a chagrined Eric started, "but today, strange seems to be the norm."

******

The Giant Shark had eaten well two days before on a minke whale it had killed. Its hunger was starting to take form but had not become overpowering yet. It had been aimlessly swimming when it heard the calls of the killer whales outside the bay mouth. Now one of the patched whales was approaching it slowly, emitting a constant clicking noise. This one wasn't acting aggressively and didn't seem intent on attacking.

******

The Pod Leader moved slowly and deliberately as it moved into the bay, always aware through echolocation of what the Giant Shark was doing. He could tell that the Giant Shark was nervous, making quick turns rather than lazy circles. He turned left as soon as he cleared the entrance and hugged the shore to put as much room between him and the Giant Shark. Slowly, very slowly, so not to further agitate the Giant Shark, the Pod Leader worked his way to the back of the bay. Once opposite the bay's mouth with the Giant Shark in between, he started to weave in big loops in an effort to herd the Giant Shark toward the entrance.

It was nerve-wracking work for the Pod Leader, knowing that at any moment the Giant Shark could charge. Knowing he was no match for the Giant Shark strained at his nerves. He knew that the Giant Shark was faster and more powerful. It could choose at any moment to kill him and there was nothing that he could do. Further intensifying the situation, the Pod Leader had to take his echolocation sense out of action to herd the Giant Shark out the mouth of the Bay. His echolocation sense was developed to sense what was in the water ahead of him. But he'd to turn his body and swim sideways to the Giant Shark in order to achieve the herding pressure he desired. The only way to keep aware of what the Giant Shark was doing was to move closer so that he could visually observe what it was doing, which meant the Pod Leader had to move within a hundred feet due to the turbidity of the water. It was a delicate balance between applying pressure but not enough to provoke an attack, while trying to stay ahead and cut off the avenues of escape of a creature that could swim faster. It took a stout heart bolstered by a burning thirst for revenge to keep pressing on.

Slowly the Giant Shark started to move toward the opening until it finally headed out through the bay mouth into the channel, its fin breaking the water, passing just fifty feet in front of the strange surface craft of the human's, and into the prepared trap beyond.

******

As the Giant Shark passed the first picket killer whale, it turned and paralleled it. The appearance of another of the patched whales made the Giant Shark even more wary. But the whales were acting differently this time. They were not as aggressive. Still, the presence of these whales made the Giant Shark nervous, so it angled away from the shadowing tormenters. With one behind it and one to its side, it continued to swim in the direction of the channel center. Soon, a third whale joined them on the left, and then a fourth. When the fourth patched whale joined the group, their behavior changed. The three whales on the left started to weave a wall up and down. When one went to the surface for a breath, the other would go low to a depth just slightly below the Giant Shark while the third whale ranged just slightly ahead, weaving up and down. The patched whale at his rear began to crowd the Giant Shark and emit a constant stream of squeals and clicks that annoyed the Giant Shark, causing it to swim faster and faster. The Giant Shark was now exerting significant energy to swim faster until it found an uncomfortable speed where the patched whales seemed to harass it less. Little did the shark know, this speed was faster than its cruising speed, causing the Giant Shark to expend more energy and carbon dioxide to build up in its circulatory system faster than its gills could expel the gas.

This traveling wall encountered other patched whales at regular intervals. As it did, the leading whale slid back and joined the two weaving beside the Giant Shark, the newcomer taking the lead whale's position. Then one of the weaving whales would drop behind the Giant Shark, and the whale that had been trailing would drop away and disappear. In this manner, the Giant Shark was always hemmed in to its left and pressured from behind.

Once or twice, the Giant Shark tried to chase away the patched whales. But when it turned into the whales, they scattered, being smaller, more nimble creatures, while the whale at his rear surged ahead until it was dangerously close to the Giant Shark's flank ,with a better interception angle due to the Giant Shark's turn. This forced the Giant Shark to break off his aggression and turn back in the direction it had been forced to swim. The same happened when the Giant Shark tried to dive.

******

Eric and Chuck watched the LIDAR screen, but not much seemed to be happening with the whales in the channel. Slowly, a new underwater object began to creep on to the screen. White laser returns started to materialize on the edge of the narrow sweep to which Chuck had set the unit. Chuck was the first to notice it. "It looks like the single male is coming out of the bay to join the others," he said, pointing to the blip that was materializing.

But as they watched, the blip suddenly grew to a size much larger than the killer whales, followed by a smaller blip. "The lone killer whale must have flushed a humpback whale out of the bay," Eric offered as an explanation for the new blip. "Hey, George! Keep your eyes open for a humpback whale that just swam past us heading out into the Channel."

"OK!"

As the humpback whale swam further and further out into the channel, the killer whales of the picket began to swim alongside the humpback but always to one side, one just to the side, and one behind, below. But the wall of three killer whales always stayed in formation. As the whale sped up, it overtook the next killer whale in line while one of the flanking whales dropped off.

Eric continued to watch this scene unfold while trying to analyze what he was seeing.

"This just didn't make sense. I've seen plenty of resident killer whales, which were fish eaters. Why would they harass a humpback whale? Why would they help transient killer whales kill the larger whale?"

As he watched, the humpback whale put on a tremendous burst of speed, a burst of speed beyond what any humpback had ever been recorded.

'*This whale's got to be on steroids,*' Eric thought, '*to achieve that – or have been shot from a rocket launcher.*' Then recognition started to set in; Eric had so believed that the giant shark had died from killer whale attack, that he let himself be blinded to the reality of what had just swum by his boat. The creature in the center of the whale lines was the giant shark. Or maybe the killer whales had killed one giant shark and this was another. It now all made sense why this pod was all males and mixed tribes. The killer whales had united to hunt down and kill the giant sharks and he had a front row seat to the proceedings.

"I'll be a sonofabitch," burst suddenly from Eric without warning. "George," he yelled outside, "did you ever see the humpback come up for air?"

"Not yet."

"Sonofabitch!"

Chuck had started to grow used to such outbursts today, excitedly asked, "Now what?"

"That." Eric pointed wildly at the screen. "That sonofabitch right there is the giant shark. It swam right past us and we didn't even see it. Goddamnit." Eric was mad. Not mad at his boat members. They had all been distracted by the appearance and antics of the whales that they had lost focus on what they were supposed to be doing. He was just mad at his circumstances. His biggest career opportunity and scientific discovery had just sauntered by while he was asleep at the switch.

"Are you sure?" questioned Chuck, not wanting to believe that such a large fish could waltz right past them after all the days of fruitless searching.

"Positive. No whale that size is capable of swimming as fast as that thing is sprinting.

"You'd better turn the boat because the shark is about to swim off the screen's edge," warned Chuck.

'It'll be faster to start the engine than try and turn the boat by sail,' Eric calculated, as he reached down and hit the glow plug starter and then hit both starter buttons on the diesels without even letting the glow plug get up to temperature. The diesels cranked for three or four seconds before they caught. Without even letting them warm, he rammed the engine throttles into forward and spun the wheel in front of him at the inside steering station. The *Pacific Chanteuse* jumped as if scalded, and Eric saw George lurch wildly, caught off-guard by Eric's panicked actions.

As George righted himself, he yelled at Eric "What's going on?"

"Hold on!" Eric yelled belatedly.

Chuck was working the LIDAR controls furiously, trying to keep ahead of the shark and Eric's wild maneuvers.

"You still got it?"

"Yeah, I got it."

Eric was powering the *Pacific Chanteuse* at full throttle with her dagger boards down and sail unfurled out into the center of the Channel to stay in range of the LIDAR. The boat had not been built to be sailed like this. The dagger boards made the boat twitchy under power, and even though the sails were loose, they still caught an awful lot of breeze that fought Eric for control of the boat.

Black smoke poured from the underwater exhaust ports of the diesels because the cylinder temperatures were below normal operating temperature and the engines were laboring.

Eric muscled the *Pacific Chanteuse* into the center of the channel and Chuck talked him through putting the bows on the shark. Eric cut the engines and raced out into the cockpit where he frantically set the sails, bringing the boat back under sail power.

The wind was quartering to a reach and the *Pacific Chanteuse* was eager to dash at full speed, but Eric only needed half of that so he furled the jib and trimmed the main loosely. He only wanted enough power to keep the *Pacific Chanteuse* in steerage while spinning like the hub of a wheel to track the giant shark. Chuck called out heading changes to keep the bow on the shark.

"George, take over the wheel, please. I need to go see what's happening on the LIDAR."

"Alright, I've got it," he said as he slid behind the wheel and put his hand on it.

"Thanks." Eric hustled back into the salon to join Chuck at the LIDAR screen, asking, "What's happening?" as soon as his head cleared the doorway.

"Not much. See for yourself," Chuck replied as he made room for Eric at the screen. "They just seem to be swimming along together. As they roll up on another killer whale, one of them drops off."

Eric studied the screen intently. The line of killer whales was now markedly starting to curve at the end because the shark had been swimming slightly to its right.

"Put the LIDAR on wide sweep. Let's see what the killer whales that were following the first batch are doing."

Chuck turned a couple knobs, and the screen changed to show what was happening in a one hundred eighty degree arc in front of the boat. It showed the picket line of killer whales was bowing from the right while the line of killer whales on the left had bowed in the opposite direction and the two would shortly connect just in front the shark.

Eric watched for the next forty-five minutes as the shark raced around an oval track of the killer whales' making. It slowly dawned on him what their intent was. He remembered a paper he'd read a couple of years ago that described the hunting patterns of transient whales when hunting large whales. What he was seeing had all the hallmark characteristics. "I think I know what's going on," he said to Chuck. "I think the killer whales are trying to run the shark to ground."

Chuck didn't understand the metaphor. "No, they are keeping themselves between the shore and the shark."

"No, what I mean is, what they're trying to do is to tire the shark out. If I'm right, they're going to kill the shark." Eric let that sink in for effect before resuming. "First they'll exhaust it, and then they'll overwhelm it with superior numbers. It's how the transient whales hunt large whales in the open ocean. They run them ragged for a couple of hours, and then they move in and rip it to shreds, often eating their prey before its dead. It looks like they're doing the same.

"Here, see on the screen how they've formed a circle

around the shark? They are forcing it in an ever tightening loop, tiring the shark out."

And, he added to himself, *'Great, I've found the shark only to watch it get ripped to shreds right in front of me. How ironic is that?'*

"If that's true," pondered Chuck, "we're going to lose the body of the shark," he said with realization, "and with it, all real, physical evidence to determine its origin." The bitterness of this possibility washed sour in Chuck's mouth. He wanted desperately to know if this was the shark that had ruined his scientific career before it ever started and through its recovery, rekindle his scientific credentials. "Do you have a plan, if that's what the killer whales are trying to do?" he asked Eric.

"Maybe we can make this work for us," Eric said as a realization came to him. The words of Sid, his boss, came back to him. Sid had been giddy about the prospect of bringing in a body of the shark. Eric had dismissed it because he knew that the *Pacific Chanteuse* could never kill something that large. It would take an explosive-head harpoon cannon to kill something that big. But if they let the killer whales do the work for them, there just might be a ray of hope in this situation for them.

"The only thing that we can do is to try and put as many tracking tags into the shark as possible rather than just one. Then we can trigger the gas recovery bags. Maybe if we get enough on the shark, it will be enough to float the carcass when the killer whales are done with it."

"That might just work. Shark bodies are only slightly negatively buoyant. They rely on oils manufactured and stored in their livers to give their bodies buoyancy. It shouldn't take much to tip the scales and make it positively buoyant. It may not rocket to the surface, but it doesn't have to. It just has to come up, as long as it gets there. Once we get it to the surface, we can tie bumpers and the skiff to it for flotation and tow it back to town to land it. I'm sure I can make arrangements with one of the canneries to store the body in one of the cold-storage units."

"In order for this to work, the speed of the chase will have to diminish and we'll have to have the wind on either a reach or a following wind to get our fastest speed. Right now, the killer whales are chasing the shark faster than we can go at top speed. I make that they are chasing the shark at about twenty knots. Under optimum conditions, the best the *Chanteuse* can do is fifteen, tops. We need to wait until they're going slower if we're going to have a chance."

Chuck nodded assent.

The one thing that Eric didn't say was how much he hated this plan. It was dangerous enough maneuvering the *Pacific Chanteuse* close enough for one shot. But trying to hold the boat in position long enough for three shots? That was just begging for disaster. The only thing he hated more than the plan was the thought of losing the shark, so Eric went outside to tell George of their plan.

"It looks like killer whales want to chase the shark for a while."

"Yes. They'll chase if for hours if they need to," George finished the thought for Eric. "When their prey is tired and weak, they will kill it."

Eric was surprised at George's knowledge of killer whales. His surprise must have showed on his face.

George continued, "My people have seen killer whales take prey this way many times over the centuries. We call them 'the Wolves of the Sea' because, like wolves, they use teamwork and relays to run down their prey, making their prey grow weak while they grow strong, resting while others of the pack chase the prey. And like the wolf, when the time comes they will savage and shred it without remorse."

Eric thought this analogy was very accurate. He was reminded again of how much understanding of animal behavior was intertwined in the culture of the Alaskan Natives. He explained what they intended to do, then came back in to watch the drama unfold with Chuck. They watched for an hour as the killer whales chased the shark around the circuit, probably twenty miles or larger, one full time without the shark's speed diminishing.

A third of the way into the second lap, they started to see the speed of the shark fall off very slightly. As they watched, it exited the distant corner of the oval. Now they saw a further decrease in its speed, but their anxiety was building. They didn't know when the killer whales were going to attack, and their only hope was to tag the shark before they moved in for the kill.

"I think that the shark will be tired enough by the start of the third pass." Eric voiced his opinion, trying to convince himself as well as Chuck. "I don't think we can wait much longer than that. Our best chance is to try and catch the shark in the straightaway of the oval on the first leg. That way, we'll have good wind and good speed, sailing on a reach. If we wait to try and catch the shark on the far corner, we'd have a good following wind, but the window for top speed will be much smaller, and we'd constantly have to change course on a curve. I think the killer whales will attack somewhere on the backstretch. I'm afraid if we wait until then, it might be too late."

Chuck was silent, studying the LIDAR screen and pondering Eric's statement. He'd noted the slowing progress of the shark's speed on the LIDAR, and looking at Eric, nodded his head once. "I agree."

"I think the best place to start our run will be to return back to the bay mouth that the shark swam out of, let them swim past and then sprint as best we can to overtake the shark and get as many shots off as we can."

"I'm in," Chuck said excitedly, now that they were moving from observing to action.

"There's only one hitch. In order to position ourselves, we're going to have to turn our backs on the chase for a while. We'll be blind until the shark comes around in front of us. If the killer whales attack before then, we'll miss everything, including a last ditch opportunity to swing in and get some tagging shots off."

"Everything is a trade-off, Eric," Chuck counseled. "It's the best we can do with imperfect information. It was luck that you survived the first attack of the shark, and it was luck that put us in the middle of the killer whales' hunting party when they cornered the shark. All we can do is take our best shot and hope that our luck holds out."

"Luck has nothing to do with it," George inserted, having come down into the salon doorway to hear what they were talking about. "I told you that you would need me if you were going after the Spirit Fish and that you would need me and the patron spirits of my clan and tribe. Just look at what it has brought to you; the greatest warriors of the sea have gathered to help you in your quest. Even now, they seek to tire the fish so that you can get your instruments on it. I don't know what more proof you need. I've been watching," George waved the binoculars he was carrying in the air, "the killer whales for several hours and I can see no other explanation, can you?"

Chuck and Eric were silent; they had no ready answer to counter George's claims. Eric nodded, but he was sure that Chuck, principled in science as he was, felt the same way. Counting on luck or native voodoo was no way to do scientific research. He was already operating way outside his comfort zone. Eric headed out the door to the cockpit. "George, get your camera ready. We're going shark hunting. I've got the wheel," he said as placed his hand on the rudder wheel. "COMING ABOUT!"

Eric brought the *Pacific Chanteuse* around sharply to head for the bay's mouth. He brought all the boat's sail to bear as he raced ahead to get to the starting point before the shark did. George put fresh batteries in the camcorder and copied the video in its memory to Eric's laptop.

Eric set the autopilot and then went to the salon where he switched on the diesel engines, letting them idle to warm, before returning to the cockpit.

Meanwhile, Chuck placed the rifle's case on the galley table and opened it. He took two cylinders and slipped them into his right front pocket and then loaded the last cylinder into the gun, waiting to prime the pressure system that fired the gun until he was ready to shoot, to lessening the chances of an accidental discharge. The light streaming in from the windows glinted coldly off the weapon's barrel, portending of the coming violence for which it was built.

37

In short order, the *Pacific Chanteuse* had arrived at the starting point of its run. "COMING ABOUT!" Eric dumped tension on the sails and spun the boat to face in the direction he intended to chase the shark in. His gut was telling him that he was only going to have one shot at this, so he pre-positioned all his lines and the traveler for the main sail. When all was ready, he used the diesels to hold the boat on station and to pivot the boat using the engines to swing the bows in arc so that Chuck could find the shark on the LIDAR.

"Found it!" he said excitedly. "About three miles out...and heading this way! They've really slowed down."

Relief showed in Chuck's and Eric's faces. Now, more than ever, Eric was convinced that this would be the shark's final lap, one way or another.

"How much time do we have?' George asked.

"Probably ten or fifteen minutes," Chuck estimated as Eric joined him at the LIDAR screen.

"Good," said George, putting down the camera and dashing down the stairs to his room. He appeared two minutes later tugging his ceremonial garb into place with one hand while donning his hat with the other. He rushed out to the starboard bow where he immediately started to chant while kneeling with his hands on his thighs, arms akimbo. The rhythm of his chant didn't change but the words and the loudness cycled from high to low and back again.

Eric and Chuck watched through the window of the deck cabin as the wind carried George's chants in through the door. Chuck had not yet seen the brightly colored red and black outfit. He stared intently at the beautiful regalia. They watched with interest as George continued to apply himself to the Spirit World of the Tlingit people. A sense of thanks and appreciation suddenly washed over Eric; he felt an odd sense of assurance knowing that George was appealing for assistance from a higher source, and right now he felt he needed all the help he could get if they were going to pull this off.

Eric felt an elbow jab him in the ribs. He turned to see Chuck pointing at the LIDAR screen. It was getting close. But he didn't want to interrupt George's supplications, at the risk of offending any gods or shorting them of any assistance. He waited for a few more moments, as long as he could, but it was time to go. He'd just chosen his words with which to interrupt George when he stopped and stood up. Then he did something unexpected. He clasped his hands together, bowed his head and said a short prayer, after which he started to walk back toward the deckhouse.

Eric reached down and killed the diesels before going out to the cockpit. "Time is getting short, George. No time for a change of clothes." As he stepped into the cockpit, Eric put a hand on George's shoulder as he stepped by. "Thanks. I appreciate you covering all the bases for us. And don't forget to put your life preserver vest back on."

"Get ready," Chuck yelled from inside.

Eric could see the dorsal fins of the killer whales approaching. He thought he could see a gray body in the water on the other side of whales. The *Pacific Chanteuse* sat in the water like a relay runner waiting for the baton to be passed. As the procession passed two hundred yards in front of the *Pacific Chanteuse*, Eric killed the diesel mains, then hauled in lines on the sails as the boat jumped into the chase.

******

The Pod Leader, after completing his second chase of the Giant Shark, had leisurely swum back to its starting position in front of the mouth of the bay where he'd found the Giant Shark. He sensed the odd boat approaching as he rested in the water. His curiosity was still aroused by the creatures that were assisting them in the hunt for the Giant Shark. He swam over close to the boat when a brightly colored human appeared and settled on one of the craft's two points. It appeared to him that the human was again trying to talk to him. Again, he didn't understand what the human was trying to say, but this time his voice carried a rhythm and pitch modulation that he could relate to; it sounded familiar, like the language of the whales.

But he could hear the sounds of the chase approaching. The Giant Shark was tiring quickly now, its approach much slowed. Soon it would be time to start the killing. He was rested and ready to take on the Giant Shark one last time.

******

The *Pacific Chanteuse* accelerated quickly and was up to full speed in a quarter-mile under Eric's expert hands. The shark could clearly be seen ahead of the boat, its great dorsal fin plowing through the water, followed by the caudal fin swishing from side to side. The killer whales' strategy had worked; the shark's speed was down to less than ten knots. The *Pacific Chanteuse* was closing the gap steadily.

George was on the starboard bow with his camera documenting the whales, the shark and the chase, his inflatable life jacket with air horn strapped on over his ceremonial costume. Chuck was standing out on the cross member between the two hulls holding onto the jib's furling device, waiting until they were a little bit closer before taking his position on the smaller spar that anchored the mainsail mast support cable.

******

The human craft crept up on the killer whale that was in the chase position. The whale had been so focused on the shark that it was unaware of the silent boat's approach. The startled whale momentarily broke off its harassment and swam to the inside of the oval track until the craft passed. The other whales of the picket to the left were confused by the appearance of the boat in the middle of their program. The Pod Leader didn't know what the humans were trying to do exactly, but he knew they were there to help. He spoke to the other whales telling them not to run, to hold and watch; the humans were there to help.

******

Eric adjusted the sails, easing off some power. The shark was in front of the boat now with the *Pacific Chanteuse* gaining foot by foot.

Chuck started to get in position. Although the green waters of the Pacific were glass smooth, the *Pacific Chanteuse* was under full sail and on a reach. The wind gently rocked and plunged the boat as speed, friction, leverage, and buoyancy all fought for supremacy one moment to the next. Chuck held the tag gun in his left hand while holding onto the jib unfurling device in his right, sliding his feet along the bow sprite spar until he was able to hook his wrist and gun over the mast guy wire. He let go with his right hand to grab the guy wire and shuffled his feet up the four-foot span of the spar to its tip. He brought the gun to his shoulder firing position while hugging the guy wire. After he charged the air system, making the gun hot to shoot, he gave a thumb up to let Eric know it was time.

Eric used one of the hand winches at the front of the cockpit to tighten the line on the jib just a crank to add a fraction of power. Foot by foot, the *Pacific Chanteuse* crept forward, straddling the shark with its two hulls.

******

The Giant Shark swam on, too tired to care about the silent boat creeping up from behind. It could sense the boat but the signal was small, constant and rhythmical which didn't unduly alarm it. This was less irritating than the squeals and clicks of the patched whales.

******

The giant tail of the shark passed under Chuck, flicking from side to side in a six-foot arc. The shark was swimming just a couple of feet under the water. The power of its tail sent water sheeting over its back. Its huge dorsal fin was creating a small wake and bow waves angling from its front edge where it cut the surface.

Eric watched as the big tail slide, flicking from side to side between the hulls of the *Pacific Chanteuse*, measuring how close each flick came to striking the inside of the sponson hulls. If he didn't keep the *Chanteuse* perfectly centered over the shark, even the slightest contact with the hull could crush it or lead to a catastrophic outcome at this speed.

Chuck was going to try and set the transmitter as close to the base of the dorsal fin as possible. The giant fin was now seven feet in front of him. Chuck sighted the gun. But the shark was swimming just deep enough that Chuck didn't think the transmitter could punch through the water and affix to its back. *Time for Plan B*, Chuck thought. He retargeted the gun higher on the fin six inches below the water line, and pulled the trigger.

The gun gave considerable more recoil than Chuck had expected. With a lurch and a very loud pop, the transmitter punched through the water with a loud plop and banged into the shark's dorsal fin a foot above its base. The sharp barb punched through the shark's tough, thick skin and set. The slipstream of the water flowing over the shark's body grabbed the transmitter and dragged it backwards, playing out the plastic tether from inside. As the last of the tether played out, it flipped a switch, activating the unit.

Eric saw the projectile leave the gun's barrel and strike the shark. This was the instant he feared. If the shark flinched, one flick of its tail could damage or sink his boat.

The shark did nothing to respond to the probe stuck in its back.

******

The Pod Leader watched as the boat positioned itself over the shark, two humans positioned on the front. It looked like the humans were poised to attack the Giant Shark in some manner. The Pod Leader felt kinship for the warriors of the boat who were not afraid to make the first strike on the Giant Shark.

******

Chuck let go of the rifle with his right hand and groped for the breach release catch to crack the gun open. As he flicked the breach release, the gun flopped open. With his left hand hooked around the guy wire, he fumbled in his pocket for another transmitter. His fingers fumbled to grab onto the tube, but he finally managed to pinch out the tube so that he could wrap his hand around it. Given his precarious position, he made several attempts to slide the cylinder into the breach.

"C'mon, c'mon," Eric muttered under his breath, "this is taking way too long." Eric split his focus on the shark in front of the boat and the giant tail fin that was missing the inside hulls by just mere feet with each flick.

Chuck finally got the next transmitter into the firing chamber and clanked shut the breach. He primed the air system to charge the gun for his second shot. The shark had crept in a little closer as it was losing energy and speed. George was still on his perch on the starboard bow, camera stuck to his eye taking it all in. Eric saw the slowdown of the shark and was frantically adjusting the sails to slow the boat. Chuck brought up the gun to his shoulder and sighted the gun. The angle was a little steeper, but it was relatively the same shot. Chuck squeezed the trigger. The gun popped loudly and the transmitter flew. This time, it found its mark six inches below the first.

"C'mon, c'mon, c'mon. Hurry," Eric chanted.

Chuck groped again for the breach release. He fumbled even longer this time trying to corral the lone transmitter left in his pocket. The transmitter slid from one side to the other as Chuck stabbed his thumb and forefinger into his pocket. Finally, the transmitter lodged diagonally in his pocket. With difficulty, he was finally able to dig it out and maneuvered it into the breach.

"Jesus Christ, Chuck! You're taking too long! C'mon, c'mon!" Eric was loosing the battle trying to stay behind the shark. It was fading fast. The *Pacific Chanteuse* had crept up over the shark now with most of it between the hulls. The shark's tail fin had slid from Eric's vision and was now somewhere below the main mast.

Chuck primed the gun again and shouldered it. The giant dorsal fin was now directly underneath his feet. He would have to shoot straight down, a difficult shot from the shoulder in his precarious position. Then Chuck had an idea. This was a point blank shot. He would just hang the gun from his side with one hand and shoot.

Just as he was pulling the trigger, the shark rose and a patch of its back cleared the water's surface just below the barrel of the gun.

POP!

The transmitter, fired from four feet with no water to slow its impact, struck the shark full force, the barb plunging deep into its back. The shark flinched hard at the sudden pain in its back and flicked its tail hard to its right, swatting the starboard hull with a horrifying smack, and smashing the boat to starboard several feet.

Eric was thrown to the port side of the cockpit by the force of the shark's tail, the deck shoved out from under his feet. Instinctively, he grabbed onto whatever was close by to maintain his balance, but at that moment, it just happened to be the boat's wheel. Eric's momentum jerked the wheel hard to port, only to be shoved hard to starboard as he tried to correct. In slow motion, Eric watched as George and Chuck were launched from their spots as he struggle with his own balance.

George felt the deck disappear from beneath his knees and the video camera fly from his hands as he reflexively thrashed his arms for balance. George's first reaction was to dive after the camera flying to his left. In less than half a heartbeat, he realized that that had been the wrong choice as he found himself flying through the space in front of the boat where the giant shark swam beneath him. He twisted in space to face the cross-member between the hulls and threw his arms out to try to catch it. The cross-member struck him in the chest with his arms over the top of the cross-member, his hands grasping the netting mesh. His feet were dangling, just skimming the surface of the water.

Chuck had reflexively let go of the gun and tried to grasp the guy wire with his freed hand. The lurch of boat took the spar from beneath his feet. He'd been able to throw one leg over the spar as he fell towards the water, his free hand catching the guy wire.

The force of the shark's tail snapped the starboard dagger board where it entered the hull. Only the thin sheet of fiberglass cloth imbedded on one side in the polyester resin kept the dagger board from tearing away. It folded up along the outside half of the hull before the rushing water of the boat's slipstream caught the broken half and snapped it on the hinge of fiberglass cloth back to its original upright position where it fluttered in the slipstream.

Both Chuck and George were crying out for help, but Eric was frozen in place. He'd lost sight of the shark.

'Where's the shark! Where's the Shark!' Eric's mind screamed.

Not knowing meant he had to steer the boat straight to prevent any further collisions. If he steered left or right, he could ram the shark and spill both Chuck and George into the ocean for sure. He was afraid to dump the sails because the sudden loss of power could also dump them into the sea, plus he would lose steerage. All he could do was to hold the boat steady until everybody was hauled back on board. He frantically searched for any sign of the shark in front of the boat, but all he could see was Chuck and George clawing to get back aboard the safety of the *Pacific Chanteuse*.

38

The Pod Leader watched as the Giant Shark quickly exhausted, and the humans hovered over it for several minutes. He didn't know what they had done to the Giant Shark, but he saw it flinch in pain and use the last of its reserves to push itself ahead of its antagonists, diving slightly, before slowing drastically and letting the boat overtake it again. Judging by the shark's exhausted response to the attack of the humans, it was time to call the pack together for the attack. He lowered his head and gave the War Cry: *TTTTHHHROOOOM click-click-click-click, TTTTHHHROOOOM click-click-click-click, TTTTHHHROOOOM click-click-click-click*. It was killing time.

******

Chuck started to pull himself up, throwing his dangling leg over the spar and using the guy wire he was able to plant a foot on top of the spar and the do the same for the other legs.

George's position was painful, causing him to breathe in forced spats. The round spar was making him bear all his weight on the crest of the spar. Like a fulcrum, it was bruising and crushing the tissue around the middle of his biceps. To relieve the pain, he was alternating between arms, releasing the net and trying to claw his way further up. But leverage and his center of gravity were against him. He just didn't have the strength necessary to pull himself up.

Chuck inched his way across the spar until his hand could grab the jib furler.

"Where's the shark? Can you see it?" Eric yelled at Chuck.

Chuck turned slightly to peer into the water. He pointed to the massive body in front of the boat.

Eric couldn't tell from Chuck's gesture if it was safe to turn. It looked like Chuck had pointed in front of the boat. So he continued to steer the boat straight ahead.

The pain became unbearable for George, his position untenable. He slipped his hands back to hang from the cross member spar. His feet were now dragging a foot deep in the water.

Chuck finally stepped onto the web decking and rushed to help George who had just dropped further into the water. The current of water flowing around George's feet was dragging his body at a backward angle under the web decking.

"Hold on, George," Chuck said as he threw himself down on the web decking and leaned over the cross member. He grabbed George's forearms and tried to haul him in. As he was tugging on George, the *Pacific Chanteuse* overtook the shark again which had risen to the surface. The shark started to pass beneath George's feet. George didn't see, but Chuck could see it all.

Eric also saw the *Pacific Chanteuse* straddle the shark again now that it had risen to the surface. He could see that the shark would pass quickly under the boat. Now, for sure, there was no way he could dump the sails and stall the boat over the slowing shark. He would just have to sail on.

"Eric," Chuck yelled, "I need your help. I can't pull George in."

As Chuck was yelling, the shark's back slid under George's feet. Surprised at finding solid purchase under his soles, George looked down as the shark's giant dorsal fin slid past him to his right, his feet tracing a line along its back heading for the shark's head and jaws.

"Awwwwww, awwww!!!" George's terror escaped from his mouth uncontrollably. He started to swat at the shark with his feet, then jabbing it with his heels, trying to kick it away.

Eric reached down on the console to flip on the autopilot. He had to wait a few seconds for the autopilot to stabilize before he could let go. As he was waiting for stabilization, he heard George's terror, unaware the shark was underneath him.

"Hurry, Eric!" screamed Chuck.

Eric hurried to the point of panic. He let go of the wheel and tried to vault straight to the right side deck over the cockpit seats. He didn't make it all the way. One foot landed clean, but the other hit the edge of the deck and then slipped to the seats as Eric's weight came to bear. The sudden loss of one foot spun Eric as he tried to find his balance. As he spun and staggered, his right foot got caught in the haul line of the main sail, kicking it free of the quick-grip cleat that held tension on the line.

George's feet were now pounding on the shark's head.

The shark's head fully slid past George's feet. He continued to swat his feet at it, trying to make it go away.

The shark felt the blows on its back. Though not painful, it wasn't used to being struck and this agitated it toward the creature doing the striking. The blows pitter-pattered off its head and dropped into the water in front of it as the creature continued to struggle. Though totally spent, the sight of a struggling, black and bright red creature inches from its nose triggered every predatory instinct in its brain. Its eyes rolled back in its head as it opened its mouth, extending its five foot wide jaws and used the last of its feeble strength to surge ahead. Like a trout rising to a fisherman's fly upon the water, the shark took in the black and red lure, its feet hitting the back of its throat, before the shark tugged it free of the boat.

Chuck saw the five-foot wide maw of the razor sharp serrated teeth rise from the water and engulf George. He shrieked and jerked back involuntarily, crab-walking on his back, skittering away to leaving George alone to his fate as the jaws came inches from where he'd been holding onto George's forearm.

George felt his feet being lifted from below, pile driving his knees into his chest. For a fraction of a second he felt as if he might be catapulted to safety. But pressure and darkness clamped his body. He understood what was happening to him, having seen the terror in Chuck's eyes before he disappeared. The scream just barely left his mouth before the darkness engulfed him. The last thing he was aware of, before the darkness was complete and the intense bolts of pain in his forearms blotted out his consciousness, was his life preserver inflating; the pull-tab caught on a tooth of Chagatash.

The turbulence of the shark's last surge was more than the damaged, fluttering dagger board could handle. It fluttered once and then turned minutely broadside in the slipstream enough to overstress the remaining fiberglass cloth fibers that had not yet been broken by the fluttering. The dagger board ripped free and was carried backwards by the slipstream and momentum of the boat. Or more accurately, the dagger board ripped free and hung motionless in the water while the starboard rudder slammed into the broad side of the broken dagger board.

In a fraction of a second the autopilot was overwhelmed by the sudden force on the rudder and its microcircuit, disengaged. The twin rudders were steered and linked by a hydraulic circuit, so both rudders acted in unison. The dagger board slammed the starboard rudder full right, forcing the port rudder to do likewise.

Eric was still staggering when he felt the boat suddenly lurch to starboard, the direction he was already wobbling in still trying to recover from his misstep. His concentration on his feet, he never saw the mainsail boom swing. Caught by the wind, unfettered by the haul line's restraint, and added impetus by the boat's sharp turn in the same direction, the boom stuck Eric in the side of the head with enough force to topple his body over the guard rails and into the waiting sea below.

The big plank of the dagger board, hung up in the rudder, acted as a big brake and drug the *Pacific Chanteuse* to a slow stop, almost keeping the boat positioned over the shark.

Chuck had rolled back away as the shark surged, and was further thrown off as the boat lurched to the right. Once he was able to get his wits about him, his first thought was George. He'd heard a brief cry from George and thought surely he was hurt. "George?" he called out, he crawled on his hands and knees to George's hands on the cross member and flopped himself over to help him. As he gazed over, what he saw stirred first confusion and then revulsion. Both of George's hand were clamped to the cross member in a death grip, both arms neatly severed at mid forearm.

Chuck rolled away from the arms, came to a stop on his hands and knees, and then proceed to throw up through the mesh decking. When he was done heaving, he noticed the *Pacific Chanteuse* was just coasting to a stop. He looked up to see where Eric was. But, he was nowhere to be seen. "Eric? Eric?" Chuck called, already thinking the worst. He got up and started to walk into the salon hoping to find Eric lying on the cockpit deck or in the salon. He was about to step down into the cockpit, when he caught sight of something out of the corner of his eye. He turned to the starboard deck railing to see Eric's life preserver, strap broken, tangled in the top wire.

'*No. No! NO!*' Chuck's mind screamed.

He rushed to the side and looked down. Eric wasn't there. Chuck ran to the stern of the boat to see if Eric was floating in the water behind the boat. But he could see nothing. "ERIC!" He yelled, panic starting to edge into his voice. But his call was met with only the muted sounds of killer whales blowing in the distance.

39

The Pod Leader saw the brightly colored human attack the Giant Shark and die for its efforts. He also saw the leader of the humans on the boat get battered into the water. He was gravely concerned. His echolocation sense told him that the human leader wasn't moving, and was floating only fifty yards from where the exhausted Giant Shark was milling about.

More killer whales were arriving every ten or fifteen seconds from all quadrants. There were enough killer whales now surrounding the Giant Shark to cut off any escape attempt. The Pod Leader no longer needed to hold his position to ring in the Giant Shark. He felt that he could go assist the human leader if he were not already dead. The Pod Leader felt pity for the human leader, another warrior sacrificed in hunting down and killing the Giant Shark.

******

Eric snapped to consciousness to find himself floating face down, peering into the depths of green water. His solar plexus had been stunned by his collision with the boat's guardrail and wouldn't function. His body was screaming for oxygen. He didn't know which way was up, even though he was only three feet from the surface. He thrashed about wildly not fully in control of all his senses yet, the main sail boom striking his head scrambled everything but his most rudimentary functions. His mind, low on oxygen was desperately ordering the lungs to inhale, but the stunned muscles of his solar plexus could not obey, which saved him from filling his lungs with water and drowning. At the rate he was struggling and using what little reserves of oxygen available in his circulatory system as Eric's vision started to gray at the edges. He knew he was only moments from death.

******

The shark was a creature of instinct. Utterly exhausted, barely able to create enough forward momentum to get water and life-giving oxygen to flow over its gills, the strange irregular thrashings in the water inflamed its already aroused predatory instincts and triggered its hunting response. Its simple brain reasoned that if it had to move forward to breathe, it might as well move in the direction of the wounded creature it could sense and see on the edge of its visual range. The shark had only enough strength to turn in small increments as it trudged forward, spiraling into the threshing creature. Exhaustion tempered its appetite; it was torn between eating and resting. Having just swallowed a bite to eat moments ago, it was content just to bump the agitated prey or perhaps just mouth it with its teeth just to get a taste.

The Giant Shark closed in until it was just twenty feet away.

Eric was so panicked by his dwindling oxygen and inability to breathe, that although he saw the shark coming at him, he didn't really register it. His diaphragm had recovered and he could barely contain the urge to fill his lungs with water. He continued to thrash, but much more slowly now. His peripheral vision was starting to narrow as his brain started to shut down from lack of oxygen. From below him, a black and white blur raced at him at an astonishing speed.

******

The Pod Leader had been watching the dead human leader, pondering its fate, when it suddenly jerked to life. He'd been watching as the Giant Shark altered his course to the quivering human leader. He realized the human was in trouble and needed help to the surface, but the Giant Shark made it impossible to swim directly to its assistance. The Pod Leader made a split second decision. He charged straight down in the water at full speed and then cranked his pectoral fins into a one hundred eighty degree climb and accelerated to full speed in a vertical power climb directly under the human, all the while blasting a constant stream of echolocation clicks at the Giant Shark and the human in an attempt to frighten off the killer fish from its prey. He was determined not to let the shark get the human, but he was putting himself within less than half a body length of the Giant Shark's jaws.

******

As the Giant Shark approached Eric, its dorsal fin and tail rose to cut the surface's calm as it adjusted its depth to that of the thrashing prey just below the surface, its black eyes locked on to the creature that was slowly becoming less agitated.

******

Eric's eyes grew wide as the black and white form materialized and then slammed into his abdomen and chest. The blow was slightly buffered by the bow compression waves in the water that built up in front of the killer whale's blunt forehead, shoving Eric in the direction of the whale's travel before its body slammed into him. Unfortunately, a significant percentage of the force of eight tons traveling at thirty-five miles per hour still transferred to his body, and Eric felt as if ten heavyweight boxing champions had slugged him at the same time. He thought he heard ribs crack. His body conformed and draped around the killer whale's head; his feet dangling over the whale's jaw and down its throat, his chest and head draped across its bulbous forehead, and his arms spread to the side.

The cool, rubbery feel of the killer whale's skin registered against Eric's as he felt himself propelled out of the water and into the sky with the whale. Near the apogee of the flight, Eric separated from the whale and once again within the course of less than a month, he found himself flying through the air in an uncontrolled arc over water, time blurring to slow motion. The pain from the blow of the killer whale wracked his body as he tumbled slowly in the air.

******

The Giant Shark sensed the killer whale's onrush and knew that the whale wasn't aimed at it, but instead at the thrashing creature in front of it. Since it wasn't being attacked, and it was too tired to react with much vigor, the shark just turned a few degrees away from where the struggling creature that had been snatched from the water and continued on at its best speed, which was nothing more than a crawl.

******

The Pod Leader had no plan other than to push the human out of the Giant Shark's path. The killer whale's momentum carried it close to twenty feet out of the water. At the top of its flight, the human separated from its nose and the Pod Leader arched right to re-enter the water nearly sideways. As he arched over and the ocean below him came into view of the one eye closest to the water, he saw that the Giant Shark was going to pass under him, right where he was going to land. He tensed his body for the impact.

******

The Giant Shark was a marvel of nature with all its sensory capability to understand what was happening in the sea around it. The one thing that it wasn't equipped to detect was whales falling from the sky. The black and white body crashed down upon the Giant Shark, striking just behind the juncture where the Giant Shark's skull joined its cartilage spine.

******

Like a professional wrestler launching himself from the top of a corner turnbuckle to deliver a flying body slam to a prostrate opponent, the Pod Leader struck the Giant Shark like a brick of solid muscle, hitting the Giant Shark with his body just behind his right pectoral fin. Almost all of his eight tons of weight, multiplied by gravity, was delivered to the point of impact, snapping the Giant Shark's head back, driving it deep into the ocean.

The impact left the Giant Shark stunned, floating motionless, head down in the water. The Pod Leader, too, was stunned by the colossal impact. He lay floating on the surface near the Giant Shark, breathing hard to cleanse his body of the pain that the shock waves of collision spread from his lips to his fluke.

Eric continued to fly in a much higher arc before slamming into the water uncontrolled feet first. The pain in his wracked body made him oblivious to all about him. After the initial plunge, Eric struggled weakly to the surface, where he dog paddled feebly, able to only keep his face above water to breathe. He was aware of the large male killer whale thirty feet away, lying motionless and breathing loudly through his blowhole.

While all this had transpired, most of the killer whales of the hunting pack had arrived and witnessed the Pod Leader's presumed assault on the Giant Shark. Many took this as the opening assault and hurled themselves at the stunned fish. The first killer whale to take up the attack charged at full speed and rammed the Giant Shark, slamming his head into the Giant Shark's side just behind the gills and directly over the heart. Another killer whale rammed the Giant Shark from the other side in the corresponding spot a few seconds later.

The assembled hunting pack cut loose with war cries and became a frenzy of whales hammering the Giant Shark with heart, gill, and head shots delivered with all their weight behind each blow.

The Giant Shark swung from side to side, head down in the water, like a boxer's punching bag before the delivered blows.

******

The Pod Leader groggily started to swim to where Eric hung in the water. Eric saw the killer whale's dorsal fin approaching. He was too incapacitated to do more than watch. He was still not clear on whether the killer whale had attacked him or was trying to save him.

'I suppose if he wanted me dead, he would have used his teeth,' Eric reasoned. With that realization, whatever apprehension remained melted away. The whale gently brushed up against Eric's side while his hand stroked the whale's rubbery skin. The whale paused, and the two looked at each other through the ocean's surface.

It was an odd, wonderful moment for Eric, who had watched these creatures from afar all his professional life, to be examined by animal so large, so close. Something passed between them, but he wasn't sure what it was. He hoped that someday he would. The whale rolled slightly to bring his pectoral fin to near the surface and moved forward until Eric was cradled in the juncture where his fin joined his body and started to swim slowly towards the approaching sailboat.

Once the boat had lost enough speed, the broken dagger board had fallen off the jammed rudder. Chuck had gotten the *Pacific Chanteuse* turned around slowly in the breeze to look for Eric. He'd only learned to tack in the last two weeks, but never had he been required to reverse the boat's course. It took him several tries before he learned that he needed the boat's forward momentum to carry it through a complete turn while slacking the sails, rather than trying to use the sails during the maneuver.

The result was that he was late in arriving to the events. He didn't know where Eric was until the saw him launched from the nose of a massive male killer whale in the face of the shark. Chuck tracked Eric through the air and adjusted course to bring the boat close to where he thought Eric was in the water.

Now, to his amazement, it appeared that a killer whale was carrying Eric toward the boat on one of his fin. "Good God almighty," escaped from Chuck's lips, unbeknownst to him.

'If this isn't the first day of first -- I don't think I will be astonished by anything else I see today. But this...this has got to be the most bizarre – Eric being delivered to the boat by an eight-ton killer whale,' was all that Chuck could think of.

He was so emotionally drained from fear of losing Eric, revulsion at watching George be consumed, the excitement of the chase, and elation at finding the shark, that he waited too long to dump the sails and the boat glided past the killer whale on the starboard side. The whale turned with Eric still cradled and brought him to the rear of the boat as it coasted to a stop. Chuck raced to the stairs on the starboard hull's rear and leaped down them to the little platform just above the waterline. He arrived just in time to see a pained and cold Eric delivered to the boat's platform.

Eric put up a hand and Chuck heaved him up, moaning as he was lifted, ribs on both sides flaring in pain, so he could sit on the platform dangling his feet in the water.

"Think I've separated or broke some ribs," he half mumbled to Chuck. The killer whale lay still in the water until Eric was seated safely on the platform, his head protruding out of the water so that his eyes were above. Eric looked down into the eyes of his savior and for the second time that day he was at a loss of what to say or how to communicate with a killer whale.

The killer whale solved the problem for him by rolling slightly to its side so that a pectoral fin came clear of the water, and then the killer whale started waving at him. Reflexively, both Chuck and Eric raised their hands and waved back.

"Thank you, friend," Eric said, as he examined the dorsal fin and recognized it as the same killer whale that had spied him just before the *Pacific Chanteuse* joined the chase several hours ago. Up until now, he thought that all that had transpired had been random acts by different whales. Now he realized that his rescue had been the deliberate act of one creature. An electrical shock went through him as the potential of this interspecies connection hit him.

"He's been looking out for me the whole time,' Eric thought in wonderment.

The Pod Leader rolled and put his fin back in the water, turned to see what the hunting pack had accomplished, and started to swim back in the direction of the attack in progress.

Eric studied the dorsal fin intently, committing to memory every scar, wave and nick in it so that he would recognize his friend should they ever meet again. As he scrutinized the fin, he realized that this fin looked familiar to him. He knew he'd seen this individual recently, but where? The waters of the south end of Southeastern Alaska had been oddly vacant of killer whales as they had searched for the shark. Until today, he hadn't seen one live killer whale in the last two weeks or better. Then he realized that the operative word was live. He'd seen this whale on the TTAC video of the shark's attack on his favorite little breakaway pod. He was the Pod Leader of that new pod!

Eric hoped he would see his friend again one day with a new family.

40

As the Pod leader approached the scene of the killer whales' attack on the Giant Shark, he saw that it had been spun and battered repeatedly by the killer whales. Although they were smaller than the shark, their blows hurt, doing considerable damage to the Giant Sharks internal organs. The Giant Shark was motionless in the water, blood leaking heavily from all ten of its gill slits. The cumulative damage from the killer whales' blows had crushed much of the lamellae, the super thin structures of the gills where gases were exchanged with the water, crushed major arteries and veins on both sides, and massively bruised the muscles of the heart. The Giant Shark was dying.

When the killer whales sensed the Giant Shark was done for, they set upon it with their teeth. Their mouths weren't designed to open wide enough to take in the wide, round contours of the Giant Shark's body, so they used the teeth on one side of their mouths to scrape and shred its flanks and back. Others tore at the numerous fins that projected from the Giant Shark. The nose of the Giant Shark was removed, as was most of its tail fin. The blood lust was upon them and all satisfied their anger and lust for revenge until only a shredded carcass remained, barely recognizable as a shark. The Pod Leader could see that three silver barnacles were attached by short tethers to the dorsal fin.

All but one whale contributed to the rendering. The Pod Leader swam to the side, content to watch the others rake the flesh from the Giant Shark's body. Today's events put to rest his desire to avenge the deaths of his loved ones and the members of his Clan. Today, he put behind him the bonds of those murdered and forged a new bond with the humans that had bravely fought beside him. It brought peace to his heart. He turned and started to swim north.

In ones and twos, as the killer whales exhausted their bloodlust, they broke off to find their way home without fanfare or goodbyes. The contacts and relationships built by their endeavors were uncertain. It was unclear whether the tribes would return to their status quo or build upon them.

******

"Help me up the stairs, will you?" Eric asked Chuck. As he was pulled up, another groan escaped his lips.

"Let's get you inside and dried," Chuck said patiently. He gingerly moved Eric across the boat and into the salon before depositing him in the pilot's chair in front of the wheel. He raced down the stairs to his bunk and pulled off his bed's blankets, which he took back and wrapped around Eric.

"Here, you get dry and warm. You can watch what's happening on the LIDAR. There's something I've got to do." Then Chuck paused. "Where are your garbage sacks?"

"Under the sink, on the right. Why?"

"Remains recovery, I've got to get what's left of George for his family."

Eric felt a stab in his heart. What a clod. He'd been so wrapped up in his own physical pain and suffering, he'd forgotten to ask about George. He'd just assumed that Chuck had been able to haul George back onboard and that he was in his room or bunk recovering. "What happened?"

"The shark got him before I was able to pull him up." Chuck was troubled by the images in his mind as he relived them in slow motion, totally forgetting about Eric. Willing himself back to the present, he started again, "It bit him off in mid forearms. His hands are still holding onto the cross member."

Eric watched in silence as Chuck went to the starboard side of the front cross member and kneeled on the web decking. It took both hands for Chuck to free the remains, which he gingerly placed in the plastic garbage bag. He tightly tied the bag closed and then placed it in another bag, tying it off also.

Chuck brought the remains back in and headed for the galley. "I'm going to need to put this in the freezer."

Eric nodded silently. As Ship's Master, he was responsible for everybody's safety and well being. It was he who was going to have to report the fatality upon his boat to the Coast Guard. With a heavy heart, he turned to the LIDAR to watch the shark's death barely able to focus on the screen as he thought of George.

There was much commotion on the surface as the whales jockeyed for position or came up to breathe. The

LIDAR wasn't much help. There were so many bodies circling, swimming in tight quarters, which made it impossible to see what was happening.

Chuck came up the stairs from the galley and joined Eric in staring at the confusing screen.

"What am I going to say to the Coast Guard, Chuck?" Eric asked while staring blankly at the screen. "He had an accident? An 'industrial accident'? Is that what we'll call it? With what? What could I possibly tell them he could have had an accident with on this boat that would cut off his arms? We can't tell them a giant shark bit him off at the arms. They'll never believe us."

"They will if we get the shark's body back," he reminded him. "Besides, I work with them on a near daily basis. If I confirm the story, whatever it is, they will accept it."

They watched in silence as the killer whale's fury dissipated and they started to peel off and head in different directions. Once they started to leave, it didn't take long for all of them to clear out.

They watched on the screen as shark's body had sunk lower and lower in the water during the killer whales' attack until it glided to the bottom of the three hundred foot deep channel. When it hit the muddy bottom, they knew within minutes, sand fleas, the sea's equivalent of fly maggots, would descend upon the corpse. They would enter the body through the gills and mouth first to eat the blood rich membranes of the shark's respiratory system. It wouldn't take long before the shark's body was being devoured by thousands upon thousands of tiny mouths.

Using the LIDAR, they were able to track it until it hit bottom and the LIDAR could no longer distinguish it from the seabed. But they were able to find its location using the sound gear following the three tracking beacons.

Eric was recovering from his encounter with the charging killer whale and had changed his clothes. He and Chuck set about preparing the boat to blow the recovery gas bags and retrieve the body. They released the skiff from its davits, loading it with prepared ropes and boat fenders for flotation. When all was ready, they met back at the sound gear display on his laptop computer at the navigational table.

"Here it goes. Cross your fingers," Eric said, his finger hovering over the "Enter" key. His finger descended, hitting the keyboard, which the computer translated into an electronic impulse that the underwater speakers converted to sound.

The sound traveled through the water and was received by all three tracking transmitters. In near perfect unison, tough plastic bags shot out from the rear of the little silver cylinders and were filled by little gas canisters within.

The bags instantly strained at their tethers, the gases trying to reach the surface. But even with the added buoyancy of George's inflated lifejacket lifting in the belly of the shark, it wasn't enough to lift the corpse. The gas recovery bags had come critically close to achieving positive buoyancy but had stopped just twenty pounds shy of neutral and twenty-one pounds shy of positive buoyancy.

"Any movement?" Chuck asked anxiously.

"Nothing," Eric said, peering intently at his laptop screen.

"Maybe it's stuck in the mud," Chuck offered hopefully.

"Maybe."

Eric and Chuck waited for a couple of hours, hoping their patience would be rewarded. It was getting late and they needed to leave to find a place to anchor for the evening.

"You know, Eric, I've been thinking," Chuck filled the silence with his inner musings, "This whole trip has motivated me to go back to school again and try and get my Ph.D. After the Dr. Katzburg fiasco, I just kind of lost my love for academics. But seeing that monster today has got my juices flowing again. Whether we get the body back or not, I've learned enough today to go in new directions with my dissertation. I've got a whole new line of investigation formed in my mind: the conflict between sharks and mammals as apex predators. I don't think that's ever been clearly studied. People always ask why sharks have been so successful for millions of years. I think the answer is that although they are presumed to be apex predators, the reality is that it's the non-apex predator species that have carried them through the ages. Apex predators tend to go extinct. The line of species survives because in each age of earth's evolution, enough non-apex predator sharks survive to spawn apex-class predator shark species that adapt and specialize for each millennium. It's not that they're the most efficient platform in the sea, it's just that, as a species, they seem the quickest to adapt to environmental changes," Chuck concluded as both went back to staring at whatever had been occupying them before Chuck's disclosure.

Eric thought about what he'd said with studied silence. "Great," he finally muttered, with a tinge of moroseness in his voice. "I'm glad *something* good came out of today that might have some positive spin-off." And then, as an afterthought, he added, "Just as long as you send a copy of your dissertation to my friend, Dutch. Of course, he's not going to be very happy with me when I tell him that I knew about the shark but never said anything. Hopefully, the case of bourbon I plan on taking him will help ease him through his anger once I explain everything."

"But you know what's really eating me?" Eric asked, introspectively.

"What?"

"All this talk about science...I mean, I'm a man of science. I look for facts and make the best interpretation of them, never overstating what the facts can bear."

"Yah, so..."

Eric paused before continuing, as he searched for the right words. "I'm faced with a dilemma. I have no rational explanation for today. I saw killer whales that aren't even supposed to run together working for a common purpose. I saw whales that are supposed to have different dialects and unable to communicate with each other collectively stop on a dime when I hit that new call. Clearly, it meant something to all of them, which means they can communicate with each other. I have no explanation for this, but George did. He believed. He had an explanation. And when you add it all up, his explanation is no more valid than anything that I can offer, and no less. So where does that leave all this science we're talking about?"

"Yah," Chuck agreed, "I see your point."

"After everything I witnessed today, it comes down to faith: faith in science that in time we might be able to explain today, or faith in the mysticism of a shaman's charms."

Both men lapsed into silence as they each mulled over their own quandaries. The Alaskan evening crept upon them slowly until the sun paled and pinked near the western horizon. Eric was the first to break the silence.

"I think that we need to face the facts," Eric finally voiced what both of them had been thinking for the last hour. "We're not going to be able to recover the shark's body. We gave it our best shot, but we're going to come up dry."

Neither one wanted to admit it, because both had so much riding on proving the shark existed. But at the end of the day, they had no conclusive evidence: no body, video lost over the side when George fell, a bunch of ambiguous recordings on the LIDAR that could just as easily be interpreted as killer whales hunting another whale, and some really interesting sound recordings of different killer whale types mixing together; and one fatality. Both Chuck and Eric were gagging on the bitterness of it all.

"I guess you're right," Chuck agreed, "maybe it's time

to leave. Besides, we need to get George's remains home."

Eric shut the lid of his laptop, effectively powering it down to standby, and headed out to the cockpit, where he set the sails and turned north towards Ketchikan.

******

On the bottom of the channel, in the mudflats where the shark's body had come to rest, the tides had changed and the current was really starting to build. With the shark's near neutral buoyancy and the corpse's large cross section, the shark was starting to be buffeted around. As the tide's current picked up, it began to roll the shark's body along the flat, muddy bottom until it landed upon a small rock outcropping jutting from the seabed and settled, belly first, on the rock. The tide continued to pin the shark's body against the rock, increasing the pressure, driving jagged rocks into the underside of the corpse. Had Eric left on his sound gear, he might very well have heard the muted air horn on George's life preserver blowing as a rock pressed just hard enough on the button to empty the whole can of compressed air into the shark's stomach.

The shark's sides swelled as the stomach was inflated and the body achieved positive buoyancy, allowing it to float free of the rock outcropping and rise to the surface. Twenty minutes later, the shark's body broke the surface. It was sunset, but there was still enough light to see the *Pacific Chanteuse* sailing well off to the north.

The corpse bobbed there on the surface until just a little past dark, when one of the sea's scavengers arrived to take a bite from the body. It was just one of many that would show up that night and in the following days to feast on the corpse. Satisfied with the first bite, the salmon shark rolled its eyes back and took another.

THE END

Coming Soon
from Scott William:

The Last Emperor's Scepter
A Neptune's Trident Novel

Go to
www.scottwilliambooks

for the back stories on this and other Scott William novels
and to see what novels are in the works.

An Excerpt from: The Last Emperor's Scepter

July 25th, 1943

"You are being sacked. I no longer desire or need your services as Prime Minister. Please vacate your office forthwith so that Marshal Pietro Badoglia can take over your post."

"But, but..." the short, heavyset man with short cropped salt and peppered browned hair sputtered, "you can't fire me. I'm The Leader," said the man known to his people as Ill Duce, his ire continuing to build. Taking a moment to smooth the sleeves of his khaki military uniform adorned with black epaulets before he said, "For twenty-one years the people of this land have elected me as their Supreme Leader and asked my party to govern them."

"Yes, that's right. You were elected to represent them in *my* government. May I remind you, this is a constitutional monarchy, and I, King Victor Emmanuel III, King of Italy, King of Sardinia, Cyprus, Jerusalem, Armenia, Duke of Savoy, still rule this land. You serve the people at my pleasure. And," he paused for effect, "you no longer please me. For that matter, it seems that your Fascist Party doesn't want you either. The Grand Council of Fascism voted yesterday on your ouster and asked me to assume my full constitutional powers."

"They have no power over me; they're merely an advisory…"

The King cut him off and waved to the opulent room in which the throne sitting on raised dais was situated. "Take a look around you, Benito Mussolini."

Huge silk tapestries adorned the richly paneled walls and the floors; the shades on the lights were made of cut crystal and ground opal; gilded paintings and golden statues picketed the walls, creating a stunning perimeter of masters' work capped by a ceiling covered in an ornate fresco painting.

"Just where do you think you are? In some stadium filled with drunk, adoring fascists paid or bullied into attendance? No. You are in The Royal House of Savoy, *my* Palace, the seat of power in Italy for the last century and a half. Take a good look, for it is the last time you will ever sully these halls that have known great artist, philosophers, statesmen and leaders - none of which you even remotely resemble. Making the trains run on time is not a mark of greatness. Now remove yourself, or I will have the guards do it for you."

The four guards standing to either side and slightly behind the throne dais neither twitched nor batted an eyelash at the King's mention of them, so intent were they on watching Mussolini so that he did not harm the King. They had been instructed before allowing Mussolini into the room to search him thoroughly to remove anything that could be used as a weapon. This even included fountain pens. This directive was highly unusual and had sharpened the guards' attention to every gesture of the now defunct premier.

Benito Mussolini stood there, his arrogance and certitude deflating with each pump of his mouth that uttered no words. Finally, with stooped shoulders, he turned for the long walk across the polished marble floor to the double doors at the end of the great hall, his footsteps echoing ominously as he receded into the distance. Two more guards at the door opened the chamber's doors as the once great and mighty Benito Mussolini exited, a de-fanged dictator.

As soon as the guards closed the door behind him, a commotion could be heard from the hall. It was the sound of Mussolini's protests as guards in the hall placed him under arrest.

"That was quite a performance, your Excellency," came a voice emanating from behind one of the tapestries to the right and behind the dais. The tapestry fluttered for moment before it was pulled back by a dapper, tall man wearing a black formal military uniform with a white silk sash. Several rows of ribbons and medal encrusted the upper left front of the uniform. Upon one shoulder was the braided rope and tassel signifying that he was an aide de-camp. His name was Duke Albertino Costanzini, and he was much more than the aide de camp to the King. He was the King's confidante and closest advisor. He strode confidently to the front of the King's throne, careful to never let his head get higher than the King's. This was more difficult than it seemed, since the King stood only five feet four inches when standing and he was now seated. Waiting patiently, he listened to the King's summary, hoping he gave him an opening to interject his concerns into the conversation.

"One has to use a firm hand with the common born. They can be so loutish and base. And he was one of the worst. His arrogance was maddening. But, he is gone now. As you know, I have been planning for some time to dismiss that bag of wind; the vote of the Grand Council of Fascism just gave me all the impetus I needed.

"We will need a new Prime Minister. Summons Marshal Pietro Badoglia so that I can make his appointment as the new PM official. Then notify the parliament, Albert," the use of his pet name for the Count was a sign of affection.

"Of course, Your Excellency." He paused before broaching what was truly bothering him. "Your Highness, I am troubled that today's dismissal may not necessarily be the last we see of Mussolini."

"Of course it is. I have spoken and there is nothing else to say on the matter. He has brought defeat after defeat upon our nation. He has ruined our Army, Navy and Air Force. The people no longer believe in his visions of grandeur and conquest. He has not brought prosperity or prestige to the people of Italy as he had promised. Instead he has brought fear and despair to the people and loathing from the rest of the world upon my country. The people no longer support him, and why would they? And now, the Allied Forces are poised to invade my country. No, that is the last we have seen of him."

"I'm not so sure. Hitler and he feed from the same

fascist trough. As swill-mates, Hitler may not be happy to see his only European supporter summarily dismissed."

"But what can Hitler do about it? I'm the sovereign ruler of this land and am acting with the authority of our constitution."

"While that may be true, your Highness, Hitler has fourteen divisions of German troops in our country. That amounts to one hundred twenty-five thousand soldiers. Our Armed Forces are in no shape to expel them if they do not want to go. So, if Hitler wants Mussolini to stay, he has the military strength to force the issue. Our only hope is to strike an accord with the British Crown. Surely, as one sovereign to another, they can understand the danger of letting the masses have a say in the governing of a country. The inquiries we have directed to various noble families of the Italian Court to the British Court on reconciliation and accord on an armistice have all been positively received.   No, the best thing that can be done now is to strike a conciliatory tone with the British Monarchy, especially if Hitler decides to use his military strength to take over the country. Hitler is peasant born and has no respect for nobility. He may very well decide that he prefers fascist to nobility and use his army to impose his viewpoint. And if he does, there is no way we can stop his armies in time before they loot your castles and steal the Crown's treasures. I have no doubt that we can spirit you away to safety in time, but it sears my soul a thousand times over to think of your precious art works being taken by an ugly thug like Hitler. It is too painful to contemplate the thought of some low-born's hands wrapped around the Emperor's Scepter."

"Yes, I see what you mean. Perhaps a gesture of good faith between two noble houses is in order. The British Monarchy could hold the most precious jewels and other works of fine arts until we deal with the Nazi problem." King Emmanuel III seemed to ponder this notion for several moments before reaching a conclusion. "Albertino, I want you to send out a feeler to the King George VI in the next round of negotiations on the armistice to see if he would be willing to help. And more importantly, what's his price for such generosity."

"I'll send a communiqué to our Ambassador in Spain. He can pass it on to the British Embassy there in Madrid."

"Excellent."

Made in the USA
Charleston, SC
07 January 2016